continued . . .

The Diva Paints the Town

"[Davis] handles this tricky tale with aplomb and fills it with a cast of eccentrics . . . And the three animals are endlessly amusing. Davis includes several recipes, and although the novel takes place during a Virginia winter, the strawberry daiquiris will have you pretending it's summer." —*Richmond Times-Dispatch*

"Davis plates up another delectable whodunit, complete with recipes. Indeed, her novels are every bit as good as Diane Mott Davidson's Goldy Schulz mysteries." —*Shine*

"Davis's latest is an enjoyable mystery that includes decorating tips, a few pets, an unusual bequest, and recipes . . . Once again, Krista Davis brings us interesting, fun characters." —*Lesa's Book Critiques*

"Ms. Davis immerses the reader into the world of interior design." —*TwoLips Reviews*

The Diva Takes the Cake

"*The Diva Takes the Cake* does just that—takes the cake." —*The Romance Readers Connection*

"Mistaken identities, half truths, buried secrets, missing jewelry, wedding jitters, and family squabbles are whipped into a sweet froth in this second of the Domestic Diva Mysteries . . . [A] fun little bonbon of a book to enjoy on the beach or as a break from any wedding plans." —ReviewingTheEvidence.com

"Sure to thrill cozy fans." —*Fresh Fiction*

"Davis has devised a delightful romp, with engaging characters and a nicely crafted setting in which to place them. The author sets just the right tone to match her diva's perfect centerpieces, tablescapes, and lighting effects." —*Shine*

The Diva Runs Out of Thyme

"[A] tricky whodunit laced with delectable food . . . [A] fine mystery that's stuffed with suspects—and a reminder that nobody's Thanksgiving is perfect." —*Richmond Times-Dispatch*

"A mouthwatering mix of murder, mirth, and mayhem, nicely spiced by new author Krista Davis."
—Mary Jane Maffini, author of
The Busy Woman's Guide to Murder

"This cozy mystery delivers a plethora of useful household tips and mouthwatering recipes immersed within a keep-you-guessing plot filled with suspicious-acting characters, and twists and turns around every corner. Davis's smart writing style and engaging characters are sure to garner fans."
—*AuthorsDen.com*

"Filled with humor, delicious recipes, and holiday decorating tips, *The Diva Runs Out of Thyme* is a lighthearted mystery that is sure to get you in the Thanksgiving mood . . . [A] must-read to prepare for the holiday season!"
—*The Romance Readers Connection*

"[A] fun romp into the world of food, murder, and mayhem."
—*Armchair Interviews*

"*The Diva Runs Out of Thyme* is as much comedy as mystery . . . [A] really good book . . . [A] series worth watching."
—*Mysterious Reviews*

"An entertaining mystery novel with charming characters. The plot of the mystery is well drawn out . . . Davis is an excellent mystery author." —*MyShelf.com*

"The beginning of a good culinary cozy series with some interesting and different characters." —*Gumshoe Review*

The Diva
Frosts a Cupcake

KRISTA DAVIS

BERKLEY PRIME CRIME, NEW YORK

THE BERKLEY PUBLISHING GROUP
Published by the Penguin Group
Penguin Group (USA) Inc.
375 Hudson Street, New York, New York 10014, USA

USA | Canada | UK | Ireland | Australia | New Zealand | India | South Africa | China

Penguin Books Ltd., Registered Offices: 80 Strand, London WC2R 0RL, England
For more information about the Penguin Group, visit penguin.com.

THE DIVA FROSTS A CUPCAKE

A Berkley Prime Crime Book / published by arrangement with the author

Berkley Prime Crime Books are published by The Berkley Publishing Group.
BERKLEY® PRIME CRIME and the PRIME CRIME logo are trademarks of
Penguin Group (USA) Inc.

For information, address: The Berkley Publishing Group,
a division of Penguin Group (USA) Inc.,
375 Hudson Street, New York, New York 10014.

ISBN: 978-0-425-25813-2

PUBLISHING HISTORY
Berkley Prime Crime mass-market edition / June 2013

PRINTED IN THE UNITED STATES OF AMERICA

10 9 8 7 6 5 4 3 2 1

Cover illustration by Teresa Fasolino.
Cover design by Diana Kolsky.
Interior text design by Laura K. Corless.

This is a work of fiction. Names, characters, places, and incidents either are the product
of the author's imagination or are used fictitiously, and any resemblance to actual persons,
living or dead, business establishments, events, or locales is entirely coincidental.
The publisher does not have any control over and does not assume any responsibility for
author or third-party websites or their content.

PUBLISHER'S NOTE: The recipes contained in this book are to be followed exactly as
written. The publisher is not responsible for your specific health or allergy needs that
may require medical supervision. The publisher is not responsible for any adverse
reactions to the recipes contained in this book.

ALWAYS LEARNING   PEARSON

For the Plothatchers,
who always have an answer, a suggestion, or a great idea,
and are there no matter what.
They are my watercooler when I need a break,
a shoulder to lean on, and have become
my very dear friends:
Janet Bolin, Peg Cochran, Kaye George,
Daryl Wood Gerber, Janet Koch,
and Marilyn Levinson.

ACKNOWLEDGMENTS

Very special thanks to Laura Owens, D.V.M., for explaining the treatment of chocolate ingestion by dogs. Many thanks yet again to Lucy Zahray for her amazing knowledge and helpfulness about poisonous plants. And to my mother, Marianne, and my friends Betsy Strickland, Susan Erba, Amy Wheeler, and David Erba for patiently testing cupcake after cupcake without ever complaining about sugar rushes. I must thank my brilliant editor, Sandra Harding, whose edits always result in a stronger book, even when they present challenges. My agent, Jessica Faust, has been supportive and helpful and is always very wise. What would I do without Sandy and Jessica to keep me on track? Teresa Fasolino has painted another fabulous cover for Sophie and her friends, this time depicting the heart of Old Town so beautifully. Special thanks to Andy Ball for his eagle eye in catching my errors. As always, any mistakes are my own. I am grateful to all of you.

~❦~

CUPCAKES and PUPCAKES
Gala Eight-Course Dinner

Black Tie

By Ticket Only. Sold Out.

~❦~

Guests

General Euclid German
Alex German
Nick Rigas
Clarissa Osbourne
Maurice Lester
Mars Winston
Myra Liebling
Humphrey Brown
Francine Vanderhoosen
Officer Wong
Bernie Frei
Martha (Chihuahua)
Daisy (mixed hound)
Guinevere (gray cat)
Buddy (black-and-tan
rescue dog)

Bakers

Sugar Baby Cupcakes
  Renee Gatewood
  ~~Joy Bickford~~
  Muffin Pruitt
Cupcake Saloon
Natasha
Cake My Day
  Spenser Osbourne
Sugar Mama Cupcakes
  Joy Bickford
The Laughing Hound

CUPCAKES & PUPCAKES
Dinner Menu

Amuse Bouche
Asparagus Mini-cupcake

Appetizer
Avocado and Black Bean Cupcake

Fish Course
Salmon Cupcake

Les Légumes
Spinach Cupcake

Entrée
Rosemary Bacon Corn Cupcake
Bison Lasagna Cupcake

Cheese Course
Blueberry Cheesecake Cupcake

Fruit
Strawberry Cupcake

Dessert
Salted Caramel Cupcake
Coco Loco (Chocolate Coconut) Cupcake

CHAPTER ONE

Dear Sophie,

I am lactose intolerant, so I avoid cream cheese and buttercream frostings on cupcakes. The bakery near my office sells delicious mocha cupcakes that I eat all the time without problems. My grandfather's new wife swears there's no cream cheese or butter in the frosting of her mocha cupcakes, but I get sick every time I eat one. I'm worried about what she might be putting in them . . .

—Hold the Milk Please in Cream City, Ohio

Dear Hold the Milk Please,

Many cupcake recipes call for milk or cream in the cake portion and that could be the cause of your discomfort. If you're truly concerned that she's adding something more sinister, you might wish to have one of her cupcakes analyzed.

—Sophie

The creepy sensation of being watched overcame me. I was standing in line to buy coffee at a take-out window in Old Town, far too early in the morning for my taste. Shivering in the chilly spring weather, I gazed around and snuggled deeper into my rose-colored fleece pullover.

A few people ahead of me in line, a slender woman observed me. She didn't avert her piercing eyes, even when I looked straight at her. Brunette with deep auburn overtones, her freckles shone through a thin dusting of makeup. A long ski-jump nose brought perkiness to her face, and laugh lines had begun to develop around her mouth. She seemed vaguely familiar to me, and I sought to place her. She wore understated Old Town chic—dark brown jeans with a green suede jacket. The chunky gold bracelet on her wrist might have been costume jewelry, but the casual leather bag that hung from a long strap over her shoulder said *money* in no uncertain terms.

She strode over to me. "I defended you for dating Wolf. Under the circumstances, it seemed reasonable."

I braced myself. Her tone was level, but I detected a note of hostility. Why would she declare such a thing? My relationship with my boyfriend, Wolf, had recently come to an abrupt end because of a very complicated situation. I'd heard that some people felt I never should have dated him, and in hindsight I had thought that myself. Did she want me to thank her for standing up for me?

"I guess I was wrong. Apparently you lack the character I attributed to you. Have you no morals? No shame?"

As shocked as I was by her words, I was even more painfully aware of the interest of everyone around us. "I . . . I'm sorry. I have no idea what you're talking about."

"Let's not add insult here by feigning ignorance. We both know what you have done." She lowered her voice to a whisper, and her tone grew hard. "Just know that I will fight you. I might not look like much, but I can play dirty—and I will if I have to."

She strode away with her head held high, completely unflustered, as though pleased with herself. I, on the other hand, could feel my face flushing hot.

All the eyes watching her turned back to me. A few eyebrows rose. I tried hard to smile and managed a shrug. I wanted to think she had mistaken me for someone else, but the part about Wolf led me to believe she had the right person. My relationship with Wolf had broken off about nine months earlier. What on earth could I have done to upset her so much? Better yet, who *was* she?

The thought of turning and running crossed my mind, but I really did want coffee, and I had promised my best friend and across-the-street neighbor, Nina Reid Norwood, that I would bring her some. Besides, whatever dreadful thing the woman thought I'd done—I had a completely clear conscience. Part of me hoped our paths wouldn't cross again, yet I also hoped I might see her from afar when Nina was around. Maybe Nina could place her.

Gasps and whispers about Sugar Baby drew me out of my thoughts about the angry woman.

Frowning, I turned in the direction of the bakery. Just down the side street, I could see the familiar pink awning with chocolate polka dots and trim.

"Excuse me," I said to the man in front of me. "What's going on with Sugar Baby?"

"Look across the street. Renee and Joy split up, and Joy pulled a fast one. Cupcake war has begun in Old Town."

Sure enough, a new storefront had appeared directly across the street from Sugar Baby. A blue awning with brown polka dots and trim hung over a large window. Even from a distance, I could make out the name of the business—*Sugar Mama*. Except for the blue color and the one word name difference, it was *identical* to Sugar Baby.

I tried to hear what the people in line for coffee were saying.

"Apparently their business partnership broke up over a man."

"It must have been more than that. They're such nice women."

"Joy has a temper. Were you ever in the shop when something went wrong? I saw her throw a cupcake once!"

"I wonder who their assistant, Muffin, went with? She's the one with the real talent."

"I'm sure it was a fight over money. It always is in partnerships."

No one seemed to know. Not that it was any of my business. Still, it would be the talk of the town for a while.

I tried to shake my troubled mood, ordered three grande lattes, and carried them across the street to Market Square, where Nina waited with my mixed-breed hound, Daisy.

"Humphrey still hasn't shown up." Nina glared at me as though I were responsible. "He promised he would help us."

It *was* odd. Humphrey might be a bit of a nerd, but he was always reliable and punctual. It worried me that he hadn't arrived. I didn't dare say that though, out of fear that it would send Nina into a tailspin.

At six in the morning, only a few early birds had started to set up their booths for Cupcakes and Pupcakes, Nina's first major fundraising event. Tension ran from her tight lips to her clenched fists, all the way down to the sneaker-clad foot that twisted nervously on the red brick plaza.

On Friday, Saturday, and Sunday, the general public could buy cupcakes at booths operated by bakers who had come from all over the metropolitan Washington, DC, area, and then cast a vote at Nina's booth for the best cupcake.

Dog and cat owners would browse through rainbows of leashes, beds, and clothing for their little darlings. A portion of all the profits would be donated to local animal rescue groups.

Tickets for Saturday evening's gala event had sold out weeks ago. The highlight of the weekend, it featured an eight-course cupcake dinner in a park on the Potomac River. Dogs were invited, naturally, for their own special eight-course dinner of pupcakes. Local bakers and chefs were providing the fabulous fare.

"You didn't have breakfast, did you?" Nina was always hungry but never cooked. I knew I should have brought food, but I'd rolled out of bed at the last minute, secure in the belief that there was no point in baking muffins when we were going to be surrounded by cupcakes anyway.

She sipped her latte. "Where do you think Humphrey could be? He's going to throw us off schedule."

She had a much bigger problem to deal with. I had to tell her about Renee and Joy splitting up. Sugar Baby was supposed to provide a cupcake course for the gala dinner tomorrow night.

I told her in as calm a voice as I could muster.

She responded with a deer-in-headlights look. "One of them had better make the cupcake course they promised for tomorrow night! Why did this have to happen right now? They couldn't have waited until next week? Just a couple of days?"

"You go get the dogs and cats, and I'll have everything set up here by the time you return. Then you can talk to Renee and Joy to straighten out that mess."

"Not by yourself, you won't!"

Technically, she was right about that. "Humphrey will be here any minute, I'm sure. Now go!"

The heavenly scent of our freshly brewed coffee wafted to me. I sipped the hot liquid, savoring the rich brew with the slightest note of hazelnut. If Nina would finally leave, I could scare up a little breakfast for her to chow down on when she returned. Renee Gatewood of Sugar Baby Cupcakes was already setting up her booth. Maybe I could buy some cupcakes from her before she was officially open for business.

Nina spotted her at about the same time. Poor Nina was so stressed that her elbows and shoulders pumped when she hustled over to talk with Renee.

I set to work, flipping out the legs on a table. Nina returned in time to help me turn it upright and tug it into a spot that would be the front of the booth.

"At least tomorrow's dinner isn't a problem. Renee says she committed to supplying cupcakes, and she'll have them there on time." She blew a loud breath of air out of her mouth. "One problem resolved. I can't wait around for Humphrey any longer, though."

I grabbed Daisy's leash and walked Nina to her car, trying to calm her by assuring her everything would work out fine. As soon as she left, I navigated the booths being set up, and was headed toward Sugar Baby's booth to buy cupcakes when I spotted Humphrey.

He was pitching in all right—over at Renee Gatewood's Sugar Baby Cupcakes booth! Had he forgotten about Nina's adoption booth? I marched over to him. "What are you doing *here*? Where's Renee?"

"Morning, Sophie!" sang Humphrey. I'd never heard him sound so cheerful.

Red spots flushed his pale cheeks, reminding me of a painted porcelain doll's face. He had snapped his navy blue jacket at the neck against the chilly air. The dark color emphasized his pasty skin and hair so blond it was very nearly white. Renee was nowhere to be seen, but Officer Wong was eyeing the cupcake assortment.

As I recalled, the African-American policewoman was a huge fan of cupcakes. On the petite side, she had the well-rounded figure of a woman who liked to eat, causing her uniform to stretch tight. She sported a new hairstyle of soft curls, shorter toward her neck and longer on top. One curl dared to curve down on her forehead, giving the look a touch of sass. I had always envied her flawless complexion.

Wong glanced at me. "Have you tried the Mint Cookies and Cream Cupcake or the White Chocolate Raspberry Cupcake?"

"I haven't tasted either one." They sounded delicious, though. I looked around for Renee. "Is she open for business?"

Humphrey placed a Mint Cookies and Cream Cupcake and a White Chocolate Raspberry Cupcake into a box with ease, as though he'd done it all his life. "Renee had to go back to the bakery, so I'm filling in. I'm sure she wouldn't mind if I sold a few cupcakes. Don't worry, I didn't forget about you and Nina. As soon as Renee returns, I'll be over to help you."

Wong reached for the box Humphrey handed out to her. "I don't know what got into all these cupcake bakers. First Joy and Renee split up"—she looked over at me—"who'd ever have expected that? And some idiot broke into Cake My Day last night."

CHAPTER TWO

Dear Natasha,

I am one of your biggest fans and never miss your show. My five dogs are my babies. I wish you would do a show with your dog. Do you cook fabulous gourmet dishes for her? I bet you've built her a one-of-a-kind dog bed. Please do a show on dogs!

—Goldendoodle Mom in Dog Walk, Kentucky

Dear Goldendoodle Mom,

Dog cookies are baking in the oven as I write this. My sweet dog is always dressed in an adorable outfit, and she sleeps in a four-poster bed with a canopy. Thanks for your suggestion for a "dog show"!

—Natasha

As soon as Wong said *Cake My Day*, I knew who the irate woman had been. The angry face that had stayed with me like a persistent raincloud belonged to Clarissa Osbourne. She and her husband, Spenser, owned the Cake My Day chain of cupcakeries. "Someone must have had a major cupcake attack," I joked. "Why would anyone break into a cupcakery?"

"Same reason they burglarize other stores and people's homes—they're after money." Wong opened the box, lifted out a cupcake with pink frosting, and smelled it. "Ahh, doesn't get any better than this." She bit into it and pretended to melt.

I handed Humphrey some cash. "Bring breakfast when you come. What's in a breakfast cupcake?" I peered at something crumbed on top of the frosting.

"Maple buttermilk cake with maple frosting, sprinkled with bacon." He rattled it off like a pro.

"Are you moonlighting at Sugar Baby?" I teased.

Humphrey blushed. "Of course not. But I've tried all their flavors."

"I think I'll pass on the ones with bacon, but Strawberry Lemonade sounds good."

He waved me away. "They're on me. I'll be there as soon as Renee comes back."

"Don't forget to bring cupcakes."

Daisy and I returned to our own booth. I hooked her leash onto a table leg and flipped out the legs of two more tables. It turned out they weren't at all difficult to flip upright by myself.

Humphrey soon arrived and helped move them into position under the tent awning, creating a U-shaped booth.

"Give me a hand with the cages?"

They weren't particularly heavy, but the cat cages were large and unwieldy. We placed them on the table in the back where the canopy would shield the cats from the sun, and had just lined up the cages when Humphrey grabbed my arm, and whispered, "Whatever Myra wants, help me get out of it."

"Myra? Who is Myra?"

Humphrey nudged me with his elbow.

A woman with generous curves descended upon us. Her teeth shone such a bright white I feared they might glow in the dark. Black eyeliner rimmed her expressive eyes and turquoise waves decorated her eyelids. Big, jet black hair sported an occasional turquoise tip. Her fuchsia and black zebra-striped leather jacket would have been sufficiently eye-catching on its own, but she had paired it with fuchsia leggings that hugged her body like a second skin. She turned heads as she sashayed her way toward us, the tight leggings showing off more than I wanted to see of her swaying hips. A purse decorated with a rainbow of hearts hung on her forearm, and interlocking heart earrings dangled down to her shoulders.

"Humphrey," she scolded sweetly, "you didn't come to work last night. I was hoping I'd see you because I have an extra ticket to the cupcake feast tomorrow. Would you do me the honor of accompanying me?" Her voice surprised me. Soft and gentle, it didn't match her bold appearance.

Behind her, I could see Renee Gatewood in the Sugar Baby Cupcakes booth stretching her neck and leaning a bit to see what was going on.

"Sorry, Myra. I bought a ticket months ago." Humphrey's shoulders relaxed.

"Oh! You bad, bad boy. Now what will I do with my extra one?"

Maurice Lester, a curmudgeon if I'd ever met one, ambled up. His nose arced outward rather prominently and was as narrow as he was thin. In dire need of a cut, his white hair hung limply along the sides of his face.

Maurice was so fixated on Myra that I didn't think he noticed anything else. "I'll go with you, my dear. I would be honored to be your escort."

Myra cringed at his words. "I thought you already had a ticket."

"No matter." He smiled, revealing long, horsey teeth. "They've been sold out for months. I can probably sell it for twice what I paid for it."

I stepped in to save poor Myra. "I believe scalping tickets is illegal. I'll just refund your money, Myra." Good thing I'd brought some extra cash for shopping. I held the bills out to her.

Maurice reached for them, but Myra snatched them away from him, and in spite of the heavy makeup, I could see gratitude in her expression.

"The tickets were ridiculously expensive," Maurice complained.

I bit my lip to keep from saying what I thought—*No one forced him to buy one.* Besides, it was all for a very worthy cause.

Myra edged away from Maurice. "Well, I'll see you later." She touched Humphrey's sleeve, showing off long green fingernails with flashes of blue sparkle.

The pink circles on Humphrey's cheeks radiated larger.

If Myra thought she would lose Maurice by leaving, she was dead wrong. He turned on his heel and hurried to catch up to her.

"I can't believe you didn't tell me about Myra." Poor Humphrey had the worst luck with women. It probably didn't help that he looked like the proverbial ninety-pound weakling and that he was as timid as he was pale, a shrinking violet, really. Totally clueless about women but painfully knowledgeable about many other things. We'd grown up together in a small Virginia town. When we were in school, he'd had a huge crush on me. Immersed in my own childhood issues, I had no idea about his young love until a few years ago when he confessed. Humphrey reminded me a little bit of a dog, in a good way—a loyal friend, on the ball and protective but prone to making a mess in the wrong yard.

Now that I looked at him more carefully, it dawned on me that his fleece pullover was hiding a little paunch. He'd put on some weight in his face, too. It filled him out a little bit and looked good on him.

"A woman is interested in you? Why didn't you tell me?"

"Myra works at the funeral home with me, but she's not my type. She's nice enough, but she's rather boisterous. Draws too much attention to herself."

What a shame. Finally, a woman who liked Humphrey, and he was being picky? "Have you gone out with her? Maybe she's not so bad. She certainly seems to like you." I returned to work, placing cerise cloths over two of the tables.

"At the office Christmas party last year she drank too much and started slinging her bra over her head like it was a rodeo lasso."

Ouch. I bet she regretted that in the morning—in more ways than one. "Maurice certainly seems interested in her."

"I loathe that man. He's as cheap and tawdry as they come. He hangs around at the funeral home all the time to be near Myra. She hates it. Half the time she hides from him."

"Can't you put a stop to that?"

"He claims he's there for the viewings that are open to the public."

Humphrey was setting out the stack of adoption forms when Renee Gatewood rushed over. Every bit as petite and sweet as the cupcakes she baked, even her ruffled pink apron with chocolate polka dots and the Sugar Baby Cupcakes logo on it screamed sugar. "Humphrey, sweetie, could you do me a big favor? I'm short-handed and, as you well know, *everything, just everything*, has gone wrong."

Sweetie? Had I entered some alternate universe where Humphrey actually attracted women? I lifted the box for best cupcake votes and took my time placing it on the table next to the adoption forms so I could watch what happened.

She brushed hair the color of light brown sugar out of her eyes. Her pixie face wrinkled with worry. "I found a desk for sale that I really need." She gazed my way and angled toward me. "It's so cute and dainty, with a fold-down writing area and the most darling little cubbyholes. I'm stuck here all day, and I have to bake cupcakes tonight. Could you be a dear and pick it up for me?"

"Of course!" Humphrey agreed fast. Too fast.

"Oh! You're wonderful. Just wonderful!" She flitted back to her booth, sold a box of cupcakes, and returned. "Here's the check to pay for it, and this is the address. I've asked

Muffin to unlock the back door for you at the bakery, so you can swing it by whenever you have the time. I don't know how I'll ever thank you."

From the look on Humphrey's face, I had a pretty good idea that dating him would be thanks enough. Or were they already dating?

"It's nothing. Glad to help."

The second she flew back to her booth, Humphrey turned to me in a panic. "May I borrow your car? Mine isn't big enough to transport a desk!"

I shouldn't have laughed, but he was so desperate and earnest. "Yeah, sure. So what's going on between you and Renee?"

His pale face flushed again. "Nothing."

I dragged a dog pen to the open side of the booth. "Here, hold this. If nothing is going on, how come you were helping her set up her booth?"

"You and Nina weren't here when I arrived this morning. Poor Renee was frazzled, so I offered to lend a hand. You needn't sound so suspicious. All I did was help in the shop while Renee carried cupcakes over from the bakery."

"I saw Joy's new shop across the street."

"Renee had no idea that was coming. The poor thing didn't get any sleep last night. Joy blindsided her. It was a double whammy because they lived together. She lost her business partner and roommate."

"She must have known something. When did Joy put up the big awning?"

"It was covered for days!" Humphrey sounded scandalized. "She did everything she could to hide her plans from poor Renee."

Tugging, I unfolded the pen into an octagonal corral with a gate. Several dogs would fit easily. I handed him one end of a banner to attach to the poles that held up the back of the booth.

"I always thought Joy was such a nice person," he continued. "But she left Renee high and dry. Didn't even let on that she was leaving. Joy packed up her things and moved out."

I frowned at him. Why did I think he might not know the full story? Renee must have suspected something. Surely they'd had a disagreement or a falling out.

We didn't finish the booth a minute too soon. I was admiring the banner that said *Cupcakes and Pupcakes Adoptions, Adopt a Pet and Save a Life, Donations Welcome,* when a honking car horn caught our attention.

Nina had pulled up in a van. She reached out of the window and waved at us.

Minutes later, five dogs eagerly sniffed the corral from the inside, tails wagging, while Daisy welcomed them from the other side.

When four cats and seven kittens were safely caged and already being observed by admirers, Nina unfolded a chair and collapsed into it. "What a morning! It's not even nine o'clock yet, and I'm ready for a nap. Are those cupcakes? Is one for me?" She selected one and peeled back the cupcake paper without waiting for an answer.

"Maybe I can pick up the animals tomorrow morning," I offered.

She gave me a dark look. "That was the easy part. Besides, I need your help for the big cupcake feast tomorrow. If I ever want to do a fundraiser like Cupcakes and Pupcakes again, please shoot me and put me out of my misery. My phone has been ringing all morning. As soon as I finish one call, another one comes in." She moaned so loud that the dogs stared at her. "People are crazy, nutso, cuckoo, and just plain weird. I'd rather work with a dog or a cat any day."

I grinned at her exaggeration. As a professional event planner, I knew what she was going through. Last-minute cancellations and broken promises were the norm. "Is there anything I can do to help?"

Nina leaned back in the flimsy chair, her legs stretched out in front of her. "More coffee, please. And more cupcakes. I'm begging you. We're surrounded by them, but I don't have the strength to browse at the moment."

It didn't take much coaxing, because I'd been itching to have a look around now that everyone was set up.

I strolled past several cupcake booths, admiring colorful cupcakes set out in amazing displays. Renee at Sugar Baby had piped artistic kitty faces on her cupcakes. At Sweet Cakes, they had topped their cupcakes with dog faces made of icing and sprinkles. Heavenly Cupcakes had placed fat little marzipan dogs dusted with brown and gold colors atop their cupcakes. No two were alike. Some of the featured cupcakes were works of art. I couldn't imagine biting into little frosting schnauzers and bulldogs. There were cupcakes representing every imaginable breed of dog and cat. Everyone had joined in the swing of things. Nina might be exhausted, but she had pulled off quite an extravaganza.

The buying had already begun, with Old Town's dog owners eagerly browsing through booths with their pooches, purchasing dog outfits and toys from vendors geared to canine needs.

I picked up more lattes to boost our energy. On my way back, I bought three Dark Side Chocolate Cupcakes that were chocolate cake with chocolate frosting. Darling white puppy and kitten faces cut out of fondant adorned the tops. Just in case chocolate didn't appeal to Humphrey and Nina, I also bought three Caramel Spice Cupcakes with white icing. Tiny signs that said *Woof!* jutted out of the icing at a slant. And so Daisy wouldn't feel left out, I bought her a barley apple pupcake iced with cream cheese.

Juggling my purchases, I found myself dodging dogs and their people. A medium-sized white dog with black freckles across his nose resembled one of the dogs in the corral. In the company of a young couple, he pranced by me, his tail wagging so hard it smacked everyone within close range.

I finally scooted behind the booth and set down the cupcakes and lattes. Nina was kissing the forehead of a basset hound mix. The dog shuffled off happily with a new owner. I looked for the freckled dog. It was gone.

"Two adoptions already?" I asked Nina.

She latched onto a latte and pulled back the top. "And a kitten, too." Nina beamed. "You wouldn't believe how wonderful people have been. They walk by with a dog, stop to see ours, and want to adopt another dog on the spot. All local people whom I know, so I was able to approve the adoptions right away. Humphrey is helping someone with that gorgeous Siamese cat." She took a long swig of latte. "Mmm." Peeling back the paper on a Caramel Spice Cupcake, she said, "I'm going to pick up a couple more dogs in a few minutes." She wolfed down the cupcake. "These have to be from Cupcake Saloon. They make the best cupcakes in town." Her voice suddenly lowered several notches. "Don't look now," she whispered, "but what is Maurice Lester doing?"

CHAPTER THREE

Dear Sophie,

I want to rescue a mixed-breed dog from the shelter, but my husband insists on a purebred bulldog. How can I convince him to adopt a mixed breed?

—Dog Crazy in Bulldog Crossing, Illinois

Dear Dog Crazy,

Buy a purebred bulldog to keep hubby happy, and adopt a mixed breed, as well! Don't forget that purebred dogs often end up in shelters, too.

—Sophie

"You know, they say Maurice used to be in the cupcake business," said Nina, nodding in his direction.

At the Sugar Baby booth, Maurice was arguing with Renee. The lank white hair that hung in his face reminded me of an old man in a horror movie. I shivered at the thought. Poor Myra, to have a guy like him interested in her. "Is he haggling with

Renee over the price of a cupcake? He's already been by here once today. I hope he skips us this time."

Renee handed him a cupcake and waved her hands at him, apparently refusing to accept any money. He headed straight toward us.

"Well, what have we here?" Maurice peered at the dogs in the pen. Dark hollows sank in under his high cheekbones and bushy eyebrows dramatized his melancholy brown eyes. "Mutts." He spat the word as though it were distasteful to even speak it. He peered over the table. "Don't you two have dogs?"

"I have a hound mix," I said proudly, hoping to shame him.

Daisy must have sensed my reaction, or perhaps Nina's, because she growled and backed out of her position under the table.

"Good heavens! One of them is loose. There's a leash law, you know." Maurice postured protectively. "You really ought to put her in the pen."

"That's Daisy. She belongs to Sophie and is very friendly," Nina assured him. "Besides, her leash is hooked to the table."

Maurice focused on me. "Reaaally? I would have pegged you for a purebred type. Hmm, I believe I've seen Mars running with it. Natasha must loathe having a mongrel."

My mouth dropped open. It was true in a way, because Natasha didn't like anything with four legs. Neither my ex-husband, Mars, short for Marshall, nor I could bear to give up Daisy in our divorce, so we shared custody of her. Every other week, Daisy stayed with Mars and Natasha. Mars doted on her while Natasha barely tolerated her. But to come right out and say it like that! The nerve of Maurice! What a snooty guy. I edged closer to Daisy and rested my hand on the scruff of her neck. "She's the most wonderful dog."

"Why don't you have a dog, Nina?" Maurice peered at the cats in the cages.

"My husband travels constantly. We plan to adopt a couple when he retires. But until then, there are so many who need help. I'd rather foster them until they find homes. I can save more animals that way. I'm glad you're coming to the big cupcake feast tomorrow night. It should be a lot of fun."

How clever of her to change the topic before I said something I might regret.

"You should be ashamed asking those prices. I do love a cupcake, though." He returned to watch the dogs in the pen. "I hope the money doesn't just benefit mixed-breed dogs like these." He pushed back a hank of white hair and cast a disparaging eye on the three dogs in the pen, all happily wagging their tails. "I'm a cat person. Black tie ought to be reserved for elegant creatures."

For my job, I arranged black-tie events constantly and had nothing against them, but every word this man uttered elevated him a notch on the too-pompous-to-live scale.

I reminded myself that I didn't have to do anything with him, other than smile and act gracious.

His nostrils flared. "Nina, darling, I *must* warn you. Nick Rigas, you know him, don't you? Everyone does. Anyway, Nick has been making noises about acquiring a canine companion. You should be aware that he's four months behind in rent. He won't leave the premises, just laughs at me in that condescending way of his when I bring it up. I'm going to have to evict him. So if he comes sniffing around for a hound, keep in mind that he'll be homeless himself in fairly short order."

I supposed it was good for Nina to know that, but it was distasteful of him to be so public about Nick's inability to pay his rent.

Spenser Osbourne ambled up carrying a huge box of cupcakes from Sugar Baby. Rather odd, since he owned Cake My Day, the biggest cupcake chain on the east coast, and could surely have as many as he wanted free of charge from the Cake My Day booth. He immediately reached out to pat the head of a huge black and tan dog. Its fur and size reminded me of a Bernese mountain dog.

The two men were a study in contrasts. Spenser's round face was as open and friendly as Maurice's was closed and sour. By nature, Spenser was stocky and muscular. He wasn't particularly tall, a few inches shorter than Maurice, and he tended just a bit toward pudginess.

"Sugar Baby Cupcakes?" sneered Maurice. "Well, well. It says a lot when the owner of a cupcakery buys the cupcakes of his competition. Are you trying to duplicate Renee's recipes? The ones you stole from Colleen weren't enough?"

Colleen? I mouthed the name and looked at Nina, who shrugged.

Spenser released a long breath and appeared to consider his response. "Good to see you, Maurice."

"It's never good to see *you.*"

Maurice was known to be a first-class grump, but this display of uncalled-for animosity was just plain rude.

Spenser flicked a glance at Nina and me. He bore the slight nobly, though I suspected it pained him.

"All these dogs and cats are up for adoption," said Nina.

Spenser reached over the pen and stroked the dog again. "What a big guy. Reminds me of a dog I had as a kid. You're a special boy." The dog's tail wagged, and he licked Spenser's hand. "I hope you'll get a great home, buddy."

"Buddy!" Nina spoke cheerfully. "That would be a cute name for him."

I saw what she was doing. By acting like Spenser had named the dog, she was getting him invested in Buddy.

"I'd love to adopt you . . ." His voice trailed off, and he stared at the dog while rubbing its ear. "Well, maybe!" he declared with enthusiasm. "Maybe I can work something out!" Clutching the cupcake box, he leaned over the rail of the corral, bringing his face close to the dog, whose feathery tail whipped back and forth with joy. "I'll be back, Buddy," he whispered.

"Hurry," said Nina. "I can't hold him, you know."

Spenser lumbered away.

The second he was out of hearing range, Maurice said, "I want that dog."

CHAPTER FOUR

Dear Natasha,

My wife insists on dressing our dog. If you ask me, a dog shouldn't have to wear anything other than a collar and a leash. Would you please tell her to quit buying doggy pajamas?

—Cat's Pajamas in Hounds Ear, North Carolina

Dear Cat's Pajamas,

She buys them? Why isn't she sewing them herself? Ask her to sew you a matching pair so you won't be so jealous.

—Natasha

Nina looked at me in shock before focusing on Maurice. "I beg your pardon?"

"I want to adopt that big dog."

Nina's mouth bunched up in anger. "You just said that you don't like mutts."

Smooth and slippery as butter, he said, "I'm selective."

"So am I—and I'm holding him for Spenser." I'd never seen Nina so angry.

"You can't do that. You just said you can't hold dogs." Maurice opened the dog pen. "I'm here, ready and able to adopt. I insist on this dog!"

I raced to his side to prevent the dogs from wandering out of their little fence.

"Fine." Nina addressed him in a sugary tone. "Here's an adoption form for you to fill out."

Behind his back, I waved my hands at her. How could she let this horrible man adopt a dog he clearly wanted only to spite Spenser?

She wiggled an eyebrow at me. I hoped that meant she was up to no good.

Maurice flipped through the adoption form. "I don't have time for this!" His thin lips twisted to the side. "I'll be back shortly."

He loped away in the direction Spenser had gone.

Nina sucked in a deep breath and released it. "I'll adopt that poor dog myself if I have to. Imagine having the nerve to try to adopt it after he just insulted dogs." She patted the stack of applications into a neat pile. "I probably ought to take him back to the shelter, but then no one will see him and adopt him. Poor fellow. Honestly," she huffed, "what could Maurice be thinking? If he comes back, tell him that the dog has already been adopted."

"Like he'll believe *that*." I stroked the dog. He would be hard to place because of his size. He deserved to be here so people would see him. Hiding him would only delay the process of finding a home for him.

I grabbed my wallet and dashed over to a nearby dog apparel vendor. Eyeing their wares, I purchased a yellow dog bandanna with adorable pink cupcakes on it. A little girly for such a macho dog, but it would have to do. Looking over my shoulder for Maurice, I raced back and tied it on the big dog's neck. "There. You can tell him that means this guy has been adopted."

"He's so cute! I'm hoping Maurice will just forget about it."

"Fat chance."

Nina stepped away to assist someone who was interested in one of the dogs.

I gladly hurried to help a little girl who was exclaiming over the kittens. Happily, her two friends wanted kittens, too, and after prolonged phone calls between all their mothers, three fuzzy little balls of fur went home with their doting new owners.

~~~

By noon, the spring day hadn't warmed too much. A huge relief, because we didn't have to worry about the cats and dogs overheating. Old Town's residents flooded Market Square with their dogs. It was perfect weather for dog walking.

Renee used Humphrey as her personal gofer, sending him back to the bakery several times and asking him to fill in for her while she took bathroom breaks. Humphrey blushed every single time she asked him for a favor. She flitted her hands like a baby bird trying out wings and fawned over him like she was smitten.

Even busy Nina noticed. "Do you think Renee has the hots for Humphrey?"

"I'm not sure." I wasn't. Renee had obviously found herself in an unenviable position now that Joy had left. I hoped she didn't think she'd also found a source of free labor. Humphrey was so eager to have a relationship that he might misinterpret her need for help as interest in him. "I hope she's not taking advantage of him. Do you know her very well?"

"I know she bakes a great cupcake. And I'm about ready to strangle Joy." Nina held the top of her head with both hands as though she feared it might explode. "I can't believe this is happening. Everything was planned so far in advance, and now Joy is demanding her own course at the dinner tomorrow. I already managed to secure a spot for her booth"—she pointed with her entire hand—"way over there, but how can I invent another course for the dinner?"

"Let's go over it. Appetizer, salad"—I laughed aloud—"give

her a soup course. How could anyone do soup as a cup-cake?"

Nina glared at me.

"All right, all right." I tried to be serious about it. "We have an appetizer, a fish course, vegetables, a main course, a fruit, and two desserts. Oh! How about an after-dinner cheese course? Very elegant and French."

"Perfect! Hold down the fort while I go tell her."

Humphrey returned again and my elderly neighbor, Francie, showed up with her golden retriever, Duke, for her shift at the booth. Hair the same color as Duke's but the texture of straw stuck out from under Francie's hunter green canvas hat. She'd dressed it up with a pin in the shape and color of a golden retriever. Francie wore her jacket open, revealing a bright yellow long-sleeve T-shirt and loose drawstring pants. "It's cold out here! I'm your lunch relief, so you'd better go grab something to eat. Bring some back for me, will you?"

"Soph, could we pick up the desk for Renee while we're out getting lunch?" asked Humphrey. "It's not far from here."

I didn't imagine we would have more time later. Not to mention that we would be worn out.

Humphrey retrieved my car and picked me up. Leaving Daisy in the care of Nina and Francie, I hopped into the passenger seat to give him a hand with the desk. We cruised a mere six blocks away. Humphrey parked the car in front of a typical Old Town red brick town house. Located on a corner lot, it was four stories tall if one counted the basement and attic. Small dormer windows peeked out of the third-floor attic, and tiny basement windows showed just above the sidewalk. I gauged the steps to the front door that we would no doubt have to negotiate with the desk. Five steps—wide, but steep. A fan-shaped window graced the top of the front door, and a topiary sat on the stoop.

Humphrey plunked change into the meter. From the sidewalk we could hear someone yelling, one of the drawbacks of living so close to the street. A woman's voice shouted angrily, but I couldn't make out the words.

"Maybe we should come back another time," I said.

"What if it's coming from the neighboring house?" asked Humphrey.

I didn't think it was, but before I could dissuade him, he trotted up the steps and rang the bell.

Somewhat leery, I followed him.

"I don't want to disappoint Renee," he explained.

The door opened immediately, and a woman yelled, "What do you want?"

There, right before us, stood a steaming mad Clarissa Osbourne—the very same woman who had been angry with me when I was getting coffee.

She took one look at me, and her mouth opened wide. She threw her hands in the air and shook her head. Her hands flailed in anger. She closed them into fists, and snorted like a bull. *"You! How dare you come to my home?"*

Humphrey took a step back.

Clarissa ran her hands through her hair, mussing it into a wild mess. Breathing heavily, she said, "So it's come to this, has it? Perfect timing. Just perfect!" Her eyes searched the floor, and she pumped her fists on her waist. Meeting my eyes, she shook a trembling forefinger a bare inch from my nose. "I'm not through with you. You will rue the day you did this to me."

Spenser approached her from behind. She whipped around, screamed in his face at a pitch that caused Humphrey to stick his fingers in his ears, then she pounded up the stairs, her heels kicking out to the sides like a child's.

The color of Spenser's face reminded me of a purple tomato, but he forced a feeble smile. "Sorry about that." His forehead creased. "Sophie? What are you doing here?"

Humphrey's hand shook much as Clarissa's had when he held the check out to Spenser. "We came for the desk."

"We could come back later," I offered. "This obviously isn't a good time."

"It's the right time. You saved me from another agonizing hour of that tantrum." Spenser pulled reading glasses out of his shirt pocket and peered at the check. "What desk?" He leaned forward and looked around. "Is Renee with you?"

"She can't get away, so we're picking the desk up for her," explained Humphrey.

Spenser examined the check again. "I don't know anything about a desk. If you'll excuse me for a moment, I'll ask Clarissa."

"Look, if this is a bad time—"

He was already halfway up the stairs when he interrupted me. "No," he said softly. "This is fine."

We waited quietly. I hoped the screaming wouldn't begin again.

The Osbourne's entrance hall was barely larger than the width of the door. Marble tiles alternated in a black and white checkerboard on the floor. An English-style table with turned legs and three drawers straight across the top held an assortment of blue and white pitchers and vases. Two oriental rugs lay end to end, stretching to the bottom of the stairs. A third oriental runner padded the stairs. To the left of the stairway was a tiny upholstered bench. The sun shone through windows in a back room, probably the kitchen.

Spenser returned, looking perplexed. "I apologize for the confusion. I had no idea that Clarissa had agreed to sell my grandmother's desk. I'll need a hand bringing it up from the basement."

I followed Spenser and Humphrey down the hallway and into a modern kitchen decorated in a colonial style. The stove was set in an old-fashioned brick nook, designed to appear like a colonial fireplace. Shiny copper pots with black handles hung on it. Sunshine flooded through a window over a farmhouse-style sink and tiny pots of seedlings basked in the rays.

Spenser opened a door that led to a lower level. Only partly finished, it was being used as an exercise room.

He stared at a petite lady's writing desk at the bottom of the stairs. Rubbed to a shining polish, the cherry wood gleamed. He took a deep breath and held it, his lips mashed together, wrinkling his chin. Finally, he nodded his head. "Humphrey, if you can carry one side, I'll get the other, and Sophie, maybe you could close the door behind us?"

We trooped up the stairs, the men huffing and puffing. As

they carried it outside, I realized that Clarissa was watching from the bend in the upper staircase. If looks could kill, I'd have keeled over dead.

We made it out to the car, and I breathed a little easier, relieved to be away from Clarissa. I opened the back hatch and the guys slid the desk inside.

"Spenser," I said, "Clarissa seems to have some kind of beef with me. I can't imagine what I've done to upset her."

He made a point of looking into the car and touching the desk one last time as though he was parting with something dear to him. "She's watching from the window?"

Humphrey and I looked up. Clarissa stood against the window like a hawk-eyed sentry, her arms crossed over her chest.

"Yes," I said.

Spenser avoided my eyes and directed his response to Humphrey. "Everything's fine. She . . . has her moments. Sophie, would you tell Nina that I'm coming to get Buddy, the dog I liked so much?"

"Fantastic!" I worried, though, that it could have been news of the dog that had set off Clarissa's screaming fit. If she didn't want the dog, maybe the adoption wasn't such a good idea.

I felt unsettled as we drove away. Something was clearly wrong. Nevertheless, I phoned Nina to tell her Spenser intended to adopt the black and tan dog.

Humphrey blocked traffic by double-parking in front of Sugar Baby. Horns honked at us immediately.

"Isn't there a back entrance?" I asked.

Humphrey hopped out of the car, flipped open the back hatch, and struggled with the desk. He had it partway out when I said, hoping he would catch on, "Isn't there a delivery alley behind Sugar Baby?"

He paid me no heed whatsoever and continued to struggle with the desk, apparently oblivious to the protesting horns and the blocked traffic. People were looking out of shop windows to see what was happening.

"Humphrey! For heaven's sake, someone is going to shoot you if you don't move this car!"

"Huh? Could you give me a hand here?"

Was he really so besotted with Renee that he couldn't hear me or the honking horns? I waved apologetically at the car behind us.

"Renee lives upstairs over top of the shop," he said. "Think we're strong enough to carry it up the stairs?"

"Yes. But only if we park in the alley!" I shoved the desk inside the car and slammed the back door shut. "Let's go!"

Humphrey finally figured out what I'd been saying. "Oh, I see. The alley *would* be easier." He drove around the corner and into the alley that ran behind the stores, parking in back of Sugar Baby.

Once again, he struggled to pull the desk from the car. I wedged in next to him and tugged on the other side. It slid toward us.

The delicate desk was far heavier than I'd expected. I appreciated the fact that it was made of solid wood, but the weight would make the stairs hard to negotiate.

A Saab that looked like a station wagon with a hatch in the back rolled into the alley and parked. Spenser stepped out. "I thought you might need a hand getting it up to Renee's apartment. Sorry to be so late. Traffic was at a standstill."

Summoning every bit of strength I had, I didn't mention who had caused the traffic to stop.

Humphrey gladly accepted his offer. The men removed the desk from the car and carried it to the stoop. I opened the back door of the building. The three of us entered a small foyer, which smelled heavenly, thanks to cupcakes that were baking.

Muffin Pruitt emerged in the hallway wearing a cute pink Sugar Baby apron over a white polo shirt and a jean skirt. Black Mary Jane shoes adorned her feet. She looked like an adorable advertisement for happy baking. "Hi! Renee said you'd be coming by." She opened a door and pointed. "Just take it up the stairs, if you don't mind. Renee will be so thrilled to have it."

I led the way up to a small landing that opened into an empty living room with two French doors overlooking the quaint street.

Huffing and puffing, the guys reached the living room and set the desk down. The delicate desk seemed even smaller in the empty room.

Spenser leaned against the wall to catch his breath. Humphrey, not at all used to physical activity, bent over, his hands on his knees.

Spenser choked out, "What happened here? There's not even a sofa or a TV."

Humphrey glanced around before whispering, "Joy must have wiped her out."

His breath coming hard, Spenser asked, "Didn't she have furniture of her own?"

Humphrey straightened up. "I thought Renee and Joy were good friends. Maybe I should have a word with Joy?"

"Humphrey," I cautioned, "you probably shouldn't get involved in someone else's argument."

"I disagree, Sophie. Someone should intervene on Renee's behalf," said Spenser. "Something isn't right here."

"You bet it isn't," said Muffin.

I hadn't heard her feet on the stairs.

"I might look like a little mouse," she said, "but I'm not one to stand by idly when I see someone wronged."

She opened the slanted lid of the desk, which folded down into a writing area. Inside, adorable cubbyholes, delicate carved columns, and tiny drawers filled the back wall. "This is beautiful."

A bell tinkled downstairs.

"Oops. That's a customer. Just leave the desk against that wall," she suggested. "Renee can slide it wherever she likes when she comes home."

The guys still breathed heavily as we left the building.

"Do you think Renee would mind if I left my car here temporarily?" asked Spenser. "I'll never find another parking space close by with Cupcakes and Pupcakes going on today."

"Maybe we should do the same," said Humphrey. "That way, one of us can give Francie a lift home later."

The mind is a strange place. He couldn't see that he'd been

blocking traffic, yet he had enough foresight to realize that elderly Francie might be too worn out to walk home?

"Fine with me, as long as it's not towed," I said.

"I'll clear it with Renee." It was an authoritative declaration. Humphrey felt empowered by his relationship with her.

Spenser frowned at him, as though he didn't quite understand. I couldn't blame him. I didn't, either.

I made Humphrey promise he would return to the booth immediately, so Nina wouldn't stress out. Meanwhile, I went in search of lunch.

People and their dogs packed the streets. A line had formed on the sidewalk outside the little deli where I thought I'd pick up sandwiches, so I wound my way through the throngs on the sidewalks to The Laughing Hound. Bernie, the best man at my wedding to Mars, ran the popular restaurant. None of us ever expected footloose Bernie to settle down in one place, much less manage a successful restaurant, but he had. Bernie's hair was always disheveled and his nose sported a bump that suggested it had once been broken, yet he exuded a friendly British charm that endeared him to those who knew him.

Located in a tall town house, The Laughing Hound featured dining rooms on several levels. As usual, the place was packed. I waltzed past the hostess and trotted down the few stairs on the right to the bar. Even the cozy lounge area overflowed with customers. Weaving my way through the crowd, I reached the bar, leaned toward a balding bartender I didn't know, and asked if I could place a take-out order.

"Sure. I don't have a menu, though." He handed a customer a glass of white wine and a mug of beer. "It's been a zoo in here, what with the cupcake-pupcake thing going on."

"I don't really need a menu."

That stopped him in his tracks. He stepped toward me and took a closer look. "Sophie?"

"Yes?" Did I know this guy?

"Bernie said to be on the lookout for you. Be right back." He disappeared through a swinging door that I happened to know led to the kitchen. In less than a minute, he returned with five take-out boxes that featured The Laughing Hound's logo on the top. "You're to try these and let Bernie know what you think."

I took them from him, wondering what was going on. "Okay. What do I owe you?"

He grinned and held up a little note penned in Bernie's handwriting that said, *On the house.*

"Thank Bernie for me. Why are there five boxes?"

The bartender shrugged. "That's what Bernie told me, lunch and dessert for five."

The crowd behind me was growing restless. I thanked him again and made my way up the steps and out the front door, relieved to be outside. How could Bernie have known I would be coming by for take-out lunch?

I walked past people browsing through Old Town with their dogs. Nina's event had certainly drawn a lot of attention. I was within two feet of the adoption booth when I heard someone scream.

"Stop! Stop that dog!"

All heads turned as a tiny white dog shot between feet, heading for the street. She wore a robin's-egg blue dress with white polka dots, and a blue sash around her waist. Two tiers of ruffles flounced on her haunches as she made her mad escape.

I tossed the take-out boxes onto the table and stepped into her path. I hunched over, ready to nab her. She veered . . . I lunged . . . fell over . . . and miraculously managed to wrap my arms around a wriggling mass of dog.

The crowd applauded, and someone offered a hand to help me up. I took it and looked up into blue-gray eyes that made my knees weak.

CHAPTER FIVE

Dear Natasha,

Over my vehement objections, my husband and son brought home a puppy—a very hairy puppy. You have a dog. How do you keep your floors clean?

—Tired of Sweeping in Furry, Arkansas

Dear Tired of Sweeping,

You're cleaning the wrong thing. Buy a pet-grooming attachment for your vacuum and gently vacuum the puppy daily before he can drop fur all over your clean floors.

—Natasha

"Whoa!" He wrapped his other arm around my waist so I wouldn't fall backward. For a moment it was as though we were in a romantic dance dip. He smiled as he helped me to my feet. Thick, neatly trimmed cocoa brown hair topped a strong forehead, great cheekbones, and a determined chin. Everything about him from the white shirt with a button-down collar that he wore under a casual maroon crew neck sweater to chinos with a crease pressed into them made a dashingly clean-cut impression.

General Euclid German looked on and clapped his hands together. A familiar face around Old Town, the retired general who published a newsletter for military retirees was one of the biggest contributors to Cupcakes and Pupcakes. "Excellent catch!" he said.

I wasn't sure if he meant me or the gorgeous guy who still held my hand. The silly dog wriggled, forcing me to withdraw my hand and grasp her more tightly.

"Sophie's a tough one to catch," said the general. "Are you all right, young lady?"

The cute guy said, *"Sophie?"* softly, and I could hardly breathe. "This is Sophie?" he asked, a tinge of wonder in his voice.

The general slapped him on his back. "Sophie Winston, I would like to introduce you to my nephew, Alex German. Alex is relocating, and I'm trying to talk him into making his home here in Old Town. Looks just like me, doesn't he?"

The family resemblance was unmistakable. Even though the general was well into his seventies, he stood erect as a twenty-year-old. He had a couple of inches on Alex, but they shared intelligent, kind eyes and a marked jawline. The general appeared fatigued, though, and perhaps a bit sallow. Probably the result of entertaining a younger relative.

"The general has been after me to meet you. I had no idea the old buck had such exceptional taste in women."

I was savvy enough to know that guys as stunningly good-looking as Alex were flirts, and that he would have said something just as flattering if I had three eyes and elf ears. But that didn't stop me from being captivated.

I managed to choke out, "Is this your dog?" She licked my cheek, which I imagined was the color of a cayenne pepper. I could feel the heat in my face.

"No, she's not. But she's cute, too."

I tore my eyes away from him long enough to take a better look at the dog. Fluffy white fur covered her head. Toward her ears it turned ever so slightly ivory. Her tiny nose was jet black, and she had darling lively eyes.

"Martha! Martha!"

I recognized *that* voice. I didn't need to turn around to know Natasha was behind me.

She strode up and stopped next to me looking glamorous in an impeccable knit suit of robin's-egg blue adorned with pearl buttons set in gold frames. I'd felt svelte in my dark purple T-shirt, which hid the elastic waist on my black jeans, but suddenly they seemed drab and gloomy. Why hadn't I worn something chic, or at the very least—spring colors?

"Sophie! What are *you* doing with my dog?" she asked.

Daisy lay in the shade under the table, and her head lifted at the sound of Natasha's voice.

Francie clutched at her throat and staggered backward into Nina. "Dear heaven, tell me I heard that wrong."

Natasha didn't bother taking the dog from me. She had spotted Alex. She held out her hand to him and tossed her dark tresses back seductively with a mere shake of her head. "Helloooo," she sang. "I'm Natasha. I don't believe we've met before."

Natasha and I had grown up together and competed at everything as kids. Everything except beauty pageants, where she was on her own. She excelled in them, as she did in most things she set her mind to. Unlike me, she was tall and model thin, with dark hair that was always perfectly coiffed. She never tucked her hair up with a big clip to get it out of the way, or left the house without makeup like I had that morning.

When my husband, Mars, and I divorced, Natasha had set up housekeeping with him, and they moved into a house on my block. I had wanted to think that she had nothing to do with the end of my marriage, but some of my friends and family blamed it on her, and as the years went by, I wasn't so sure myself. Making matters worse, Natasha and I wrote rival domestic advice columns for newspapers.

I had come to terms with her relationship with Mars, sort of. He and I had shared a romantic moment in almost this exact spot not that long ago. The heat in my face welled up again at the mere thought. I'd avoided being alone with him as much as possible since then. It was the chicken's way out to avoid addressing what had happened, but I was afraid to open that door and see what lurked behind it.

Natasha usually meant well. If only she didn't think she was always right about everything. I blamed that on her adoring fans, who thought she was perfect because of her local TV show about all things domestic. At the moment, she teetered on five-inch heels, difficult under any circumstances, and impossible on Old Town's brick sidewalks.

Alex shook her hand. "Alex German."

"German? Euclid! You never told me you had such a handsome brother."

Oh, puh-leeze! Why was she buttering him up?

Francie sputtered and hacked at Natasha's flattery of the elderly man.

In a Southern accent, the general drawled, "You flatter me, Miss Natasha. Alex is my nephew, darlin'."

She flapped the air with fingers that sported a gleaming French manicure. "I don't believe it. You must be the baby in your family, sir." Wrinkling her nose coyly at Alex, she added, "I'm a bit of a local celebrity."

I didn't mean to snort. *Really, I didn't.*

Natasha bristled. "Well, I am! I have a TV show."

The general beamed at her. "Natasha"—he pronounced her name as though she were a bug, Gnat-ash-a—"will be one of the cupcake bakers at tomorrow night's feast. What kind of cupcakes can we look forward to, Natasha?"

Tucking her chin in slightly, she said, "I wish I could tell you, but mean old Sophie would have me disqualified."

The general roared. "I must confess that I am partial to Spenser's cupcakes at Cake My Day. In fact, I have a standing order there, but I imagine you'll give him a run for his money, Natasha. I noticed your name wasn't on the list of bakers, Sophie. Why aren't you baking cupcakes for the competition?"

"Because I don't own a bakery." And I didn't feel the need

to compete with everyone about everything like Gnat-ash-a did. She glared at me. Of course, she didn't own a bakery, either, but she would never pass up an opportunity to compete.

"It's a haute cuisine event," said Natasha.

Although she hadn't said it explicitly, I knew she meant I wasn't worthy of baking for it.

Alex stroked the little dog's head. Her tail waggled back and forth.

"Did you say this is *your* dog?" I asked Natasha. "You hate dogs!" My own dog, Daisy, watched her wicked stepmother from under the table. Natasha didn't like anything that might shed fur, and unless I missed my guess, this little dog would shed plenty. I had heard no end of complaints about Daisy's fur. Natasha didn't have the best record with animals. None of her friends would soon forget the time she'd lost two kittens outdoors on a cold winter night.

Natasha flashed a wild-eyed look my way and checked around to see if anyone had overheard. She responded smoothly, "Now that's not true. I love sweet little dogs like this. I named her Martha after my idol, Martha Stewart. Isn't she adorable?"

Martha was the picture of a perfect lapdog. She wriggled impatiently. I held her out to Natasha, who averted her eyes and leaned away.

"She's from the finest show stock," said Natasha.

I persisted, practically jamming the dog into her, until Natasha finally took her dog in her arms.

Martha growled. Daisy left her spot under the table to take a better look at Martha.

"I don't dare tell Mars—" Martha bit down on Natasha's arm. The muscles in Natasha's neck tightened, but the smile never left her face. She finished her sentence. "—how much she cost."

Snarling, Martha gnawed Natasha's arm through her soft knit sleeve with a vengeance.

"Gahhhhh." Natasha held Martha out to me. "Take her," she wheezed.

It seemed pretty clear to me that Martha wanted to make another mad dash. Natasha had managed to buy a high-energy dog. "Do you have a leash?"

"Isn't she darling? I can carry her around in a purse!" Rivulets of blood running down her wrist, Natasha pulled a leash out of her bag and handed it to me. Blue with white polka dots, it matched Martha's dress. I snapped it on her and lowered her to the plaza.

Martha ran directly to Daisy and serious sniffing ensued.

"Give me a tissue, please," hissed Natasha.

The general's deep voice boomed, "Darlin', I believe you'd better get that cleaned up. Alex, you don't mind carryin' that pup."

The general offered Natasha his arm and gentlemanly strode her across the plaza toward the street.

Alex lingered. "I presume I'll see you at the dinner tomorrow night?"

What did he want with me? Gorgeous guys like Alex went out with women like Natasha. "I'll definitely be there."

"I'm looking forward to it." Alex ruffled the fur on Daisy's head before picking up Martha. His eyes met mine, and he grinned. "She's not biting *me* . . ." Taking long strides, he followed the general.

Nina scooted over next to me. "Be still, my heart! Some guys have it all. If I were you, I'd grab him."

"You steered me toward my last boyfriend. Need I remind you what a mess that turned out to be?"

"Who could have foreseen that? Okay, we'll do a little sleuthing about this guy first. If you can wait that long. Women will be after him like he's the last cupcake on the plate. Military, don't you think? He has that same regal posture as the general." She gazed around. "Where did Humphrey go now? I'm getting a little miffed that he's spending so much time at Sugar Baby. Not that Renee doesn't need help, but have you noticed that she keeps asking him to fill in while she runs back to the bakery?"

"No kidding," said Francie. "This time she sent *him* to the bakery."

"Sophie, would you go get him? I have to make another run to pick up dogs and cats, but we're so busy that I'm afraid to leave unless Humphrey's back to help."

"Sure." Lunch on my mind, I hurried back to Sugar Baby. This time I entered through the front door. The walls and countertops of Sugar Baby Cupcakes were frosting pink, which provided a soft contrast to the lovely milk chocolate brown of the hardwood floors and the base of the cupcake display. Five old-fashioned tables with pink Formica tops and adorable brown bentwood chairs upholstered with pink fabric sporting brown polka dots offered places for a cupcake snack.

Humphrey stood behind the counter, holding cash in his hand like he worked there.

"Are you stealing Renee's money?" I joked.

Humphrey didn't smile at my question. His brow furrowed, and he said, "I can't find Muffin."

CHAPTER SIX

Dear Sophie,

I always manage to make a mess when I pour batter into a cupcake pan. It ends up everywhere. A spoon doesn't work much better. Help!

—Messy Moyra in Kitchen, West Virginia

Dear Messy Moyra,

Cut the tip off the bottom corner of a large freezer bag, roll the top back over your hand and fill it with your cupcake batter. You can squeeze out exactly as much as you want into each cupcake liner.

—Sophie

"She must be here somewhere. Did you check in the back?" I asked.

Humphrey tilted his head. I could read his expression—he wasn't that dumb!

"Muffin?" I jogged upstairs and peeked into the bedrooms.

One was almost empty. A tangle of wire coat hangers lay on the floor, along with a few scraps of paper and a partial roll of leftover Christmas gift wrapping paper. A pile of clothes was heaped in a corner. Jeans and colorful tops peeked out, and a black fleece jacket lay on top. It appeared that someone had emptied drawers but forgotten the contents.

The other bedroom was so adorable that I wanted to curl up on the bed with a book. Gauzy white curtains billowed gently at two tall windows overlooking the alley. Tiny jewelry boxes clustered together on a dressing table. Renee clearly loved miniatures. Petite cat statuettes were displayed in a case on the wall. Teeny teapots and saucers sat on the dresser in an artistic arrangement. A glass shelf contained a collection of miniature cupcakes.

The white headboard and dresser shone against barely pink walls. A cushy armchair had been upholstered in a pink and white toile with a ruffle around the bottom. The duvet cover was a brisk, clean white, like the dust ruffle, but the pillows on the bed were a darling mixture of patterns that ran from pale pink to red.

The largest and most prominent pillow was in the shape of a cupcake. The white bottom had been stitched to look like a cupcake wrapper. Pink icing swirled to a peak, and tiny clear beads had been sewn onto it as though they were sparkling sprinkles of sugar. Part of the frosting looked so real that I paused to examine it. How had they done that?

I touched the frosting on the pillow. It smeared under my finger. That was odd. Anyone with a room this tidy would never leave icing on a pillow.

"Sophie!" called Humphrey. "Come down here."

I ran down the stairs to the back foyer. Voices drifted to me from the bakery, and I followed them.

Humphrey stashed money in a drawer. "I just sold some guy a blueberry cupcake."

"I didn't see her upstairs. Maybe she stepped out. Did you check the restroom?" I marched to the restroom door, knocked, and flung it open. "Not a soul in there."

I opened the front door and peered up and down the street,

but didn't see her outside, either. When I closed the door, a scorched smell wafted to me. "Is something burning?"

Humphrey sniffed.

I joined him behind the counter and peered into an oven. "There are cupcakes in there!" I promptly jerked the door open, located oven mitts, and yanked out two pans of scorched cupcakes. "Those are toast." I set them on a stainless steel worktop next to a tray of baked cupcakes and a mixing bowl full of pink icing. Only two of the cupcakes had been frosted.

"She must be nearby," I said. "No one would put cupcakes in the oven to bake and then leave."

"Maybe she ran over to Market Square and something delayed her along the way?" Humphrey postulated.

I didn't think so. "And left the doors unlocked so anyone could walk right in and help themselves to cupcakes and the cash register? Seems unlikely."

"This place isn't very big," said Humphrey. "Let's split up and have a good look around. If we don't find her, we'll, uh, decide what to do next."

"Is there a basement?" I asked. "Maybe a door slammed shut, and she can't get out?"

"Wouldn't we hear her screaming?" asked Humphrey. "Sophie, you check upstairs. I'll take the main floor and look for a basement."

The upstairs wouldn't be hard to search. There wasn't a thing in the living room but the desk. I hadn't seen the kitchen or bathroom, though.

I took the steep stairs faster than I should have and breathed heavily at the top. On the alley side of the apartment, the sun shone in through a kitchen window over the sink. Galley style, it was small but well outfitted. No sign of Muffin, though. Dashing through the apartment, I flung open closet doors just to be on the safe side. No Muffin. The pink and black bathroom was dated, like my own, but it gleamed squeaky clean. Still no Muffin.

Joy's old closet had been emptied. The last place to check was Renee's closet. Packed to the gills, I didn't think anyone could have wedged herself in there. I sighed when I shut the door and leaned against it. We were searching as though she was hiding, which made no sense. She must have had some overwhelming reason to leave the cupcakery—some kind of personal emergency that caused her to forget about the cupcakes in the oven. I couldn't imagine what that emergency might have been, but there wasn't any other logical explanation.

I peered out the open window in case Muffin was catching a quick break out back. Spenser's car was gone, but there was no sign of Muffin.

My gaze fell on the cupcake-shaped pillow. I walked to the bed and picked it up. Once again, I ran my fingers over the frosting. If it were old icing, it would have hardened and felt crusty. This was fresh enough to rub off on my fingers. I turned the pillow around. Two dark smudges marred the base of the faux frosting. I was sniffing them for a clue when the toe of my shoe hit something under the bed.

A scream burbled up my throat, and I jumped away from the bed. A glob of pink frosting had somehow landed on top of my shoe. I stared at it stupidly. How could frosting be under the bed? Idiotic thoughts flicked through my head. Did Renee store frosting under the bed? Had she hidden it from Joy so she wouldn't take it? And then it came to me that someone must be hiding under the bed. I backed toward the door, chills coursing down my arms.

Footsteps banged on the stairs. Humphrey raced into Renee's bedroom.

"Did you find her?" asked Humphrey.

Trying to keep my cool, I said, "There's someone under the bed. He . . . she just dumped a little dollop of frosting on my shoe."

Humphrey's shoulders twitched at the thought. He grabbed a heavy doorstop and bravely dropped to his knees. He lifted the bed skirt and peered underneath, holding the doorstop at the ready to swing it down on someone. "Oh noooo."

He pulled two legs out from under the bed, and I felt as though my heart had plummeted off a cliff. They wore girlish Mary Jane–style shoes.

I knelt and helped him tug Muffin out from under the bed.

Humphrey placed two fingers on the side of Muffin's neck. Ever so softly, he said, "No pulse." He tilted Muffin's chin back and blew into her mouth.

I hustled to the telephone and called 911.

A siren wailed in the distance almost immediately. I was still on the phone when the bell tinkled downstairs and someone shouted. The woman on the phone said, "There's an officer on the premises." I hung up and scrambled down the stairs.

A young police officer peered into the back hallway. He must have been close by when the call went out. "Something burning in here?" he asked. "I thought someone was injured."

I explained as succinctly as I could.

He remained calm, but when I showed him the stairs, he wasted no time and was all business. "Stay down here and show the EMTs where to go." He hustled up.

Emergency medical technicians arrived a scant minute later. As they chugged upstairs, I could hear voices in the bakery. People had begun to come in to find out what was going on. I shooed them outside, locked the front door, and flipped the open sign to closed.

Fearing they would peek in the back door, I rushed through the hallway, only to find Humphrey sagging against the wall, his shoulders curled forward.

He wiped his eyes with his sleeve. "Why would anyone hurt Muffin? She wasn't much more than a kid."

I rubbed his arm in a futile gesture of comfort. "Is she . . . ?"

"They're still trying to resuscitate her, but . . ."

He didn't need to say more. As a mortician, he knew.

He snuffled. "She was going home to see her family in Tucson next week."

Obviously, he had known Muffin well. I'd seen her around town but knew nothing about her.

"I'm going over to tell Renee," he said. "She shouldn't hear about this over the phone."

I locked the back door behind him.

Footsteps on the stairs caught my attention.

The young officer emerged. "Don't touch anything. This place is officially a crime scene. Where's Mr. Brown?"

"He went to tell Renee about Muffin."

His mouth swung to the side in annoyance. He took down explicit notes about how we happened to find Muffin's body, including my name and contact information.

He squinted at me. "You seem nervous."

"I am! I just found Muffin, who was probably murdered!" I couldn't exactly tell him that I was afraid my old boyfriend Wolf, a homicide investigator, would knock on the door any second. Besides, finding Muffin had rattled me. Cupcakes usually baked in my oven in sixteen to eighteen minutes. The cupcakes I removed from Sugar Baby's oven had baked into rocks. I'd have to run a test to be sure, but my guess was that Muffin had been murdered within the last hour. It was even remotely possible that the killer had left when the bell on the front door tinkled due to Humphrey's arrival.

"I didn't mention murder." He held his breath and studied me.

"Why else would she be under the bed? Clearly someone bothered to hide her."

He made a note on his pad. "I'll probably have more questions for you later."

He hustled me out the front door and latched it. A crowd had gathered outside, including Clarissa Osbourne and Maurice.

They pummeled me with questions.

"Who is it?"

"Did Joy murder Renee?"

"Is Joy dead?"

No one even mentioned poor Muffin. I pushed past everyone and made my way back to Nina's booth on Market Square.

Nina hugged me fiercely. "Humphrey told us what happened. He's taken over for Renee at her booth so she can go back to the cupcakery."

Tear trails stained Francie's face. "I liked that young woman. How dare someone snuff out her life like that?" She held on to her golden retriever as though she found solace in his presence.

"Do you want to go home?" asked Nina. "It must have been quite a shock."

If going home could have brought Muffin back to life, I would have run all the way. "Thanks, but I'd rather be busy and useful here."

"Maybe you should eat something. Bernie sent over quite a feast!" Francie pointed to the take-out boxes.

I reached into the dog pen and slid my hand over Buddy's head. Just thinking about him having a new home soothed my ragged nerves. "Hey, Buddy, your new dad will be coming by to take you home soon." He wagged his tail and panted.

"Where *is* Spenser? I'm so afraid that horrible Maurice will be back." Nina scanned the crowds milling through the booths.

As though the mere mention of his name caused him to materialize, Maurice emerged from the clusters of people, and appeared to have Officer Wong in tow. Pointing a long, bony forefinger at us, Maurice said, "They refuse to give me that dog."

CHAPTER SEVEN

Dear Natasha,

My daughter says she wants cupcakes as favors for her sweet sixteen party. That's okay with me, but what do I put them in? I can't just hand out cupcakes as the guests walk out the door.

—Baking Mom in Sixteen Acres, Massachusetts

Dear Baking Mom,

Buy cupcake favor boxes and personalize them to suit the occasion with a little bling, and ribbon imprinted with your daughter's name!

—Natasha

"Are you kidding me?" Wong placed her fists on her ample hips. "There's a murder less than a block away, and you haul me all the way over here because of a dog adoption? Have you lost your senses?"

I thanked my lucky stars it was Wong he'd dragged over. She wasn't easily fooled. In fact, Maurice might rue his decision to involve the police.

"So what's the story here?" Her gaze drifted up to the adoption sign.

"Hi, Wo—"

I elbowed Nina. It probably wouldn't be smart to let Maurice know we were chummy with Wong. What could I say to get him to malign dogs again so she could see Maurice for what he was?

Nina coughed. "Sorry, Maurice. The other interested party has confirmed. The big black and tan dog is taken. That's what the bandanna means."

Wong nodded her head. "Okay. Why don't you take one of these other dogs? That one with the brown spot around his eye is awfully cute."

Maurice drew himself as erect as he could. Wong and I were on the short side, and Nina was only a couple inches taller than me. Did he think he could intimidate us?

"I was told they would not hold a dog."

"Is that true?" asked Wong.

"We don't usually hold them, but in this case we made an exception, since the person notified us that he is on his way to collect the dog." Nina licked her lips, and I could tell she was gearing up for Maurice's next accusation.

"I don't see him anywhere. I am here, ready to adopt." Maurice sneered at us.

Nina shot back, "He refused to fill out the adoption form."

Wong sighed. "What is *wrong* with you people? I have better things to do. Mr. Lester, fill out the form already."

I had to do something before she told us to hand over Buddy! Wong *had* to see Maurice for what he was. Trying to act casual, I strolled to the gate on the pen, latched a leash onto the cute dog with the brown spot around his eye, and let him out. He wriggled all over with excitement. I edged toward Maurice. Bingo. Cute as could be, the dog sniffed Maurice's pant leg.

Maurice shrieked as though the dog had bitten him, jumped away, and pulled his foot back to kick the poor little dog. I bent to sweep the dog into my arms, and the toe of Maurice's shoe clocked me in the eye, hard enough to knock me over onto my side.

The ensuing chaos was all a little fuzzy. I held on to the dog so he wouldn't get away.

"You kicked her! That's assault!" Wong's hands reached out to me. "Sophie? You okay? Let me see that eye."

"I can't believe you did that," said Nina. "You monster! You would have kicked a defenseless little dog?" Nina gently removed the dog from my arms.

With Wong's help, I stood up, holding my hand over my eye.

Maurice barely flinched. "You set me up. You intentionally threw yourself in the path of my foot. My lawyer will hear about this."

He opened the gate to the dog pen and tried to remove Buddy.

Wong blocked his path. "I'm very sorry, sir, but I'm not sure that *you* should adopt a dog at all. Sophie, do you want to press charges?"

"No." After all, I *had* meant to trick him into saying something vicious, I just hadn't anticipated that he would try to kick the poor dog.

Maurice sputtered something incoherent and slunk away. Nina secured the dogs in the pen while Francie and Wong examined my eye.

They didn't say anything until Nina joined us, and said, "Man, but you're gonna have a shiner!"

I covered my other eye. I could see fine. Francie pulled a mirror out of her purse. I peered into it. Sure enough, the skin around my eye was turning all sorts of pink and blue colors. Swell.

"Okay, everybody, I'll be fine." I wanted to focus their attention on something else already.

Wong's radio spewed something unintelligible to me that appeared to have meaning for her. "I'll come back later to check on you."

"Hey! Anyone hungry?" I asked to get their minds off me. "I'm starved! We're supposed to tell Bernie what we think."

I opened the boxes to find enough food for eight people, even though Nina and Francie had already eaten some of it. I could see ham, turkey, roast beef, various cheeses, sprouts, lettuce, tomato, cucumber, and mustard in assorted sandwiches and roll-ups. There were a few tubs of a mouthwatering chicken salad with mangoes and avocados, as well as some with pasta that appeared to contain spinach and little specs of some sort of red pepper.

Nina whisked a fork into the chicken salad. "Oh! Oh!" Her mouth full, she murmured, "It's a good thing I'm married, or I would latch on to Bernie and hang out in the restaurant all day."

A couple ambled up to admire the cats. Nina set her food down to talk with them.

Francie excused herself for a powder room break, and I rushed a box of food over to Humphrey.

"How's Renee?" I asked.

"She took it hard." He craned his neck to get a better look at me. "What's with your eye?"

I didn't feel like going into details with people listening in. "I banged into something."

"It looks terrible."

He slid a cupcake into a box and accepted payment for it from a young woman. "I'm still having trouble believing that I saw Muffin with my own eyes, and that she's dead."

"It seems impossible. She just met us in the back when we delivered the desk. All cheery and adorable. How could this have happened?"

"I'm almost out of cupcakes." He said it in a disconnected way. Like he was struggling to cope with mundane reality. "I don't think Renee will be able to bake more. It would be unreasonable to expect that of her under these circumstances."

As I passed him the box from The Laughing Hound, I realized Nina would have a new problem to deal with. "Renee was a featured baker for the dinner tomorrow night. And Joy worked with Muffin, too. I doubt either one of them will be up to baking."

I cringed to have even considered anything of the sort. Muffin had been killed, and I was thinking about cupcakes and a massive dinner party.

Humphrey set the box aside. "Thanks for the lunch, but I'm not very hungry."

I drifted back to the adoption booth, thinking through the ramifications of Muffin's untimely death. People had come from all over, including bakers. It wasn't like we could cancel Cupcakes and Pupcakes now.

Francie returned, and we had just begun to chow down when Bernie showed up with a baggie of crushed ice. "Heard you encountered an angry shoe."

He handed it to me and insisted on examining my eye.

Nina told him the story, barely able to stop eating long enough to get it all out. I sat down and ate slowly, hampered by the ice I pressed against my black eye.

"Maurice, eh? He's an odd one. Comes into the bar all the time expecting other people to pay for his food and drinks." Bernie helped himself to a tub of pasta. "So how's the lunch Moe made?"

We assured him it was terrific.

"I thought you would be stopping by for a bite today. I've had a rotten streak of bad luck with employees lately. I'm giving Moe a trial run. He claims he can cook, bake, make oven-fired pizza, schedule employees, and tend bar."

"With all those skills, why is he on probation?" asked Francie.

Bernie swallowed a bite of the roasted red pepper and spinach pasta. "Nice flavor in this farfalle salad. Because, in my experience, when a bloke claims he can do it all, he usually can't do any of it well."

"He didn't appear to be flustered by that mammoth crowd in the bar today," I offered.

"He can cook. That's for sure," said Nina, selecting a lingonberry turkey sandwich.

"He uses interesting ingredients, but sandwiches aren't much of a challenge." Bernie cast a critical eye over them. "We'll be busy with the cupcakes for the gala dinner tomorrow. I might give him a shot at the grill."

Spenser ambled up. "What a day! Nightmare after nightmare. I suppose you heard about the murder at Sugar Baby."

"Definitely murder?" asked Bernie.

Even though that came as no surprise to me, just hearing the word *murder* sent tremors to my fingers.

Spenser nodded. "That's what I hear. A cop came by to ask if there's anything someone would want to steal from a cupcakery. Cake My Day was hit last night. I guess they're trying to figure out if there's a connection."

"Is there?" asked Francie.

"None that I know of. But the worst thing—" Spenser steadied himself by leaning against a table. He closed his eyes and a jagged breath shuddered out of him. "—I think I heard Muffin arguing with her killer. I was there! Dear heaven, I was there, but I didn't go in. I'll never forgive myself. I picked up my car and headed over to my cupcakery."

"You couldn't have known . . ." Nina's voice tapered off, and her eyes met mine.

"Of course not." Francie scowled at him. "People argue all the time. There was no way you could have known. And maybe you're wrong. Maybe that argument was with someone else." She shook her forefinger at Spenser. "I'll hear no more of that. Don't blame yourself!"

"She's right, you know. But what did you overhear?" asked Bernie.

Spenser swallowed hard. "Muffin was shouting at someone about taking advantage of people. And then there was something about a ring."

Joy! When we'd left Muffin earlier, she'd said she intended to speak to Joy about her treatment of Renee. "Did you hear who the other person was?"

Spenser shook his head.

"If I had heard what you just described, I wouldn't have butted in," I said. "Don't blame yourself. How could you have foreseen that it would end tragically?"

"Thank you all for being so comforting. I fear I'll never get over the fact that I didn't intervene." Spenser looked at the dogs in the pen. "Where's Buddy?"

Nina sprang out of her seat, knocking the pasta salad over. "He's gone!"

CHAPTER EIGHT

Dear Sophie,

I'm always seeing flyers about lost pets. It would break my heart if I couldn't find one of my fur babies. How can I protect them?

—Worried Mom in Catts Corner, Maryland

Dear Worried Mom,

A collar is the place to start. Hang a tag on it with your contact information. They also make tags with QR (Quick Response) codes that can be scanned with a smartphone to access your contact information. Or consider a microchip implant, so that veterinarians, shelters, and rescue groups can contact you if they find your pet.

—Sophie

"Maurice!" Francie breathed the name that jumped to my mind.

"How could that have happened?" I asked.

"I bet he kicked you on purpose," said Francie. "To create a distraction."

"Bernie, you stay here, because you don't know what Buddy looks like." Nina motioned to Spenser, Francie, and me in a frantic gesture. "Everyone spread out. Maybe they're still here."

Seemed unlikely. If I had swiped a dog, I would have left the area immediately. But we had to try. It was our only hope.

I took the outer perimeter of booths, peering over tables and under cloths. Anyone could have marched Buddy out without a soul noticing. There were dogs of every shape and size in every direction I looked.

Joy, newly of Sugar Mama Cupcakes and Renee's former business partner and roommate, exclaimed over my eye. A ponytail the color of dark mocha hung halfway down her back. She must have been planning the split from Renee for some time, because she already wore a blue and brown apron imprinted with the words *Sugar Mama*.

I promised her that my eye wasn't too bad. "I'm so sorry about Muffin. It's a terrible tragedy."

Her brown eyes reflected true sorrow and were rimmed red from crying. "I begged her to leave Renee and come with me. I can't help wondering if she would be alive now if she had."

The thought sent chills down my back. It must have been a major decision for Muffin. If only she had chosen differently. But no one could have anticipated that she would die because she stayed with Renee. And we didn't know what had happened. Maybe her killer would have sought her out across the street at Sugar Mama.

I wanted to dally longer, but we had no time to lose. "One of the dogs that was up for adoption is missing. We're looking for him. A big black and tan dog, wearing a yellow bandanna with pink cupcakes. Let me know if you spot him."

"Oh no. Poor baby. Nick! Nick?"

Like magic, Nick emerged from the crowd. I'd seen him around town. His pretty boy face, smoldering eyes, and easy smile made him very hard to ignore. Joy told him about Buddy, and I described the dog to him.

"I'll scout around. If I see him, I'll bring him to the adoption booth."

Thanking them, I hurried on. Dog owners had brought their best friends with them. Dogs were everywhere I looked. Still, among all the dogs, there was no sign of Buddy.

I trudged back to the adoption booth, fearing the others had as little success as I. Their grim expressions confirmed the worst. No one had seen Maurice or Buddy.

"How could he have pulled that off?" asked Francie. "We were all here. How is it possible that no one noticed him?"

Nina scowled. "He must have been watching us, and moved fast when I had my back turned to deal with the cats and you two left for a few minutes. I never did like that man."

She pulled out her cell phone. "I'm calling Wong. She saw how he acted and that he tried to take Buddy without my consent before. Maybe she can go to his house and demand Buddy's return. I'm so sorry, Spenser!"

He nodded, but the disappointment on his face made his feelings painfully clear. He'd been taken by that dog.

Bernie offered him a sandwich.

Spenser took it and thanked him. He sat down in one of our chairs and held the sandwich in his hands. "They say trouble comes in threes. This was number three for me today. I only saw one of them coming."

"What's going on between you and Maurice?" Maybe I shouldn't have asked, but the words came out of my mouth before I considered them.

Spenser turned his sandwich around in his hands as though he was studying it, but I had the feeling he wasn't seeing it.

"He blames me for his misfortune, but I've never done a thing to the man."

"I got hold of Wong," Nina announced. "Spenser, want to come with us?"

He reflected for a moment, before saying, "Maybe it will go better if he doesn't see me."

Nina took a selection of sandwich halves with her to share with Wong and left me in charge of the booth. So far I'd managed to make a royal mess of things.

Bernie and Spenser went back to work, and a darling boy fell in love with the dog with the brown spot around her eye.

I hitched a leash onto her collar. She couldn't have been more than six months old and wanted to kiss everyone. Fortunately, she kissed the right little boy. His dad filled out the adoption form while I waited with the boy and his mom, kneeling next to the puppy. A masculine hand with strong fingers slid over the puppy's head and ever so briefly grazed my hand.

Alex had squatted on the other side of the puppy. His eyes opened wide in shock when he saw my eye. "Are you all right? That looks painful."

"I'm fine."

"I'm not!" We looked up at Natasha, who was showing off her bandaged right arm. "I don't understand why she bites me."

"Where *is* Martha?" I asked.

"Right here. Isn't this the smartest thing?" She pulled a dog stroller from behind her. Martha growled and bit at the mesh front.

I could imagine great uses for them, but this puppy needed to wear herself out by walking and running. At least she wouldn't escape again.

"I brought you a little present," she trilled, handing Alex a box wrapped in her signature robin's-egg blue and tied with a lacy bow. "It's a DVD of my best shows."

Alex stood up and accepted it graciously, pecking her on the cheek.

"Maybe you'd like to come to the studio with me one day? And you simply must come to dinner while you're visiting. I'll set it up with the general."

"Thank you. That's very thoughtful of you."

"Did Sophie tell you I was a beauty queen?"

"She must have forgotten to mention that. I can't say I'm surprised."

I admired his deft handling of Natasha, but she irritated me. She already had Mars. Would she *never* go away?

"Look over there. Isn't that a photographer from the newspaper?" It was a lie. A terrible, mean thing to do. But it worked. Natasha spun that stroller around faster than Superman could fly and propelled it across the plaza.

"Is this your dog?" Alex asked the little boy.

The boy gazed up at his mom for reassurance. Nodding, he wrapped his arms around the puppy's neck.

"What are you going to name her?" asked Nick.

"Princess Isabella von Humperdink," the boy answered without hesitation.

His mother smiled. "I'm thinking Bella."

I promised their application for adoption would be on the top of the pile. When they walked away, Alex promised I would keep Bella for the boy.

Francie had a twinkle in her eye and nudged me. "He's adorable!" she whispered.

I knew she didn't mean the kid. Alex seemed too nice to be true.

Francie held out her hand. "I'm Sophie's neighbor, Francine Vanderhoosen. What's your marital status, young fellow?"

I wanted to dive under the table with Daisy. She had other ideas, though, and belly-crawled toward Alex to sniff his shoes.

He reached down to pat her and didn't seem a bit perturbed by Francie's nosiness. "I'm separated from my wife."

To anyone else, that might have been a good thing, but to me it meant he wasn't available yet.

Francie crossed her arms over her chest. "Hmpff. And what is it you do for a living?"

His grin was enchanting. How dare he be so charming when he wasn't single yet?

Clearly amused by Francie's question, he said, "I'm an attorney in Richmond. Three hamsters, two step-kids, one cockapoo. My mom taught fifth grade, my dad was a CPA. They're retired now and spend half the year in a fancy motor home. I make a Bloody Mary that you won't believe, and I'm an expert on the barbecue grill, if I do say so myself. Did I omit anything?"

"You seeing anybody?" She observed him with a dubious squint.

"If you need a date for the cupcake feast tomorrow night, I would be honored to escort you."

Francie, his senior by a good twenty or more years, tucked her head and wiggled her hand in embarrassment. "Pick me up at five thirty. I don't want to be late and miss out on anything."

Alex wrote down directions to her house and promised to be on time.

As he walked away, she leveled a stern look at me. "If you don't date that boy, I will!"

By the time Nina returned an hour later, several adoptions awaited her approval.

"Well?" Francie and I couldn't contain ourselves, even though we were eager to see the other dogs and cats in homes.

"He claims he doesn't have Buddy." Nina smiled at people waiting to adopt, and started processing their applications. "He refused to let us into his house. If Buddy was there, he wasn't barking."

My heart sank. What had he done with that poor dog? Was Buddy wandering the streets? I had to push away thoughts of what might happen to him.

In a slow trickle, we emptied the dog pen and the cat cages.

The timing proved perfect. The next shift arrived with new dogs and cats for adoption.

Nina whispered to me, "I've never been so glad to turn anything over to someone else. I'm beat."

She told them the heartbreaking news about Buddy. "Watch out for Maurice Lester. He's tall and gangly with white hair that hangs down to his chin. Don't be fooled—he doesn't like dogs. Do not allow him to adopt any animals and keep an eye on him. I can't imagine that he would steal another dog, but you never know. Also, I've been told not to adopt to Nick Rigas, but I'm not sure about the validity of that one, so if he comes along wanting to adopt, have him fill out the adoption form and tell you'll get back to him."

She smoothed the fur on Daisy's head. "I know you're exhausted . . . and you've been through a terrible trauma today, but could you please help me put up missing flyers about Buddy?" Nina cocked her head at us with the saddest expression I'd ever seen.

"Don't be silly. I'm behind you all the way." I couldn't bear the thought of what might be happening to Buddy.

Nina handed me her phone. Would you round up some volunteers? I'm going to set up a flyer and make copies across the street. I'll meet you back here."

"I'm going to stretch my legs and buy some treats for Duke. I'll be back in a few minutes," said Francie. The set of her mouth told me she was determined to find the missing dog.

I headed to the Sugar Baby booth to recruit Humphrey, but on the way I spied a cute cat hammock for my Ocicat, Mochie. A throwback to one of his American shorthair ancestors, Mochie's fur didn't have spots. He had the classic M on his forehead and spots on his tummy, though. The hammock had the Ocelot-type spots Mochie lacked, and I thought he would enjoy the comfort of the hanging bed.

I paid for it and hurried on to Sugar Baby. Humphrey had put up the closed sign.

"Are you wrapping up here?" I asked. "Nina's putting together a posse to post flyers about Buddy."

"I heard about that. Maurice is a menace! The nerve of him to steal a dog! Sure, I'll help. There's not much I can do here. Nina hired someone to keep an eye on the booths overnight, so I'm not breaking it down yet. I can't imagine that Renee will have cupcakes to sell tomorrow, but I also don't know where to take all this stuff. Do you think the cops would let her bring it into the bakery?"

I doubted it. "Probably not while it's a crime scene. You haven't heard from Renee?"

"Not yet. I went over there a little while ago to see what was going on, but I couldn't get in." He leaned toward me and spoke in a low tone. "Do you mind if I ask you a personal question?"

CHAPTER NINE

Dear Sophie,

Everyone in my family raves about my cupcakes. I'm baking
four hundred for my niece's wedding, but I'm a little nervous
because I'm not used to making so many at once. I hate to
be up all night before the wedding to bake them. Is there an
easy way to bake a lot of cupcakes at once?

—Overwhelmed in Bride's Hill, Alabama

Dear Overwhelmed,

Some bakers freeze cupcakes when they have to bake a large
quantity. Many cupcakes thaw very well and will taste
freshly baked. However, it's best not to frost them until
the day they'll be served.

—Sophie

"What is it that women see in a guy like Nick Rigas?" asked
Humphrey.

Across the plaza, Nick was eyeing cupcakes at Sugar

Mama's booth. Joy Bickford opened a box of cupcakes and showed him the contents. I couldn't hear their conversation, but Nick selected one.

Joy ran her fingers around her neck and laughed.

Nick said a few more words and moved on without paying, wolfing the cupcake in four bites.

"Is it his hair?" asked Humphrey.

Nick had been blessed with an abundance of dark hair. Medium height and not particularly athletic-looking, he lacked some of the typical attributes thought to be particularly handsome. Women coveted his long, lush eyelashes. His warm chocolate eyes coupled with an easy grin that made everyone feel special. "Humphrey, I think it's the smile. There's something boyish and captivating about it." I watched as Nick turned his charm on a woman who was old enough to be his grandmother. She giggled at something he said and swiped a hand through the air in his direction.

Humphrey grimaced at me like a jack-o'-lantern.

"What's wrong?"

"That was my boyish smile."

"Don't do that! You'll frighten women away."

He slumped. Unfortunately for Humphrey, Nick was still in my line of sight. "Maybe it's not the smile. Nick carries himself as though he expects everyone to like him. There's a comfortable assuredness about him." Of course, it didn't hurt that his features came together in a remarkably appealing way.

Humphrey frowned. "How do I do that?" He turned his head slightly, raised his chin, and posed with his hands held waist high, palms down.

"Now you look conceited and like you're trying to keep people away from you. Just relax and be yourself."

"Being myself hasn't worked. I think I'd be better off trying to be someone else for a while."

I pulled him into a big hug. "I don't know why you think that. It's obvious that Myra likes you just the way you are."

"Eh, Myra." He spoke her name like he was talking about broccoli.

I made a few phone calls to friends, asking them if they

would help post flyers about Buddy. Half an hour later, Spenser, Mars, Bernie, Francie, Humphrey, Nick, and a host of our Old Town friends met to pick up flyers. Humphrey had drawn a grid of Old Town. He assigned each person an area, and we all dispersed with flyers in hand. Humphrey had thoughtfully given elderly Francie the route back to the block where we lived. I drew the area behind Market Square, along North Pitt Street and North St. Asaph Street.

Word about Muffin had spread quickly through Old Town. As I popped into stores, asking them to post the flyer, everyone inquired about Muffin and about my eye, which, from the comments, must have become considerably more pronounced.

Daisy and I dragged home, exhausted. Mochie, who had slept all day, met us at the door, full of energy.

I set his new hammock on the tile floor in the sunroom. He circled it, examining it from all sides before he jumped into it. But when I set out a fresh bowl of kitty salmon, he readily abandoned the hammock for his dinner.

I curled up on the loveseat in the sunroom for a nap, but no sooner had I dozed off than someone slammed the knocker on my front door. I dragged myself to the door and opened it to find Detective Kenner.

His usual disapproving expression turned to a mix of wonder and horror at the sight of me. "What happened to you?"

"Don't worry. I have witnesses. It had nothing to do with Muffin's death." Once my nemesis, he no longer frightened me. I held out my arms and he readily hugged me. I invited him in, but Daisy growled at him.

"Why doesn't your dog like me?"

"They say dogs are good judges of character."

A hint of a grin emerged, softening the hollows under his cheekbones.

"Could I offer you some tea or coffee?"

"No, thanks. Busy day. Tell me what happened at Sugar Baby."

He sat down at my kitchen table. Daisy sat next to me, her gaze never wavering from Kenner. I ran through the details for him.

"Can you be any more precise about the times when Humphrey or Renee left Market Square?"

"I wasn't watching them or a clock. All I can tell you is that she was alive when we delivered the desk."

"Thanks. Does Francie still live next door?"

"Absolutely."

I walked him to the front door.

"I don't see much of you anymore," he said.

"Trying to keep my nose clean and stay out of trouble."

He nodded. "Try harder."

I closed the door behind him and gave up on napping. A peek into the fridge revealed a beautiful flank steak that I'd forgotten about. If I knew Nina, she would order takeout for dinner or just eat four cupcakes and call it a day. When I phoned her, she and Humphrey were still at Market Square. I felt like a sloth. The least I could do was feed them.

≈≈≈

Dusk was beginning to fall over Old Town when Humphrey, Nina, and I gathered in my outdoor room. Humphrey insisted on building a fire but clearly had never achieved a Boy Scout merit badge for fire building.

I coached him on the use of kindling, but I could tell he wasn't paying attention. "Are you thinking about Muffin?"

"Sophie, I deal with death every day. I've come to terms with it for the most part. But Muffin shouldn't be in the morgue yet. She wasn't meant to be there. Someone snuffed her out, but I can't imagine why. It can't have been for money, because she didn't have anything." He stood up. "We have to find out who it was. *We have to!*"

I wasn't altogether keen on his use of the word *we* in that context.

"I couldn't agree more." Nina stirred an icy concoction in a pitcher. "I hope you don't mind, Sophie. I used the rest of your strawberries in the margaritas."

She poured drinks for the three of us and settled into a chaise longue.

Humphrey switched on the little lights in the lofted ceiling overhead while I placed the steak on the grill. Potatoes had been baking for almost an hour, slathered in butter, sprinkled with salt, and wrapped in aluminum foil. I had marinated the flank steak briefly in bourbon, oil, sea salt, and freshly ground pepper. A raid of the refrigerator had yielded the ingredients for a salad of fresh baby spinach leaves, sliced strawberries, red onion, and creamy avocado, with a strawberry and orange blossom honey vinaigrette.

"I don't mean to sound self-centered," said Nina. "Let's face it—Muffin was murdered—it doesn't get worse than that. But honestly, if I could find the person who did it, I'd wring his neck myself. You can't imagine what a ruckus this has caused in regard to the dinner tomorrow night."

"So we'll have fewer cupcakes," I said. "Surely everyone will understand. Is Joy still baking her cupcakes? She knew Muffin very well, having worked with her."

"Not only is Joy baking her cupcakes, but Renee will be presenting cupcakes, too."

Humphrey gasped. "Renee is baking anyway?"

"Turns out they were already done," said Nina. "Get this. She baked her cupcakes in advance and froze them. All she needs to do is frost them."

"Are they still at the bakery?" I asked.

"Spenser is so generous. He's setting her up in the Old Town branch of Cake My Day." Nina poured herself another drink. "Wong and one of the detectives accompanied her to be sure she didn't destroy evidence when she removed the frozen cupcakes from Sugar Baby. I think that was just a formality, or maybe a way to get her to loosen up. They probably peppered her with questions the whole time. But don't you think that's suspicious? That she baked them in advance and froze them?"

Humphrey scooted so far forward on his chair that he almost fell off. "Are you suggesting that she baked the cupcakes in advance because she knew Muffin would be murdered?"

Nina tilted her head from side to side. "Just sayin'. Plus, I would have been a wreck. I can promise you that if someone close to me had been murdered, I would not be producing cupcakes for a banquet the following day. No way."

"Did you know that Renee is a micro-manager? One of those people who is always a step ahead of the game?" A defensive edge had crept into Humphrey's tone.

Time for me to jump in. "I hate to spoil your theory, Nina. But a lot of bakeries bake very large orders ahead of time and freeze them. It's not that unusual."

She seemed disappointed. "Maybe so. But would they deliver cupcakes the following day?"

"Stop that!" shouted Humphrey. "You're making it sound as though Renee killed Muffin."

Nina met his eyes dead on but didn't deny it.

He lowered his voice. "She couldn't have. She was busy at her booth."

"Humphrey, sweetheart," Nina drawled soothingly in her North Carolina accent, "once you left to pick up the desk, I don't think anyone watched her constantly. I know for a fact that she put up the closed sign for a few minutes. I guessed she slipped off to the restroom, but I *don't* really know. I didn't go with her."

"That would have been very daring of her, Nina." Using tongs, I placed the hot potatoes on a plate and the steak on a carving board and carried them over to the table. "She knew we would be bringing the desk. It wouldn't make sense for her to risk being caught. If she had planned to kill Muffin, wouldn't she have waited a day or even a week to have the desk delivered?"

"All the more reason to shove poor little Muffin under the bed." Nina unwrapped her potato, sliced it open, and plunked a pat of butter inside. "Did she know you were going for the desk right then?" She gasped. "What if Renee planned to pin it on Humphrey? If he had brought the desk all by himself, he would have been the prime suspect." She leaned over the table toward Humphrey. "It's just lucky that Sophie and Spenser were with you!"

From his expression, I gathered Humphrey wasn't at all pleased with the discussion. "I don't think anyone could have carried that desk up the stairs by himself. Sorry, Nina. You're wrong this time."

"Don't be so sure. There are rumors that Muffin and Renee were after the same man. After all, they were arguing in Renee's bedroom."

The candle on the table flickered.

Humphrey hadn't taken the first bite of his dinner. "What man? How do you know they were arguing?"

"Spenser heard them."

"He only heard Muffin." Humphrey's chest puffed up. "That's nothing but an assumption!"

I mustered a calm voice. "There are also rumors that Renee and Joy split because of a man. You can't believe everything you hear. Muffin could have been arguing with Joy or, for that matter, Spenser himself."

Only after I'd spoken did it dawn on me that Humphrey might have been the man who came between them. Surely not.

"That's ridiculous," said Humphrey. "How could Spenser hear himself?"

"What if he's lying?" I asked. "What if he said he heard an argument in case someone else heard him arguing with Muffin?"

"You mean he could have left his car there on purpose knowing he would return? It gave him an excuse to be at the scene of the murder!" Humphrey gripped a steak knife in his fist like a weapon.

Poor Humphrey needed to eat. I turned the conversation to the cupcake dinner the next night. In spite of our lovely meal and spring air that held the promise of warm summer nights, Muffin's death hung over us, dampening our spirits.

We broke up early since we were all exhausted and the next day would be busy. I had returned to the outdoor table to retrieve the remaining dishes when I heard Daisy's collar tags jangle. She loped to the back gate. It creaked open, reminding me to oil the hinges. In the shadows of falling darkness, I made out a stocky figure entering my yard and closing the gate behind him in haste, as though he was trying to avoid detection.

CHAPTER TEN

Dear Sophie,

We'd like to take our dog on the road with us this summer, but I'm worried about where we'll stay. We've never traveled with a dog before.

—Timmy in Collietown, Arkansas

Dear Timmy,

Plan your route ahead of time so you can make reservations at dog-friendly hotels. Be sure to ask about weight or size restrictions. Happily, many hotels offer special amenities for dogs, like bedtime treats on their pillows and doggie room service.

—Sophie

The person paused and leaned over to pat Daisy, which made me feel like he must be friend, not foe. But his demeanor left me a little bit wary. I made a mental note to start bringing my cell phone outside with me.

I couldn't quite make out his identity in the dark. Had he come to see me, or was he dodging someone and had simply snuck inside my fence to hide? I watched him for a moment. He turned around.

"Sophie!" It was a loud whisper. He'd clearly seen me.

As he drew near, I realized it was Spenser. "Hi! What's going on? Is it about Buddy?"

"I wish it were. I'm heartbroken about that dog. If only someone would find the poor guy." He took in my outdoor room, gazing up at the lofted ceiling and twinkling lights. "Nice place."

"Thanks. I think there's some margarita left. Could I interest you in one?"

"Yes, please!"

I fetched a clean glass, poured a drink, and handed it to him. "What brings you here?"

He rested on an Adirondack chair and focused on the margarita. Was he avoiding my eyes?

"Sophie, you're a very nice woman. And attractive, too!"

He said the last part in a rush, which made me smile. He was greasing me up for something with those compliments.

"Under other circumstances, I would be flattered by your interest . . ." He peeked up at me, turning his face slightly as if he were afraid of my response.

I laughed. "My interest? What are you trying to say, Spenser? Spit it out!"

He chugged back half the margarita. "I can't date you!"

I hadn't expected *that*! What on earth? Did he think I was in the habit of dating married men because of my relationship with Wolf? There had been extenuating circumstances. Why didn't people realize that? I worked at keeping my tone friendly. "Of course not. You're married, and I don't date married men." *There. I'd said it up front—clear as could be.* Not that there had ever been any question of dating him, or any indication of anything of the sort. He'd caught me off guard. Why would he have imagined such a thing? I racked my brain for anything I might have said or done that could have misled him. Had I told him I was in love with his cupcakes?

He heaved a great sigh. "I believe I've put my foot in it. You're not chasing me, are you?"

I was tempted to say what he had—that he was a nice man *and attractive, too*! Instead I asked, "Does this have anything to do with Clarissa being so angry with me?" I sipped my drink.

"She thinks we're having an affair."

I spewed margarita.

"And two other people have asked me about it, as well."

Dabbing my shirt with a napkin, I said, "No wonder you had trouble broaching the subject. Why would anyone think that?" It certainly explained Clarissa's odd outbreak at the coffee place and her ire when I showed up for the desk. No wonder she thought I had nerve to come to her house.

Spenser acted bashful. "I thought maybe you had a little crush on me, and . . ."

This time I choked. Coughing to clear my throat, I sputtered, "You thought I told people that we were having an affair?" I wiped my watering eyes. "What would that accomplish? Besides, don't most people try to keep their affairs under wraps so people *won't* find out about them?"

Looking much relieved, Spenser sat back in his chair and crossed a leg over his knee. "You can imagine how well it went over when you turned up at my house with Humphrey today."

"Actually, I didn't realize we were going to your house. After my brush with Clarissa this morning, I would never have intentionally visited your home."

Spenser sipped his margarita and frowned. "If you didn't suggest it to anyone, then I don't understand. It's not like we could have been seen together anywhere, thus raising suspicions."

I sighed. "It's possible that my split with Wolf has made me Grade A Prime meat for the gossip mill. Sounds like you were the unwitting victim. I'm so sorry, Spenser. I'll talk to Clarissa about it tomorrow and straighten her out."

Spenser rose. "Thanks, Sophie. I'd appreciate that. See you tomorrow night at the cupcake feast. Call my cell if there's any word about Buddy. I'd love to bring him to the banquet tomorrow night."

He let himself out. I finished cleaning up and put out the fire but couldn't get Buddy out of my mind. Old Town was in for a rollicking weekend. Would he hide from people or come out in search of food? Or had Maurice locked him up somewhere?

I was tempted to take Daisy for a drive through Old Town to look for him. Only then did it finally dawn on me that I had forgotten all about my car. It was still parked behind Sugar Baby.

I found my spare key, since Humphrey still had the other one, latched a leash onto Daisy, and walked toward Market Square. An occasional breeze brought scents of irises my way. Within a few blocks, though, I approached the heart of Old Town, and it buzzed with Friday night fever. The restaurants teemed with people.

A deep bark made Daisy's ears perk up. She tugged at the lead and rounded into the circular drive of a very upscale hotel. Could it be Buddy?

A yellow lab pranced happily in the driveway and barked again. So much for that. But there, wearing a big smile and watching the lab, was Spenser. He ambled past the dog and up the main steps into the hotel.

It wasn't too late to be out and about. But it was a bit late for a business meeting. I felt incredibly guilty for imagining anything inappropriate, but what else could I think? I watched from the street for a moment, trying to convince myself that it wasn't what it looked like. Maybe he had a friend who worked there. Maybe he was meeting someone visiting from out of town. Or maybe Clarissa was right about him having an affair. She just had the wrong woman.

I was being silly. Cake My Day was in competition for best cupcake. He'd probably brought some people in from other stores to help with the baking and was having a drink with them in the hotel bar.

Shaking my head about the fact that I had become so suspicious of everyone, I walked on.

A memorial to Muffin had appeared in front of Sugar Baby.

Flowers, candles, and the occasional teddy bear stretched all the way across the storefront. Ominous yellow crime scene tape on the front door fluttered gently in the breeze.

Someone had blown up a photo of Muffin wearing her Sugar Baby apron and propped it in front of the door, under the yellow tape. She'd been so young and full of life. A few people slowed down to read the messages and tributes to Muffin.

Daisy and I walked farther up the street and turned behind the row of buildings.

The alley lay quiet and a bit forbidding. An occasional light by a back door shone in the night, but no streetlights or spotlights brightened the area. Fences blocked the rear view of some buildings, while others were clearly businesses with off-street parking in the back. A door slammed somewhere. A man and a woman raised their voices in an argument about whose turn it was to walk the dog. I couldn't tell where they were, but reflected that their neighbors knew everything about them when lovely spring air moved them to open their windows.

Daisy sniffed the side of the alley, no doubt smelling the scent of other dogs who had walked that way earlier in the day. A dog barked behind one of the fences. Daisy and I swung around to look. But something else distracted Daisy. She turned and growled.

A shadowy figure emerged in the darkness. Tall and lean, he loped toward us. I shrank back and pulled Daisy closer. I could see the back of my car. If we made a run for it, would we be able to jump inside before he reached it?

CHAPTER ELEVEN

Dear Sophie,

Cupcakes are all the rage at the parties my kids attend. Some of these moms could rival Natasha in the cupcake-decorating department! I have neither the time nor the talent. How can I dress up cupcakes with less fuss?

—Exhausted Mom in Sprinkle, Texas

Dear Exhausted Mom,

Pour sprinkles or colored sugar into a shallow bowl. Apply frosting to your cupcakes with a knife, or spatula, ending with a little peak in the middle. Before the frosting sets, roll the edge of the cupcake in the sprinkles or sugar. Adorable in no time at all, and no talent required!

—Sophie

Would it be better to run in the other direction, toward the street?

Too late. Evidently, he hadn't noticed us before, because

he screamed—a short, ear-splitting howl—like he'd seen a ghost.

"Sophie!" Maurice Lester slammed a hand over his heart. "What are you doing here?"

Me? I had every right to be there. Then again, so did everyone else in the world, including Maurice. The alley was open to the public. Moving so slowly that I hoped he might not notice, I edged toward the SUV. "I came to get my car. What are you doing here?"

The dim light did nothing to enhance his appearance. His eyes sank into dark cadaver-like holes. His stringy white hair seemed to glow. "I brought flowers for Muffin from my garden. I, uh, well, I didn't want anybody to see me putting them out. There's a big crowd out front, so I thought I'd bring them around back, where it's more private and solemn."

We'd done a semicircular dance, with me moving toward my car and him moving toward the alley exit. Now I felt like a heel. He'd done something thoughtful and kind. Why hadn't it occurred to me to bring flowers from my garden?

This was a side of Maurice I had never seen or heard about. Could his grumpy behavior be a cover-up for a human being with a heart? I took a chance. "Look, Maurice, everyone is upset about the disappearance of that black and tan dog—"

"I don't have it," he shouted. "Stop acting like I do. The *police* came to my house about that worthless mutt." His voice rose in pitch and volume. "I didn't take it!"

With that, he sprinted off into the night.

So much for him having a heart. I hurried Daisy to my car. Although she usually jumped in from a back door or the rear hatch, this time I urged her over the driver's seat and clambered in behind her as fast as I could. I mashed the lever that locked all the doors, turned on the ignition, and felt better when the headlights illuminated the alley.

I toyed with the notion of calling the police, but other than the fact that Maurice had been in the alley, which certainly wasn't against the law, I really couldn't justify notifying them. What would I say? *A grumpy man was in back of Sugar Baby leaving flowers.* Big deal. They would want to know why I had returned and would likely think I was the one acting peculiar.

I turned the high beams on and angled the SUV so I could see the back of Sugar Baby clearly. Police tape sagged across the door, and a spray of pink flowers lay on the stoop. It looked like a branch from an azalea bush.

There was nothing else to see, and I was beat. I drove out of the alley and merged into the traffic that crawled through Old Town. I caught a light and watched as people crossed the street in front of me. Maurice Lester hurried across the intersection and almost ran into Alex, who appeared to be waiting for someone at the corner. Funny, I'd been under the impression he didn't know anyone in Old Town.

Wishing I could find Buddy, I drove home and parked in the garage. Either he was wandering the streets, or the person who'd stolen him had confined him somewhere.

⌗

The next morning I rose leisurely, thankful I didn't have to rush off anywhere and looking forward to the cupcake feast in the evening. I was mincing onion for my breakfast when my ex-husband, Mars, rapped on the kitchen door. Through the window, I could see Nina dashing up behind him.

Mars stepped inside with Martha, Natasha's little Chihuahua, and set her on the floor. "Ouch! Your eye looks painful."

"It looks worse than it feels."

Nina made a beeline for the coffee on the counter and promptly poured it into two mugs.

Daisy eagerly sniffed Martha. My cat, Mochie, approached her from behind, very politely. But Martha whipped around and yipped at him. He retreated to the cushioned window seat in a huff and washed his fur with smug feline indifference.

"I see you're already in charge of Martha." I hauled cremini mushrooms and more eggs out of the refrigerator.

"I thought I'd pick up Daisy and take them both for a run. Can you believe Natasha bought a dog? Normally I'm partial to bigger dogs, but Martha is quite a character." Mars bent over to adjust Martha's rhinestone collar. "We have to watch her like hawks because she loves to grab things and run off with them. Last night she managed to jump up on Natasha's vanity. She pawed open one of those little compacts with powder. Natasha saw her digging in it, and when she tried to take it away, the little scamp jumped to the floor with it in her mouth and ran like the wind. I thought we'd never catch her. The funny thing is that she hid it or dropped it somewhere, and now we can't find it." He chuckled and watched her like an adoring dad. "But I'm worried that Martha is a replacement for Vegas."

"Vegas left?" I asked Mars.

Natasha's distant teenage relative, Vegas, had lived with them for a couple of years while her father served in the military. The poor kid's mother had disappeared without a trace.

"Her dad is back. They're living out in Sterling, so it's not like we'll never see her again, but I think Natasha is taking it harder than she lets on. This dog thing, for instance. We have Daisy every other week, and Nat never wants to walk her, feed her, or even have her in the house. I don't understand her new fascination with tiny dogs."

Nina handed a mug of coffee to Mars. "You don't read Natasha's column, do you? Some of her fans have been asking about her dog."

Mars ran a hand up his forehead and through his hair. "I had no idea. That explains everything. Why couldn't she just use Daisy?" He reached over and hugged Daisy. A sad sigh escaped his lips.

I couldn't help feeling sorry for him. Mars was a good guy. I still didn't quite understand his attraction to Natasha, but then, who can explain why any two people are attracted to each other? One thing was for sure, the saga of little Martha was only beginning, and I was fairly sure she would end up being in Mars's care.

Nina was watching me like Daisy did when I was making her dinner.

"Hungry?" I asked.

"Starved! What are you cooking?"

"After all that sugar yesterday, I thought nice savory eggs with onion and mushrooms would be good for breakfast."

"Sounds great." She set the table while Mars perched on one of the fireside chairs, observing Daisy and Martha playing.

"Shouldn't you be working on tonight's dinner?" I asked Nina.

She laced her fingers together and proudly flexed them in the air. "Everything is under control. The tent is up. The weather is supposed to be almost summerlike. The chairs and tables are being set up as we speak. I have one hour before I have to return to check on everything. After yesterday's disasters, I expect it to go swimmingly tonight. The only problem is Buddy's disappearance. And we know who has him. We just can't prove it."

Mars shook his head. "I heard about that! Maurice is a weird guy anyway, but who would steal a shelter dog unless it belonged to him?"

I hadn't thought of that. "Nina? Could that be the case?"

"I seriously doubt it. Wasn't it odd the way he didn't even notice Buddy until Spenser made a fuss over him?" She shuddered. "Creepy!"

"Do you think they're having some sort of spat over Clarissa?" asked Mars.

I slid the eggs into the oven. "*Eww.* Why would Clarissa be interested in Maurice? I doubt it. Besides, Clarissa thinks I'm having an affair with Spenser."

Nina laughed hysterically, but Mars asked, "You're not, are you?"

The fear that flashed in his eyes reminded me of the romantic moment we had shared. It had been well over a year ago, so I'd hoped that it was a mere aberration—the consequence of a stress-filled moment in our lives when everything had gone haywire. But the look he leveled on me as he waited for my answer shook me, and I wondered if everything was completely over between us after all.

"Don't be silly. If there is one thing I have learned about myself, it's that I am not cut out to be the other woman." Even if the man in question was my ex-husband and he hadn't married the woman with whom he lived.

"She only dates murder suspects," jested Nina.

"Not funny!" I protested vehemently. Her reference to my most recent beau, Wolf, prompted me to add, "No men who are married, separated, have missing wives, or are murder suspects."

"No one else I know has that kind of problem." Mars laughed and Nina joined in.

"Do you two want brunch? I'd recommend not teasing the cook if you're hungry." They didn't seem one bit worried. "What are you doing here anyway, Mars? Did Natasha kick you out of the kitchen?"

"She's a terror right now. Totally stressed about tonight's cupcake banquet. I feel sorry for her assistant, Leon. She's working him to death and, unlike me, he can't escape."

"Which course does she have?" I asked.

Nina mimicked a game show buzzer when a contestant provides the wrong answer. "No one is allowed to know except for me. I even gave the bakers identical paper cupcake liners so no one can vote for their favorite bakery. It's all going to be anonymous."

≈≈≈

Nina's departure after brunch left me exactly where I didn't want to be—alone with Mars. I rinsed the dishes and he stacked them in the dishwasher, annoyingly like we were married again.

Eager to get out of the house, I pulled on walking shoes and told Mars I'd walk partway down to the park with him and the dogs. Besides, I had one major errand to take care of before the dinner.

The temperature had soared into the mid-eighties and people flooded Old Town's sidewalks. We were pleased to see a stellar turnout at Cupcakes and Pupcakes on Market Square. To my total shock, Renee was back selling cupcakes at her booth. Even more astonishing, Humphrey was helping her.

Mars leaned over, and whispered, "That Renee is one tough cupcake."

"Humphrey's crazy mad about her, but I'm worried that she's taking advantage of him."

"Are you sure you're not jealous?"

"What?"

"He's been chasing you for years. Are you certain that you're not feeling a little bit miffed that someone else has his attention?"

"Of course not." That was ridiculous. But it might not be a bad time to straighten out Mars about our relationship. "Humphrey and I are just friends. Like you and me."

"Uh-huh. Go ahead and tell yourself that. Our relationship doesn't begin to equate to a friendship."

What did that mean? He grinned at me, which I found annoying and worrisome. I didn't have a chance to retort, though, because he wiggled his eyebrows and took off at a slow jog with the dogs.

Aargh. I was going to have to sit down with him one of these days and straighten things out. I should have done that immediately after the big kiss, but I'd let it slide, hoping it would just dissipate like the gas in a balloon. Obviously it hadn't. And I didn't like the fact that I'd been such a chicken about it. If it had happened with anyone else, I'd have confronted the situation head-on. Why did I try so hard to avoid that with Mars?

I left Market Square and walked the six blocks to Spenser's house. Along the way, I couldn't help thinking that what I was doing was a perfect example of preferring to tackle a problem directly. The last thing I wanted was for Clarissa to blow up at me again in public.

The day had grown warm, and the sticky humidity more typical of summer air made my skin moist as I walked up the stairs to Spenser's home and knocked on the door.

Clarissa opened it about four inches. She appeared alarmed to see me.

"I hope you don't mind my dropping by, but I'd like to clear something up."

Her lips turned inward. She poked her head out and looked up and down the street nervously.

CHAPTER TWELVE

Dear Natasha,

My cupcakes look beautiful when I take them out of the oven, but then they deflate! What am I doing wrong?

—Sagging in Flat Lick, Kentucky

Dear Sagging,

Most likely you're not baking them long enough or your oven is too hot. Most cupcakes bake in 16—18 minutes at 350 degrees. Buy an oven thermometer to check the temperature inside your oven.

—Natasha

Clarissa stepped outside, leaving the door open just a sliver behind her. "This isn't a good time." Her eyes narrowed to bitter slits.

"I'll be quick. Spenser told me that you think we're having an affair. Nothing could be further from the truth."

"Uh-huh. Okay, buh-bye." She wedged inside as though

she didn't want to open the door all the way, and closed it with a snap.

Of all the things in the world she might have said or done, I hadn't expected that. What happened to the screaming woman? The one who told me she'd fight? I knocked on the door.

She opened it a crack. "What now?"

I wasn't sure what to say. "Are we okay, then? You accept that I'm not sleeping with Spenser?"

"Do you think I'm an idiot? Of course I don't believe you. It's all over town." She closed the door. I could hear her locking it and sliding a chain across to secure it.

Did she think I was going to force my way inside? I stepped away and looked back at the house. This time, she wasn't peering from any windows. Feeling unsettled again, I walked away, hoping she wouldn't make a scene at the banquet. Could she be on medication that was causing her to behave erratically? Surely Spenser would have mentioned it or warned me if that was the case. Maybe she had a drinking problem?

What a nuisance. Why hadn't she believed me? I massaged my forehead as I walked. Poor Spenser. He must have a miserable life. Clarissa had always seemed so friendly. It just went to show that people weren't always what they seemed on the outside.

The big dinner was scheduled to begin at six with cocktails. Anticipating that something would go wrong, I showered and changed early so I could help Nina. I blew my hair out, popped hot rollers in it, and swung it all up in what I hoped was an elegant French twist. I applied eye makeup that wouldn't run and did my best to cover up the black eye that had bloomed into a remarkable shiner overnight. There was little hope of covering the red semicircle under my eye, but dabbing the black portions with thick concealer helped enormously. I hated the feeling of plastered makeup, but I had no choice. After I'd covered as much as I could, I studied my closet for an appropriate dress. In the spirit of springtime, I wanted to wear coral, but since Alex would be there, I conceded that black would be more slimming. He might not be divorced yet, but that didn't mean I shouldn't look my best. He *was* very enticing. With a sigh and a millionth resolution to take off some weight—*after I ate my way through the cupcake dinner, of course*—I selected a long, sleeveless black dress with a sweetheart neckline that skimmed my figure without hugging any of the bulgy parts. I dug through a drawer in search of a necklace someone had given me. An artistic rendering of a dog paw print pave'd with rhinestones that hung on a gold chain. If this wasn't the right event for it, there would never be one. Finding earrings that could stand up to the necklace proved to be a challenge. I settled on large rhinestone clips from the fifties that had belonged to my grandmother. The cascading marquise-cut stones weren't really my style, but they were pretty, and I figured that anything goes at a black-tie Cupcakes and Pupcakes feast. The earrings kicked up my black dress a notch, and I thought they looked rather chic now that 1950s clothes were back in style.

I slid my feet into comfortable black flats in case I had to do a lot of walking to be helpful to Nina.

Mochie napped in the sunroom. I nuzzled with him a little bit, taking care not to cover my dress with fur. I added chicken in gravy to his food bowl, locked the door, and left. Mars would bring Daisy to the feast later on. I knew he was grateful to hide out at my house while Natasha was in a baking frenzy.

My phone rang the second I stepped out the door. I hustled back into the kitchen and answered it.

"Sophie!" Nina screeched at someone and returned to the phone, her tone an octave higher than normal. "Thank goodness you haven't left yet. How can you stand doing this for a living? Natasha makes me so mad. She used robin's-egg blue icing so everyone would know which cupcakes were hers. And just in case they didn't know that blue is her signature color, she stuck a big *N* on top of each one. Can you believe her nerve? That doesn't even match the theme. But that's not my biggest problem. I can't reach Joy. After that huge fuss she made, I don't know if she's bringing her cheese cupcakes or not. Could you go over to the bakery and see if she's there? Find out what's going on?"

I assured Nina I would take care of it. Instead of heading to the park, I drove the few blocks to Sugar Mama's.

Across the street, people continued to stop at the makeshift memorial to Muffin.

A closed sign hung on the door to Joy's bakery. I tried it anyway, but it was locked. Two possibilities sprang to mind. Either Joy was inside baking, or she was at Market Square selling cupcakes from her booth. I guessed the latter might be the case.

I looked for a bell to ring and was thinking that I ought to check her booth at Market Square when a flash of blue caught my eye. I cupped my hands around my eyes to see through the glass more clearly. Joy, wearing a blue apron, walked out of sight. I rapped fiercely on the glass.

Joy returned, waving her hands and shaking her head to signal that the cupcakery was closed. I rapped harder. She pointed at the sign. Even at a distance, I could tell she'd been crying.

She must have finally recognized me, because she hurried to the door and unlocked it. "Sophie! I'm sorry, people have been knocking all day, and I've done my best to ignore them. I'll probably lose business as a result."

Her long brown ponytail had been pinned up into a bun, and she wore a hairnet. Her eyes weren't just rimmed red from crying, the whites of her eyes appeared bloodshot, too. "And to be honest, I'm a little jumpy after Muffin's murder."

"I'm so sorry about Muffin. You must have been close to her."

She sniffed. "I can hardly bear to look out the window. It's inconceivable to me that she's not there anymore, that she won't come running up to me with a fantastic idea for a new recipe or to tell me about one of her spying excursions to try out the cupcakes of our competitors. She was just like a little sister to me."

"What do you think happened?"

Staring at the floor, she adjusted the hairnet. "I can't imagine. Everyone liked her. The cops asked if we had any weird guys who hung around. We had regulars—that creepy

Maurice, Humphrey, and I did think it odd that Spenser came by so regularly when he has his own cupcakery, you know?" Her expression changed, and she rested a hand on my shoulder. "I'm so sorry! Humphrey is a friend of yours, isn't he? I didn't mean anything by that, but he came to the cupcakery every day."

That explained Humphrey's weight gain. "Did she date anyone? Did anyone seem obsessed with her?"

"You sound like the police." Joy shook her head. "I've been racking my brain about that. So many people come into the shop, you know? And when it's busy you can't remember them all. The police were surprised that we don't have surveillance cameras. I told them if more of them bought cupcakes instead of doughnuts we could afford them. We don't even have alarm systems."

I looked around. "I guess there's not much to take."

"Exactly. You have to pinch pennies in a startup business."

The fabulous aroma of baking cupcakes drifted to me, reminding me of my mission. "Nina has been trying to reach you. She sent me over to be sure you're up to baking cupcakes for the gala tonight."

Joy smacked her head. "No wonder you're all dressed up. Nick will be delivering them for me. I baked through the night, and I'm beat. I managed to find someone to sell cupcakes at my booth today. Honestly, I feel like I'm calling in favors from everyone. I knew it would be tough going out on my own, but"—she licked her lips and wiped away a tear—"it's all overwhelming. They say that work is good for you when tragedy strikes, but I'm so broken by Muffin's death that I can hardly think straight."

She promised to have the cupcakes delivered in two hours. I left in a hurry so she could finish them and drove to the site of the Cupcakes and Pupcakes feast.

Parking in Old Town was always an issue. I found a spot two blocks from the waterfront park. Assorted vendor trucks lined the street, blocking the flow of traffic.

The tent for the banquet was gorgeous. Passersby gathered to admire it and check out what was going on. The white top swept upward to three peaks. Round-topped window panels lined the walls. A smaller tent without windows stood nearby.

Dodging trucks, I hurried across the street. A walkway had been rolled out for the guests, but I cut across the grass to the small tent, where long tables had been set up for cupcake deliveries. So far only half of the bakers had brought their cupcakes or pupcakes. Table number holders marked sections of the tables with cards stating the type of cupcake, but not the name of the bakery. A banquet menu card lay on an empty table.

I wandered over to the main tent to see what was going on. Round tables draped in coral dominated the room. A dog or cat topiary graced the center of each table. Some of them stood and some were in sitting positions, but each one wore a coral bow with white polka dots. White, pink, and orange tulips surrounded the topiaries. At each place setting, a small white tub with coral paw prints walking across it overflowed with dog and cat treats.

At the far end, a small stage and podium had been set up. An oversized white poodle and a cat the same size flanked the podium. They were made of carnations and sported the same coral bows as the topiaries on the tables. Along one wall, a table of auction items nearly overflowed.

"Sophie! Thank goodness you're here." Nina closed her eyes, and I suspected she was counting to ten to calm down.

"Would you hang out at the cupcake tent?" She crooked a finger at me.

As we walked toward the smaller tent, she whispered, "Would you *please* make sure they keep the dog dinner pupcakes separate from the human cupcakes as they're delivered? I live in fear of someone like Maurice complaining because his cupcake tastes like liver."

We watched as a baker delivering cupcakes sauntered toward us, tripped, and a tray full of cupcakes flew through the air and landed upside down. "They'd better have brought extras," Nina growled.

"I'll take care of it." I strolled over to the young red-faced fellow, probably an assistant, and held out my hand to help him up.

He gazed at the cupcakes. "They'll kill me. I'll lose my job!"

"Are you sure they didn't send extras, just in case of a mishap?"

He brightened up. "You think?" He picked up the ruined cupcakes and trudged back to the delivery van.

I heard him yelp, "Yahoo! I think you're right!"

Cupcake deliveries came fast and thick. The bakers had been wonderfully clever, decorating the cupcakes to fit their courses and the theme of the event. Cupcakes decorated with artistic little fish with cute scales and kissy lips had to be the fish course. Pupcakes featured frosting mice and bunnies. One guy promised his cupcakes for people were *pawsitively* delicious because he had cut out pieces of marzipan in the shape of dog paw prints as a decoration. Another brought dog treats shaped like hearts and dipped in carob. I assumed that was the dog dessert course, but it turned out to be their appetizer. I hoped someone was planning to keep the waiters on track—and I hoped it wouldn't be me. I was itching to try all the people cupcakes.

A big Cake My Day van pulled up. The driver unloaded two types of cupcakes. One kind featured dog faces. No two were alike. The others were white kitten faces with amber tiger stripes. I had no idea which ones belonged to Cake My Day and which ones might be Renee's cupcakes.

When the van pulled away, I couldn't help noticing Clarissa watching from across the street.

CHAPTER THIRTEEN

Dear Sophie,

After all the scares about tainted dog food, I would like to cook for my three dogs. My girlfriend says that's crazy because they have complicated nutritional needs. What do you think?

—Riley, Casey, and Chloe's Mom in Paw Paw, Illinois

Dear Riley, Casey, and Chloe's Mom,

Dogs are omnivores, like people. They can eat most people food! Think of it like feeding your child. They need balanced meals—with meats, veggies, and healthy carbs. No skimping and serving fast food! Your vet can give you information on canine dietary needs and supplements, as well as a list of foods they should never eat, like onions, grapes, and chocolate.

—Sophie

Had Clarissa positioned herself there in the hope that she would catch me with Spenser? She nibbled on the side of a fingernail.

Spenser had bought tickets for two tables at the banquet. I imagined he had invited all his local employees. Why wouldn't Clarissa come across the street and have a seat or mingle with the early birds?

If she noticed me watching her from across the street, she didn't show it. Clarissa twisted and turned impatiently, watching cars as though expecting someone to arrive. She'd chosen to wear a drab olive green dress that looked like it cost ten times the amount I'd paid for my dress. Although the color seemed more suited to a military maneuver, she had certainly dressed to impress. She'd been to the hairdresser since I'd seen her earlier in the day, and wore her hair upswept. Unlike my rhinestones, I suspected the gems glittering on her ears and neck were the real thing.

Two little noses snuffled my shoes from behind. Daisy and Martha had arrived in their finery. Martha wore a pink dress embellished with a sequin cupcake. Glittery ruffles shone on her haunches. Daisy sported a bright red collar with a rhinestone buckle and a heart charm that I had never seen before.

"Where did this come from?" I asked.

Mars, looking disquietingly handsome in a tuxedo, said, "I didn't want her to feel like she was the ugly stepsister. Something told me she might not go for a dress like Martha's, though. I imagined it in shreds."

He was right about Daisy. "I'm surprised Martha tolerates wearing a dress. If you start them young enough, I guess they can get used to anything. Is she still biting Natasha?"

"You know about that, huh? She's the sweetest little dog, but she can't stand Natasha." He bit his upper lip, but that didn't prevent him from cracking up.

He wasn't the only one. A lot of people had limited patience for Natasha because she acted so imperial. It was mean of me, but I found it amusing, too. Daisy was as sweet as could be, but Natasha treated her like she was a nuisance. Natasha had finally found a dog she deemed worthy of her, and it had an aversion to her. "Martha's probably just teething, don't you think? She'll get over that gnawing stage."

Out of the corner of my eye, I noticed Clarissa proudly walking into the large tent, her arm linked with Spenser's. She made a point of looking at me, tilting her head back as if to lord her ownership of Spenser over me.

"How well do you know Clarissa Osbourne?" I asked.

Mars shrugged. "She's always been very pleasant to me. But then, I'm not having an affair with Spenser."

I smacked his arm playfully for his sarcasm. "I went over there this afternoon to clear things up. She acted odd then told me she didn't believe me."

Mars laughed. "Surely you didn't really expect her to take your word for that. Why would she? Doesn't everyone deny affairs? Especially the people engaging in them?"

He was right, of course. If I were having an affair with her husband, I wouldn't proudly admit it. I would try to keep it quiet. But then, I wouldn't boldly go to her home and deny it to her face like that, either. I sighed. Some people probably would. I needed to put Clarissa and her ridiculous ideas out of my mind. After all, I knew the truth. I had nothing to hide and no reason to be ashamed. But that was far easier said than done. I would simply do my best to avoid Spenser during the feast.

Natasha's assistant, Leon, scrambled out of an SUV and carried cupcakes toward me. He held them carefully at arm's length, probably to be sure he didn't soil his designer tuxedo.

Mars raised an eyebrow. "Where's Natasha?"

Leon, who was generally of good cheer, grumbled, "Nina forced us to change the icing and *N* adornment on our cupcakes. Beware. There is no placating Natasha at the moment. Since Nina forbade us from using Natasha's signature color or initial, we had to scramble."

We followed him into cupcake central. He removed the cover to display the cupcakes. Natasha's anger shone through. She'd gone with a dog face. The basics were good—three dimensional ears and noses—but the piped icing looked more like the sinister wolf from "Little Red Riding Hood" than a sweet dog.

"Good heavens!" Mars exclaimed. "I knew she didn't care for dogs, but these are scary."

I was taken aback by them. "Let me guess. You were responsible for the noses and the ears."

Leon sighed. "She wouldn't let me pipe the faces. I tried to talk her into letting me do the expressions, but she insisted on doing the tongues and teeth. Did a dog bite her when she was a kid or something?"

I'd known her since we were small children. "I never heard anything about an incident involving Natasha and a dog. Maybe there's a shrink among the guests tonight who can analyze this."

"So, where is she?" Mars appeared concerned.

"She had to change her gown to match the cupcakes."

"What matches werewolf?" The words slid out of my mouth, and I was mortified that I'd been so unkind.

Fortunately, Mars and Leon snickered. The remaining cupcakes arrived all at once. I shooed Mars away and motioned like the traffic police, waving bakers over and pointing them to their tables.

Nick Rigas, prettier than ever in his tux, winked at me when he brought Joy's cupcakes over. He paused for a second, and dimples appeared when he grinned at me. "Thank you for taking the time to talk with Joy. She felt better after your visit."

I couldn't imagine why that would be the case. I certainly hadn't offered much in the way of consolation, but at the moment, I didn't have time to dwell on it.

Within half an hour, all the food had been delivered, waiters in black and white uniforms had arrived, and Nina had given the headwaiter instructions on when to serve the various courses.

Relieved of my duties, I wandered into the big tent, greeting friends who milled around with drinks in their hands. Dogs sniffed each other, and an occasional yip sounded from somewhere in the tent.

As he'd promised, Alex had brought Francie as his date. What was it about tuxedos that made men so astonishingly gorgeous? If they knew how much women loved that look, men would wear them every day. Alex didn't need help in the good-looks department, but in a tux, he was competition for George Clooney.

Francie clung to his arm, proudly parading him about the tent. I'd never seen her dressed so elegantly before. Ornate beading adorned the round neckline and waist of her emerald green gown. She wore a matching jacket with beading on the wrists as well as along the front and bottom.

Alex appeared to be a good sport about being her escort for the night. In fact, he seemed to be enjoying himself as she introduced him to her friends.

Mars had found Natasha. While she might be annoying, she had good taste, and her werewolf brown dress was so glamorous that it must have been couture. I never could have pulled off all the varying folds that crisscrossed down her torso and ended in a little kickable tail-like flounce. She was gorgeous. True to form, she managed to bring in her signature color by wearing robin's-egg blue earrings and a stunning necklace of three large blue stones. Topaz, if I had to guess, but it didn't matter—she was perfectly beautiful.

I collected Daisy from Mars and made a point of telling her how pretty she was in her new glam collar.

Natasha observed me, her arms crossed, her hands gripping her upper arms. "You do know that she doesn't understand you. Why bother talking to her?"

"She understands much more than you realize. Research has shown repeatedly that dogs understand anywhere from one hundred and fifty to five hundred words."

"Puh-leeze. Now if you were to tell *me* how gorgeous my dress is . . ."

Nothing like fishing for compliments. "It's stunning. And so is the jewelry."

Natasha touched the large stones just below her collarbone. "Isn't it beautiful? I'm still surprised that Clarissa wanted to sell it. Robin's-egg blue is a good color for her. I thought she ought to keep it, but she said she would sell it on the Internet if I wasn't interested."

"Looks like you got lucky."

We made our way to the cocktail bar, where I ordered a Tiger Paw and offered Daisy one of the baked chicken cookies for dogs. Daisy snarfed the biscuit, which was in the shape of a tiny chicken.

Francie drifted by, and whispered, "I can't keep Natasha away from Alex. She's making me nuts."

Not far from us, Myra turned her back on Maurice and wound through the crowd wearing a stormy expression. Her hair seemed even bigger than I remembered, but gentle tendrils curled around her face, softening the look. Her makeup appeared toned down, or maybe it just wasn't as noticeable, since everyone had gone heavier on eye makeup for the evening event. She wore a flashy violet halter-style gown, cut to her navel but cinched together under her bust by a matching ribbon, giving the effect of a keyhole underneath. The beaded top, holding her considerable cleavage, glistened under the lights.

Maurice trailed after her. If he'd made any attempt to tame his mop of white hair, it certainly wasn't evident. Instead of an elegant tuxedo, he'd dressed in gray and black plaid trousers, a black suit jacket, and a bow tie and suspenders imprinted with cat faces. The outfit suited him. It rebelled by not being a tuxedo, yet the cat motif on his accessories revealed a desire to play along. He carried something pink that I couldn't quite make out at a distance.

Daisy and I cut through the crowd to intercept Myra and, hopefully, save her from Maurice. "Myra!"

She raised her head and waved. In spite of Humphrey's feelings about her, there was something about Myra that I liked. She might be a little bit bold and brassy, but she struck me as sweet and genuine.

"I understand you work at the mortuary with Humphrey," I said.

Her eyes lit up when she smiled at me. "I started out doing hair and makeup, but I'm taking classes to be a bereavement counselor. There's such a need for them. It breaks my heart to see the way people suffer. Not all of them, but so many don't know how to cope. Sometimes people have a priest or preacher to turn to for comfort. Too often, they don't know where to turn."

Her voice was so soft and gentle that I could imagine she would be comforting to others.

"Is Maurice watching?"

I glanced his way. "Yes."

"I shouldn't have worn this dress. My mother says the reason I love bright colors and flashy things is because I'm around death all day, and I have a need to celebrate life when I'm not at the mortuary." She giggled. "I think she might be right."

"You're reminded every day that we have to make the most of our lives."

"You should see my condo. It's all yellows and pinks and happy colors. I wore this because it usually attracts men, but I wasn't thinking of sour old Maurice."

She reached out to pat Daisy. "Sophie," she whispered, "how do you get rid of men who won't leave you alone?"

"I don't have a very good track record with that. I usually tell them I'm involved with someone else." I doubted this was the first time Myra had ever dealt with an overly zealous suitor.

She released a deep breath. "I'd like to be involved with someone, but he has eyes for another."

I followed her gaze across several tables. Humphrey was ogling Renee like a lovesick teenager while Renee chatted with someone else, laughing, and ignoring Humphrey.

Just past them, Nick appeared to be admiring Clarissa's necklace. He slid a seductive finger along the jewels on her neck. Was she trying to sell that necklace, too? Unfortunately for Myra, Maurice joined us. In his arms he held a large gray cat wearing a pink wig and a tiny cat crown along with a necklace of glittering pink stones.

"Who is this?" I asked.

"Gun . . . ivere."

"Gunivere? That's unusual."

"It's different." Myra edged away from him.

He snorted. "What's wrong with you two? Guinevere?"

I was certain he'd said *Gunivere*. "How does the crown stay on her head?" Daisy had once worn a wreath of flowers, but not for very long. One good shake of her head, and a bejeweled tiara would have flown to the floor.

"He had it made specially for her." Myra's words came out flat. She didn't seem to be impressed.

"Is it attached to the wig?" I was curious about the crown, but, more important, I was wondering if Myra could get the truth about Buddy, the missing dog, out of Maurice. He was clearly smitten with Myra. Would it be too much to ask of her?

"Of course not. Her head is the perfect shape for a crown," insisted Maurice.

I edged toward Guinevere's right to see behind the crown, which was actually a tiara, since it didn't have a back. No clips of any sort were visible.

Maurice shot me a smug smile before turning his attention to Myra. "I think we'd better take our seats, dear."

I wished I could rescue Myra, but many of the tables had been reserved for entire groups, and it was too late to switch things up. As Maurice turned away, he adjusted his grasp on Guinevere, and I saw a little bit more of Guinevere than I was probably supposed to see. I wondered if Maurice knew that Guinevere was really a Lancelot.

Spenser and Clarissa had purchased two tables for their employees. They were already sitting at one of them, chatting animatedly with the people sitting close by. If I hadn't been privy to some of their problems, I would have imagined them a perfectly happy couple.

The general had taken his place at his table with his boxer. Francie and her golden retriever, Duke, sat between the general and breathtakingly handsome Alex. I sidled over to their table to say hello just as Joy and Nick took seats there.

Alex rose to speak with me. "You look beautiful."

I knew that was impossible for a host of reasons, but it was sweet of him anyway. "Black eyes are de rigueur for black-tie affairs."

He leaned close to speak to me in the noisy tent, his breath soft and warm on my ear. "Brunch tomorrow?"

I nodded.

"I'll pick you up at ten."

It didn't escape me that Mars frowned at me from our table.

I had mixed feelings about that. Mostly I thought this was none of his business, but some tiny part of me was glad he cared, and I didn't like that about myself.

Natasha loomed beside me in her super-high heels. She gushed over Alex. Maybe I'd been wrong about Mars. Maybe that frown reflected his feeling toward Natasha's incessant attention to Alex.

Nina stepped up to the podium, and I hurried Daisy to our table.

Nina made some introductions and thanked everyone for their support, but kept her remarks short. The centerpieces on the tables, as well as the slew of other items along the wall, were up for auction after the dinner. When she took her seat, the waiters poured wine, offering a choice of cabernet or chardonnay. One featured a dog label and the other bore a cat label. They soon brought around tiny pupcakes for the dogs and the amuse bouche, a bite-size cupcake. The human first course, a Tex-Mex-style cupcake, was made of black beans and onion. The baker had incorporated cumin and a teeny kick of chipotle. The icing on top was a cool, creamy avocado that went perfectly with the spicy cupcake.

"Black beans and avocado?" Natasha broke off a small corner and tasted it. "Ugh. As dreadful as I expected."

Not everyone shared that opinion. Nina and Bernie wolfed theirs down with gusto.

"Mmm. Those were great." Mars snatched the remainder of the cupcake on Natasha's plate. "I hope that bakery starts making them on a regular basis. I'd eat a couple of them for lunch any day."

"Oh, Mars," grumbled Natasha. "Your palate is just so primitive."

Daisy eagerly ate the tiny dog appetizer and sniffed around for more.

Natasha frowned as she scoped out the room. "I'm quite taken aback by the lengths people go to for their pets. I thought Martha's cupcake outfit would be adorable, but it's rather plebian compared to the flashy gems and tiaras some of these dogs are wearing. Hmm."

"Did you see Maurice's cat?" asked Bernie.

The fish course arrived with a small fish-shaped cookie for the dogs and another cupcake for the rest of us.

Natasha rolled her eyes. "Salmon Cupcakes? Really? Couldn't they have thought of something more clever?"

"What would you have baked, Natasha?" asked Bernie. "Anchovy cupcakes?"

"Puffer fish?" suggested Nina, in reference to a deadly Japanese delicacy.

"She's very partial to black squid ink." Mars's voice was so droll, that everyone at the table laughed hysterically.

"Are you making fun of me?" asked Natasha.

"Are you going to complain about every course until we hit yours?" responded Nina.

While salmon certainly wasn't an ingredient I would think of for cupcakes, the coral-colored icing with little scales and fish lips was so cute that I hated to bite into it.

It wouldn't win my vote for best cupcake of the banquet, but fish was a tough category, and I thought the baker had done a remarkable job with it.

The entrée arrived on larger plates. The lasagna was surprisingly delicious.

Natasha scoffed at the Rosemary Bacon Corn Cupcakes. "These are cornmeal muffins. They're not cupcakes at all."

"Go with the flow, Nat," muttered Mars.

"Honestly, they ought to be disqualified. They're nothing more than seasoned corn muffins. Dotting the top with butter and jamming a piece of bacon into it does not make them cupcakes!"

Uh-oh. I saw a fight coming on. "Then don't vote for it, Natasha."

"But other people might not realize that it's not a cupcake. And this lasagna thing. It's not a cupcake at all." Natasha pushed it to the side of her plate. "Nina owes it to everyone to disqualify the ones that aren't truly cupcakes."

Nina did not look happy about the direction of the conversation.

"What's the difference between a cupcake and a muffin

anyway?" asked Mars. "I buy blueberry muffins from Big Daddy's Bakery that come in little paper wrappers like these. Is it icing? Muffins don't have icing and cupcakes do?"

As though she were an expert on baking, Nina stated, "The line is becoming somewhat imprecise. Technically, a muffin has a coarser texture while a cupcake should be finer, like a cake."

Her knowledge surprised me. Nina had been known to dirty pots and pans so her mother-in-law would think she had prepared a dinner that was actually takeout. When had she become an expert on baking?

"I didn't realize that you watch my show," exclaimed Natasha. "I'm delighted that you have learned so much."

"I hate to disappoint you, but my education on the subject has come from the bakers themselves," Nina explained.

While they chatted, I nonchalantly observed Alex. Francie was giggling at something he said. Not every guy would take out a woman old enough to be his mother and be a good sport about it. I barely knew him, but that impressed me as an indicator of a kind and thoughtful person who wasn't so self-absorbed that he had to parade around with a supermodel type on his arm.

Joy had engaged the general in a discussion. Nick piped up now and then. As I watched their table, it dawned on me that Nick looked strikingly like Alex and the general. The dark hair, the full lips, even the rounded tips of their noses.

I nudged Nina, who was still busy defending the corn cupcakes. "Is Nick Rigas related to the general?"

"What an odd question. I don't think so." She glanced in their direction and did a double take. "I see what you mean. That's one handsome gene pool. Is it the lighting in here, or is the general looking a little bit green?"

General German gave a little jolt, like he'd been kicked in the abdomen. He stared straight ahead, seemingly oblivious to Joy's chatter. He opened his mouth as though he couldn't get air, and braced his hands on the table.

CHAPTER FOURTEEN

Dear Sophie,

My neighbor, who believes everything she hears, told me that chocolate is bad for dogs. My Rhodesian ridgeback loves it and has never had any ill effects. Is this true or just an old wives' tale?

—Chocoholic in Hershey, Pennsylvania

Dear Chocoholic,

Never feed chocolate to dogs. The theobromine in chocolate can make them very ill and even lead to death. If your dog loves that chocolate flavor, look for treats made with carob instead. Should your dog accidentally eat chocolate, contact your veterinarian immediately.

—Sophie

General German tried to push himself up into a standing position. He teetered forward, overcompensated, and fell backward, pulling the tablecloth with him. Glasses spilled and china crashed to the floor.

Screams pierced the air. I tossed Daisy's leash into Bernie's lap and rushed to the general's table with Nina. He lay on the floor breathing heavily.

Alex knelt over him, dissuading everyone from taking action. Turning down all offers to place a spoon on his tongue, sit him up, or carry him outside for air, Alex remained admirably calm. "Please call 911. Everyone, stand back."

Nick hovered behind Alex, seemingly at a loss.

Natasha wedged her way in and nearly fell over the general.

Officer Wong was already on her phone calling an ambulance. Even in a strapless red gown, she cut an authoritative figure. When she hung up, she spoke with a commanding voice. "Let's move back, folks. Give the man air."

Alex positioned the chair on which General German had been sitting so that it formed a bit of a barrier to the onlookers. Sirens sounded nearby.

The attendees had stepped back when Wong asked them to, but they still formed a tight horseshoe around the table.

Joy cried out and jumped forward a couple of steps, wiping the rear of her dress. "Something stung me."

Appropriately solicitous, Nick examined her dress. "I don't see anything."

A couple of women closed in behind her. I feared the crowd wouldn't part for the rescue squad. Nabbing Mars and Bernie by the hands, I tugged them away and recruited Spenser, Leon, and Humphrey as I walked.

Shouting to be heard over the din, I said, "We need to move everyone back so help can get through."

Each of them took up a position. Spenser and Bernie held their arms out to the sides, moving the crowd like pros. I skittered through the space that opened up and met the rescue squad outside.

People inquired about the general as I returned, but I had nothing to tell them other than the fact that he'd been taken ill. When I reached the table again, I overheard one of the paramedics say the general had a weak, rapid pulse.

Before long, the general had been loaded onto a gurney and carried out through a whispering crowd. When they passed by me, General German's eyes were closed, and he lay as still as a corpse.

Alex and Nick trailed along behind him. Alex gently reached for my arm. "Would you mind seeing Francie and Duke safely home?"

I assured him I would take care of them. Given the circumstances, I thought it extremely telling about his character that he even remembered his elderly date.

Nick was equally considerate and insisted Joy remain. She assured him she could walk home or catch a ride with someone.

The relief that swept through the tent was palpable. The general was in good hands, and the din rose again.

Wong clinked a fork against a glass a few times. "May I have your attention? Does anyone else feel sick?"

As unobtrusively as possible, I moseyed over to the general's table and examined it. Wong had prevented the waitstaff from cleaning up the mess, but there was no telling who had eaten what, since everything had landed on the floor.

Daisy had been passed along to Francie. I leaned over, and whispered to Francie, "Did you notice what the general ate?"

"It was the oddest thing. I watched him all evening because he was so quiet. He refused wine and didn't eat a bite. I asked him if he wasn't hungry, and he said his stomach was giving him some problems."

A wave of relief washed over me. It was unlikely that whatever caused him to be ill had come from the cupcakes.

But then someone spoke up. "I do. I feel sick."

Everyone turned to look—at Maurice. Of course. Who else?

"You do *not*!" I couldn't help myself. The man would do anything ornery. He probably wanted a refund.

Wong held up a hand to stop me from saying anything more. "What's the problem, Mr. Lester?"

"I'm queasy. Sick to my stomach."

"In that case, we'd better get you to the hospital, too. No point in taking any chances," said Wong.

At least it would get him away from poor Myra for a while.

A murmur spread through the tent like a wave. A few people rose and left. Nina buried her head in her hands. Poor Nina! This wasn't supposed to happen.

"Anyone else feel sick?" asked Wong.

I held my breath. Nina peeked through her fingers. Not a soul. Nina and I accompanied Wong over to Maurice.

"Do you need an ambulance, Mr. Lester?" she asked.

"Will Cupcakes and Pupcakes pay for it?"

I *knew* he wasn't sick. What a crumb. Someone who was truly ill wouldn't stop to ask if it was a free ride.

Wong must have had thoughts along the same lines. "Mr. Lester, do you need medical attention or not? I am not inclined to tie up ambulances and rescue squads with phony illnesses."

Myra leaned away from Maurice as though she didn't want to be associated with him.

His eyes shifted to her. Moaning, he grabbed his stomach. "Maybe Myra could drive me home."

Clearly appalled by the thought, the corners of her mouth jerked downward. She spoke softly. "I am not your date. And the only way I'd go anywhere near your home is in your dreams."

"Besides, she promised to help with the auction." It was a big, horrible lie, but I liked Myra, and despised Maurice for being so obnoxious to her.

Myra jumped to her feet. "I should be sitting at your table then, shouldn't I?"

"First Spenser poisons me with his cupcake. Now you're embarrassing me in front of my girlfriend." Maurice stood up and bent his slight frame, clutching his stomach.

Seated at the next table, Spenser clearly heard Maurice's accusation. "For pity's sake, Maurice. Let it go already. Besides, I didn't bake any of the cupcakes. They were all baked by my trusty crew here." He smiled at the people seated at his table.

In her soft voice, Myra protested, "And I am *not* your girlfriend. Stop saying that. People will start to believe you."

"Aw, snookums." He reached out and grasped her arm.

She stepped out of his reach. "Get away from me. It was bad enough having to sit beside you. Please just leave me alone."

"I'll see you at home later." He raised his head proudly. "I'd like the rest of my cupcakes, please."

He was nuts. Wong shot me a look that suggested she was thinking the same thing. He claimed to be poisoned by the cupcakes, but now he wanted more of them? The man twisted everything.

Nina held her hand just below her neck. She swallowed hard, her jaw muscles tense. "I don't know what to do," she whispered.

"I think Wong has it under control. Why don't you leave it up to the guests? I'll handle Maurice. You talk to the guests."

Nina made her way to the podium. The loudspeaker crackled as she picked up the microphone.

Wong walked Maurice to the entrance of the tent, and I followed, listening to Nina apologize to the guests. She was up front with them, saying she wasn't sure if we should call off the rest of the feast. A chorus of boos filled the tent. Behind me someone yelled, "Bring more cupcakes!"

Applause broke out as everyone got back to their merriment.

I asked the headwaiter for Maurice's share of the remaining cupcakes. Fortunately, Nina had thought ahead and provided cupcake boxes and doggie bags for those who wished to take home some of their dinners.

I handed two boxes to Maurice. He had trouble holding them with Guinevere in his arms.

"I'll carry them to your car for you." I didn't want to, but frankly, I was glad that he was leaving, and was willing to do whatever might be necessary to speed up his departure.

"You'd like that, wouldn't you?" He loomed over me. "I don't have a dog in my car!" With that odd comment, he seized the boxes and strode off into the night.

While it had never occurred to me that he might have Buddy in his car, his strange outburst piqued my curiosity. I waited until he was a good distance from me before I followed him. Two blocks later, he stopped by a small car and unlocked the door. He was careful and gentle with Guinevere. He folded himself into the driver's seat and hastily closed the door, no doubt so Guinevere wouldn't spring from the car.

His head nearly hit the interior roof of the car. If he'd had Buddy, the silhouette of the big dog's head would probably have been visible in the back seat. With a sigh, I returned to the party.

Bernie had pulled chairs up to our table for Myra and Francie during my absence.

The second I sat down, Nina asked Myra, "How do you feel about spying?"

Myra thought a moment. "I suppose it's politically necessary. To be honest, I've never given it much thought."

Nina held up her forefinger. "Necessary! That's exactly it." She lowered her voice. "You're the only one who can get into Maurice's house."

"You couldn't get *me* in there for anything."

Nina launched into the sad story of Buddy's disappearance, ending with "and he hasn't been seen since."

"And you think he's in Maurice's house?"

All eyes focused on poor Myra.

"Oh! I see now. No, no, no. I don't think so. Alone with him in his home? No way! Isn't there someone else? He rents the upstairs apartment to Nick Rigas. He's a slimy sort. Maybe he'd snoop around."

"At the very least, he might have heard Buddy bark," I said.

"Too bad he left with the general. I'd like to find out what he might know about Buddy." Nina bit into her cheesecake cupcake.

Natasha picked a corner off the cheesecake cupcake and

sampled it. "At least no one can blame me for making the general sick. My cupcakes hadn't been served."

I thought Nina might explode. "Why don't you go right on up to the loudspeaker and announce which ones are your cupcakes?"

Natasha glared at her. "No wonder Sophie didn't bake cupcakes. She probably knew what a pill you would be."

Gritting her teeth, Nina hissed, "It's not a popularity contest. People should vote for the cupcake that tasted the best— which you should be glad about, because if it were about popularity, Sugar Baby or Cake My Day would probably win."

Although I had enjoyed the savory cupcakes, I had to admit that the sweet ones were my favorites. The Blueberry Cheesecake Cupcake was delicious, though perhaps a bit too much like cheesecake. The Strawberry Cupcakes and Natasha's Coco Loco Cupcakes, which combined dark chocolate with coconut, were superb. I wanted to love the Salted Caramel Cupcakes, but something wasn't quite right. The base was a yellow cupcake with a hint of caramel and just a wisp of saltiness. The baker had carved out a divot in the center of each cupcake and filled it with caramel. That part was fabulous. But the icing, which contained caramel, tasted like paste. Whoever made them had used the caramel to make kitty stripes and piped the icing to look like fur. I felt sorry for the baker, because the little faces were so artistic, but the flavor of the frosting was far too much like elementary-school glue. A quick glance around confirmed that I wasn't the only one who'd left most of that cupcake on my plate. I'd seen them come in on the Cake My Day truck, which meant they'd been baked by Spenser's bakery, or by Renee. As much as I might have liked the others, the indulgence of sweet, creamy strawberry frosting, a tiny bit of a luscious strawberry surprise inside, balanced with a tiny portion of moist cake could not be beat. I voted for the Strawberry Cupcake.

A team of waiters collected ballots, and when Nina trotted up to the podium for the auction, I stole away to the small tent with Humphrey and Francie to tabulate the results. When Nina selected her counting team, she'd taken care to choose people with no stake in the outcome. Of course, that was well before anyone realized that Humphrey had a thing for Renee.

Only when he walked into the small tent did it occur to me that Renee's interest in Humphrey might be directly related to his position as a counter of the ballots. It wasn't like there was an incredible award at stake, just the honor and a very cute trophy. A black block base with a gold inscription— *Cupcakes and Pupcakes Gala Dinner Best Cupcake*. On top of the base sat a cupcake statuette consisting of a gold wrapper topped with enamel that looked like white frosting, topped with chocolate frosting, topped with raspberry frosting with a cherry on top.

The three of us sat down at a table. Francie pulled out her reading glasses. "I'll call them out," she said. "Sophie, you keep track of the cupcake votes. Humphrey, you keep track of the pupcake votes."

It didn't take long to realize that a lot of people felt as I did. The sweet cupcakes took the lead, though all the cupcakes received votes.

The pupcake votes went in the savory direction. While the dogs liked their desserts, the chicken liver pupcake won their hearts.

We wrote the winners on cards and returned to the banquet tent, where the auction was still in progress. In spite of the general's illness, life and laughter had returned to the festivities, and bidding between Spenser and another well-heeled Old Town resident had become spirited. Spenser finally conceded and allowed the other man to win. Applause broke out, as did a chorus of barking.

I handed the results to Nina and returned to my seat. Natasha gripped Mars's hand. I hadn't seen any physical contact between them in a very long time. The pang that I felt at their tiny display of togetherness tore through me in a way I would never have expected.

I barely noticed Nina congratulating the baker of the Strawberry Cupcake—one of Bernie's employees at The Laughing Hound.

The united hands at which I stared broke up when Natasha

yanked her hand out of Mars's, stood up, and said, "I demand a recount. Humphrey was biased because he's smitten with Renee, and Bernie is his friend."

Renee drew a sharp breath and appeared on the verge of tears. Had Natasha's outburst offended her so deeply?

Bernie ran a hand over his face. "Blimey, Natasha! Couldn't you lose gracefully just once in your life?"

Mars rose and placed a hand on Natasha's shoulder, which looked to me less like support and more like restraint. Martha took that opportunity to leap onto Natasha's empty chair and up onto the table, where she nabbed the remainder of a Coco Loco Cupcake. Hands reached for her from all directions, but the clever dog evaded them, hopping down so fast she was little more than a blur.

Bernie rose to chase her, shouting, "Stop that dog. She has dark chocolate in her mouth. It could kill her!"

CHAPTER FIFTEEN

Dear Natasha,

I have never been fond of cupcakes. They're just too sweet for my taste. I've been asked to bring them to our next bridge club party, but I can't bring myself to make that sweet, fluffy icing. Are there any alternatives?

—Savory Gal in Sugartown, New York

Dear Savory Gal,

Dip your cupcakes in melted chocolate. Or drizzle them with a glaze and sprinkle chopped nuts on top. The added bonus is that the frosting lovers won't ask you to bring cupcakes to bridge club again.

—Natasha

Mars, Daisy, and I collided directly behind Bernie. We chased after Martha, but in single file we weren't effective. When we reached the entrance of the tent, we came to an abrupt halt. This time, Martha had made good on her escape.

Silently, the three of us scanned the park and surrounding area. Cars lined the street, providing plenty of shadows where Martha could hide. Not to mention the trees and bushes in the park. The streetlights offered ample light for walking, but not for locating little dogs.

"Will she come if we call her?"

"I doubt it," said Mars. "We've only had her for a couple of days."

Nevertheless, we all called her name.

"What if we split up and carry dog treats? Something she'd smell—like the chicken liver pupcakes," I suggested.

"It's worth a shot," said Bernie. "If she ate that chocolate cupcake, she'll be in trouble soon."

"If we ever find her, I'm going to rename her Trouble," grumbled Mars.

I handed Daisy's leash to Mars and poked my head into the cupcake tent. Luckily, a couple of the liver pupcakes remained. I grabbed them and returned to hand one to Mars and half of one to Bernie. We divided the area. Mars offered to check the cars along the street. He insisted on taking Daisy with him, saying she might alert him if Martha was hiding underneath a car.

Bernie took the left side of the park, and I strolled out to the right.

When I reached the edge of the river, I wished I had a flashlight. Even though the lights of the tent were bright in the distance, the dark river's edge seemed a little sinister. A wind kicked up, and the water gurgled. I'd grown up in the country, so there was no reason for me to be afraid of the thickets of bushes, but I was uncomfortable nevertheless. Someone crashed through the brush. I paused, thinking it could be Martha, but heard a strange singsong voice.

Instead of calling out Martha's name, I shouted Bernie's.

"Did you find her?" he asked.

Relief swept over me. I ran in the direction of his voice.

"I don't have her, sorry. Just got a little spooked. Someone is creeping around out there."

Bernie slung an arm around me. "Are you okay?"

"I'm fine. I just wish we could locate Martha. Especially since she's so small."

I could feel him nodding. "The smaller the dog, the darker the chocolate, the more dangerous the situation. Maybe we should come back with flashlights. She could be a meter away and we wouldn't see her."

We walked across the grass and rounded the tents. Guests flooded out to their cars. Nina had arranged for valet parking as well, and a polite line had formed for that.

Mars and Daisy met us. "From your empty arms, I'm guessing you didn't find her," said Mars.

Daisy nuzzled my hand for the liver cupcake and ate it with gusto.

"It's too dark back there. I suggest we go home, change clothes, and return with flashlights."

"That's about all we can do right now," said Mars. "You know, Maurice is a very strange egg. After that fuss he made about not feeling well, would you believe he was out here on the sidewalk? It was bizarre. When he saw me, he took off down that way and disappeared in the dark."

"Sophie, I bet that's why you were creeped out," said Bernie. "Maybe you got a vibe that he was lurking in the bushes."

"Eww." Chill bumps rose on my arms at the mere thought. "But why? Why run from Mars, and why hide?"

"He didn't want me to recognize him? Or to know he wasn't really sick? Beats me. I'll watch Daisy while you go home and change. Do you have any stinky meat or cheese?"

I could have called Mars on that, but I knew what he meant. "I'll sniff the fridge."

Instead of taking both cars, Bernie gave me a lift home. I changed into jeans that had enough spandex in them to make them feel comfortable and soft, even after a ten-cupcake meal. Mochie watched from my bed, but he'd curled up into a soft ball that indicated he planned to stay there for a nap. I found a teal three-quarter-sleeve T-shirt with a V-neck and managed to slide it on without messing up my hair. A pair of running shoes, and I was set to go. In case Nina wanted to join in the hunt, I stuffed drawstring pants and another Tee into a bag. She wore a larger shoe size, so I hoped she might have taken a pair of sneakers with her for the prep work before the dinner.

Mochie purred when I stroked him, and I assured him I'd be home later. He didn't seem worried.

I took a minute to sniff the fridge for anything with a powerful scent. The best I could do was leftover lamb steak and a block of sharp cheddar cheese. When I grabbed my favorite flashlight, which pointed straight as well as down at my feet so I could see where I was stepping, it dawned on me to bring leashes, too, in case one of us nabbed her.

Leaving a light on in the kitchen for Mochie, I locked the front door. Bernie pulled around in minutes. He drove to the park slowly so we could be on the lookout for Martha, and Buddy, too.

He hit the brakes. "Do you see that?"

I bent forward to look past him. In the dim recesses of an alley, a slender figure darted crazily from shadow to shadow. "Is that Maurice?"

"I certainly hope he's not up to no good. What peculiar behavior."

"I think he's hiding from someone. What other reason would he have to run into the shadows and lurk like that?"

"Martha's more important than that nutter, Maurice." Bernie drove on. "He's off his trolley!"

By the time we reached the park and the tent, only Nina, Francie, Natasha, Mars, Spenser, and Clarissa remained along with cleanup and break-down crews. Bernie passed out flashlights, and I handed out leashes, cheese, and chunks of lamb. Nina changed clothes.

Natasha pulled me aside. "Will she really die from eating chocolate? I think Mars and Bernie are trying to scare me as punishment for contesting the results, which I'm certain were wrong."

"I'm sorry, Natasha. It doesn't take much chocolate to be lethal to a tiny dog like Martha."

It was rare for me to feel sorry for Natasha, but she looked so sad that I hugged her. "Maybe we'll find her in time. Don't give up hope yet."

"I feel so guilty. I . . . I was thinking about returning her to the breeder, but I didn't want her to *die*."

"Natasha, it wasn't your fault. She's a fast little devil."

"It was the fault of the person who didn't finish that cupcake."

That was ridiculous, too. But I didn't point that out because she was already miserable.

Nina returned, and we spread out in a line to canvas the park. Natasha still wore her beautiful gown, so she kept watch on the street and the tents with Francie and Clarissa while the rest of us ventured toward the river flicking our flashlights across the grass and under bushes.

We neared the spot where I'd heard a strange voice. Loud and clear, someone was speaking gibberish. I aimed my flashlight into the bushes but didn't see anyone.

It was a woman's voice I heard, and she continued speaking. "Come back to me. I can see you there, glittering. Why can't I reach you? Nana? Oh, Nana! Don't hate me."

We inched forward, and there at the edge of the river, on a rock that jutted out toward the water, stood Joy, her arms outstretched as though she were reaching for something in the depths of the river.

Bernie whispered, "I hope she's not planning to jump. Sophie and Nina, get as close to her as you can without endangering yourselves. Mars, Spenser, and I will walk around in back of her. When you see my light flash twice, distract her, and we'll move in to grab her."

Branches cracked as they plowed through the bushes. Nina and I eased forward. We reached the edge of the river, and didn't dare go farther. One more step and we would have fallen several feet and slid into the water.

Two quick bursts of light flashed behind Joy.

"Joy?" I started with a very soft singsong voice so she wouldn't be alarmed. "Joy?"

"Nana! I'll get your ring back."

I had no idea what she meant. What if I said the wrong thing, and she plunged into the river?

Nina whispered, "Tell her to take a step back."

"Joy . . . step back. It's Nana, Joy. I want you to step backward."

"I hurt her," she moaned. "It was evil of me." Her wail turned into a nightmarish scream, like she had been attacked.

I feared she had jumped.

Nina shone her light directly on Joy. Thank heaven. She'd cried out because Bernie had grabbed her around the waist. She kicked her legs like a wild woman and fought him. He turned around and passed her to Spenser, who held fast while Mars tried to calm her.

They carried her out of the brush. She stopped fighting them but talked nonstop. None of it made any sense. She tried to walk, but staggered as though the earth were sliding away underneath her.

For the second time that night, we called 911.

While we waited for the rescue squad to arrive, she answered our questions politely, but seemed embarrassed when she had trouble finding words. She also conversed with people who weren't there, which I thought extremely worrisome.

Mars pulled me aside. "I found Nick's number on the cell phone in her purse. He's waiting for her at the emergency room." He glanced over at Natasha. "I know it's my turn to take Daisy, but given the situation with Martha, I think it might be better if Daisy stayed with you tonight. Is that okay?"

"It's always okay." I was glad to know someone would be looking after Joy, too. "Do you think this has anything to do with that sting she complained about earlier?"

Mars shrugged. "It's very bizarre. Bernie says he's seen people act like this under the influence of hallucinogens. I hope it's not related to what the general has, or we could all be in trouble. Do you feel funny?"

"No." I hadn't given it any thought, but I felt fine.

"Me, either."

Bernie joined us. "Did you hear her say that she hurt someone and it was evil? Could she have been talking about Muffin?"

"Muffin? You think Joy murdered Muffin?" asked Mars.

"Shh. It's possible." I watched Joy play patty cake with

someone who wasn't there. "Those were pretty condemning words. On the other hand, maybe the person who murdered Muffin slipped Joy something tonight."

～～～

The paramedics made quick work of securing Joy to a gurney. They asked us questions about what she'd had to eat and drink, but none of us were experiencing anything remotely similar. I relayed the information about the sting she'd felt earlier, but other than that, there wasn't much we could do. Our panic over her condition waned a hair when the ambulance pulled away.

"Could we all take different routes home tonight?" asked Mars. "Just in case Martha is running along the street somewhere."

Mars had grown attached to her. Even Natasha seemed upset. Their long faces left no mistake that they were heartbroken.

I walked Daisy to my car. We hopped in, and I rolled down the rear windows. It might be silly to think she would bark if she saw Martha, but she had barked at dogs on the street before. It couldn't hurt.

We drove to the tent to pick up Francie and Duke. On the way home, we scanned the quiet streets, on the alert for dogs.

We arrived at my garage without seeing a single one. Francie and Duke went home through the gate that joined our properties, and I trudged to my kitchen door with a heavy heart.

Mochie greeted Daisy and me with a long kitty stretch and a yawn. I picked him up and carried him to my den to check for messages. Nothing.

It was too late to call anyone to check on General German. Other than prowling the streets of Old Town, there wasn't much I could do. I suspected worry about the general, Joy, and Martha would prevent me from sleeping. The night air had been cold, so I heated milk for hot chocolate. I spooned rich powdered chocolate and sugar into a mug and added just enough water to dissolve them before stirring in the milk. I turned off the lights and padded into the sunroom where I curled up on the loveseat. Daisy sprawled at my feet, and Mochie jumped up on the loveseat, forcing me to change my position so he could snuggle on my lap.

I stared out into the dark backyard, lighted only by a few strategically placed solar lights that were mostly just decorative.

Mochie purred as I sipped my hot chocolate and contemplated the evening's disasters. Normally, Humphrey would have stayed with us and helped search for Martha. But he'd left with everyone else, undoubtedly at Renee's urging. Mars would say that I was jealous. I smiled at the thought. That was complete nonsense. I cared about Humphrey, though. He'd become a close friend, and I hated to think he might be hurt by Renee. I didn't like the way she'd appeared to ignore him at the feast, or the way she'd used him for everything from running her booth to fetching her furniture. Helping friends was fine. I had nothing against that. But chances were good that either she or Joy had killed Muffin during an argument. I'd dismissed the possibility that Renee might have planned to pin the murder on Humphrey, but maybe I'd been too hasty. She had no problem using him for everything else she needed.

Joy's delusional comments had propelled her into the number-one suspect spot in my mind, though. She was probably still blathering on at the hospital. Maybe she would make a full confession. Would it be valid if someone had doped her up?

Better yet, who would have wanted to do that? Muffin's killer? Hadn't Spenser heard Muffin shouting about a ring?

The milk in the hot chocolate began to make me drowsy. Mochie, Daisy, and I headed upstairs and went to bed.

What seemed like only minutes later, the phone on my nightstand rang, waking me from deep sleep. It was Mars, who quickly blurted out, "Humphrey found Martha and took her straight to the twenty-four hour veterinary clinic. We're with her now."

I blinked at the clock. Just past midnight. "I'll join you as soon as I can."

"There's no use in anyone else coming, I just wanted to let you know."

I hung up and eased back onto my pillow. Maybe there was still hope for Martha. Comforted by that tiny bit of good news, I waited for the phone to ring again with an update. Alert in spite of my exhaustion, I didn't think I would be able to sleep, but I soon dozed off.

⌘

Morning dawned with the promise of summer. Unseasonably warm air drifted through the window I'd left open a crack. I stretched leisurely until I remembered the events of the night before. What had happened to Martha? Had she survived? What about the general and Joy? Alex was probably staying at the general's house. He'd be more likely to tell me how the general was doing than the hospital.

I slung on a light bathrobe and stumbled down the stairs behind Daisy and Mochie. I let Daisy out into the fenced backyard, put the kettle on, and scooped Nell's Breakfast Blend coffee from Newman's Own into my French press. I hurried back to the den, with Mochie dancing around my ankles all the way.

A quick search of my personal records produced a home phone number for General German. It wasn't even eight o'clock yet. Did I dare call this early? What if the hospital had released him, and he was still sleeping? The kettle screamed, and I decided to wait until nine to make calls.

I poured the hot water into the French press, thinking how grateful I was that I didn't have to man a booth on the final day of Cupcakes and Pupcakes. Nina had talked me into counting the ballots for best-tasting cupcake and cutest cupcake. While it seemed like that might be a rerun of the previous night, more bakeries were involved, as well as a wider range of testers, since anyone could vote. Nina and the other Cupcakes and Pupcakes planners wanted to be as inclusive as possible and give all the bakers a chance.

Voting closed at noon. I'd thought I could pick up the ballot box on my way home from brunch. But given the general's illness, I suspected that my brunch with Alex was cancelled.

I pushed on the French press, watching it shove the coffee grounds to the bottom. The aroma wafted up to me as I poured it into a mug. A spoon of sugar and a little milk—perfect. I was reaching for a loaf of rye bread I had baked when someone tapped on the kitchen door.

Humphrey opened the door to let Daisy bound inside in front of him. "I'm sorry to come by so early. You're not even dressed yet."

"Come on in." I cinched the belt of the robe tighter. "Coffee?"

He checked his watch. "I'd love some to wake up. I'm not used to so little sleep. Ugh, have you looked at your eye? It's in full bloom."

I poured a mug for him but let him add the milk himself. "I heard you were the hero who found Martha last night."

"She was blocks away from the river, near Cake My Day. It was just dumb luck that I spotted her. I didn't think she would come to me, but Renee and I were able to corner her. Have you heard anything about her condition?" He sat down on the banquette that ran behind my kitchen table.

"Not yet."

"I probably should have called, but I'm about to do something awful to you, so I wanted to explain to you face-to-face."

Oh no. I eased into a chair across from him, dreading what he was about to say.

"I wish to withdraw from the tabulating committee."

The weight of unknown fears dropped away. It could have been so much worse! "I'm sorry to hear that. Because of work?"

"Because I wish to avoid any scenes like the one Natasha made last night at the banquet. I was mortified. Not only was it embarrassing in front of Renee, but now all of Old Town will think I'm some sort of swindler."

Natasha had put me in embarrassing positions more than once in my life. I understood Humphrey. But it meant we would be short a ballot counter, and there wasn't much time to find a replacement. "I can't say that I blame you. No one will think you're a swindler, though. Most of those people know Natasha."

"All the same. I don't want her saying things like that about me. Ever. I'm very honest. You know that. I won't put myself in the position of being accused of bias."

"You know that Natasha isn't a contestant in today's voting. She didn't have a booth."

He brightened up. "I forgot about that!" His face fell again. "But Renee is involved. If she wins, someone will accuse me of preferential treatment."

"So this is getting pretty serious with Renee?" I held my breath.

His pale face flushed like a cherry. "She has no place else to live, what with her bakery being a crime scene."

"She's staying with you?" I needed a lot more coffee to brace myself for that kind of news.

"Now don't go telling your mother, because she'll tell my mother, and that would ruin everything."

"Mum's the word, I promise. But don't you think your mother would be happy that you've finally found someone you care about so much?"

Humphrey blinked at me like he couldn't believe I'd said something so stupid. "You know my mother. No one will ever be good enough for me. If she gets wind of it, she'll be here in a heartbeat to mash any hope of my happiness to a pulp."

I wanted to be reassuring, to pooh-pooh his belief, but he was right. Mrs. Brown would chase away any woman who might be interested in a relationship with Humphrey. "Where is Renee now?"

"Back at her booth. Detective Kenner has been really hard on her. She's already distraught over Muffin's murder, and Kenner had to hammer away at her like he thinks she did it!"

I'd been through his interrogations in the past. I could understand her distress. Underneath, Kenner wasn't such a bad guy, but he never believed anyone was innocent until it was proven. "Did he question you, too?"

"Yes, of course. I'm not quite as delicate as Renee. She's in such a bind, Sophie. Joy took all the money in the Sugar Baby bank account. Wiped her out! Plus, she can't get into her own bakery to bake or sell cupcakes. She baked all last night at Cake My Day. Early in the morning, when Spenser's employees arrived, she came to my house and caught a nap. Now she's back at her booth selling her little heart out. It's just lucky that Spenser has been so accommodating to her."

"Joy took all their money? Why would she do that? Shouldn't they have divided it equally?"

"One would think so. And without Muffin, Renee doesn't have anyone to assist her. Spenser and I have been pitching in. I'm not much help, but I'm learning. Spenser is much more useful. He's a wizard at piping frosting. Although, after last night's disaster, she doesn't know if she can recover her reputation."

"Disaster?" There'd been too many. I didn't know which one he meant.

"With her frosting. Half the cupcakes had frosting that tasted like paste. It was all she could do to hold back the tears until we got into my car."

"Didn't she taste the frosting?"

"Of course she did! The one she tried must have been from the good batch."

His phone jingled. "It's Renee." He pushed a button and said, "Hi, cupcake."

I wanted to barf. *Cupcake?* Seriously?

"I'll be right there." He clicked off. "Something's wrong with the cupcakes. People are bringing them back and complaining about them."

CHAPTER SIXTEEN

Dear Sophie,

I saw a photograph of your cat walking on a leash. How did you train Mochie to do that?

—Catwoman in Whiskerville, Pennsylvania

Dear Catwoman,

It's best to start when they're kittens. Most kittens will object to a harness initially, but once they associate it with going outdoors, they'll come running when they see you bring the harness out. Don't expect them to walk like dogs. Cats have their own ideas. Allow them to sniff and have fun at their own speed.

—Sophie

Humphrey rushed out the door faster than I'd ever seen him move. I watched him from the window. While I didn't want to be like his mother and crush his happiness, I couldn't help feeling that something wasn't quite right.

Over the past two days, Renee had lost just about everything. Not only had she lost her assistant in a cruel murder, but Muffin had died in Renee's bedroom. *Ugh.* Would she ever be able to live in the apartment over the bakery again? I couldn't imagine wanting to sleep in that bed or in that room anymore. And then Joy had taken all their cash and opened a rival bakery across the street. What a scummy thing to do. Couldn't she have found a place a few blocks away? I had liked Joy. I didn't know her very well, but taking all their joint funds was really low. Opening a store across the street that was almost identical was nothing short of despicable.

What would I do if I had lost everything? I shuddered at the thought. Renee was to be admired for forging ahead. She had to be devastated by Muffin's death, yet she had jumped into her work, trying to dig a way out of the financial hole in which she found herself.

Then why did I feel like she was taking advantage of Humphrey? Maybe she was as smitten with him as Myra was. Still, something wasn't sitting right with me, but I couldn't put my finger on it.

It sounded as though Renee thought someone had sabotaged her cupcakes. She'd frosted them at Cake My Day. Humphrey wouldn't have tampered with the ingredients, but hadn't he said Spencer had helped, too? *Uh-oh.*

Would Spenser have stooped that low? His offer to let Renee use his bakery seemed so generous. Had he done it just so he could tamper with her cupcakes? I pondered his motives as I washed Mochie's food bowl, looking out the window over the sink.

Across the street, on the corner of the next block over, a commotion was taking place. The lovely mansion on that corner had belonged to Mordecai Artemus and had sat empty since his demise. A van bearing the logo of The Laughing Hound restaurant was parked in front, and people were carrying things into the house. Surely they weren't catering a function. I'd have heard about it if the mansion was available as a party rental.

I dashed up the stairs, hopped in the shower, and, wrapped

in a towel, scanned my walk-in closet with brunch in mind—
just in case it hadn't been called off.

The truth was that I had grown tired of wearing gloomy
black all the time. It might be more slimming, but I wanted to
feel summery, and I pawed through clothes until I landed on a
berry red dress. If I wore sandals, I wouldn't be overdressed
no matter where we went. Happily, it zipped up the back without a problem. I added gold earrings and a delicate chain. So
what if the necklace had been a gift from Mars when we were
married? I happened to like it.

But there was no fixing my black eye. I packed on makeup,
but to no avail. I slid my feet into beaded sandals and rushed
back downstairs.

Clicking a leash onto Daisy's collar, I opened the front
door, and casually walked toward Mordecai's house to find
out what was going on.

We crossed the street and were on the opposite sidewalk
when I realized that people were unloading furniture from
the van and carrying it into the house. Bernie strolled out.
Perfect! It wouldn't seem as nosy if I asked him what was up.

We crossed to the house, and I flagged Bernie down.

He patted Daisy. "Morning! Don't you look lovely."

"Thanks! Who's moving in?" I whispered.

"Me."

I was dumbfounded. "Seriously?"

He nodded. "The chap who owns The Laughing Hound
wanted to buy it as an investment. They dropped the price,
and he bit. I'm bringing my cats over this afternoon. I was
tired of living in tiny quarters over Mars and Natasha's garage
anyway, and I've had enough of Natasha. Her rudeness last
night at the banquet . . . I don't know how Mars can stand it.
That was embarrassing."

I held out my hand. "Welcome, neighbor."

He laughed, took my hand, and kissed my cheek. "Now I
can watch your comings and goings! Hey, I could use some
help buying furniture for the place. There are a lot of empty
rooms."

"Shopping with someone else's money! Sounds like fun."

"My mum has been making noises about a visit. I've stalled her for a bit, but I'd like to get a couple of guest rooms in shape. Don't know how long I can hold the old girl off."

"I'm looking forward to meeting her." His mother had been down the aisle more times than Elizabeth Taylor and had lived in exotic places like Shanghai. "Where is home for her these days?"

"I honestly thought she might settle in Sydney, but she's in Tokyo at the moment."

"Daisy!" Mars waved at us from the front of my house. He jogged over. "There's my girl. Want to go for a run?"

I handed him the leash. "How's Martha?"

"Just got off the phone with the vet. She's doing great. They induced vomiting, gave her activated charcoal, and monitored her overnight, but she can come home later today."

"It's so lucky that Humphrey spotted her! Heard you lost your tenant, though."

"I don't blame him for wanting a bigger place. Besides, Natasha has plans for the apartment over the garage. So, what's with you and the general's nephew?"

I'd forgotten all about him. "What time is it?"

Bernie nudged me. "I'd guess it's time for him to pick you up. Isn't that him?"

Sure enough, like a scene in a movie, Alex stepped out of a flashy metallic red BMW convertible and gazed straight at my house.

"That, gentlemen, would be my cue to go." I hurried across the street and waved. "Alex!"

When I caught up to him, I said, "I wasn't sure we'd be on after the general fell ill. How's he doing?"

"It's a little dicey. I'll tell you about it over brunch." He walked to my kitchen door with me.

Leaving him in the kitchen, I grabbed my purse, locked the front door, and hurried back to the kitchen, where I stopped cold. Through the window, we could see Natasha sashaying her way toward us. "Do you want company?" I asked.

"I'd rather it was just the two of us."

"Follow me." We heard the door knocker bang against the front door as we slipped out the French doors in my living room and rushed out my back gate, into the alley.

When we came around the front corner of my lot, we saw Natasha dash through my side gate, toward my backyard. Giggling like schoolkids, we did our own hurrying before she reappeared. When we passed by the mansion, Bernie and Mars watched us from Bernie's front porch like a couple of gossipy old women.

Alex had selected a restaurant on the river. Immediately after we both ordered eggs Benedict, I asked him about the general again.

The waiter brought Bellinis and poured coffee into our mugs.

"This isn't exactly the kind of thing a guy likes to talk about when he's trying to impress a lady."

He needn't have worried. Those wise eyes and that mouth that looked like it might break into laughter had me mesmerized. I couldn't imagine anything he could say that would turn me off at that moment.

"Although our last name is German my family is actually Greek."

Aha. That explained the dark hair and good looks.

"Some people from the Mediterranean have a genetic quirk, a gene that makes them—us—resistant to malaria."

He could have launched into a discussion of anything and I would have found it interesting. But being genetically malaria-resistant was a new concept to me, and I found it fascinating.

"Unfortunately, there's a flip side. The condition is called favism, because we're unable to process fava beans. Well, broad beans in general, but especially fava beans."

"So you're allergic to fava beans?"

"Since it's a genetic thing, it's not technically an allergy, but I shouldn't eat them."

I thought back. What had he ordered for brunch? Eggs Benedict—no beans in that.

"In the simplest sense, they make us anemic. It appears that's what has happened to the general."

"You didn't ask if fava beans were in anything on the menu."

He laughed. "Hannibal Lecter's tastes notwithstanding, they're not all that popular or common on menus. I've eaten a bite or two by mistake—I feel crummy a few hours later, but so far, as long as I don't eat more of them, I'm right as rain by the next day."

"The general has this condition and ate fava beans?"

"That's what the doctors think."

"But there weren't any fava bean cupcakes served. Did you feel ill?"

He smiled broadly, the tops of his cheeks crinkling up ever so slightly. "I'm fine. I thoroughly enjoyed the cupcake banquet. The general is severely anemic. To have gotten to this point, we think he must have been eating them regularly for some time."

I thought back on what little I knew about anemia. "Then he'll be okay as soon as he gets a blood transfusion?"

"Not quite. That has already helped, but there are additional complications, especially at his age."

"Joy's condition isn't related then? She doesn't suffer from favism?"

"No. The doctors think she'll be fine, but something entirely different was going on with her." He inhaled deeply. "She was suffering from hallucinations. I don't know what caused that, but it wasn't favism. It was just serendipitous that they sat at the same table." He paused and gazed around before leaning toward me, and whispering, "They seemed to think she might be in the habit of taking recreational drugs and that she had a bad reaction to something she took."

The waiter arrived with our orders. I cut into an egg, piercing the yolk, and ate a bite coated with creamy, rich hollandaise sauce.

I examined Alex's plate very carefully, even though we'd ordered the same thing. Chili, stews, tacos, salads—there were plenty of dishes he needed to be careful about. On the other hand, he was right about fava beans. I didn't often see them on a menu.

Alex politely asked me about my life and managed to convince me that he was interested. It was fun brunching with someone new, who hadn't heard all my stories before.

When the dessert cart came around, we both went for the fruit tart—photo perfect rings of blueberries, raspberries, and strawberries in a shining glaze. A sweet custard underneath was the perfect complement to the berries. We took our coffee the same way, too, which meant nothing, yet made me wonder if we shared other tastes.

Eventually the topic of conversation returned to the general, since Alex planned to visit him in the hospital after we ate.

"Surely the general was aware that he had this condition. After all, you know that you have it."

Alex nodded. "Everyone in our family is aware of it. My sister passed it on to her sons."

"Then why would the general eat fava beans? Making a mistake once is understandable, but every day? It's like he wanted to be sick."

"That's something I've been thinking about since the diagnosis. He's a very intelligent man, a graduate of West Point, and a brilliant businessman. He would never intentionally eat fava beans day after day. Never."

Alex looked directly into my eyes. "It could only happen if someone intentionally fed him fava beans every day—without his knowledge."

CHAPTER SEVENTEEN

Dear Sophie,

How do I make a filled cupcake? I love that extra surprise when I bite into one.

—Cupcake Mom in Lemontree, Arizona

Dear Cupcake Mom,

After the cupcakes have been baked, cut a small cone out of the middle. I use a paring knife, but an apple corer also works. Don't worry about it being perfect, because the frosting will cover it. Fill the spot with jam, whipped cream, lemon curd, chocolate, Nutella, Marshmallow Fluff—the options are endless. You can eat the little cone as a snack, or stick it back on top of the filling. It's up to you.

—Sophie

I could barely tear my eyes away from Alex's. But when he reached across the table and took my hand, my gaze moved down in amazement.

"Aside from wanting to see you again, I didn't cancel today's brunch because I'm told you're pretty good at solving crimes."

I snatched my hand out from under his and leaned back in my chair. *Aha*. Well, it wasn't like I didn't know from the very beginning that guys as handsome as Alex didn't go for women like me. I should have realized that as soon as I saw his BMW. He was used to sleek sports cars, and I was a VW Beetle.

Alex cocked his head. "Have I offended you?"

"No." He'd disappointed me a little, but I'd sort of expected as much. "I don't know exactly what you've heard, but I'm not a private investigator. I just got lucky a few times. You're an attorney—I'm sure you can figure out what's going on. Considering how you phrased that, I'm guessing you think someone is trying to kill the general?"

He appeared to hold his breath for a moment. "I don't want to think that. But since the general wouldn't have eaten fava beans, I have to think they were disguised in some way. There is the possibility that someone has unknowingly continued to offer him a dish containing fava beans, but—" he paused and slowly shook his head "—it seems like an awfully big coincidence that fava beans would happen to be in the dish. When's the last time you cooked fava beans?"

"Never."

"Precisely. There are a few sweet widows who bring the general homemade goodies. They're adorable. He's still popular with ladies. I can't say that one of them doesn't innocently make a dish with fava beans in it, but it just seems so unlikely. I'm planning to track them down this afternoon to find out. Three of them called early this morning as soon as they heard he was in the hospital. None of those have ever cooked fava beans. Most of them know he has a thing for sweets. They bring him brownies and cobblers, the kinds of dishes that wouldn't contain legumes."

"Maybe one of them is a health food type who makes him salads or casseroles?"

"Could be. I'm definitely going to find out." Alex rubbed

his chin and looked away. "The alternative is something I'd rather not contemplate, but I think I have to."

"Is there anyone who has it in for the general?"

Alex leaned back in his chair. "I'm at a loss. I don't live here, so I'm not familiar with his life and the people he knows."

"Any family other than Nick?"

Alex froze. He stared at me, but I couldn't read his expression. Had I said something disturbing?

"No. Just Nick. How did you know? He has a different last name, because his mother is the general's sister."

"You're his brother's son, then?"

He nodded.

"Wasn't hard to guess. Nick was seated at the general's table last night. There's a strong family resemblance among the three of you. Was it supposed to be a secret?"

Alex placed his elbows on the table. "Not really. Nick likes to keep it quiet, since he works for the general. He's sensitive about people knowing he's related to the boss. You know, nepotism in the workplace."

I could see it in his eyes. He was afraid Nick had slowly been killing the general. "Do you know who will inherit the general's estate?"

"No, I don't. It's a pretty lousy time to ask him, don't you think?"

The waitress came around one more time to see if we needed anything else. I checked the time. "I need to pick up a ballot box, and I guess you'd better check on the general."

We walked back through the booths on Market Square. They were still doing big business, with throngs of people browsing and buying. We stopped by the adoption booth so I could pick up the ballot box.

Nina could barely contain herself. She raised her eyebrows at me and whispered, "I want full blow-by-blow details later."

I glanced over at Renee's Sugar Baby booth, but no one was there. "Did Renee shut down?"

Nina cringed. "There was a major problem with her

cupcakes. I tasted one, and they were weird. Now isn't that odd after the catastrophe last night with her frosting?"

"Humphrey told me that Renee made the horrible Salted Caramel Cupcakes."

"And now there's something wrong with all her cupcakes." Her face pulled into an unpleasant distortion. "They taste like a really bad recipe—like I baked them! I was all for her shutting down. Wong took a few of the cupcakes for the police lab, just in case anyone turns up sick."

"Do you feel sick?"

"No, and neither does anyone else. In spite of the problems last night, I've heard nothing but raves from the people who attended. Some are hoping we'll make this an annual event."

Alex carried the box for me on the way back to my place. It wasn't heavy, but it was a nice gesture. We left Market Square, heading for my house, and he asked about the flyers regarding Buddy that were hanging everywhere.

I explained what had happened. He paused, lifted my chin a tad with gentle fingers, and studied my eye. "You sure you don't want to bring charges?"

"I set Maurice up. He never should have kicked a dog, of course, but I was trying to get him to say something horrible and, well, I really don't think he meant to kick me."

"What a worm. Why does that name sound so familiar to me?"

"He's the one who made a fuss about feeling ill after the ambulance came for the general last night. Oh! But you were gone by then."

He stopped walking for a moment. "Maurice . . . any chance that he could be Nick's landlord?"

"Yes, I believe he is."

Alex resumed a comfortable pace. "That figures. He wants to throw Nick out. Apparently Maurice went to the general for Nick's rent, which provoked some fireworks. All three of them were furious." He shot me a knowing look. "One doesn't ever ask the general for money. He has plenty, but he likes to remind people that he is not 'The Bank of General German.' "

I wanted to ask if the general had paid Nick's rent, but decided that was just plain too nosy.

Alex peppered me with questions about life in Old Town.

"You're serious about moving here?" I asked.

"I've almost decided to make the move. I've extended my trip a few days because of the general's illness. Tomorrow I hope to check out some properties. Wouldn't it be great to set up a law practice in one of these historic town houses?"

What with all the news about favism in his family, I hadn't asked him about his work. "What kind of law do you practice?"

That enticing grin appeared. "Your favorite—criminal law."

We were laughing when we passed Bernie's new house. Alex walked me to my front door and reached for my hand. For an awkward moment, I thought he might kiss it. But he leaned toward me for a kiss—

"There you are!" Natasha had changed into a stunning blue and beige dress that showed off her figure. I didn't know how she managed to walk on those five-inch heels. "I just missed you before. Alex, you simply must come over for a tour of my house."

He still held my hand, and although his face revealed no distress, his hand clenched mine tighter. "I'm afraid I have to get to the general, Natasha. He's still in the hospital. You understand. Another time, perhaps?"

She actually had the nerve, the chutzpah, the brazenness to lean toward him for a kiss.

He obliged her with a perfunctory peck on the cheek— while still grasping my hand!

Natasha walked him to his snazzy car. I could hear her exclaiming about it nonstop.

As he climbed in, I realized that Bernie and Mars had witnessed the whole thing from Bernie's front porch. Maybe having him so close by wasn't such a great idea after all.

I unlocked the house, left the ballot box on the console in the foyer, and crossed the street to Bernie's. The front door stood open. I rapped on it and walked inside. Someone had kept the house clean, but it was so empty that Bernie's and Mars's voices sounded like they were in a cavern. I found them in the family room I had once decorated for a show house. Francie rested on a sofa, holding Daisy's and Duke's leashes. The dogs strained toward me. Bernie was exclaiming over the carved wall-to-wall bookcase. They had already hung the TV in a niche.

"I'm so glad you didn't tear this out," said Bernie. "You just don't see this kind of hand-carved work much anymore."

"Have a nice brunch?" asked Mars in a vexed tone.

"It was lovely, thank you very much."

"I see you're dating married men again."

The nerve of him! "I am not. In the first place, he happens to be separated from his wife, and in the second place, it was just brunch, not a date."

"I dated him last night," said Francie. "Whoo, is he adorable!" She winked at me. "But I only got a kiss on my wrinkled old cheek."

Bernie and Mars stared at me, their arms crossed over their chests.

"I have a completely clear conscience. No one calls it a date when I have lunch with one of you."

"You boys get over yourselves," said Francie. "Mars, I'm not one of Natasha's fans, but it's time for you to tie the knot. Quit making cow eyes at Sophie. You already made your bed."

I held my breath. I was so sure no one had known anything about the spark left between us.

Bernie laughed at Mars.

"Not so fast, Bernie," she added. "Dana is a perfectly darling girl. I can't imagine why you broke things off with her. You and Mars need to quit giving Sophie a hard time. Besides, Alex's wife is the one who caused the marriage to fail. She's the one who started sneaking around to see someone else. Poor Alex."

"How did you find that out?" I asked.

"You young people are too hung up on niceties. If you'd tell each other what you think and come out and ask questions, you wouldn't have to pussyfoot around so much. I asked Alex why he was getting a divorce. Sometimes, if you just ask, it's pretty amazing what people will tell you."

I hurried to change the subject before Mars could start in on me again. "I came over to see if you'd like to help count ballots with Francie and me. Humphrey had to bow out. Neither of you has a dog in the race. How about it?"

"I'm in," said Bernie.

Mars acted a little sheepish, not the norm for him, but he nodded. "Sure."

Bernie locked his front door and handed me a key. "Just in case of emergency."

At the bottom of his porch steps, he bent over and reached out to examine seedlings that were coming up.

"Don't you dare touch that with your bare hand!" Francie seized his arm and tugged at him. "That's jimsonweed."

Bernie straightened up. "I'm not familiar with that plant. What happens if I touch it?"

"You die," said Francie grimly. "Okay, maybe you wouldn't die right away, but the whole plant is extremely poisonous."

"How can you tell what it is?" The seedlings looked unidentifiable to me.

"I was standing in this very spot when Mordecai planted it. There was a bit of a discussion between Mordecai and my husband because of its dangerous properties. We felt he should plant it in the enclosed yard in the back, where children wouldn't be tempted to touch it."

Mars peered at it. "Why would anyone want such a dangerous plant?"

"Are you sure Natasha doesn't have one?" asked Francie. "They're gorgeous. The blooms are four inches long and look like trumpets. They're quite popular as ornamental plants. The name *jimsonweed* is thought to have come from 'Jamestown weed,' because it was so prevalent there. Some people call it thorn apple, mad apple, or devil's trumpet."

"I don't believe we have this delightful killer in England," said Bernie.

"You must. If memory serves, Agatha Christie used it in

a couple of books. It's part of the nightshade family. Shamans around the world reportedly used it to induce visions."

Bernie scowled. "I really don't care how beautiful it is if it's that deadly. I'll dig it up this afternoon and dispose of it."

We trooped across to my house. While Bernie, Mars, and Francie settled around the kitchen table, I put on a kettle of water for tea. Bernie had fed them takeout from The Laughing Hound for lunch, but I thought a little dessert nosh might be in order. Fortunately, I had a batch of my favorite new oatmeal cookie recipe frozen in a roll. I preheated the oven, then cut off fat rounds that I quartered and placed, pointy side up, on parchment paper spread over a cookie sheet. I slid them into the oven to bake.

I poured organic black tea for everyone except Francie, who asked for green tea. They moaned appreciatively when the cookies came out of the oven. The smell was so mouth-wateringly scrumptious that I wanted to bite into one even though they were still too hot. When everyone had a mug of tea, and the platter of cookies was on the table, we commenced with the tabulation of the ballots.

It was a close call between Joy's Monkey Business, a banana walnut cupcake with chocolate frosting, and Spenser's Raspberry Vanilla, a raspberry-laced cake with raspberry filling and vanilla icing. But in the end, after a recount to be absolutely, positively sure, Spenser's Raspberry Vanilla won the public opinion taste test for Cake My Day.

At three o'clock, we ambled up to Market Square. I couldn't help noticing that the cupcake vendors appeared to be dwindling. Renee had not reopened, and Joy's booth was closed as well. I had expected them to shut down when they heard about Muffin's murder, but they'd carried on like troupers, in spite of their sorrow. I wondered if it was more than coincidence that they'd both had to shut down their booths early. Maybe I was reading too much into it. They'd tried too hard to keep going. Maybe they'd both finally taken time to grieve.

When I handed Nina the envelope containing the winner's name, she seized my arm, and whispered, "I'm worried about

Humphrey. Word around town is that Joy claims she was poisoned."

"By a cupcake? One of Renee's cupcakes?" What a nightmare. A couple hundred people had attended the cupcake feast. Would Humphrey know how many she'd sold at her booth?

"No, no. Where did Nick go? He was eating a cupcake . . . Nick!"

He must have heard her shout his name, because he loped toward us.

I wasn't sure which of the general's nephews was better looking. Nick might have been a few years younger than me, but the way women chased him, his age didn't appear to matter to them. He had the same lush hair as Alex, as well as the dark masculine eyebrows. Alex held his shoulders squared and his chin high. He had a sense of humor but was clearly the more serious of the two. But Nick was a grown-up pretty boy with a smile that lit his face. No wonder Humphrey was jealous and wanted to be like him.

"Would you please tell Sophie about Joy?" asked Nina. Bernie, Mars, and Francie crowded around us.

"I hope Joy will be okay?" I asked.

"The doctors said she'll probably be fine. It won't be long before she's released."

"So what happened?" He didn't seem very worried.

He gestured with his hands as he spoke. "They don't know exactly. The doctors think she took some kind of recreational drug that induces hallucinations, but Joy insists that's not the case. She thinks she was poisoned by something that stung her."

Nina discreetly tugged me away, and whispered, "It had to be Renee. Unless she talked someone we know and love into doing the dirty deed for her."

CHAPTER EIGHTEEN

Dear Sophie,

My wife and I are arguing about the proper shape of a cupcake. I think it should have a round curve on top. She says
it should be flat. There's a batch of cupcakes riding on this.
Who has to bake them?

—Rangers Fan in Round Top, New York

Dear Rangers Fan,

It doesn't matter. You're going to hide the top under frosting
anyway. Bake the next batch together!

—Sophie

I couldn't have been more stunned. "Please tell me that you
don't mean Humphrey?"

Nina had the decency to look like she felt guilty for suggesting such a thing. "Desperate people sometimes lose their
sense of what's right and wrong. I'm not being mean! Humphrey is an easy target. He wants to have a relationship with

a woman more than anything in the world. There's no telling what he might do to make Renee happy."

I shivered at the thought. Not Humphrey! He'd creeped me out a few years ago when my mother invited him to Thanksgiving dinner without telling me. But I'd gotten to know and treasure him as a close friend. What Nina was suggesting was too far out of Humphrey's value system. Even if he *was* desperate for a relationship, I couldn't see him doing anything so vicious. He didn't have it in him.

It didn't escape me, though, that something horrible was happening to the women who had been associated with the original Sugar Baby cupcakery. The only one who hadn't suffered physical harm was Renee. "In my wildest imagination, I cannot imagine Humphrey hurting anyone. But it can't be a coincidence that Muffin was murdered, and now someone has apparently tried to injure Joy." I sighed, hating that I was even thinking such a thing. "Sort of leaves Renee as the culprit, doesn't it?"

"How are we going to get Humphrey out of her clutches?"

"You're scaring me!" But she was right. "I've had this bad feeling about the way she was treating Humphrey from the beginning. Did you know that she's staying with him?"

A squeal escaped Nina's lips. The dogs and cats up for adoption looked in her direction. "This is far worse than I thought. If she has moved in, it's too late to rescue Humphrey."

"Stop that!" I scowled at her and lowered my voice so no one would hear. "Renee has always seemed very sweet. We don't know that she's a monster."

"Not yet, we don't. But I'd be willing to bet on it."

A couple of people called to Nina. "*Ack!* I forgot all about announcing the winner. Look at all the cupcake bakers around the podium, waiting for the results. "Is it Joy? I hope it is. She could use some good news."

"Humphrey said Joy cleaned out Sugar Baby's bank account. I wonder what was going on there behind the scenes."

Her mouth hanging open, Nina hurried to join the people waiting for her. Renee had shown up, but without Humphrey. Nick winked at Renee, but she turned a cold shoulder and said something to Spenser, who was also waiting for the results. He laughed, caught sight of me, and waved.

"I saw that."

I looked over my shoulder. Spenser's wife, Clarissa, had snuck up behind me.

"Maybe he was waving at you."

"Oh, please. Don't bother trying to fool me. Though I found it fascinating that you've managed to dupe Natasha. She thinks no man could possibly be interested in you."

That was so typical of Natasha. What she'd said was insulting, but in this case, fortunate.

"I haven't duped anyone. If Spenser is having an affair, it's not with me. He seems like a nice guy. Why don't you cut him some slack?"

"How stupid do you think I am? I followed him to your house on Friday."

I wondered if she had also followed him to the hotel, but thought I'd better keep that to myself. I really didn't want to be involved in their marital problems. If I said she must have seen him leave my house, too, then I would be admitting that he visited. At two in the morning, a clever retort would undoubtedly come to me. At the moment, all I wanted was to get away from her. No matter what I said, she wouldn't believe me anyway. And then I said words I never in my life would have expected to hear from my own mouth. "Listen to Natasha."

At that moment, Nina announced Spenser's cupcakery, Cake My Day, as the winner. "You must be very proud." I gave Daisy's leash a little twitch and walked away, wishing I knew how to prove that I had no connection to Spenser.

It wasn't until I was walking home that I remembered Mars was supposed to have Daisy for the rest of the week. I didn't go back, though. He'd probably come by for her later.

I spent the rest of the afternoon cleaning house and catching up on work. Mars never showed up. With all the commotion about Martha, they must have forgotten about Daisy. That was fine with me. After a long walk and a light dinner, we hit the sack early.

I tossed awhile, thinking about Humphrey and Renee. Was

it possible that Muffin had changed her mind and decided to work for Joy? Was that why Renee had killed her? What kind of warped mind would think that way? People had killed for less, though. Had Renee made an attempt on Joy's life, too?

I bolted upright in bed. Could it be that Joy had a history of drug abuse, and that was the reason the doctors thought Joy was doing recreational drugs? That would explain a lot of things. If Joy was using drugs, maybe Renee couldn't deal with it, and that was the real reason behind their split. It would certainly explain why Joy drained Sugar Baby's bank account. And maybe it *was* Joy who'd killed Muffin. After all, she was the one who had said she'd done something evil. I would have to make some discreet inquiries.

Feeling a little bit better about Humphrey's relationship with Renee, I relaxed. Now, who was feeding the general fava beans?

⌘

"Sophie?" Humphrey's voice was soft, almost timid. Not terribly surprising, since he'd had the nerve to call me at ten minutes past four in the morning.

I grunted and lay back on my pillow, calculating that I could sleep for another hour and fifty minutes before my alarm went off.

"I'm in jail!"

CHAPTER NINETEEN

Dear Natasha,

You display cupcakes so beautifully on your show. I have a cupcake stand, but it never matches the theme or colors of my parties. Is there a way to make my own?

—Cupcake Diva in Paris, Tennessee

Dear Cupcake Diva,

Make your own in any color and theme by using three sizes of cake boards and two equal-sized cake dummies. Cover the cake boards with heavy paper and glue ribbon on the edges. Cover the smaller cake dummies with ribbon and stack them between the cake boards. Voila! Your own personalized cupcake stand.

—Natasha

I jerked upright in my bed. "You're where?"

Mochie jumped to his feet and looked around. Daisy ran to the window and barked. They must have picked up on the panic in my voice.

"Can you pick me up? I need somebody to bail me out." I could hear hysteria in Humphrey's voice, even though he was making perfect sense.

"Of course! I'll be right there." I started to hang up, then thought better of it. "Humphrey? Humphrey? Are you still there?"

"Yes."

"Don't talk. Don't tell the cops anything." I wanted to think it was a mistake. It *had* to be a misunderstanding. But Nina's words hung in my head and, no matter how hard I tried, I couldn't shake them. Had he done something heinous to win Renee's affections? The possibility frightened me. I wasn't scared of Humphrey, I was scared *for* Humphrey.

I swung my legs over the side of the bed and rushed to my closet. It would be nippy until the sun rose. I pulled on a pair of jeans with a lot of stretch in them, struggled to fasten the waist in spite of that, and slipped a dark green fleece top over my head. Not bothering with makeup, I clipped my hair up without stopping to brush it, and pounded down the stairs.

I let Daisy out in the backyard while I checked the computer. *Bail bondsmen!* I had never needed one of those before. Why wasn't Alex an Old Town attorney already? He would know what to do.

Good grief, bail bonding must be a lucrative business, because there were dozens of them. I chose one based on its Old Town address. The male voice on the phone promised someone would meet me at the police station.

Daisy waited at the kitchen door to be let in. I told Mochie and Daisy to be good, grabbed my purse, and flew out to my garage. I drank in the cold night air, thrilled that I didn't have to walk four blocks to my car now that I had a garage. I climbed into my hybrid SUV, backed out into the alley, and was on the deserted street in minutes.

Historic Old Town still slept as I cruised along Duke Street to the adult detention center. I parked in haste and ran inside.

"Hi, I'm here to pick up Humphrey Brown?"

The female officer at the desk nodded knowingly. "He's a bit agitated."

I didn't doubt it. He usually took crises calmly, but this was way out of his norm.

True to his word, the bail bondsman walked in seconds after I did. He clearly knew the drill and shifted into paper-work mode.

"What's the charge?" I asked.

A door swung open, and Officer Wong walked in. "Sophie! Did you come for Humphrey?"

"How is he?"

It wasn't polite of me. I should have asked how she was doing. Fortunately, she didn't appear to mind. "He's been better."

"What happened?" I waited for the worst. Had they connected him or Renee to Muffin's murder or Joy's poisoning?

She tugged at her ear and grimaced like she wasn't quite sure about something. "Grand larceny . . ."

"Of what? That has to be wrong!" I calmed down. "There's a mistake." There was simply no way Humphrey would steal anything. It was better than the murder charge I'd feared, though.

Wong wrapped an arm around my shoulders and squeezed. "I hope there's something peculiar going on, otherwise our sweet nerd is actually one slick criminal. See if you can get the real story out of him. If he wasn't involved in the burglary, they might drop the charges to possession of stolen goods."

It was almost eight o'clock in the morning before I walked out the door with Humphrey, newly accused of burglary.

He climbed into the passenger seat of my car without a peep. But once he started talking, words streamed out of his mouth like a flood. "I'm so sorry, Sophie. I didn't know what to do. I told them I was a friend of Wong's, and I think that may have helped a bit. She suggested I call you."

We were at a light, so I turned to face him. "Okay, suppose you tell me what you allegedly stole."

"Thank you for saying *allegedly*, because I have never sto-len a thing in my life. Well, there was the time Benton Monroe was in the locker-room shower, and I took his clothes."

Humphrey waggled his finger. "But that wasn't theft, because I hung them neatly on a hanger and hooked it onto his locker. I never would have done it if he hadn't been such a bully."

The light changed and I focused on the street. I remembered Benton. He'd been a menace to everyone. I could imagine how he had probably tortured Humphrey. He deserved to have his clothes taken. "Did you relocate something this time?"

"No! To be honest, I'm still quite clueless about it all." He sat quietly for a moment. "It seems there was a valuable cupcake in my car. I just can't figure out how it got there. From their questions, I gather it was stolen in what must have been an alarming burglary."

I had to bite my upper lip to keep from laughing. A cupcake? "Oh, Humphrey! Who would steal a cupcake? A little kid? How much could it have cost?"

"Fifty thousand dollars."

I glanced over at him. "That must be some cupcake! How is that possible?"

"I don't know exactly. I've been pondering that myself. The nature of the police questions led me to believe it's studded with gemstones."

"Could someone have put it in your car?"

"That seems rather obvious, doesn't it?" He sounded testy. "How else would it have appeared there?"

Which led me to another question. "Let's put that aside for the moment. How did the police know it was in your car?"

His eyes opened wide. "Good point! The police must be the ones who planted it on me!"

I thought that unlikely. Not out of the realm of possibility, but why would they pick on Humphrey? "Is anyone angry with you?" As soon as I asked, I thought of Clarissa's ridiculous beef with me. Sometimes we had no idea that someone was upset with us.

"Maurice Lester doesn't care for me."

"Maurice? He doesn't like anyone." His name seemed to be popping up a lot. First, he stole Buddy because he didn't like Spenser, and now he was trying to pin something on Humphrey?

"He's jealous of me because of Myra. He resents the fact that she's fond of me."

"Are you saying that Maurice stole this valuable cupcake and planted it in your car to get rid of you because he's in love with Myra?"

"I wouldn't put it past him, but . . . no, as revolting as I find the man, I have no reason to believe he's a thief."

"How does Maurice make a living?"

"I don't know. But he has way too much free time on his hands." Humphrey's head bowed forward, as though he couldn't look at me. For the most fleeting of seconds, I wondered if he *had* stolen the cupcake. That couldn't be the case. Not Humphrey.

He spoke in a small voice. "My life is over."

I pulled up in front of his house. "Would you like me to come in for a while? Make you a cup of tea? You must be starving."

His shoulders rolled forward. "How can I ever face anyone again?"

"Humphrey! Now stop that. We'll get to the bottom of this."

"They could suspend my funeral director's license."

"But you haven't been convicted of anything."

He rubbed his eyes with the heels of his palms.

"Humphrey! Look at me!"

He turned his bowed head just enough for me to see misery etched on his face.

"Did you or did you not steal that cupcake?"

"No." His tone quivered in that one word, so timid and simple that I had to reach over and hug him.

"Then you'll be fine. I promise we'll help you figure out what happened. The charges will be dropped, and everything will be okay. It's probably all just a big misunderstanding." At least I hoped so.

I couldn't leave him alone in this condition. He was wearing a business suit. Summoning as much cheer as I could, I said, "Hop inside and change clothes. We have some sleuthing to do. Hurry!"

He blinked at me. "Are you sure? I don't want to be a bother."

I nodded vigorously. "Go on!"

He bounded from the car.

Much better. I followed along behind him. Humphrey's town house didn't fall into the historic category, but the architect had done a great job of ensuring that it blended in with the neighborhood. Humphrey unlocked the front door, shouted, "Make yourself at home," and took the stairs two at a time.

Humphrey's house was spotless. The L-shaped kitchen counter gleamed. Stacks of Sugar Baby cupcake boxes were lined up like soldiers. Probably the leftover empty boxes from the booth. Beyond the kitchen, a combination dining area and living room stretched out to French doors flanked by windows. A tiny fenced patio lay beyond. Even the garden bordering the flagstone patio was tidy.

I perched on the sofa. Across from me, a wall of bookcases surrounded the fireplace. The titles reflected Humphrey's diverse interests, from the classics to physics. A TV blocked a small portion of the bookcases.

Certainly not the home of a person in the habit of stealing expensive objects.

While he was upstairs, I phoned Nina and brought her up to date.

Humphrey returned, dressed in surprisingly snug jeans. It wasn't like him to show off his bottom like some young stud. His navy blue Henley-style pullover did a good job of hiding his shape, and I realized with a start that his jeans were snug because of the weight he had put on.

He opened a drawer in a side table and removed an iPad. "I'm ready," he announced.

I drove home and parked in my garage. Wordlessly we walked to my kitchen. When I opened the kitchen door, Nina and Francie shouted, "Humphrey!" so that it sounded like a cheer. Some of his anguish appeared to wash away as they fussed over him. While he told them what had happened, I dashed back to my den and checked over my schedule for the day. There wasn't anything I couldn't reschedule. It struck me as odd, though, that I had cupcake tastings down for a few organizations. Cupcakes were in high demand for functions. Humphrey came first, but sometime I would have to find out what was happening with Renee and Joy, because cupcakes had been requested by a couple of my clients for their dinners and receptions.

A few quick phone calls to move engagements, and I was back in the kitchen.

Proud as an eight-year-old, Nina said, "Look, we made coffee!" She poured me a mug, added milk and sugar, and held it out to me.

I sipped, prepared to gush over it, even if it tasted of salt. "This is good. Really good! Thanks."

"Humphrey would like Ebelskivers after his ordeal in the slammer," said Francie. "Do you think you could make some?"

"No problem." I happened to be a fan of the tiny filled pancakes. I pulled eggs, fresh spinach, pork sausages, and blueberries out of the fridge.

Humphrey, Nina, and Francie tried to find mention of the gem-studded cupcake on Humphrey's iPad. I was whisking eggs when I heard a collective exclamation. Carrying the bowl, I rushed over to look.

The cupcake in the photo would have been at home in a museum. The paper part on the bottom had been fashioned out of eighteen-karat gold. The jeweler who created it had lasered an intricate pattern of curlicues and hearts all the way around the gold and set it with diamonds. Smooth pink-enameled gold formed the frosting. Colorful gemstones had been artistically placed over the swirling icing to resemble sprinkles. It reportedly stood about two inches tall. According to the information, the top was hinged and opened to accommodate a tiny pendant version.

"*That* was in your car?" I asked. "It's incredible. Where on earth did it come from?"

Humphrey scanned the iPad. "Spenser! It was stolen from his home during a burglary last year."

CHAPTER TWENTY

Dear Sophie,

I'd rather have cupcakes at my wedding than a wedding cake. My mother is pitching a fit. How can I convince her?

—Fit to Be Tied in Romance, Wisconsin

Dear Fit to Be Tied,

Cupcakes have become a popular change from the traditional wedding cake. Talk to your baker. She'll probably have pictures of lovely wedding cupcakes. Maybe it will help mom compromise if the very top of the cupcake display features a small traditional cake with flowers or a cake topper.

—Sophie

"I remember that," said Francie. "Spenser was out of town on business. Clarissa had the fright of her life when some man broke into the house and took their things. I heard she hid under the bed so the man wouldn't see her."

My concern for Humphrey heightened. All the recent

troubles had involved a small circle of cupcake bakers. I didn't understand what was going on, but it seemed like Humphrey had stepped into a nest of yellow jackets, and one of them had stung him. I set the bowl on the counter and sat down with my friends. One person's name rattled around in my head— Renee. Humphrey would balk as soon as I mentioned her. He would deny her involvement. How could I get him to see what I was thinking without shoving it down his throat?

"Who has been in your car in the last couple of weeks?" I gave him a window, so he wouldn't fight me right away.

"No one."

We stared at him.

"Renee." He spoke her name like he was doomed. "And Natasha's dog, Martha."

Nina gasped. "That's why Renee killed Muffin!"

There could be a connection, but I didn't see it. I waited for her to go on.

"Muffin found the bejeweled cupcake in Renee's apartment and accused her of burglarizing Spenser's house."

"Or maybe Renee stumbled upon it and was going to return it to Spenser. I need to talk with Renee!" Humphrey rose from his seat.

"Maybe you should eat breakfast first. Where is Renee anyway?" I rose and folded the egg whites into the batter.

Francie poured more coffee for everyone. "If a man burglarized the Osbourne home, then he must have given it to Renee. Maybe she doesn't know that it was stolen."

"Why would she be carrying it around?" asked Nina. "I would have that thing in a safe, or at least well hidden."

"She stayed at my house for a couple of nights while her place was a crime scene," said Humphrey. "She probably brought it with her for safekeeping and it slipped out in the car. Oh my gosh, I bet she's frantic about losing it."

I heated the pork sausages and warmed the Ebelskiver pan. The scents of spinach and pork mingled with the coffee aroma, and I realized how hungry I was.

Unbidden, Nina set the table with a blue tablecloth, round white Fiesta ware plates, and chocolate and blue toile napkins that boosted the elegance of the table setting immediately. She located the maple syrup in the fridge and brought it to the table.

It warmed my heart that Nina pitched in without asking—and she even knew where to find everything!

Squeezing the moisture out of the spinach, I considered my mixed feelings about Renee. I'd liked her and had no problems with her until she started using Humphrey as her personal assistant. That wasn't reason to suspect her of murdering Muffin, though. Or of stealing the cupcake. Her bedroom was packed with miniature collectables but I hadn't noticed any of that caliber.

I poured a teensy bit of cream and mixed a tablespoon of butter into the spinach, added salt, pepper, and a dash of nutmeg, and gave it a whir with an immersion blender to chop it up and incorporate the seasonings. I spooned a small portion of batter into each of the round Ebelskiver indentations in the pan. On top of each, I added a tiny bit of the spinach mixture, then added a little bit more batter to cover it. I flipped each Ebelskiver to cook on the other side and fetched a serving platter. The pork sausages went in the middle and the spinach-filled Ebelskivers formed a circle around them.

I set the platter on the table and started the next batch of Ebelskivers, this time with a Nutella filling. After that, I made one more batch with blueberries, dusted them very lightly with powdered sugar, brought them to the table, and sat down.

The food had brought conversation to a dead stop. Nina helped herself to more of the savory spinach Ebelskivers. "As much as I love sweets, these have to be one of my favorites. They're like spinach crepes, only in little balls."

Humphrey chowed down, apparently not any worse for wear after his incarceration.

Francie had finished with the savory portion of her breakfast and eagerly helped herself to sweet Ebelskivers. "Mmm." She swallowed a bite. "I never know what to do with Nutella other than spread it on toast. These are sinful. Humphrey, I hope you'll ask Sophie to make Ebelskivers more often."

I appreciated their enthusiasm, and had to admit that the

chocolatey hazelnut flavor of Nutella wrapped in a tiny warm pancake was hard to beat.

If only Humphrey's problem wasn't hanging over our heads like a sword dangling on a loose cord.

My fear was that Nina had been right in regard to Renee's connection to Muffin's murder. So far, we hadn't heard about anyone who might have a motive to murder poor Muffin. No one except Renee or Joy. And I wondered if even they had motives. After all, they were the ones who'd put her in the position of having to choose between them. It seemed impossible to imagine that Joy had been so upset by Muffin's decision to stay with Renee that she'd resorted to murder, unless she had a drug problem and hadn't been thinking clearly.

Or maybe Joy was right. Maybe someone had tried to poison her. The most likely candidate for that was, once again, Renee.

Trying to sound oh-so-casual, I asked, "So Humphrey—what's the story behind the split between Renee and Joy?"

"I already told you. Joy moved out without any notice to Renee."

"What's with the ring I keep hearing about?" I asked.

"Joy claims Renee stole her grandmother's ring, a valuable family heirloom. That's nonsense, of course. What's worse, Joy cleaned out the business bank account, so Renee didn't even have money to pay the rent!"

I watched him carefully. Had he paid the rent for Renee? How could I delicately inquire?

Francie coughed. "Good grief. I hope she didn't hit you up for rent money."

I froze. Trust Francie to cut to the chase.

Humphrey didn't seem put out in the slightest. "She did not. I offered to pay it for her."

"A loan, I hope?" asked Nina.

"Not at all. If you were in a financial bind, and I was able to help, I would do the same for any one of you."

Glances shot around the table between Francie, Nina, and me.

"That was very kind, Humphrey." He'd never see that money again. I cut into a blueberry Ebelskiver.

"No wonder Renee tried to knock off Joy!" Francie shook her head. "What was Joy thinking, taking all their money? It's like a bad divorce."

This time Humphrey bristled. "Francie, please. I won't have you speaking that way about the woman I love. You have no reason whatsoever to think that Renee had anything to do with Joy's illness. And frankly, I'm not sure that the rumors of poisoning are even true. The doctors think she may have taken something that caused her hallucinations."

"The woman you love?" Nina choked on her coffee.

I had seen this coming. I *so* wanted to be happy for Humphrey, but I'd had misgivings from the start. Now that so many horrible things had happened, and Renee seemed to be in the middle of them, Humphrey's adoration of her worried me.

"I'm going to ask her to marry me."

Forks clattered on dishes around the table as they fell from our hands.

"How long have you known Renee?" I asked.

"Over a year."

"You've been dating her that long and never said anything about it?" How did we miss that? How could we not have known?

Humphrey raised his forefinger. "Known . . . dating, that's a distinction without a difference."

Uh-oh. He was in for another huge letdown.

"Oh, Humphrey! How can you be so naïve?" Nina smacked his hand.

His forehead crinkled. "I am not naïve. For instance, Sophie and I have never dated, but I've known her most of my life. There's probably not much I don't know about her."

"Apparently you don't know how shocked she would be if you asked her to marry you." As usual, Francie had hit it on the head.

Humphrey turned his head ever so slightly toward me. "Is that true? You would be shocked?"

"Yes! I have male friends, but marriage—well, that's a completely different thing." I dared to ask, "Is your relationship with Renee . . . romantic?"

"Actually, it is."

I relaxed a little bit. Maybe I'd gotten the wrong idea about Renee.

"You can't imagine what fun we had selling cupcakes in the booth. Tight quarters, you know, so we couldn't help brushing against each other now and then. And the laughs we had when we baked cupcakes at Cake My Day with Spenser! I'd say we've been quite close."

Once again, looks flitted between Nina, Francie, and me.

Francie set her coffee mug on the table with a little thud. "Have you been intimate, son?"

"We have engaged in warm embraces." He scowled at us. "I believe a gentleman never discusses such things."

"Oh dear heaven!" Nina bit back a smile. She'd said exactly what I was thinking.

Francie *tsk*ed at us. "Now, now. There's nothing wrong with being a gentleman. In my day, we didn't plop into bed with whomever came along. We allowed feelings and mutual respect to develop. You don't have to rush into anything, Humphrey. But, son, you can't just marry someone because you've baked cupcakes with her."

I felt for poor Humphrey. He'd had so little luck with women that he saw the most ordinary behavior as special. "What's important right now is to figure out how Humphrey came into possession of that expensive cupcake and how to clear his name."

"And while we're doing that, we still need to find poor Buddy!" Nina eyed Humphrey. "Do you think you could sweet-talk Myra into going into Maurice's house? I tried, but you might have more sway with her."

"I forgot all about him. That poor dog! Of course, I'll ask Myra. She's really a very good-hearted person." He checked his watch. "In fact, she should be at work right about now."

Francie rose. "I'll come along with you. I've always wanted to see the inner workings of a mortuary."

When Humphrey excused himself for a moment, Francie said, "Somebody's got to look after that boy. I've never met anyone so smart who was more clueless about women. Besides, I've always wanted to match someone up with the right partner. You know, where they thank you in the wedding toast."

"You're going to try to help him with Renee?" asked Nina. She sounded appalled.

"Do you think I'm daft? It's that Myra girl that *I* like!" She raised her voice. "Humphrey! Don't take all day!" She winked at us and met him in the foyer.

I stood up and began to clear the table. I was holding three dishes when Humphrey dashed back into the kitchen and hugged me. "Thank you, Sophie. In spite of your concerns about Renee, you're a very good friend. No one else would rescue me at four in the morning."

Nina cleared her throat dramatically.

"Except for Nina," said Humphrey. He pecked her on the cheek and hurried back to the front door, where Francie was hollering his name.

The second Nina saw them on the sidewalk, she grasped my arm. "He is in so much trouble! Do you think that cupcake was planted on Humphrey or dropped in his car by mistake?"

"It could have happened either way. The only thing I'm certain about is that he didn't steal it." I rinsed the dishes and slid them into the dishwasher. "How would you feel about making some inquiries?"

"I'm in. As soon as I shower and change. Half an hour?"

Nina and I met on the sidewalk in front of her house. I'd left Daisy at home with Mochie, since we were planning to visit bakeries. After the busy weekend, complete with doggy gala, I figured she had some sleep to catch up on anyway.

Fresh spring air invigorated us. We both wore running shoes, rather a joke since neither of us was inclined to run, except when no other alternative appeared reasonable. But we walked at a nice clip, and even though we talked about Humphrey and Renee, we slowed occasionally to appreciate the scent of blooming flowers or a particularly spectacular azalea.

The center of Old Town bustled with people. We turned right and faced the rival bakeries, Sugar Baby and Sugar Mama.

"Joy first?" asked Nina.

"She might not be back at work yet. How are we going to find out more about her taking Sugar Baby's money? It's not like we can come right out and ask."

"We should have brought Francie. She doesn't seem to care about being polite. What if we tell her that we're worried about Humphrey and his relationship with Renee? Maybe she'll tell us the scoop about her."

Armed with that intention, we proceeded to Sugar Mama. The door was locked, though, and the closed sign hung on it.

"Do you guess she's home from the hospital?" asked Nina. "Maybe she's still recuperating from the poison."

"Or the drugs."

We jaywalked across the street to Sugar Baby, easy to do in Old Town, where cars didn't move very fast. Even before we entered, I could see Renee smiling at customers. She wore her trademark pink apron and looked as though nothing terrible had ever happened there. The makeshift memorial to Muffin had already vanished, along with the police tape. How quickly we moved on. It wasn't fair to Muffin or her memory.

I pushed the door open, and the little bell tinkled merrily. The customers left, and Nina and I caught Renee alone.

"Looks like business is good," I said.

She hurried out from behind the counter. "Where's Humphrey? I've been calling him for hours, but he doesn't answer." She didn't wait for a response. She clutched her forehead with nervous fingers. "Someone almost broke into the bakery last night. I'm scared to death."

CHAPTER TWENTY-ONE

Dear Sophie,

How can I cover cupcakes to store them? The wrap or foil always destroys the cute frosting.

—Can't Get Enough Cupcakes in Cold Spring, Minnesota

Dear Can't Get Enough Cupcakes,

Use toothpicks! Stick three to four toothpicks in each cupcake to hold the wrap away. It works for cakes, too!

—Sophie

I was inclined to believe Renee, because her chest heaved heavily, as though she was extremely agitated.

"What happened?" asked Nina.

"Did you call the police?" I motioned to a table, and we all sat down.

"It was early in the morning." Her fingers balled into little fists. "You're going to think I'm crazy, but I was dreaming about Muffin. It was as though she came to me in my dream, and she scolded me for not changing the locks. I woke up and went downstairs to be sure I had locked up. When I reached the bottom, I could hear someone messing with the lock on the back door. I screamed my head off and shoved one of these chairs under the doorknob at an angle so he couldn't get in if he managed to unlock it." She bent forward and hid her face in her hands.

Nina patted her back.

When Renee sat up, she drew her hands down her face, and she could hardly breathe. "Just remembering it is giving me chills. I called the cops and ran back up the stairs. When I looked out my bedroom window, I saw him running away. It wasn't my imagination. Somebody tried to break in."

"Could you tell it was a man?" I asked. She was so frightened that my own pulse raced.

"Not really. I guess it could have been a woman. It's dark out in the alley. I didn't see much."

"What did the cops say?" asked Nina.

"To change the locks. The locksmith is working on the back door right now. He's adding a deadbolt, and he'll do the front door next. An electrician should be here any minute to add a spotlight in the back of the store. And Spenser is sending someone over to install an alarm system."

"Spenser?" That was interesting.

"I couldn't reach Humphrey, and I just didn't know what to do, so I called Spenser. I'm sorry, I didn't mean to burden you with my problems. I've been trying so hard to keep a cheery face since Muffin's murder. It hasn't been easy, but if I don't do that, people won't come here, and I'll be out of business." She bit her upper lip. "I'm scared witless. I'll feel better once all the security measures are in place. Spenser says I'll be safer here than anywhere else. There's even going to be an alarm that goes off if someone breaks one of the storefront windows."

I wanted to ask about Joy gently, but there just wasn't any way to pussyfoot around it. "Does Joy suffer from a drug addiction?"

"Oh, my word, no! I never would have gone into business

with anyone into drugs. That would have been a guaranteed nightmare."

"I wanted to thank you for being such a trouper and baking cupcakes for the feast in spite of everything that happened." Nina smiled at her. "I was so busy searching for Martha that I never had a chance to chat after the cupcake feast."

Renee wove her fingers together over the logo on her apron. "I'm lucky most people don't know about my inedible frosting at the cupcake feast. What a disaster. Nothing like that has ever happened to me in all my years of baking. I don't know what went wrong with the frosting on the Salted Caramel Cupcakes. Spenser thinks I mixed up the flour and the powdered sugar."

"I'll take six of the Tres Leches Cupcakes," said Nina. When I looked to her in surprise, she said, "Humphrey and Francie might want one."

Renee rose and pulled out a box for the cupcakes. "Where is Humphrey? He usually stops by for a cupcake in the morning, but I haven't seen him."

"Usually stops by? Every day?" I asked.

Renee raised her chin with pride. "Some people are addicted to our—*my*—cupcakes. Humphrey is here every single day. Muffin always worried about him when he didn't show up on time."

Muffin's name had rolled off Renee's tongue easily, but a cloud passed over her sunny expression. She stopped working and winced. "I'm sorry. Sometimes I forget that she's not here anymore. I keep thinking she'll walk in the door and tell me an outrageously funny story about what happened to her on the way to work."

"It must be hard for you to sleep upstairs." The words slid out of my mouth, and I immediately regretted them.

"It is! I don't know what I'm going to do. I might just rent out the unit upstairs. Do you think I'd find a tenant? Would anyone rent an apartment where someone had been murdered? On the other hand, it's so convenient to be right here at the bakery. I never have to worry about working late or dealing with traffic. It's almost a luxury. Once the locks, and lights, and bells and whistles are installed, it will be super safe. And I love living in Old Town. But I know I'll never be able to sleep in my bedroom again." She winced. "I never wanted to look under the bed, but when the police let me come home, I found sugar ants trailing under there."

"Frosting!" I said.

"How did you know?"

"A dollop landed on my shoe."

Renee nodded. "She must have been gripping an icing bag in her hand when she was killed. Frosting was all over underneath the bed."

Nina wrinkled her nose. "Where are you sleeping?"

"Humphrey loaned me one of those big inflatable mattresses. I put it in the living room. I have to try to block out what happened to Muffin, but it's hard."

I believed her. I didn't think her distress was fake. Of course, even if she *had* murdered Muffin, she could still be distressed by it. But if Renee had murdered Muffin, why would someone have tried to break in last night?

"Do the police have any leads?" I asked.

"Not any that they've mentioned to me. Muffin was a sweetheart. No one hated her. She even slipped that dreadful Maurice Lester a free cupcake now and then."

"Why?" I asked.

Renee's mouth pulled tight. "That man won't pay for anything. He and Nick Rigas. Talk about tightfisted. For some reason, they think everyone should just hand them whatever they want. I would never have the audacity to ask for free food at a bakery. Seriously"—she waved her hands as though showing us the bakery—"do they really not understand that this is a business? Who does that? I don't go to restaurants and expect free food. And Maurice of all people! He knows how hard it is to make it as a cupcakery. I got so mad at poor Muffin, because I won't put up with freeloaders. Maurice was like a neighborhood dog—slip him a treat once and he comes by every day looking for another one."

She brushed a dusting of powdered sugar off her apron. "If he'd been destitute, well, that would have been different.

It's not as though I have no compassion for those in need, but I see no reason to feed him for free. He can fork it over as far as I'm concerned."

"That's what was going on at your booth," I said. "We thought he was acting odd."

"I gave him a cupcake as a bribe to get rid of him. He can be a pest and *mean*! I was afraid if I didn't give him a cupcake, he'd hang around and bad-mouth me to other customers." Renee came around to the front of the case. "Joy, Muffin, and I used to categorize people as cupcakes. For instance, Humphrey is plain vanilla, with a dependable plain chocolate frosting—no surprises there. Spenser is like one of these Chocolate Hazelnut Raspberry Cupcakes. He's multilayered and complex, but inside, there's a soft, sweet raspberry filling. His wife, do you know Clarissa?"

We nodded. I couldn't wait to get her assessment of Clarissa.

"She's our Peanut Butter Surprise. A familiar flavor when you bite into it. But inside, it's not jam, like you might expect. It's chipotle chocolate, and it's all nutty on top. Oh, I shouldn't bore you with my silliness!"

"This is fun!" said Nina. "Who else has a cupcake?"

"Let's see. Nick Rigas is like these, which are a huge hit with women customers—devilishly rich chocolate, with a soft dark chocolate truffle inside and this gorgeous piped top. They look so pretty, but there's a lot going on. And that cute policewoman, Wong, is definitely her favorite cupcake. Red Velvet. There's nothing ordinary about her, but what you see is what you get—a no-nonsense cupcake. And this Pink Coconut was Muffin—sweet, innocent, and yet fun and unexpected." She released a long breath, and the momentary happiness vanished. "I can't understand why anyone would have wanted her dead."

"Are you afraid that the killer was looking for you?" asked Nina.

Nina's question must have caught Renee by surprise. She stared at Nina. "I wasn't before last night. What could I have done to make somebody that angry?"

"We should be going," said Nina, paying for her purchase.

"Tell Humphrey to stop by when he has a chance," said Renee.

I debated ordering a sampler for my clients. What if she was the murderer? Would she poison us? Surely not. But out of an abundance of caution, proving to myself that I still didn't completely trust Renee, I didn't say a word about the sampler.

I waved good-bye, wondering if the adorable petite blonde in the darling apron could have murdered Muffin. When we were outside and walking away, I said, "She was so nice. No wonder Humphrey is smitten. And she couldn't be any cuter."

Nina stopped walking in the middle of the sidewalk. "Where does Joy live now? Over top of her new bakery?"

We turned to look at the second story of the building across the street.

My phone rang. I pulled it from my pocket and pushed the button to answer it. Francie's voice said, "Mission accomplished. Tonight at eight o'clock. We promised you would be outside with us."

She didn't wait for me to say anything. She just clicked her phone off.

I chuckled. "I think Francie is having a good time playing detective. Apparently Myra agreed. We're on for eight o'clock tonight."

Nina pressed her hands together as though in prayer. "I hope we find that poor dog. He weighs on my conscience. It's my fault that he's lost, because I was responsible for him. What if he's wandering the streets somewhere or was hit by a car?"

I'd had the same terrible thoughts. The image of poor, big Buddy lost and alone tore at me. "No, it's my fault. I knew you were busy, and that Francie was off to the ladies' room, and I took lunch over to Humphrey anyway. If I had stayed put in the booth, Buddy wouldn't be missing. Let's hope Myra sees him at Maurice's tonight."

Nina pointed across the street. "I don't think Joy lives over

Sugar Mama. It looks like there's an antiquarian book dealer up there. See the door to the left of the shop?"

"Rats. We'll have to ask around to find out where she is. Are you game to go to Cake My Day? I'd like to speak with Spenser."

"Sure. I'm always up for visits to cupcakeries."

Cake My Day was located a good ten blocks away. We decided that would surely work off the calories of one or two cupcakes. We didn't walk as briskly as we intended, though, because we kept stopping to window-shop.

Nina poked me while we peered at the window display of The Yuppy Puppy. "Is that Natasha?"

A woman dressed like Audrey Hepburn in *Breakfast at Tiffany's* browsed in the store. Huge, dark sunglasses covered half of her face. A scarf wrapped around her head and neck, and she wore a stunning sleeveless black sheath.

Giggling, we dodged inside. Natasha picked up item after item. Apparently she was having trouble seeing them well with the dark sunglasses. She lifted the glasses and peered below the rims, turning each item over and examining it.

"Natasha?" I called.

She stiffened. Turning casually, as though she hadn't heard me, she lowered her head to look over the glasses. Holding her head high, she marched past us and left the store.

Naturally, we followed her.

She walked a few yards, stopped, and removed the sunglasses. Gesturing madly, she hissed, "I was on a spy mission."

Nina and I laughed aloud. Surely she didn't think she was fooling anyone in that getup. In fact, she was probably attracting attention. "Who are you spying on?"

"Not who. I'm doing corporate spying." She unwrapped the scarf. "It's getting hot out here. How did women wear these things in the summer?"

"You're spying on The Yuppy Puppy?" asked Nina.

"No, I'm spying on the things they sell. I can't believe I've been so blind. All these years I've baked and sewn and crafted, but I just can't get a national TV show. I've overlooked the obvious! It's all about dogs. Dogs are the new children. I don't know how I never saw it before."

I wasn't following. Actually, I hadn't gotten over *dogs are the new children.*

"People used to do domestic things for their husbands and children. But now it's all about their dogs. Dog beds, dog clothes, dog jewelry, dog cuisine. While I've been focusing on people, the world has gone to the dogs!"

"Speaking of dogs, where is Martha?" I asked.

"Hmm? Oh, I left her in Mars's study. He doesn't mind the fur."

"Alone? You left that little dog alone?" Nina clapped a hand over her mouth.

"What's wrong with that? Daisy stays in there all the time."

"Daisy isn't a puppy," I said. "She's outgrown the chew-and-tear phase."

"What could she possibly do? There's nothing in there of any interest to anyone except Mars. You're pulling my leg, right?"

She studied us, and her eyes widened in horror. "Excuse me, I think I left something on the . . . in the . . . I have to go."

She took off at top speed for someone wearing high heels on brick sidewalks.

Nina shook her head. "What was she thinking?"

We strolled on to Cake My Day. I came to a dead stop outside. What had *I* been thinking? I'd forgotten all about Clarissa's ridiculous notion that I was sleeping with her husband. "You don't think Clarissa comes down to the cupcakery, do you?"

"Want me to go in and scope it out for you first?"

I sucked in a deep breath. "No. I have a completely clear conscience. There isn't a reason in the world for her to be upset with me. If she's there, we'll just buy some cupcakes and leave."

We walked inside. No sign of Clarissa. While I asked to speak to Spenser, Nina eyed their assortment of cupcakes.

"What do you like better?" she asked. "Cookies and Cream, Orange Dreams, or Lemon Meringue?"

"Don't you have a dozen cupcakes in the box in your hand?"

"It would be rude not to buy any!"

Spenser ambled out of the back. "Nina! Sophie! I hope this means you have news about Buddy."

Nina assured him we were working on it.

His face fell. "Oh no. I know why you're here, then."

CHAPTER TWENTY-TWO

Dear Natasha,

I want to bake cupcakes. They seem so much easier than a whole cake. Do I have to grease the cupcake pan if I'm using cupcake liners?

—New Baker in Bakers Mill, Florida

Dear New Baker,

As long as you put cupcake liners in your cupcake pan, you do not need to grease it. However, if you do not use cupcake liners, grease the pan well so your cupcakes won't stick to it.

—Natasha

Spenser beckoned to us. "There's a little spot out back where we can talk in private. Iced mocha frappé okay with everybody?" He ushered us to a back door and pointed at a tiny table with a striped umbrella. "This is where my employees take their breaks in nice weather. I'll be right with you."

"What's that about?" asked Nina.

We sat down at the table. "I have no idea, but I'm willing to hear what he has to say."

Spenser showed up in minutes carrying a tray of assorted mini cupcakes and three iced mocha frappés.

Nina swooned. "Be still, my heart. It's a good thing I'm not your wife. I'd eat like this every day. Ooo, is this lemon?"

Spenser smiled. "Meyer lemon. Clarissa doesn't much care for cupcakes anymore. When you're around them all the time, I guess they begin to lose their appeal. Given her druthers, she'd choose lobster over a cupcake any day."

Nina wasted no time biting into a cupcake.

Spenser massaged his face as though he was uncomfortable. "I feel terrible. I'm so sorry. I didn't know it was Humphrey's car. Maybe I wouldn't have called the police if I had realized that. Or maybe I would have. I don't know. It was all so unexpected, that I called the cops immediately without giving it much thought."

It took me a second to figure out what he was talking about. "The gem-studded cupcake."

He leaned back in the flimsy wire chair. "I never thought I'd see it again. Silly, I know, but of all the things that were stolen from our house, that one bugged me the most. We could replace the rest of the stuff, like Clarissa's jewelry, but you don't run into that kind of cupcake every day."

"So you saw it in Humphrey's car?" The cupcake wasn't all that big. Why had he been looking in Humphrey's car?

"Yeah. Talk about flukes. The car was parked on the street. I was out walking, looking for Buddy, and I guess the streetlight just happened to shine on it, catching my eye. I was astonished. It had to be mine. There couldn't be many of them."

"Where was it in the car?"

"Have you seen his car? It's a hatchback with a shelf in the rear over the cargo area. The cupcake was up there, sort of tucked into a corner."

"Not exactly where someone would put it if they were hiding it." Nina licked frosting off her fingertip.

Spenser nodded. "I thought about that. But it could have

rolled out of a pocket or a bag. I got to know Humphrey a little bit better when he pitched in to help Renee bake her cupcakes. He seems like a stand-up guy."

"He is." I sipped my iced mocha frappé. I had so many questions for Spenser. I didn't want to run the risk of alienating him. I made a show of selecting a mini cupcake while I thought about how to best keep him talking.

Choosing a coconut cupcake, I said, "Francie tells me you were out of town when your house was burglarized." I watched Spenser carefully. I liked him, and I didn't want to think he could have been involved, but people in financial pinches had been known to stage thefts for insurance money.

"I was in Miami. Poor Clarissa was home alone when it happened. Scared her to death. It's just a lucky thing she had the presence of mind to hide under the bed and not challenge the thief. Who knows what might have happened if she'd taken him on?" He shuddered at the thought.

"I hope everything was insured?" I also hoped my question sounded breezy and not nosy.

"Unfortunately not. We didn't have the special riders required for most of the items he took. Especially not for that cupcake! It's still in police custody, but I've already placed a call to my insurance agent about getting coverage for it."

So much for that theory. "Where did you get the cupcake?"

His eyes darted to the side as though he was considering his answer. "A guy I knew found himself in financial trouble. There's not a big market for that kind of thing, and I wanted to help him out. At the time I thought it would be a great way to . . . it would make a nice present."

"I never thanked you for offering Cake My Day to Renee so she could bake for the Cupcakes and Pupcakes dinner." Nina dabbed her mouth with a napkin. "She was in such a bind without access to her bakery."

"I was glad to do it. She might have won if she hadn't swapped the powdered sugar with the flour. I pulled all the ingredients after the problems she had at her booth on Sunday.

We had to throw out a few batches of our cupcakes, too. I can't afford to have ingredients mixed up."

He swigged back some of his icy drink. Stress fell off Spenser's face when he smiled. "Renee and I go way back. Did you know that her first cupcake baking job was at the very first Cake My Day? She worked side-by-side with Clarissa and me to get the business off the ground."

"Why did she leave?" asked Nina.

Thank goodness she asked, because I was wondering if there had been a falling-out. Given the way Clarissa had acted toward me, I couldn't help wondering if she'd also imagined Spenser involved in a romance with Renee.

"Renee dreamed of having her own place. She pinched every penny to save up. Clarissa used to cook enough for three because she was worried about Renee refusing to spend money on food. Then things picked up for Cake My Day, and we started expanding. Renee knew she could have any job in the company that she wanted, but she never let go of her dream." He slid a hand around the back of his neck. "I admire that. She's very focused. When she met Joy, they pooled their resources and took a chance."

"And now that has ended in disaster. Do you know what happened?" I asked.

Spenser sighed and raised his eyebrows. "Partnerships implode all the time. It's not easy working with someone else. Everyone has a unique vision of how a business should be run. Renee says Joy took all their money and used it to open her own shop. I gave Renee a little seed money to get back on her feet."

"You gave it to her? It's not a loan?" blurted Nina.

"Loans make for bad bedfellows. When it's an outright gift, there aren't any ill feelings, because there's no expectation of repayment."

"You're a good friend!" said Nina.

I took a chance. "Is that what happened with Colleen?"

Nina frowned at me. "Who's Colleen?"

"You don't miss a trick, do you?" Spenser sighed.

I feared I had crossed a line. "Maurice mentioned her name the other day."

Spenser heaved a deep breath. "I try not to bring it up because it's a sad story, and it does no one any good to keep it alive. Colleen was Maurice's wife."

"I didn't know he was married," said Nina.

The back door creaked open, and a male employee said, "Clarissa's here, boss."

"I hope you won't think me rude, but unless we want another big fuss, I think you'd better go." Spenser rose. "I'll coax her upstairs so you two can slip out."

But it was too late. A spatula loaded with frosting flew at me and smacked me in the head.

Clarissa stood in the doorway, pulling back her arm to launch a whisk at me. It hit Spenser as he grabbed her. He motioned toward the door with his head.

Nina and I hustled into the cupcake shop and out the front door with all the employees and a good number of customers looking on.

When we made it to the sidewalk, Nina tasted a smidgen of the frosting that had splashed over on her. "Strawberry."

"Ugh. It's all over me." I reached up and touched my head. "Oh, great," I grumbled. "It's in my hair, too." There was nothing to do but walk home and hope I didn't run into anyone I knew.

Soft snickering drifted to me. Nina and I turned to the right.

A woman at least fifteen years younger than me had stepped out of a town house that was for sale. Brunette curls tumbled around her shoulders in the latest I-just-rolled-out-of-bed tousled style. She had legs like a giraffe and a wasp waist. She tittered again and pointed to me.

And right behind her, holding the door for her, stood Alex.

CHAPTER TWENTY-THREE

Dear Sophie,

My husband complains about the tough part of asparagus. It seems that, no matter how I cook them, there's always a barely edible portion at the end. I love asparagus, but he won't eat it anymore!

   —Devoted Wife in Toughkenamon, Pennsylvania

Dear Devoted Wife,

Each piece of asparagus turns woody at a different point. But there is a solution. Hold the asparagus spear just below the top. With the other hand, snap off the bottom. Asparagus will always break at the correct location. No more tough ends.

   —Sophie

All hope of any future relationship with Alex flew away.

Doing his best to hold back his amusement, he introduced Nina and me to his Realtor, Kayla. It was with enormous regret that I realized Kayla and Alex made a handsome pair.

Alex leaned forward and lightly brushed my lips with his. His tiny, gentle gesture left me breathless and stupefied.

I wasn't the only one. Nina lifted an eyebrow in surprise.

He snagged a tiny bit of icing with his finger and tasted it. "Raspberry?"

"I think it's strawberry." Nina reached toward my face and dabbed her finger in frosting.

I wanted to bat her away, but I had a feeling that would not have improved the situation.

"Hmm, maybe you're right," agreed Nina.

"What on earth happened?" Kayla inquired.

"It was a misunderstanding." I was dying to fall into a hole or at least run away, but social graces compelled me to be polite. Besides, if I ran, he might misinterpret my reaction to his kiss. Summoning courage, I pushed frosted hair out of my face and tried to pretend everything was fine. I had a bad feeling that Kayla might be catty about the loony woman with the black eye and the frosting in her hair. Who could blame her? "Have you found anything you like yet, Alex?"

"This building is nice, but there's one closer to the courthouse that I like much better."

"It's a wonderful historic town house," said Kayla. "Besides the gorgeous office on the first floor, I think Alex likes it because it once belonged to someone called Crazy Knees Lee."

"How's the general?" I asked.

"Home from the hospital. Ladies have lined up to visit. I'm having to beat them off with a broom."

Nina tapped my hair with her finger. "I think I'd better get Sophie home. That icing is beginning to dry on her hair."

Lovely. That was just the impression I wanted to make on Alex. We said good-bye, and as Nina and I walked away, I heard Kayla ask Alex, "Did she have a black eye, too?"

After a long shower, I made a tuna fish sandwich, sharing the tuna with Mochie and Daisy. I filled a mug with hot tea, added a splash of milk and a spoonful of sugar, and retreated to my office to do some work.

While I was taking care of e-mail and setting up appointments, Humphrey called to ask if we could all convene at my house around six o'clock, since Myra was nervous about trying to search Maurice's house for Buddy. Naturally, I agreed.

At five o'clock, I returned to the kitchen to take puff pastry out of the freezer and boil water for iced tea. Natasha would have been appalled that I hadn't made my own puff pastry, but some days one just didn't have the time. I left it to thaw and dashed upstairs to hide as much as possible of my black eye with makeup. It looked better, but still couldn't be entirely hidden. Since the majority of my clothes were black to hide my extra pounds, it wasn't too hard to find a sleuthing outfit. I wasn't sure what Humphrey had in mind, but I figured black was always good for blending in at night.

I pulled on a sleeveless black top with a boat neck and black jeans with a comfortable elastic waistband. Black Keds and small gold hoops completed my morbid ensemble.

With the oven preheating to 400 degrees, I rolled out a sheet of puff pastry to fit a round pizza pan. I placed a sheet of parchment paper over the pan, laid the puff pastry on top of it, and pierced it several times before sliding it into the oven. While it began to bake, I washed and snapped the ends off fresh spring asparagus. I slid them into boiling water to parboil them and removed them within minutes.

Nina tapped on the window of my kitchen door and let herself in. "Mmm. Already smells good in here." She'd dressed much as I had, also in black, but she'd had the good sense to wear a hoodie so she could cover her hair.

"You're just in time to help me roll asparagus."

"Roll it?" She wrinkled her nose.

I mixed creamy goat cheese with minced garlic, sea salt, freshly ground black pepper, a squeeze of lemon juice, minced fresh basil, dried oregano, and chopped parsley. For just a touch of zing, I sprinkled in red pepper flakes.

"I suppose mixed drinks are a bad idea if we need to be alert?"

"Later," I promised. "For now, I thought I'd make mango iced tea."

We spread the herbed goat cheese mixture on strips of ham that we wrapped around the asparagus. Then we wrapped a strip of the unbaked puff pastry along the middle of each stalk of asparagus. We brushed them with an egg wash and rolled them in Parmesan cheese.

When the dough on the pizza plate had puffed, I arranged strips of smoked salmon in a spiral design, and sprinkled the plate with strips of Gruyère so thin I could almost see through them. Both dishes went into the oven. I mixed sweet mango juice with the tea that had been steeping, added ice cubes, and we were set.

We carried the tea, tall glasses, paper napkins with a cupcake motif, and tiny hors d'oeuvre plates to my outdoor room. Francie was already lounging there comfortably, watching Daisy and Duke play in the grass. "I figured we'd be meeting out here. Poor Myra. She's a good egg, but I think she's extremely nervous."

"Is Wong coming?" asked Nina.

"We decided that involving her might put her on the spot. None of us knew if it would be legal to send Myra in with a video camera. We were afraid Wong might try to stop us." Francie accepted a glass of tea from me.

"A video camera?" I was surprised, but maybe it wasn't a bad idea.

Humphrey and Myra showed up at that exact moment. "Something in your kitchen smells really great," said Myra.

I said hello and hurried back inside, lest the appetizers burn. Fortunately, everything was fine. I pulled the trays out of the oven, arranged our little treats on square red ceramic serving platters with a yellow and green design around the edge, and carried them outside.

Myra was showing off the video camera. About an inch across and four inches long, it had been very neatly tucked into the breast pocket of a black jacket. Humphrey had cut a small hole into the fabric for the lens.

"It was Myra's idea to pin that feathery thing on the pocket to disguise it," he explained.

The bright pink flamingo and matching pink feather

earrings that dangled to her shoulders looked more like Myra than the sedate black jacket. "It's a shame you had to cut a hole in the pocket. Now the jacket is ruined."

Myra examined the jacket she wore. "It's not really my style. While Humphrey was out buying the spy camera this afternoon, I picked up the jacket at a thrift shop just for tonight. I figure I'll have a handy spy jacket ready if I ever need one again."

Although the sedate jacket wasn't her style, she wore bright pink eye shadow in large swoops over her eyelids. Her spirited eyes were rimmed in black, and she had punched up the outfit with pink leggings that were so bright I wondered if they glowed in the dark. Her top glittered, partially hidden by the jacket, but I could definitely see swirls of pink and silver sequins.

"We'll be monitoring her on my laptop," said Humphrey. "We'll see what she sees. If she feels afraid, if Maurice gets too frisky, then all she has to do is say . . ."

"I really should be going now." Myra tilted her head and batted long false eyelashes at Humphrey. "That doesn't sound too fake, does it?"

Nina helped herself to the appetizers. "I think it's a perfect line. How many times have I said that—especially to men? Plus, you can repeat it over and over, and it still won't sound suspicious."

Francie ate a piece of the salmon puff and reached for more. "You can make this for me anytime. It's delicious. I could make a meal out of it."

"How did you get him to invite you, Myra?" I tried one of the asparagus spears and savored the saltiness, a welcome change after all those cupcakes.

Myra filled a plate and sat down. "That was easy. He comes by the mortuary every day. Instead of trying to avoid him like I usually do, I mentioned how lovely his house is. That's actually true. It has a historical plaque just like yours. I love looking through these old houses and imagining all the people who lived in them so long ago." She assessed us before she went on. "And I'm into ghosts." She watched our reactions.

Francie didn't even look up from her plate. "There's one in Sophie's kitchen. You'll have to introduce her to Faye, Sophie."

"Really?" Myra sat forward, and for a moment I thought she might run into the house.

"It's not like she speaks or anything. Her existence is debatable," said Humphrey.

"The only one who says she can hear Faye is her sister," I clarified. "On the other hand, the medium who came to our Halloween séance claimed to see her. Then again, she made up some things that we knew were fabrications, so it's hard to know what was true."

"I find that so intriguing," breathed Myra.

"It gives Myra a good excuse to ask for a tour of Maurice's house. Wasn't that smart of her?" Francie beamed at her.

"So what are Sophie and I supposed to do?" asked Nina.

"Francie and I will be in the car, parked near the front of the house. We'll be able to see what Myra is seeing—on the laptop—and we can hear her if she needs us to get her out of there. Myra and I thought you and Sophie could check out the backyard for signs of Buddy while Myra distracts Maurice."

"You mean we're the poop patrol?" I couldn't help laughing.

"And listen for him. He might growl or something when he hears me in the house," said Myra. "Humphrey and I have been calling it Project Rescue Buddy."

"That doesn't sound too bad. The backyard isn't fenced," said Nina. "It should be a snap for us to check it out."

Poor Myra would be doing the hard work. Keeping my eyes and ears open for any sign of Buddy, or his poop, was doable.

By the time we drove over to Maurice's neighborhood, clouds had moved in, hastening the darkness. We could have walked, but if we found Buddy, we would need a car big enough to hold him, so I drove my hybrid SUV and parked a block away from Maurice's house.

Streetlights illuminated the front of Maurice's home nicely.

Clad with blue siding, the house was two stories tall. I didn't imagine there was much of an attic, since the roof was very nearly flat. Small windows just above the ground indicated a basement. His house appeared to be located on a corner, but instead of a side street, the road that ran along the side of his house was an alley. His home looked to be one of the larger houses in the immediate area but lacked the charm of neighboring homes with front porches and rocking chairs. Five steps that were perpendicular to the street led to a stoop and a drab gray door.

Stationed on the same side of the street, but a few doors down, Nina and I watched Myra park her car along the side of Maurice's house. Humphrey and Francie were already parked across the street.

Myra walked up the steps and knocked on Maurice's door. It opened, and she vanished inside.

CHAPTER TWENTY-FOUR

Dear Sophie,

I would like to home cook for my cats. There are so many recipes on the Internet that my head is swimming. Where do I start?

—Cat Lover in Kitty Hawk, North Carolina

Dear Cat Lover,

Cats are carnivores. They *have* to eat meat. In addition, cats absolutely must eat taurine, which is found in raw meat. But feeding cats raw meat presents additional problems, such as salmonella. Many people successfully feed their cats a raw diet, but talk to your veterinarian first, so that you do what is best for your cats as well as for the human and canine members of your household.

—Sophie

Feeling a bit ridiculous, I hustled along the street with Nina and turned down the alley. The beam from the streetlight dwindled as we walked toward the rear of the house.

"Did you notice there aren't any windows on the sides of the houses except in the very back?" she asked.

I paused. In the dark, it wasn't easy to see. "Do you suppose they knocked down a house to make this alley?"

"Looks like it to me. Both buildings have side windows but only on their rear additions."

Pulling a penlight from my pocket, I shone it very quickly along the alleyway, but saw no sign of dog poop.

A car was parked on a pad of gravel in back of Maurice's house. Steep stairs led to a tiny covered balcony on the second floor. Inside lights illuminated a glass door and a window on the second level. On the first level, I spied two windows, one rather oddly looking out at the back of the staircase.

"Shh. What's that?" Nina stopped in her tracks.

I listened for dog sounds like a bark or a snuffle. But I heard mewing. Strong and loud. In fact, in the background, I could hear Maurice talking. Not loud enough to understand what he was saying, though. "A window must be open," I whispered.

Nina aimed her tiny flashlight at it. "There's the cat. Hi, kitty, kitty!"

"Are you nuts?" I hissed. "He'll see that."

"Calm down. It sounds like he's still on the other side of the house." She flashed her light around the parking pad. A row of railroad ties appeared to mark the edge of the property. The house next door butted against Maurice's house. Nina's flashlight flicked over the garbage cans and a sad patch of scraggly grass near the house. Maurice had absolutely no garden, not even an attempt at one. Not that I cared, except for the fact that I had been ashamed when he said he'd brought flowers from his garden as a remembrance of Muffin. I shot my light through the neighbor's yard very quickly. They used it for parking, too. He must have stolen that azalea branch, but not from them.

The lights on the second floor went out. Something squeaked. A window? Unless I missed my guess, someone was trying to stealthily open the window to the backyard.

And then someone cried out and hurtled down the steep stairs.

Nina yelped and pointed her flashlight at the person, who now lay belly down and motionless.

I ran to him. "Are you okay?"

He groaned.

Thank goodness. He was alive. "Can you get up?" I gently touched his leather jacket but didn't want to move him in case he'd broken his neck. "Call 911."

The person moaned. "No!"

Uh-oh. It definitely wasn't a man. Trying not to point my light in the person's face, I angled it so I could see. "Joy!" Her hair was tucked into the jacket. No wonder I'd been confused.

"No hospital." Her voice was weak.

I didn't want to scare her by mentioning her neck. "Honey, you need help. Can you stand up?"

"Uh-huh." But she didn't move. Not an inch.

I gave her a minute, in case she'd had the wind knocked out of her. When she made no effort to right herself, I stood and whispered to Nina, "I think we'd better . . . *Gah!*" I didn't mean to shriek, but Joy had unexpectedly grabbed hold of my ankle.

"I said *no hospital*!"

Nina whispered, "Maurice must have heard her fall. He'll be out here any second."

"I'm okay." Joy's voice was still muffled. She'd landed on her face and hadn't moved. That worried me—a lot. Then again, she'd managed to reach out and seize my ankle.

She lifted herself slightly, like someone doing a really bad push-up. She rolled to her side, and I held out my hands. Joy grasped them, holding tighter than I'd have imagined possible. She rose slowly, but I didn't want to hurry her in case she was injured.

When she stood upright, she asked with a note of suspicion in her tone, "What are you doing here?"

"We're looking for Buddy, the dog who went missing at Cupcakes and Pupcakes. What are *you* doing here?"

"I heard about that dog. It's very sad." Joy ran her hands back through her hair and briefly clutched her head. "I'm living here, staying with Nick."

"Nick?"

"He rents the apartment upstairs."

Nina aimed her flashlight at Joy's chin.

Dark circles hung under her eyes, and she appeared haggard. She blew air out of her mouth and her hands trembled. "Why are you looking for Buddy here? Did someone spot him?"

"No," whispered Nina, "we think Maurice has him."

"Maurice?" Joy shook her head so slowly I wondered if she might be dizzy. "I don't think so. I haven't seen him walk a dog. No, I would have noticed. I've been on the lookout. I would have noticed for sure."

"On the lookout? For Buddy?" Nina asked.

"Someone is trying to kill me."

"Are you sure?" I couldn't help glancing around.

"You just saw evidence of it. Muffin is dead, and someone tried to kill me with some kind of poison. Now they've tried to make me fall." She clung to the railing for support. "Sophie, would you look at the steps near the top? I tripped over something. I know I did."

I tiptoed up the stairs and flashed my little light around. Indeed, someone had tied a wire across the opening. It had broken when Joy fell, and the two ends hung loose.

I walked back down. "You're right. Joy, we have to call the cops."

Joy shot me an incredulous look. "They think I'm a drug addict. I'm not. There's no way I had anything to do with drugs. The doctors and the cops keep acting like I took something intentionally so I would hallucinate, but I'm telling you, someone pricked me with it."

"Pricked you?" Nina asked.

"At the dinner. I remember," I said. "When the general fell to the floor, you said something stung you."

"Thank goodness *someone* remembers that. I'm certain

that was when it happened. I felt fine that evening until some-one jabbed me with something. I was wearing a thin silk dress, and whatever it was just went right through the fabric. That was when I started hallucinating. It was awful. I can't imagine why anyone would want to feel that way on purpose."

And now this. It certainly looked like someone was after her. "Joy, there's evidence this time. No one would think you tied a wire up there to trip yourself. The police *have* to know about it. It's not an option. Maybe they can get fingerprints."

She let out a long breath and sank to sit on the stairs. "It would be a relief to have the person arrested. I thought they would find Muffin's killer right away, but obviously they haven't."

"What's going on out there?"

Oops. That was definitely Maurice peering from the win-dow behind the stairs. "Joy fell down the back steps," I said.

"Is she going to sue?"

"Maurice!" Myra protested vehemently. "For heaven's sake! Ask her if she's okay!"

"Are you okay?" It was a low grumble.

"I'll be fine."

The window banged shut.

Nina punched numbers into her telephone and reported the incident to 911. Joy and I listened as she explained that an ambulance wasn't necessary.

She hung up, and asked, "Are you saying that whoever murdered Muffin also wants to kill you?"

Joy appeared on the verge of tears. "I don't know. I'm ter-rified. I can't sleep. I can't go to the shop and work because I'm afraid they'll do the same thing to me that they did to Muffin."

"You're saying *they*. Do you think it's more than one per-son?" I asked.

"No. Maybe. I'm so confused. I can't imagine Re . . . any-one killing Muffin." Joy held a finger under her nose and choked out, "I feel so guilty! If I hadn't moved out of Sugar Baby, Muffin would be alive today."

Was she implicating Renee? "You think your split with Renee triggered Muffin's murder?"

"What else can I think?"

"Joy, I know it's not really any of our business, but what happened exactly? Why did you leave Sugar Baby?"

"I wanted to expand. To do what Spenser did, have a chain. Maybe a franchise. Renee didn't think we were ready for that."

"I'm under the impression that your departure came as a surprise to Renee." I tried to phrase it gently.

"I would regret that if she hadn't tried to kill me." She gasped and clapped a hand over her mouth. "I didn't just say that!" She sniffled. "But it had to be her. Who else would want to kill me? She stole my grandmother's diamond ring, too. It was from Tiffany! Why did I ever trust her? What am I going to do? I don't have anywhere else to go."

"Don't you have friends or family?" Nina sat down beside Joy.

"I thought I'd be safe moving in with Nick, you know? I could move somewhere else, except I don't have the money. I borrowed from my folks to open Sugar Mama, and I signed a lease, so it's not like I can just move out of town. This is such a mess. I wish the cops would hurry up and solve Muffin's murder." She closed her eyes and whimpered. "Then maybe I could get back to work."

I patted her shoulder. "At least you have Nick. It's nice of him to let you stay here."

Joy responded with a new torrent of sobs.

A youngish police officer arrived. He questioned us briefly before trotting up the steps to take a look. When he came back down, his attitude had changed. "I'm going to call someone in to get fingerprints. Could I speak with Joy alone for a few minutes, please?"

"Maybe we should tell Humphrey what's going on. Now that Maurice knows we're here, it doesn't really matter, right?" I headed toward the alley.

"If Maurice comes out, what do I say?" asked Nina.

I shrugged. "Tell him we came to see Joy."

Poor Joy. She was miserable and suffering from enormous guilt over Muffin's death. It had occurred to me, too, that Joy's sudden departure from Sugar Baby might have been the catalyst for the attack on Muffin. I couldn't imagine living with that hanging over me. But if she'd borrowed from her parents to start Sugar Mama, what had she done with the money she took out of Sugar Baby's account?

I rapped on the window of Humphrey's car.

He rolled it down, and I heard Francie say, "What the dickens is going on?"

I explained as briefly as possible. "How's it going with Myra?"

"Maurice has actually been fairly decent. No lecherous moves so far," reported Humphrey.

"But no sign of Buddy, either," said Francie.

I hurried back to Joy.

The cop had finished with her. "It's unlikely we'll get any prints, but if we do, we'll want you and Nick to come down to the station so we can print you."

"Will you rope it off as a crime scene?" asked Nina.

He shook his head. "No, we'll be done with it very soon. There's not much here."

I placed a hand on Joy's sleeve. "I wish I could do something to help you."

She sniffled again. "You've already been nice just to listen to my woes. Nick isn't very sympathetic. If you hear of a cheap place to live, let me know?"

"Listen, we're going to The Laughing Hound for dinner. Why don't you come with us? My treat." I looked to the cop. "Is that okay? Do you need her for anything?"

"Go right ahead. I know where to find all of you if I think of anything else."

"Come on, let's get out of here."

Joy wanted to drive herself, but after the fall she took, I insisted she go with us. Instead of fighting for parking spots, I drove home and parked in my garage, and the three of us walked back to The Laughing Hound for, as Nina called it, a Maurice debriefing.

Myra waited patiently at a table. She had ditched the jacket with the camera and looked very much herself again in the flashy sequined top. She tapped long pink fingernails against an empty wineglass. When the hostess showed the rest of us to the table, Myra lifted her wineglass, and said, "I'll have another zin, please." She patted the chair next to her. "Sit over here with me, Humphrey."

We placed our drink order and stared at Myra.

She seemed to relish being the center of attention. "One thing is for sure—you do *not* need to worry about Maurice hiding a dog. The man has fifteen cats. Maybe sixteen. They . . . are . . . everywhere. And he dotes on them. There's no way he would *ever* bring a dog into his house. It would be utter chaos. Oh, and Sophie, remember Gun-i-vere?" She chuckled. "No wonder he couldn't get her name straight. It's not even a girl cat. It's a boy named Gunsmoke!"

Nina shook her head in frustration. "That man lies about everything. Thanks for checking out his house, Myra. I know it must have been nerve-racking for you, because I was tense, and I didn't have to deal with him. We're back to square one now. What did he do with poor Buddy?"

I hated to even imagine what might have become of Buddy, much less voice it. "Did you see anything that might be a clue?"

"Honey, he lives sparsely. Like a guy in his first apartment. There's a sofa and a TV. No pictures of him, of anyone, actually. I don't think there was anything on the walls, either."

"The cats are his décor," said Francie.

"They're his family." Myra accepted the wineglass from the waitress and sipped from it. "I'm so glad that's over. I thought I would die when I had to go down into the basement, but it wasn't so bad."

"What was down there?" asked Francie. "I couldn't tell on the video."

"It's mostly a cat playroom. There's a washer and a dryer, but he was very proud of the little catwalks he built around the walls. What are those things called that cats jump on and hide in?"

"Cat trees?" Nina twisted the glass of her Berry Acai Cosmo.

"Yes! That's it. He started with a few cat trees against the walls, and then just kept connecting them until he filled the room."

"The bedroom appeared very tidy," said Humphrey.

"That's because there's so little there. The bedroom looked like a monk's quarters. A bed, a dresser, and a throw rug. Nothing personal, like cologne or a book." She rubbed her eye carefully. "I hate to say it after he's been such a pest, but I felt sorry for him. It was like that room reflected how empty his life is."

We fell silent. I studied the menu, even though I knew it by heart. Myra was right. Maurice was grating—maddening, really. He twisted what people said, and even though Spenser appeared to be kind to him, Maurice insisted on acting ugly.

"I wish I had known about this. I could have saved you a lot of trouble." Joy closed her menu. "I'm certain I would have noticed a dog around."

"What exactly happened to you in the backyard?" Humphrey placed his napkin on his lap. "I nearly had a coronary when the police rolled up. I thought a neighbor had called them and reported prowlers."

Joy explained about the wire and falling down the stairs. "It was just dumb luck that Nina and Sophie happened to be there. I wouldn't have called the cops, but now I'm so glad that they did. There's finally something on record proving that I'm not just drugging myself or imagining things."

Joy ordered the Three Cheese Ravioli with Lobster Sauce and excused herself.

I had just ordered the Pomegranate-Glazed Rib Chop when Nina leaned over, and whispered, "We've got trouble now."

Renee walked toward us. I turned to see where Joy had gone. Fortunately, they had just missed each other.

Renee waltzed up to the table and kissed Humphrey—full on the lips.

CHAPTER TWENTY-FIVE

Dear Natasha,

What's the difference between a cupcake liner, a cupcake wrapper, and cupcake papers?

—Confused in Kissimmee, Florida

Dear Confused,

A cupcake liner is the little paper cup in which a cupcake is baked. It goes into the cupcake pan, and the batter is poured inside it. A cupcake wrapper is a decorative outer sleeve for a cupcake. Some are cut into fancy designs, and some have ornate edging. However, wrappers, as the name implies, go over the cupcake liner after the cupcake has been baked. Cupcake papers may include both.

—Natasha

Myra huffed. She watched Renee with her mouth open.

I didn't relish the idea of Humphrey being taken in by a murderess, but at that moment, I was more concerned about how many glasses of wine it would take before Myra whipped off her bra and swung it like a lasso.

When Renee released her hold on Humphrey, he could barely breathe. Orange lipstick was smeared around his mouth like a clown.

Myra held out her hand to Renee and smiled pleasantly. "Hi. I'm Myra."

"Renee. You look familiar."

"Mmm. I believe I ate some of your cupcake at the dinner on Saturday night."

I watched them like a Ping-Pong match. Renee had started out strong with that ravenous kiss, but Myra had evened the score and thrown Renee off her game with that one clever reference to Renee's disastrous cupcake.

Renee focused on Humphrey. "Sweetie pie," she cooed, "where have you been? I've been calling, but you're not answering your phone."

Humphrey patted his pocket. "Um, no. I turned it off."

"I bought some furniture, and I was hoping you could pick it up for me again."

Myra sipped from her third glass of wine. "Doesn't the store deliver?"

"I buy antiques." Renee spoke so sweetly that I could almost feel the sugar rush.

The corners of Myra's mouth twitched. "I don't imagine they're open at this hour."

Francie snickered, which only made the standoff worse.

I had no idea what I could do to save Humphrey.

"I'll call you in the morning?" he said.

"Just a sec, hon." Myra dipped a napkin into her water glass. Cupping the side of his face with one hand, she gently wiped the lipstick off his mouth. "Much better. That's not a good color for you. Not for anyone, actually." And then she winked at the rest of us.

Renee appraised Myra. "Humphrey, sweetie, when you're all done here, drop by the bakery. I'll have some dessert waiting for you." She turned on her heel and hurried out before anyone could say another word.

Myra watched her leave. "I don't like that woman. She's all sugary outside, but there's something devious living inside of her. You know, like those alien creatures that explode from people's stomachs in horror movies?"

Fortunately our laughter broke the tension.

"Be careful around her, Humphrey." Myra sipped more wine. "Besides, that shade of orange never looked good on anyone. I won't use it on my clients. It makes *her* look like a ghoul."

Our dinner arrived, but Joy hadn't returned to the table. After a few minutes, I thought I'd better check on her. What if she had run into Renee on the way out?

I trotted down the steps that led to the ladies' room. From the little passage, I could see into the bar. Nick lounged comfortably on a loveseat, his hand playing with the long curls of Alex's Realtor, Kayla. She giggled and flirted. There was no way of knowing if he'd met her at the bar or they were on a date, but I had a feeling Joy was sobbing in the ladies' room.

I opened the door and let it close behind me completely. "Joy?"

"Did you see?" Her voice came from one of the stalls.

"I'm sorry."

She blew her nose. "Do you think *he* hung that wire to get rid of me?"

That frightening possibility hadn't crossed my mind. It scared me even more that she thought Nick might have done such a thing. I tried to answer benignly. "I don't know him very well. It seems unlikely. Didn't you just move in with him?"

"It's only been three days! How can he already be with another woman?"

I felt terrible. How many things could go wrong in Joy's life? She'd been sitting at home while Nick was putting the moves on another attractive woman. I'm ashamed to admit that I wondered if his cousin Alex might be like that, too.

"How could I be so stupid?" Joy emerged from the stall, wiping her eyes. She splashed water on her face and dabbed it with a paper towel. "I will never trust a man again. Never!" Her chest heaved with each breath she took, and she twisted the paper towel with white-knuckle hands.

"Come on back to the table. You should eat something." She needed strength, because she was going to have to confront Nick and have it out.

She nodded. "Do me a huge favor? I don't want him to know I saw him. Can you sort of give me some cover?"

"Sure." Everyone handled romantic disappointments differently. And if she really thought he'd strung that wire so she would fall, then I could understand why she wouldn't want him to know he'd been caught. On the other hand, if that was really the case, it seemed like she would want to move out that very second. At least, I would have.

She shot out the door and rushed through the little corridor back to the restaurant side of The Laughing Hound. I trailed along behind her, hoping that if Nick had looked our way he would have seen me, not Joy.

We resumed our meal, but I noticed Myra surreptitiously watching Joy. For dessert I ordered my favorite, The Laughing Hound's incredible smooth and creamy chocolate mousse along with a cup of hot tea. The mousse arrived with a dollop of whipped cream on top, little raspberry sauce hearts on the white plate around the mousse, and a stemmed strawberry in the cream. It was such an indulgence.

Myra had ordered the same thing, but she ignored her mousse. Her eyes on Joy, she stirred her coffee. "Well, are you going to tell us what happened, honey?"

I expected Joy to balk, to deny that anything was wrong.

"I saw my boyfriend flirting with another woman in the bar."

Humphrey laid his napkin on the table with drama, like he was drawing a sword. "What a scoundrel! I shall have a word with him."

It appeared Joy was trying to hide her amusement at his offer. "Don't bother. It was folly of me to think Nick and I had something going. I've never had a relationship that slid downhill so fast. Over dinner I came to the sad realization that he lost interest as soon as he got what he wanted from me—money."

Myra sipped her coffee. "Are you talking about Nick Rigas?"

Joy nodded her head. "How did you know?"

Myra clucked. "He's a worm. Did you make his car payment or pay off his credit card bill?"

Joy's mouth fell open. "It's like you can read my mind! His rent. He was four months behind."

Myra nodded knowingly. "There ought to be signs on all the roads leading into Old Town with his picture and a warning to women. Don't beat yourself up, honey. I fell for him, too. That girl he was flirting with? Won't be long before he taps her purse and moves on."

Francie had been silently savoring her mousse. She put down her spoon and asked sternly, "Do you think he's the one who strung the wire across the stairs?"

I feared her question would bring on a fresh torrent of tears from Joy.

She kept herself remarkably composed. It was as though seeing Nick with another woman had calmed her. Or maybe she was holding it all in right now and would go home and have a good cry. Except home was where Nick lived.

Joy toyed with her fruit tart. "Much as I'd like to, I can't eliminate that as a possibility."

"You poor thing!" Myra placed her fists on the table and leaned toward Joy. "You are not going back there tonight. Not under any circumstances. I won't hear of it. You come on home with me. Humphrey and I will get the gang from the mortuary to move you tomorrow." She waggled a finger at Joy. "Do not go home and be alone with Nick. I know how persuasive he is."

"I can't do that. You hardly know me."

"We girls have to stick together, especially when there's a predator like Nick around. No, ma'am, I'm not letting you go back. I swear he'll weasel your last cent out of you."

Joy smiled. "Too late. He's already done that. But I couldn't impose."

"Humphrey will stay over, too. You trust him, right? We'll have a slumber party and drink wine and say lots of ugly things about Nick."

"Okay. I thought I would have to spend the night at the

bakery sleeping in a chair." Joy smiled for the first time all
night. "That's so nice of you. I'm a stranger to you."

"I have a sixth sense about people." Myra slid her hand
through the crook of Humphrey's arm. "Don't I, sweetums?"

I'd never seen Humphrey quite so undone. He seemed
happy yet ill at ease at the same time. He lifted his chin and
sat up straight. "This has turned out to be quite an evening.
Now if we could only find Buddy."

Francie opted to walk home with Nina and me. I couldn't
blame her. The evening air felt just warm enough to make me
want to stroll.

When we reached my house, I asked, "Nightcap?"

The three of us settled in my kitchen with Daisy, Duke,
and Mochie. I brought out tiny gold-rimmed glasses with floral
etching on the sides and poured peach schnapps for Nina and
me. Francie preferred the rich almond taste of Amaretto.

"That was something tonight." Francie sat back and
propped her feet up on a footstool. "Maurice turned out to be
a sad, lonely cat lover, and that sweet Renee was ready to do
just about anything to get Humphrey away from Myra. Who'd
have expected that?"

Nina laughed. "Myra held her own. Did you see how deftly
she made sure Humphrey wouldn't swing by Renee's for that
dessert she promised him?"

I handed each of them a napkin. "I don't know about Myra
inviting Joy to stay with her. What if Joy is really the killer?"

"I'm a little perplexed by the breakup between Joy and Renee."
Nina savored a sip of the schnapps. "It sounds like Joy made
off with their money and wound up paying Nick's bills with it.
Yet, Renee, who was pleading poverty, is buying furniture."

"I don't understand how Renee can sleep in the apartment
where Muffin was murdered," said Francie. "I think I'm a
pretty tough ol' gal, but that would give me the willies."

"Me, too." Mochie jumped onto my lap and purred. "Joy's
abrupt departure from their business seems so underhanded.
But someone has tried to kill Joy twice. That sort of points
to Renee, doesn't it?"

"I bet Renee killed Muffin for that jeweled cupcake that

was stolen from Spenser. I didn't know Renee could be so vindictive. She comes across so sweet—all smiles and cutesy clothes and cupcakes." Nina poured herself another shot of schnapps. "But after that kiss she planted on Humphrey, which was only for Myra's benefit, it's perfectly clear that she can be jealous and domineering. Remember what Myra said? 'There's something devious living inside of her.'"

Francie snorted. "There's something devious in all of us. We wouldn't be human if we didn't feel jealousy or anger sometimes. It's not that I want to defend Renee, but I'm not sure how any of us would act under the extraordinary stress she's been through. If you ask me, it's pretty amazing that she's functioning at all. And she did keep Sugar Baby going, so she's had some income coming in."

"Or she could have sold Joy's grandmother's ring," I pointed out.

"We're overlooking something major here," said Nina. "Unless Humphrey gave someone else a ride in his car, the only person who could have left Spenser's cupcake in Humphrey's car is Renee. It's conclusive evidence."

"Spenser said he and Renee go way back. It sounded as though they were on good terms," I said. "Why would she have stolen it from him?"

"They must be good friends, or he wouldn't have allowed her to use his bakery while hers was out of commission," observed Francie.

"But don't you see the consistency?" argued Nina. "First Renee steals Spenser's cupcake, then she steals Joy's grandmother's diamond ring."

"There's something else that's been bothering me, too," I said. "Someone swapped flour for powdered sugar at Cake My Day. Renee was the one who suffered most as a result, because she might well have won best cupcake if that hadn't happened. I wonder if Spenser sabotaged her."

Francie dropped her feet to the floor. "I'm going home to bed. I hate to imagine that either Joy or Renee is sufficiently depraved to have killed Muffin. I wish we had something more concrete to go on."

Nina stretched. "I'll see you home, Francie. And maybe I'll give Wong a call tomorrow morning—see if she'll share anything."

I walked to the front door with them. "Good luck with that! I bet Wong will be zipped up tight."

＊＊＊

The next morning, I dared to sleep in a little bit, but not too long. I had a luncheon meeting with a local women's group about their fundraiser for children in need. Mochie snuggled up on top of me, which he knew would force me to get out of bed and feed him. After a cup of coffee, yogurt, and fruit, I took a walk with Daisy, then came home and went over my notes about the meeting.

I showered and hit the makeup pretty heavily. It wouldn't do to face the upper crust women of Old Town with a black eye. I chose a tailored blue dress with a round neckline and added a strand of pearls, gold earrings, and low heels, since the meeting would only be a few blocks away.

Just as I was leaving the house, Humphrey tapped on the kitchen window. I unlocked the door and let him in.

"I've been suspended from work."

"Oh, Humphrey! I'm so sorry. You expected that, didn't you?"

He slumped into one of the chairs next to my fireplace. "I don't understand how this could be happening. My name has been befouled, blackened. I am disgraced."

I looked at my watch. Why was he doing this now when I had an appointment?

The knocker on the front door sounded. It had better be a package, I thought, because I didn't have time for anything else.

I opened the door to find Natasha and Martha. They wore matching robin's-egg blue outfits.

Natasha held out the end of Martha's leash as though she expected me to take it. "You have to babysit Martha for me. Leon is at a dental appointment, and Mars had a snit and a half when he saw what she did to his home office yesterday."

She thrust a sparkly ball toward me with the other hand. "Well, take them. I'm in a hurry!"

"I have an appointment, and she's not my dog. She's your responsibility."

I started to close the door, but Natasha stuck her foot in the opening. "I take care of Daisy."

"No, you don't. You lock her in Mars's office."

"Sophie! I'm in a pinch. Can't you just do this for me?"

"Look at me, Natasha. I'm dressed for a meeting."

She frowned at me. "With you it's so hard to tell."

Humphrey dragged up beside me. "I'll watch her. I don't have anywhere else to go."

She handed Martha over. While she was warning him about Martha's habits, I shouted good-bye and took off.

Fortunately, Marilee Goldenbaum didn't live far away. I made it with one minute to spare. She answered the door and ushered me into a gracious living room where a group of woman waited expectantly. Pale oriental rugs covered gleaming hardwood floors. The walls were the color of coffee diluted with cream. Heavy white molding surrounded the windows. The furniture wore delicate lime and ecru with an occasional spot of peach for a punch of color. A huge painting over the fireplace carried on the peach color and was flanked by two topiaries.

"I thought we would start by talking about our plans for the gala, then we'll go into the dining room for lunch. I believe everyone knows Sophie Winston?" she said.

A chorus of voices said hello to me.

"Have you discussed a theme?" I asked.

Shirley Morgan, a blonde with bangs and upswept hair, spoke, gliding her hands through the air. "I envision a winter wonderland theme. Wouldn't white, blue, and silver make a fabulous backdrop for the silent auction?"

I heard a couple of groans but also saw some nods.

A hand went up. "A point of order first, please." Clarissa Osbourne rose and walked toward the sofa.

I hadn't noticed her in the back corner. My heart thudded.

CHAPTER TWENTY-SIX

Dear Sophie,

When I was growing up, we used to give our dog a few grapes when we were eating them. My sister-in-law, who is an annoying know-it-all, says grapes are very, very bad for dogs. Is she pulling my leg?

—Worried in Grapevine, California

Dear Worried,

I'm afraid the know-it-all is correct. Grapes and raisins are known to cause renal failure in dogs. If your dog should accidentally eat grapes or raisins, contact your veterinarian immediately.

—Sophie

There was no telling what Clarissa might say.

She held her head high. "I believe the rest of you will be in agreement that it would be distasteful to hire someone who is having an affair with one of our husbands."

A murmur rose in the room. I wanted to drop right through the beautiful floors. Summoning courage, I forced a broad smile. "I fully agree that it would be tasteless to hire such a person. Fortunately, that's not the case with me. Any other ideas about themes?"

"Not so fast, you little strumpet," said Clarissa. "Sophie is sleeping with my Spenser."

There were surprisingly few gasps. "That's simply not true. I don't know why you won't believe me. I've never had any kind of relationship with Spenser at all."

"Sophie, don't embarrass yourself by trying to deny it."

I looked around at the faces. "This is how ugly rumors get started. Someone makes a claim and then other people repeat it. I can't do anything more than tell you that I'm *not* involved with Spenser."

Under her breath, Clarissa hissed at me, "I told you I would fight." I noted that she didn't scream in public as she had with Spenser. Oh no, she wept with grace, like a bereaved woman. Sniffling, she asked, "Then where is he living? Why doesn't he come home to me anymore?"

Now the gasps were substantial. The thing was, I had a pretty good idea where he might be living, since I'd seen him at that hotel. Of course, I didn't know who else might be shacking up in the room with him. I debated for a split second, but decided not to mention it. Spenser was a nice guy and, except for Clarissa's groundless accusations, their problems had nothing to do with me. She could follow him if she wanted to know where he was. I picked up my briefcase, but before I left, I said, loud enough for everyone to hear, in a tone that I hoped was totally without emotion, "Why don't you ask Spenser where he spends his nights?"

Marilee saw me to the door. "I'll call you to reschedule. This is the most exciting meeting we've ever had! But you know, dear, there's no point in denying your relationship with Spenser. It's all over town."

How could that be? "Where did you hear about it?" I clutched her arm, "And for the record, it's simply not true."

"Really? I thought you and Spenser would be a cute couple

and now that you're not with Wolf anymore . . . oh my!" She must have recognized the less-than-thrilled look on my face, because she called Shirley over. "Shirl, where did you hear about Sophie and Spenser?"

Shirley gazed at the ceiling. "Oh, I know. It was at The Laughing Hound. We were in the bar, and Spenser was having a drink with someone across the room. So I said to my girlfriend that if *I* were going to have an affair, it would be with someone like him. And the bartender—the new one, Moe—said to set my sights elsewhere, because Spenser was already involved with Sophie."

Oh, swell. Just swell.

"Of course I also heard that Clarissa was paying Nick to keep quiet about an affair she had with the general. Can you imagine?" She cackled hysterically. "How do these things get started?"

I thanked them and left, knowing full well that they still believed the rumor and not me. I dragged home, so worn down that if my arms had been a little bit longer my briefcase would have slid along the sidewalk. Clarissa's lies probably wouldn't hurt me in the long run. I had enough corporate business to keep me busy. But no one likes to have false rumors floated about her.

I was so immersed in my own little problem that I forgot about Humphrey's much greater nightmare until I walked into my house. Natasha's assistant, Leon, sat on the floor of my kitchen with Humphrey, Daisy, and Martha. The rich aroma of French press coffee wafted to me.

"Sophie! You have to see this!" Humphrey wore a grin that could have lit the world.

"I made coffee. Hope you don't mind," said Leon.

"Not as long as I can have some."

"There are cupcakes, too," he said.

They looked delicious. Creamy chocolate frosting swirled to peaks. "Which bakery did they come from?" Given what we knew about Renee, I wasn't sure I wanted to eat anything from Sugar Baby.

"I baked them, silly!"

I plucked one off the plate and bit into it. "Salted chocolate with . . . pistachio?"

"Exactly!" Leon beamed at me.

"They're wonderful," I said.

"Are you going to pay attention or not?" asked Humphrey.

"Okay, I'm watching." I felt like a mom with an excited four-year-old.

Humphrey tossed Martha's glittery ball onto the floor. She scrambled to it as fast as she could, picked it up in her mouth, and kept going, right into the foyer.

Was I supposed to be impressed? I applauded, hoping that was the right thing to do.

Humphrey snorted. "You don't get it." He disappeared into the foyer and returned with Martha and the ball. He set her on the floor and tossed the ball again.

Martha tore after it, grabbed it in her mouth, and ran like a little devil. She jumped onto the banquette behind the table and nosed the ball between the cushions.

I held out my palms. "I'm not seeing the beauty of this."

Leon looked up at me. "She won't give it back. She always hides it. Sometimes she carries that thing around for hours, but she never gives it back. The only way to get it again is to find where she hid it."

"Sounds like Natasha. Maybe they're a good pair after all."

"She's the greatest little dog," gushed Leon. "I'm gaga for her. She's the best thing about my job."

"Why are you so excited about this, Humphrey?" I asked.

"Don't you see it yet? There was one other person in my car right before they found the glittery cupcake." He pointed at Martha. "She must have found it somewhere and still carried it in her mouth when I caught her and put her in my car."

Leon grinned. "Then she hid it in the car."

I was very skeptical. I plucked the ball from between the cushions and tossed it onto the floor. Martha ran after it, grabbed it, and continued into my family room. This time I followed her. She appeared to be looking for a place to stash it. I picked her up and tried to take it out of her mouth. She growled and bared her teeth at me.

"Told you," said Leon. "No one can get it from her. Not until she decides to hide it."

"I have to admit that Martha's little quirk does cast a teensy bit of doubt that Renee was the one who lost it in your car. But wouldn't you have noticed that she had something in her mouth when you picked her up?"

"It was dark! I didn't examine her when I caught her. I put her in my car and drove like the wind to get her to the vet."

We returned to the kitchen, and I poured myself a cup of coffee. "Let's say your theory is correct about Martha grabbing the golden cupcake like her ball and hiding it in Humphrey's car. Where did she get it?"

In unison they said, "At the cupcake gala."

I leaned against the counter, holding my coffee mug with both hands. "That narrows it down to a couple hundred people."

"Ouch!" Leon touched his shoulder and made a sizzling sound. "What got into you?"

"I'm sorry. I had a bad morning. Don't mind me." I needed to put Clarissa and her ridiculous accusations behind me and concentrate on Humphrey. His problem was very serious and would impact his life and career. "Why would anyone bring the stolen cupcake to the dinner? The thief would be a dolt to do that."

"Crooks aren't always the brightest bulbs." Leon picked up Martha. "I'd better get back to Natasha's. She's on to a new concept for fame and fortune."

"What is it now—gourmet dog dinners?"

"I don't dare breathe a word. She has issued death threats for less." Leon waved and let himself out.

Humphrey tapped his fingertips together as though deep in thought. "Who at the cupcake gala would have had a reason to steal from Spenser?"

"His inner circle. His employees and previous employees, which, by the way, brings Renee into the picture again."

"How about Maurice?"

"I still don't know what happened between him and Spenser."

"I bet Renee knows."

How stupid of me. "I bet she does, too." Why hadn't I thought of that? "Walk over there with me?" He nodded, and I dashed upstairs to change into Keds, which were far superior to heels for walking on the brick sidewalks.

I apologized to Daisy for leaving her at home, fed Mochie shredded chicken, and we were out the door.

Before we went into Sugar Baby, Humphrey nudged me and motioned toward Sugar Mama.

The open sign hung in the door, and Joy waved to us from the other side of the glass window.

"She's open again? She was so depressed last night."

Humphrey nodded. "Myra has a way with people."

I tried to read his expression. "So how was it with the two of them?"

"It was fun! Like a slumber party."

I still wasn't getting a handle on his feelings toward Myra. He opened the door to Sugar Baby and held it for me.

Renee rushed at Humphrey. "I'm so glad to see you!" She wrapped her arms around his neck and clung to him. "I hoped you would swing by last night. Then this morning, I called the mortuary, and they said you weren't coming in. I've been so worried."

Her concern seemed genuine. She brushed a hair off his shirt. "Where have you been? I see a fine, blond woman's hair."

Humphrey laughed. "That's from Martha—" He milked the moment. "—a Chihuahua."

She giggled, clearly relieved.

"Do you have a minute?" he asked. "We were wondering why Maurice hates Spenser so much."

"Oh. That." She motioned to a table, and we sat down. "I don't know if Maurice will ever get over it. His wife, Colleen, worked for Spenser at Cake My Day. She was so talented. She had great ideas for cupcakes and was innovative about decorating them. Anyway, she and Maurice got the notion that she was wasting her talent at Cake My Day. They thought they could make a lot more money if they did what Spenser did. So Colleen left to open her own cupcakery with the idea of parlaying it into a chain of bakeries."

"Where was the cupcakery?" I asked.

Renee smiled wryly. "Right across the street from Cake My Day. We saw what happened there on a daily basis. First they leased a space that was three times the size they needed. Then they put a small fortune into upscale décor. Very modern and sleek with fancy imported fixtures. It was beautiful but just not necessary, you know? They could have set up a darling place for one-tenth the money they spent. Then Maurice quit his job to become the brains behind the chain, sort of like Spenser is, except for one thing—he didn't have Spenser's genius for business, and he wasn't a baker. So they'd sunk all that money into location number one, and before they'd even opened their doors, they rented and starting renovating location number two."

"That's awfully bold," said Humphrey.

"Stupid, too. Cupcakes are a good business, but you have to work up from the bottom. They hired a really nice guy to help bake at the first location, planning to eventually make him the primary baker at the second location. But they were low on money," she sighed, "so they mortgaged their house."

"Oh no." I could see what was coming.

"Spenser warned them to take it slow, but Maurice resented Spenser for that and told him to butt out. Spenser couldn't believe how much money they sank into their upscale cupcakeries. They lost their house, of course. But it gets worse. Both the cupcakery locations closed, and Colleen ran off with the baker they'd hired."

"Wait a minute," I said. "Spenser didn't do anything to them. They made their own problems."

"It's such a shame that Maurice turned on Spenser like he did. Spenser did his best to help them out. He took over the lease on the second location, and there were rumors that he loaned them money, too. As near as I can figure, Maurice needed to blame someone, and he picked Spenser. Probably out of jealousy, since Spenser had accomplished what they couldn't achieve." She held up her hand and ticked her fingers as she spoke. "Maurice lost his wife, his business, his house—there wasn't anything left but anger. Meanwhile, Spenser has been expanding Cake My Day and everything in his life seems perfect."

Obviously things were not perfect in Spenser's life. I didn't know if he was really having an affair with someone, but Clarissa's screaming fits certainly didn't fit the definition of a perfect life. She put on a good show of playing the wealthy socialite, though. To people who didn't know them well, they gave the impression of having it all. "Where did Maurice get the money to buy the house he lives in?"

"He doesn't own it. He lives there rent-free because he manages a bunch of rental properties for the owner. I think it's part of his compensation."

Once again I found myself feeling a smidgen of compassion toward Maurice. I'd been grumpy after one bad meeting. What if I'd lost everything? It would be hard to put on a cheerful face every day. Maurice's thinking seemed to be warped as a result of his disappointment. He'd wanted Buddy because Spenser had indicated an interest in the dog. Was Maurice so confused that he thought he was also entitled to the fruits of Spenser's success? Could he have burglarized Spenser's home?

"Maurice wasn't all that bad looking, either," said Renee. "If he got a decent haircut and didn't have that horrible stringy white hair hanging in his face, you wouldn't even recognize him."

Renee tilted her head coyly at Humphrey. Once again I found myself wondering what her game was with Humphrey. On the one hand, I wanted to like the sweet little blonde who baked such cute cupcakes. On the other hand, while I hated to admit it to myself, I didn't trust her completely. How could I ask her about the gold cupcake?

"Do you know anything about the burglary of Spenser and Clarissa's home?"

CHAPTER TWENTY-SEVEN

Dear Natasha,

Everyone loves my grandmother's recipe for devil's food cake. How do I alter the recipe to bake it as cupcakes?

Cupcake Demon in Devil's Elbow, Missouri

Dear Cupcake Demon,

The recipes for most two-layer cakes will yield about twenty-four cupcakes. Don't mess with a good thing!

—Natasha

"Wasn't that awful?" Renee clamped her hands to the sides of her face. "Clarissa was at home! Can you imagine the horror? She . . . she changed after that. She used to be much more open and fun. I guess hiding under the bed while that guy ransacked her house was so terrifying that she never fully recovered."

"Spenser was away?" I prompted her.

"He was at another store location when that brute broke

in. Clarissa heard him coming up the stairs and hid, so she only saw boots, never his face. Honestly, just hearing someone tromping up the stairs would terrify me."

"Do you know what he took?"

"Mostly jewelry, I think. Some computer stuff that was small and easy to take with him, like laptops and iPads."

Curious, she didn't mention the expensive miniature cupcake. As a baker who collected miniatures, it seemed like she would have been particularly interested in it.

Humphrey hung his head as though he was ashamed. I hoped he wouldn't blurt out details about the cupcake and his arrest. As far as I could tell, she hadn't heard about it yet.

I needed to wrap it up before he gave anything away. Renee was still my prime suspect, no matter how passionate Martha was about hiding her ball. "Didn't you need Humphrey to pick up some furniture for you?"

She eyed him bashfully. "I thought maybe you didn't want to do it. Spenser said I can use the Cake My Day delivery van. He'd probably even help."

"Sure. Just tell me when and where."

"Thanks." She squeezed her shoulders forward and curled her hands inward so that she looked like a happy little chipmunk.

As we walked out the door, I couldn't help noticing that Sugar Mama was packed with people. I was happy for Joy. She needed to make some money to get back on her feet.

Humphrey took off to arrange Renee's furniture delivery. Having something to do would temporarily take his mind off his troubles.

On the way home, I stopped at The Laughing Hound. I walked past the hostess and down the stairs to the bar. It was nearly empty. Moe dried a glass.

He smiled at me. "What can I get for you, Sophie?"

"Nothing, thanks." I jumped up on a tall barstool.

"Meeting someone for lunch?"

"Actually, I wanted to talk with you. When I came in here the other day, I wondered how you knew me."

"Easy, darlin'. Bernie described you perfectly."

"And you'd heard my name before. I understand I'm having an affair with Spenser Osbourne."

He set the glass down. His hands on the bar, he lowered his head. "I'm sorry. Look, I know Bernie is a friend of yours. I need this job."

Moe dropped the polishing cloth and rubbed his eyes. "I didn't mean anything by it. You know, people come in, and you chat them up for tips." He shrugged. "I'm sorry if that wasn't supposed to get around."

"Who did you hear it from?"

"Uh"—he ran his hand over his head in discomfort—"that crazy guy, Maurice. Like I said, I didn't mean anything by it."

I wasn't completely unsympathetic. Even though I wanted to be furious and indignant, I had certainly repeated my share of rumors and had even relied on them for information. But I wasn't ready to let him off the hot seat yet. "What else did Maurice tell you?"

"Nothing else about you, I swear."

"He comes in for a drink now and then?"

Moe's mouth twisted into an uncomfortable grimace. "More like he comes in and hopes someone will buy him a drink. People are funny. A lot of them move away from him as soon as he sits down. The chick that was murdered? Muffin? He liked her. She never changed seats. Always treated him nice. And your Spenser is a real gentleman. Maurice acts like a jerk toward Spenser. Like he hates his guts. But Spenser always pays for Maurice's drink and dinner and asks me not to tell him. That's classy in my book."

Now we were getting somewhere. "Maurice and Muffin were friends?"

"I don't know as I'd go that far, but she was kind to him. He warned her to stay away from Nick Rigas."

From what I'd heard, that was about the only good information he'd dispensed.

A faint grin crossed Moe's face. "Of course, he also said that Clarissa had something going on with General German."

"Clarissa is having an affair with the general?"

He pointed his forefinger at me. "Gotcha! Now you're doing it. See how easy it is to fall into gossip?"

"Do me a favor, will you, Moe? I'm not having an affair with Spenser. Never have. In fact, I barely know the man. Will you start a new rumor that I'm not seeing Spenser?"

His mouth swung up on one side. "Paving the way for Alex German?"

"Nope. Just telling the truth." I tucked some bills into his tip jar and left.

❧

My afternoon appointment came off perfectly. The meeting about a huge corporate event went well. I looked forward to it, even though it would be a lot of work. And there hadn't been even the slightest mention of my love life.

I swung by the grocery store on my way home and stocked up on goodies. Now that the weather was warming, I felt like barbecuing. I bought shrimp, ribs, and a few items for the salted caramel cupcakes that I'd been craving since the gala dinner.

After the groceries had been put away, I changed into a long-sleeve top the color of the shrimp I'd bought. Khaki skorts might not be fashionable, but they were comfortable. I pulled on walking shoes, and when I trotted down the stairs, Daisy waited at the door, wagging her tail. I clipped on her leash, locked the door behind us, and patted her, wondering how little Martha was doing.

"Sophie!" Nina ran out of her house. "Wait! I've eaten so many cupcakes that I need to walk. Do you mind? I have news!"

"Spill!"

We strolled toward the center of town. Daisy happily snuffled scents as we walked.

"When I was at the deli at lunchtime," said Nina, "Myra happened to be there. She heard that Muffin was suffocated with a pillow."

I knew which one. I shuddered at the memory of that cupcake pillow with black marks on one side and frosting on the other. The black smears had probably come from Muffin's eye makeup, and the frosting must have oozed out of the icing bag in her hand.

"She had bruises on her arms and head, most likely from her assailant."

"Poor Muffin!"

"Did Humphrey and Leon show you Martha's trick with the ball this morning?"

I might have known they would show off to Nina. "What do you think? Is it possible that she picked up the expensive cupcake and ran with it?"

"Stranger things have happened. Some birds collect shiny things and hoard them in their nests."

My thoughts shifted to Humphrey. "How on earth did Humphrey get mixed up in a murder?"

Nina frowned at me. "You insisted Humphrey wasn't involved in Muffin's murder. Now you think there's a connection?"

"I don't know. So many weird things have happened. First Renee and Joy split up, then Muffin was murdered. Those are facts. It seems likely that Renee and Joy are the primary suspects in Muffin's death. Right?"

She nodded.

"Then Buddy was stolen. Maurice clearly wanted Buddy to spite Spenser. It seems pretty clear that Maurice was the culprit there. I can't imagine any way that Buddy's disappearance could be linked to Muffin's murder. Finally, Humphrey was arrested—"

"You're jumping ahead," she said. "You forgot about Joy's claim that someone pricked her and set up a wire to trip her. And the general!"

"He seems to be suffering from some genetic illness. An allergy to fava beans."

"Genetic? Does that mean oh-be-still-my-heart Alex has it, too?"

"Apparently so. And Nick, as well. But it doesn't sound too bad. As long as they don't eat fava beans or other broad beans they're fine. From Alex's description I'm under the impression that it's mostly a cumulative thing. If they eat them once, they feel sick, but usually get over it. It's when they eat the beans continuously that they become very ill, like the general did."

"I wouldn't let that get out if I were Nick. Listening to Myra and Joy last night, I gather there's more than one woman in Old Town who'd like to knock *him* off."

"And for good reason. What a crumb to use women that way. Poor Joy! She opened her shop again, did you see?"

"It's exciting. I'm so glad for her."

"None of the incidents seem related." I paused so Daisy could sniff a gate. "But Spenser was tangentially involved in two of them. He wasn't home during the burglary, but it was his home that was invaded. And Spenser was the one who *really* lost Buddy because Buddy would have been his dog."

I gasped, alarming people who were walking by us. Smiling, I assured them everything was fine, and we strolled away.

"Both of the thefts involved taking things from Spenser. And who wanted to have Spenser's possessions? Maurice! Of course. He must be the one who broke into Spenser's home. But why would he have brought the gold cupcake to the gala dinner? He needed money. Wouldn't he have sold it?"

"Maybe he couldn't sell it because it was so easily identifiable. It was too hot. Or maybe he didn't think it was real. Maybe he thought it was a cheap bauble."

"Still, why would he bring it to the dinner? Unless . . . unless he wanted to taunt Spenser with it somehow."

Nina shook her head. "But then Spenser would know who the burglar was. Oh! I see what you mean. He might have placed it on a seat in the commotion, or dropped it in Spenser's pocket or something to spook him."

"Or to spook Clarissa," I suggested. "I had no idea she was so high-strung. Renee said Clarissa was never the same after the burglary. She would have jumped right out of her skin if that cupcake had turned up unexpectedly."

"You don't think Spenser could have been behind the burglary? Maybe he set it up to happen when he would have an alibi?"

"You've been watching too many movies." I laughed. "But something is definitely wrong with Clarissa. I always thought she was nice, but she's acting so odd."

We reached the waterfront and sat on one of the benches overlooking the Potomac River.

"Do you think Joy's safe now?" I asked. "Or will Nick still come after her, even though she's moving out?"

"I don't think it was Nick who strung the wire to trip her. Think about it," said Nina. "He got what he wanted. He took her money, and now he's getting rid of her. He's free to do as he likes and move on—to another woman to rip off."

"So why bother killing her? Is that what you mean?"

"Exactly. I think someone else has it in for her."

"And once again, we're back to Renee. Why does everything seem to revolve around Renee, Maurice, and Spenser?"

CHAPTER TWENTY-EIGHT

Dear Natasha,

How come Sophie gives so much advice about dogs and cats, and all you talk about is cupcakes?

—Animal Lover in Puposky, Minnesota

Dear Animal Lover,

Sophie may dispense advice, but I can tell you how to make a canopy bed for your little doggie princess! All you have to do is cut and glue lightweight PVC to form the legs and top, and then attach a ruffled canopy! Of course, a real princess deserves a little bling, so have fun with the glue gun and rhinestones.

—Natasha

"And Joy. Don't forget Joy." Nina frowned at me. "What's bugging you?"

I told her about the meeting where I'd been ushered to the door after Clarissa accused me of having an affair with

Spenser. "So then I went to The Laughing Hound, and Moe confessed to spreading it around as idle gossip."

"Wait until Bernie hears! Is Moe still on probation? He'll lose his job. Why would Moe make up something like that about you?"

"Don't tell Bernie. Right or wrong, we all share rumors. Moe heard it from Maurice and then repeated it. Why would Maurice pick on me? I know he hates Spenser, but it's a bald lie, and why involve me?"

"Ugh. I always thought Maurice was peculiar, but I'm coming to despise the man. He fabricates everything. Why lie about his cat, Gunsmoke, being a girl? Maybe the man can't tell the truth. He probably wanted to spread an ugly lie about Spenser, and you were the hapless victim."

"That's just hateful. If Spenser and I had been seen together around town or if there were any basis for it whatsoever, it still wouldn't be right or nice of Maurice, but this is just vicious. It's bad enough that he's so ugly to Spenser, but to spread this kind of callous rumor is just plain mean. It could result in all kinds of unanticipated repercussions."

"Maybe that's what he wanted—to cause a specific consequence."

I turned my head to look at her. "What do you mean?"

"Maybe Maurice hoped that spreading an ugly rumor tying Spenser to someone else would cause a rift between Spenser and Clarissa." She raised her eyebrows and grimaced. "Looks like it worked."

"But why? Why would he want to do that?" I knew the answer before I'd finished the question. "He sees it as vengeance. Spenser said it days ago. Maurice blames his misfortune on Spenser."

"Poor Spenser!" said Nina. "Remember how Maurice wanted Buddy? He wants to deny Spenser happiness." She shook her head. "I bet he wants Spenser to lose everything, just like he did. How low can a person be?"

We strolled back leisurely, until Humphrey crossed a street in front of us, so agitated that he didn't notice us. His cell phone played a jingle, and he jerked like someone had slapped him. He pulled it from his pocket, looked at it in terror, and tossed it into the trash can on the corner.

"What on earth?" Nina picked up her pace.

I stopped and peered into the trash. Fortunately, it was full and the phone had landed on a discarded fast-food bag. I picked it up.

"Come on!" Nina waited for me. "Eww. What are you doing? That's gross."

"He didn't mean to throw it away. Do you know how much information is probably in here?"

"*I'm* not touching it." She stuck out her tongue.

Humphrey disappeared into a beer bar.

Nina grabbed Daisy's leash from me. "Hurry! Go after him. He's in some kind of trouble."

I tried to hand her his phone. For what seemed an eternity, she backed away from it.

"For pity's sake, Nina. Just take it!"

She grasped the corner with the tips of her thumb and forefinger, making a face of disgust.

I stepped inside the tavern, and stopped dead so my eyes could adjust to the dark interior. Paneled walls and few windows made for a cozy atmosphere. Labored breathing to my left turned out to be from Humphrey, who stood with his back to the wall.

"Are you hiding from someone?" I asked.

"Depends. Who sent you?"

"No one. Nina and I saw you throw your phone in the trash."

"Would you believe I need a new one?"

"No."

"I need a new number. The wrong people have the old number."

"Are you in some kind of trouble?"

"If I buy you dinner, will you protect me?"

"Nina is outside with Daisy. I think they permit dogs on the patio in the back. Is that okay?"

"The farther back the better!"

I switched places with Nina. She went inside with Humphrey,

and I walked Daisy around the corner to the unofficial doggie entrance. Ivy climbed the fence that enclosed the patio. Tables with green and white umbrellas were already crowded, but Nina and Humphrey had managed to snag a table under a tree.

Before I sat down, a waitress appeared and took our order. Medium-rare burgers for everyone, including Daisy. She passed on the beer, though.

I leaned forward to talk so the other diners wouldn't overhear. "What's going on?"

"They're tormenting me."

"Who?" asked Nina.

"Renee, Joy, and Myra. Renee calls me in desperate need of help. 'I have to go to the bank. Can you come mind the store?' But Joy sees me when I go to Sugar Baby, and before I know it, Myra has some kind of emergency. Then Joy calls. 'Can you pick up some bananas at the market and bring them over here?' Then Renee sees me at Sugar Mama and gets bent out of shape. The calls and the texts never stop." His voice rose. "Even at night. They text me in the middle of the night. Even when I was in jail! Don't they ever sleep? I can't get a moment's rest!"

He'd become so loud that other patrons were staring at us.

A sly smile crept onto Nina's face. "I thought you were in love with Renee."

"She is rapidly drowning my undying devotion. If this is what a relationship with Renee is like, then I shall be forced to reconsider my position."

"Humphrey, you're caught in the middle of their cupcake war."

"You mean I'm simply a pawn to them?" His crestfallen face tugged at my heart.

"They wouldn't fight over you if they didn't care about you." That wasn't completely true, but maybe it would help soften the blow.

"They can find another pawn, then. I'm done. What a shame I *lost* my cell phone. After dinner, I'm going home and turning the ringer off on my land line. They'd better not come looking for me." He lifted an eyebrow. "Is this one of the games women play that I've heard so much about?"

"I guess it is. You're caught in the middle." Nina drank from a pilsner glass.

He rubbed his hands together. "In that case, they'd better be careful, because this exhausted mouse might just turn the tables on them."

Nina nudged me. Across the patio, the general and Nick had just sat down at a table. Alex was headed toward us.

"Hope I'm not interrupting," he said.

"Never," breathed Nina, gazing at him like he was a movie star.

"It's good to see the general out and about. He looks great. Have you met Humphrey?" I introduced them.

"Sophie," said Alex, "would you meet me for a drink or dessert later? I'd like to discuss something with you."

"I'd love t—"

Shirley Morgan, who'd been so instrumental in spreading the dreadful rumor about Spenser and me, walked up behind Alex and interrupted.

"Alex, darlin', it was fate that you happened to be here! I'd like you to marr . . . meet my daughter, Sam. Isn't she gorgeous? Sweetheart," she said to Sam, "this is Alex. He's a *lawyer* from a very fine family."

Sam had the slim build of a runner and had to be six feet tall. Her clothes clung to her, showing off her trim figure. A person could bounce a quarter off those abs if she were lying down. She wore her hair cut super short, like a young boy. No makeup, but she didn't need it. A no-maintenance beauty. But I found it curious that her mother was pushing her on Alex, who had to be closer to her mother's age.

They politely shook hands. Shirley trilled, "Look at the two of you. I will have beautiful grandchildren."

Shirley elbowed me, and whispered, "She better snag that man before he moves to town and every single woman, and probably some of the married ones, chase him." She gazed at Nina and Humphrey. "I don't see Spenser. Isn't he here with you?"

What did it take to convince this woman that I wasn't seeing him?

Dramatically pretending she'd been bad, she cringed and held a finger up to her lips. "Sorry. I forget that it's a secret." She winked at me.

To my immense relief, Alex excused himself and returned to his own table.

Shirley wrinkled her nose at me. "He's so adorable. Don't you just want to jump him and smother him with kisses?" She walked away, fanning herself with her hand.

I tried to concentrate on Humphrey and his woman problems, but it wasn't easy. As inconspicuously as possible, I pivoted my chair so that Alex wouldn't be in my line of sight, but the mere knowledge that he was there distracted me. I could barely choke down half of my burger. Fortunately, Daisy was more than happy to eat the remainder of mine, along with her own.

≈≈

A couple of hours later, I had changed into a soft peach dress that flowed and always made me feel very feminine. I'd packed more makeup on my black eye, and tried to curl my hair the way Kayla, the Realtor, wore hers. It flopped in multiple directions, not exactly what I'd intended, but it could have been worse.

When the door knocker sounded, I smoothed my dress and took a deep breath. "Ready, Daisy? Best behavior, please." I opened the front door and found myself face-to-face with Natasha—who was flirting shamelessly with Alex!

"Look who I found on your doorstep," she trilled, walking into my foyer.

"Hello, Alex. What can I do for you, Natasha?" I had to get rid of her before she invited herself along.

She bustled into my kitchen. Alex and I followed her.

Natasha eyed me critically. "Did we wake you up? You look like you just rolled out of bed."

Not exactly the impression I had hoped to make.

"Where do you keep Daisy's things?" she asked.

"Things?"

"Her wardrobe."

It was all I could do to keep from laughing. "She doesn't wear clothes."

Natasha gasped. "What about booties?"

"She doesn't wear those, either."

"What kind of dog mother are you?"

"That's pretty funny coming from you." It slipped out of my mouth, even though I didn't want to be catty in front of Alex. I had to get rid of her. "Maybe we could do this some other time?"

She nodded and sat down.

Tilting my head, I glared at her and tried to send a message with my eyes.

Flashing me an annoyed look, she said, "Alex, since Sophie doesn't have time for us right now, why don't you come down to my house? You really ought to meet Mars." She rose, brushed past me, and whispered, "So the rumors about you and Spenser are true!"

"I would enjoy meeting Mars," said Alex. "Maybe some other time? I'm here to pick up Sophie."

"Is something wrong with your car?" she asked me.

I tried not to speak through clenched teeth. "It's a date, Natasha."

Her forehead creased between her eyes. "Wh . . . oh, I get it, you're joking. Very funny."

I didn't want to hear more. "I'll tell you all about Daisy's wardrobe another time. Okay?"

"But you just said—"

Gently taking her hand, I led her to the foyer door. "Goodnight, Natasha."

I closed it before she could protest, smoothed my dress, and returned to the kitchen. "Sorry about that."

He held out his hand to me. I placed my hand in his, unsure about his intentions.

His fingers gently caressed my neck. Before I knew it, he'd mesmerized me and cupped my face between his hands. But just as his lips brushed mine, my kitchen door slammed open.

"Aha! I finally—" Clarissa stared at us. Her original shout faded to a murmur. "—caught you." She tweaked the bridge of her nose. "I don't understand. Have you dumped Spenser? Not that I would blame you. I would dump him for someone who looks like this guy, too."

"Alex," I said, "this is Clarissa."

He stepped forward and shook her hand. "Spenser? The guy from Cake My Day?"

"Her husband."

He assessed me with a disturbed expression. "You're in the habit of kissing her husband?"

I said, "No," at exactly the same time that she said, "Yes."

I rolled my eyes toward the ceiling. There was no telling what she might say next. Facing Alex, I locked on to his eyes. I wanted him to realize I wasn't lying, and I had nothing to hide. I couldn't read much in his expression, but I sensed caution. "I am not having an affair with Spenser, and I never have. As far as I can tell, a wacky guy started this rumor, and it spread like crazy."

A crease formed between Alex's eyes. "What wacky guy? Why would he do that?"

"Maurice Lester. You might have noticed him at the cupcake feast. Stringy white hair. He was carrying a cat who was wearing a pink wig?"

He nodded, and his amused grin confirmed that he remembered Maurice. "You don't forget a guy like that. I saw him in the emergency room the night the general was sick. He came in around the same time as Joy."

"Maurice went to the hospital?" Why had I doubted that he was ill? Guilt flooded up within me. "So he really *was* sick. I didn't believe him. Now I feel terrible."

"Sick?" Alex frowned. "I don't think so. He had a dog bite on his forearm. He made quite a scene about it."

"Buddy! That's proof that he has him stashed away somewhere." We knew Buddy wasn't at his house. Where could Maurice be hiding him? Maybe at one of the other rental properties he managed?

"Why would he start a rumor about you?" asked Alex.

Clarissa moaned and collapsed into a chair by the fireplace. "Because he's envious of my husband's success. You wouldn't believe the things he's done to us." She peered at me through eyes that were mere slits. "How do I know you're not lying?"

"Ask Moe, down at The Laughing Hound." I resented her for interrupting my moment of romance, but it dawned on me that it might not hurt to keep Clarissa talking. Maybe she could shed some light on the jeweled cupcake.

"Would you mind staying here?" I asked Alex.

His head gave a tiny, almost imperceptible jerk. "I'd like that very much."

"Could I interest anyone in a drink?" I didn't wait for answers. I switched on the oven, pulled out a petite loaf of crusty bread, and hit the fridge for salty, herbed cheese with sun-dried tomatoes in it, sliced Black Forest ham, and zesty horseradish mustard.

Clarissa hadn't moved. She remained slumped in the chair, her elbow on the armrest, her chin in her hand. "I just don't understand. If it's not you, then who is Spenser seeing?"

"Clarissa," I said, slicing the bread, "was at home when someone broke into their house and burglarized it. Can you imagine the horror?" I brushed the bread lightly with olive oil and slid it into the oven to toast a few minutes.

Clarissa didn't reveal much. She explained to Alex that she didn't like to talk about the incident.

I spread mustard on the crostini, and layered thin slices of ham and cheese on top. Once the tray of crostini was in the oven, I mixed cold sparkling wine with vodka, mango juice, and peach schnapps. I *needed* a drink with Clarissa and Alex in my kitchen at the same time. I poured it into three tall champagne flutes, floated a fresh raspberry on top of each as a garnish, and brought them to the table. "The crostini should be ready in a minute." I sat next to Alex on the banquette. "Clarissa, did the police ever follow up with Maurice? It seems like he would have been the prime suspect."

"Maurice?" She said his name as though she'd never thought about it. "I'm sure they must have. Spenser dealt with the police."

I rose to remove the crostini from the oven. Arranging

them on a white oval platter, I said casually, "I saw a photograph of a golden cupcake decorated with gemstones that was stolen."

Clarissa nodded absently. "It was a remarkable piece. Spenser bought it from Maurice. It turned up recently, which means everyone is talking about that horrid night again. I wish it would all go away and be in the past."

Not just yet. I needed to pump her a little bit more. Especially now that I knew the connection to Maurice. Had he stolen it back because he felt Spenser had stolen it from him? "Maurice? It was originally his?"

"He had it designed for his wife."

Setting the crostini on the table along with napkins, I slid next to Alex on the banquette. "No faaa—"

Alex's hand squeezed my knee under the table. Was he getting frisky with me?

"Do you work in the bakery with your husband?" he asked.

Clarissa finally sat up straight and joined us at the table. She swigged back her drink, emptying the glass. "Not anymore." She wolfed down two crostini. "These are good. I haven't had dinner. Spenser and I worked side-by-side for years to get the business up and running. Now that it's a chain, I still go down to the local bakery to check on things, but mostly I'm involved with charity work, that sort of thing."

"Did you know Muffin?" I asked.

"The poor girl who was killed? Wasn't that the saddest thing? No, I never met her. I have all the cupcakes I could ever want. It's not like I go around buying them."

But Spenser did. Was that research? I wondered. Or something else?

Alex ate a crostini. "You're right about these. They're terrific. Sophie was telling me about a dish she makes with pancetta and fava beans. Do you like fava beans, Clarissa?" It was a nice setup, even though I saw straight through his lie.

Alex watched Clarissa like a hawk, but he didn't need to. Even I saw the surprise in her eyes.

After a long moment, she asked, "Are you a cop?"

Alex didn't flinch. He must be one great poker player,

because I couldn't read anything in his face. But I felt his wariness as though by osmosis. Like a dog who had spotted prey, he didn't move a muscle, letting her stew. "No, I'm not. Why would you think that?"

Clarissa relaxed. "Sophie dated a cop before." She poured herself another drink and downed the whole thing. "Frankly, I find fava beans somewhat bland and uninspired." Pushing back from the table, she rose. "Well, it's been interesting meeting you, Alex."

He stood and reached out his hand to her. "Likewise."

She shook his hand and squinted at him. "Why do you look so familiar to me?"

"Perhaps you know my uncle, General German."

Clarissa should never play poker. Her face went rigid, her teeth clenched, and her jaw tightened like a vise. After a long silence her initial shock lightened, her mouth dropped open, and she began to chuckle. "I can't say as I blame you, Sophie." Her shoulders shook when she laughed. "I presume that's your snazzy car parked outside?"

"Yes."

"Figures. Well, that explains everything."

"Sophie, could I have a word with you?" She opened the kitchen door.

I followed her outside.

She fingered her forehead and looked at the ground. Raising a skinny forefinger, she said, "You almost fooled me. It took me a while to figure it out. I didn't believe I could be so wrong about you. Wow. Dating two men at the same time. If Spenser wasn't one of them, I'd be toasting you. I'm going to tell Spenser about your relationship with Alex, of course. He'll drop you once he knows you're seeing someone else, too. Poor old Spenser. Maybe he'll come home now."

The woman was delusional. I didn't see the point in arguing with her. Maybe this was a good thing. Maybe now she would believe that Spenser was hers again, and she'd stop this nonsense.

She chuckled. "Do you believe in karma, Sophie?"

"Sure, I guess I do."

"I've got news for you. Payback is murder!" She laughed hysterically and staggered away like a drunk, zigzagging and howling.

I returned to the kitchen.

Alex was watching her through the bay window. "That woman or her husband is trying to kill the general."

CHAPTER TWENTY-NINE

Dear Natasha,

I saw you and your dog wearing matching outfits in a picture. How did you find a leash of the same material?

—Trendy Dog Mom in Hollywood, Missouri

Dear Trendy Dog Mom,

I made the leash myself. All you need is a ¾" to 1" round-eye swivel-bolt snap, fabric, cotton strapping, and some basic sewing skills. In no time at all, you can sew a collection of leashes to match your wardrobe. Even better, you can embellish them with embroidery or rhinestones.

—Natasha

"What?" I was reaching for my glass and nearly knocked it over. "Why? Why would either of them want to kill the general?" I scooched into the banquette.

He sat down beside me, angling himself so that he faced

me. "That's what I don't know. Maybe you can help me piece it together. I'm fairly sure that Cake My Day is putting fava beans in their cupcakes."

"I think there's a fava-bean flour, so that's not out of the realm of possibility, but it's hardly likely that they're using it in the vague hope that they'll kill the general."

"I know it seems a little bit far-fetched. Hear me out. The general has a standing order with Cake My Day. Every morning on his way to the general's, Nick stops by Cake My Day to pick up four Carrot Cake Cupcakes. That way the general gets his sugar fix, and he has something to serve his lady friends when they drop by."

I couldn't help chuckling. "He serves his girlfriends cupcakes?"

"The general is still quite the ladies' man. You wouldn't believe how they fuss over him. My first morning here, Nick didn't want a cupcake when he delivered them. He said they didn't sit well with him and that he much preferred the cupcakes from Sugar Baby. I didn't give it much thought, but after eating one that day, I felt a little tired and queasy. The next day, at the cupcake feast, I was apprehensive, because I didn't know which cupcake came from Cake My Day. I had no problems at all. Of course, I left before trying all the cupcakes. So this morning, when Nick brought the Carrot Cake Cupcakes, I ate one. I felt fine."

"That was dangerous!"

"It was either that or have it tested, and I figured testing could take weeks. Originally I thought they might only use fava beans in the Carrot Cake Cupcakes. Maybe it gives them a special flavor? My theory was dashed this morning when I didn't get sick. But now that I've seen Clarissa's reaction, I wonder if they've stopped including the fava beans out of fear they'll be found out."

I sat up straight as pieces came together like a puzzle in my mind. "Renee prepared her frosting for the cupcake feast at Cake My Day. Spenser claimed she had mixed up flour with powdered sugar. Then the cupcakes she baked that night at Cake My Day and tried to sell the next day had to be pitched. Spenser told me that he'd replaced all their ingredients because they couldn't afford that kind of mix-up."

Alex's eyes narrowed. "It's possible then, that someone used fava-bean flour at one time, but it's now gone."

"If someone replaced the flour with fava-bean flour, wouldn't they have realized something was amiss? How much fava bean does it take for someone to get sick?"

"It varies. Some people are very sensitive to fava-bean pollen and get sick just from inhaling it. It's entirely possible that fava-bean flour was mixed in with the bakery's regular flour. No one else would have noticed, but it would have had an impact on the general over time." His fingertips touched mine. "Do you think Spenser intentionally switched the flour with the powdered sugar so he would have an excuse to get rid of the tainted fava-bean flour?"

"I had thought Spenser might have wanted to sabotage Renee's cupcakes, but what you're saying makes so much more sense." It frightened me to think that either Spenser or Clarissa would have been so calculating.

"But why would they want to hurt the general?" he asked.

"Alex, I'm somewhat hesitant to say this, especially since I've been the victim of an ugly rumor myself, but a couple of people have mentioned a romantic relationship between the general and Clarissa." I sucked in a deep breath to build up courage. "Is it remotely possible that Clarissa has been adding fava-bean flour to their ingredients to knock off the general because he ditched her or threatened to tell Spenser?"

His chin lifted, and I feared I had crossed a line. "There's a question I can get to the bottom of. The general might be a ladies' man, but he does not lie. Not ever."

He rose and reached for my hand to help me scoot out of the banquette. "I hope you didn't think I was being forward earlier when I squeezed your knee. I didn't want you to mention my fava bean issue too soon. Sorry."

If only he knew how excited I'd been! I tried to be nonchalant, even though I wanted to leap into his arms. "No problem. I'm glad you stopped me. The look on Clarissa's face told us more than she would ever have admitted."

I slid out of the banquette and, much like the first time we'd met, he wrapped a strong arm around me. But this time, his lips—

My kitchen door slammed open. Natasha smiled at us, but Mars didn't.

Natasha sailed into my kitchen, hooked her arm through Alex's and chattered at him.

"Excuse me? What are you doing here?" I demanded.

Mars huffed a breath of hot air. "Natasha insisted on coming over to check on you."

"I'm fine, thank you. Now go away."

Natasha never took her eyes off Alex. "He was just leaving. We'll walk him out. I haven't had any time to spend with him. You must tell me—how's the general?"

I waved at Alex. When he was out of earshot, I turned to Mars. "Better hurry, or she'll eat him alive."

After he left, I latched Daisy's leash onto her and set out for a walk with a destination in mind. I didn't care if Spenser was having an affair. It wasn't my problem that he didn't come home at night. But I had some questions, and he had the answers.

We walked to the hotel where I'd seen him a few nights before. It was a dog-friendly place, so I didn't hesitate to take Daisy inside. I looked around for a house phone, found one, and asked to be put through to his room. He didn't answer.

The desk clerk smiled at me. "Dogs drink for free on our terrace."

"Thanks. I'm looking for Spenser Osbourne. You wouldn't happen to know where he went?"

"I'm not allowed to say. But if he had a dog, it would be drinking for free."

I headed straight to the terrace. Small yet inviting, it was completely enclosed by a privacy fence. A few dog owners enjoyed the spring night with their canine companions. Spenser sat at a corner table by himself, focused on an iPad.

We walked over to him. I allowed Daisy to approach him first. She nudged him with her nose and waggled all over when he petted her. "Mind if we join you?"

He set aside the iPad. "Please do."

I have to admit that I was glad to see him in a public place. No one could claim we'd been up to shenanigans in his room. I ordered a sparkling water for me and regular water for Daisy.

"Since you have a lovely outdoor room in your backyard that is much nicer than this," said Spenser, "I have to assume that you came here to see me."

"I understand that you're reluctant to talk about Maurice. But you could have told me that you bought the golden cupcake from him."

"I told you that I bought it from someone who needed money. That was certainly true. He and his wife made some poor business decisions, so I offered to buy it. It was a way of handing them some money without expecting repayment. Okay?"

Did I sense some testiness? "Didn't the police suspect Maurice when you were burglarized?"

Spenser wiped the side of his face. "He had an alibi that was confirmed by half a dozen people. He spent the evening at a local pub. I understand he even sang—out of tune—which proved helpful to him because it was so memorable."

If Maurice hadn't stolen the cupcake, then how had he come into possession of it again?

Spenser interlaced his fingers on the table and flicked his thumbs. Definitely annoyed. But I didn't care. Since he was angry anyway, I took a chance. "Tell me about you and Renee."

"There's nothing to say. She was an employee of mine once. Look, Sophie, I don't wish Humphrey any ill will, but he had that cupcake in his car. I'm happy to let the cops deal with it."

I went for guilt. "This morning, I attended a business meeting and was ushered out in shame. Your wife insisted her organization shouldn't hire me because I was sleeping with you. And tonight, when I was engaged in a romantic moment with a very fine man whom I would like to know much better, your wife barged into my kitchen because she thought I was with you. Now you may not like me making inquiries about your life. I understand the desire to be a private person, but Clarissa is being a royal pain in my neck. Frankly, I think I deserve some answers from you."

I recognized that my argument went awry at the end. Maurice was probably the source of the rumor about us, and that had nothing to do with all the peculiar things that were going on, but it was all I had.

Spenser signaled the waiter, who brought him an Irish whiskey. He must have spent quite a few evenings out on the terrace if the waiter knew his preferred drink.

Spenser leaned forward, his forearms on the table. "Do you know what they call cupcakes in England?"

I didn't.

"Fairy cakes. Renee bakes fairy cakes. They're lighter than air. Like biting into a piece of a cloud. She's a little bit like a fairy, too, don't you think? She flits around, always smiling, always cheerful. There was a time when Clarissa and I were having some problems. And I was madly in love with Renee." His eyes met mine. "I want to be clear. Nothing ever happened between us. She was my employee, and I wasn't going to play around. Besides, I was still married."

He nursed his drink. "Then Clarissa said she wanted a divorce. I agreed. Everything was quite amicable. That was when I bought the miniature cupcake. Renee loves miniatures, and it opens, so I thought hiding a ring in it would be the perfect way to propose.

"But that never happened." I'd expected him to tell me of an affair, but it wasn't that way at all. Proposing with the gold cupcake would have been charming.

"The burglary happened instead. I was away, and when I came back, Clarissa was—different. She clung to me. For a while she was afraid to be in the house alone. I didn't have the heart to leave her then. Eventually she got back into her charity work. Now she's ridiculously jealous. I think she's afraid of losing me, but the truth is"—he sucked in a deep breath—"she has driven me away with her rants and tantrums. I know they stem from her fears, but I can't live this way anymore. I moved out the day you picked up the desk."

He smiled and stroked Daisy's head. "I checked into this hotel because it's dog-friendly, and I thought I'd be bringing Buddy with me. Haven't been home since. The irony of it all was that she sold *my* grandmother's desk. If she'd sold it to anyone but Renee, I'd have said no. That little desk suits Renee. It found the right home."

"Thank you for sharing that. I hope things work out for you." I stopped short of mentioning Humphrey's interest in Renee. "I don't suppose there's any truth to the rumor that there's something between Clarissa and General German?"

Spenser guffawed so loudly that dogs and their people turned to look at him. "Aw, that's priceless. Where do people get these things? I'm afraid there's as much truth to that as there is to the rumor about us. However, I have to give the general credit. I hope I can flirt like he does when I'm his age. He has no shortage of lady friends." Spenser leaned toward me and lowered his voice. "He has a standing order with us for carrot cake cupcakes. Four a day. They tell me he makes a pot of coffee, serves the cupcakes, and entertains ladies! Isn't that grand?"

I thanked him again, paid for our drinks, and said good-night.

We left the hotel through the front door. Standing like a sentinel, directly to the right, his arms crossed over his chest, was Alex.

CHAPTER THIRTY

Dear Sophie,

I just don't get what everyone else sees in cupcakes. They're always dry, even when I bake them at home.

Parched in Dryville, Pennsylvania

Dear Parched,

That's a common problem. You're probably baking your cupcakes too long. Cut back their baking time by a minute or two.

Sophie

If Daisy hadn't wagged her tail and pulled me over to Alex, I probably wouldn't have noticed him.

His mouth grim, he said quietly, "Clarissa alert on the right at the bottom of the stairs behind the azalea bush."

"Did you follow me?"

"No. I followed Clarissa, who followed you. And I might

add that I am not pleased with you. The second I left, you ran to Spenser. Did you tell him about the fava beans?"

We walked down the stairs, Alex to my right. "I did not. Didn't even mention them."

"What did you talk about?"

"Spenser wants to be like the general when he's that age." Alex laughed. "Who wouldn't?"

"You'll probably be just like him."

"I doubt it. It's a joke in our family that I got the general's serious side, and Nick inherited his flair for women."

"Don't sell yourself short."

His fingers twined into mine. Suddenly the walk home was positively romantic, and I wished I lived farther away.

At my front door he leaned in to kiss me, but Humphrey practically barged into us.

Loaded down with a giant duffel bag and a laptop case, he said, "Quick, open the door before they see me here!"

I unlocked the door, and Humphrey hurried inside.

"Is this about Renee and Myra?" I asked.

"They won't leave me alone. *Please*, can I stay here tonight? Sleep! I need sleep!"

"Of course. Pick a bedroom and make yourself at home."

I turned to Alex, but the moment was gone. He brushed my lips lightly with his and departed. Just as well. His divorce wasn't final, and there were enough rumors about me as it was.

In the morning, I was still floating in the glow of a new romance—until I saw Mars peeking in the window of my kitchen door. I opened the door, and Daisy's tail spun in circles at the sight of him.

"I haven't had coffee yet. I hope you're not here because of a problem."

"I just came by to ask if you would drop Daisy off at my house this morning. I'm on my way to a breakfast meeting or I'd take her."

I hated to think of Daisy locked in Mars's home office all day. "Why don't you pick her up on your way home?"

"It's okay. Leon is there. He has promised me that he won't let Natasha lock her in my office anymore."

I put the kettle on and spooned coffee into the French press. My heart heavy, I agreed. It wasn't as though I had much choice. Daisy had already spent part of Mars's week with me. "Poor Daisy."

Mars kissed me on the cheek, tickled Daisy under her chin, and took off out the door.

I let Daisy out into the backyard.

Humphrey shuffled in from the foyer, still wearing pajamas. He stretched his arms above his head and yawned. "Glorious quiet. Thanks for letting me hide out here, Soph."

"My pleasure. Hash browns and eggs with runny yolks?" It was one of his favorites. I poured coffee for both of us.

He ambled over to the island and located my grater. "That would be wonderful. Do you mind if I hang out here?"

"Not at all." I handed him the potatoes. "What should I tell Renee or Myra if one of them calls?"

Daisy scratched at the door. I let her in, and she danced in excited circles.

"Hmm, would you mind if we didn't answer your phone? You have an answering machine, right?"

Daisy ran to the door to go out again.

"What's with you this morning? You were just out there. Make up your mind, Daisy."

I let her out, washed my hands, and sliced fresh strawberries for a fruit salad while Humphrey grated the potatoes. "Okay. I can hear if it's a business call. But you're going to have to face them sooner or later. What are you going to do while you're in hiding?"

"Ah! I have big plans for my uninterrupted peace. I must get to the bottom of this terrible accusation of grand larceny. I intend to make spreadsheets to consider the various possibilities."

I had never considered spreadsheets. "Good idea," I said.

"Sometimes it helps to write down the facts. To look at the information in a different way."

"For instance," said Humphrey, "are you aware that none of this started, not even Muffin's murder, until that Alex fellow came to town?"

I nearly cut my finger. "You can't be serious. He doesn't even know the people involved."

"Then why has he been hanging around Cake My Day at odd hours?"

I hoped he'd been spying on Spenser. "He's considering the purchase of a building next door to Cake My Day." My heart thudded a little bit, though. Who visited a building at odd hours? I tossed the strawberries with sweet chunks of cantaloupe and tart green grapes. A squeeze of lemon and a breeze of sugar, a couple more good stirs, and I set the bowl on the table.

Daisy had returned. I opened the door. "Are you sure you want to come in this time?"

She trotted in, wagging her tail, but she didn't settle down. She sniffed around on the kitchen floor. Looking for crumbs, I assumed.

"How can you be so sure about Alex?"

"How can you be so sure about Renee?" I heated a frying pan for the eggs. "There's no evidence tying Alex to anything. That's silly. You'd make more progress if you thought about Renee."

"As irritated as I am with her constant neediness, I still don't think she murdered Muffin. And she most certainly didn't steal that cupcake. Hey, did you take trash out to the alley last night?"

"No."

"That's strange. I could have sworn I heard you. I was exhausted, though. Maybe I dreamed it."

The potatoes sizzled in the pan and turned a crispy golden brown. Humphrey slid them onto plates, and I topped them with the eggs. I'd made an extra one that I put in Daisy's bowl for her breakfast with a little bit of the crispy potatoes.

We sat down to eat. "Is Spenser one of your suspects?" I asked.

"Should he be?"

"He seems like such a nice man. Almost too nice. Generous when his friends need help. Yet I can't help thinking that he's involved somehow."

"I'm more suspicious of Nick."

"Nick? Why?"

"You heard Myra and Joy talking about him. He took every cent Joy had. He enticed her with romantic notions of a life together and left her broken and broke. A golden cupcake would make him salivate."

"But would he have brought it to the gala cupcake dinner with him? What would be the point of that?"

Humphrey and I tossed ideas around with no success. We ate the last few bites of our breakfast, and cleaned up the kitchen.

I showered and pulled on a skort. The memory of Alex's touch came flooding back to me, and I swiftly changed into a casual sky blue dress with a square neckline. A pair of gold earrings, a necklace, and I was ready to go. It was still a little early for sandals, but I didn't care, because they looked so cute with the dress. The blue discoloration around my eye had lightened in spots to a sick yellow-green. Lovely. I managed to cover most of it with makeup, but it still showed.

And then I had to do the thing I'd been putting off—deliver Daisy to Natasha. I clipped the leash onto her harness. She pulled me to the kitchen door. It eased my reluctance to let her go. If she was that excited, it wouldn't be fair to deny her fun time with Mars.

But when we stepped outside, she yanked on the leash so hard that it slipped out of my hand. She raced for the backyard.

I could see her snuffling something by the back gate. I broke into a run. Was someone lying in my backyard?

CHAPTER THIRTY-ONE

Dear Sophie,

My wife says we should use dog treats to train our dog. I think he'll get too many and become overweight if we do that. Do you use treats as a reward for your dog?

—Dooley's Dad in Treat, Arkansas

Dear Dooley's Dad,

Daisy loves treats. The thing to remember is that dogs don't care about the size of the treat—they care about getting that little reward. Use very small treats. Dooley will be just as thrilled as he would be if you gave him a big treat.

—Sophie

I screamed. Was it a corpse? Or was he still alive? His face was a bloody mess. He wore jeans and a black leather bomber jacket. He didn't move, even when Daisy stuck her nose right over that horrific face.

I ran back to the kitchen, slipping and sliding in the

sandals. Daisy galloped ahead of me. I threw open the kitchen door. "Humphrey! Call 911! We need an ambulance right away. Tell them to come to the alley."

I slid off the sandals and wet an entire roll of paper towels. Daisy wanted to go back with me. I dodged her at the door and, barefoot, ran back to the man.

I knelt beside him, afraid to touch him. His nose was bent at an unnatural angle that made me wince. Should I wipe the blood off his face or not?

Reaching for his wrist to check for a pulse, I pulled my hand back in horror. He wore gloves. We were way past glove weather. Unless he'd ridden a motorcycle to get there, I couldn't think of a good reason for him to be wearing gloves. He'd been up to no good.

Some teeny little part of me feared he might jump at me like a bad guy in a horror movie, but he lay so still that I suspected he had died.

A siren sounded in the distance, and Humphrey ran across my yard toward me.

He gasped at the sight of the man. "Is he alive?"

"I don't know. I'm afraid to do chest compressions. What if he's bleeding internally?"

The first responders rushed in.

I moved out of their way, not having done anything to help the poor guy.

Wong hustled toward me. "Do you know who that is?"

"No. Maybe I should have looked for identification." I filled her in on how Daisy had found him.

"Have you touched anything?"

"I didn't even touch *him*. I didn't know what to do."

"I have a pulse," said one of the emergency medical technicians. "Hate to cut this sleeve, though."

Nevertheless, he sliced through the sleeve of the man's leather jacket and slid a needle for an IV into his vein.

"Must have been out here all night," said Wong. "It's too hot for a warm jacket like that now."

She walked closer to him. "What's that?"

The medical technician closest to the man's head shrugged. "Beats me. The prongs of a ring maybe?"

I edged over, trying to see without getting in the way. The shoulder of the jacket had been damaged, but so slightly that I hadn't even noticed. Tiny dots formed a circle about a quarter of an inch in diameter. The shape seemed familiar to me, but I couldn't quite place it.

They removed him in minutes, leaving Humphrey and me with a pack of cops securing the alley and my backyard.

I was about to retreat to the house for a much needed cup of tea when Wong called me over.

"Recognize this?" She pointed to a shovel.

"I have one just like it in my garden shed. I'd be willing to bet it's not there now, though."

She followed me to the shed. "Don't you lock these doors?"

"No. There's nothing in here except garden equipment."

Exactly as I had expected, the shovel was gone.

Humphrey and I returned to the kitchen. I put on a pot of tea and thanked Daisy for alerting me. She eagerly accepted her reward of a homemade dog cookie in the shape of a bone.

※

The last thing I wanted to do was take Daisy over to Natasha's house. But when she called and insisted, I had no choice. In a gloomy mood, I walked Daisy over to Natasha's.

I rapped the knocker on the door. Martha yipped inside.

Natasha opened the door a crack, quickly stepped outside, and pulled it almost shut behind her. "You brought Daisy. Thank you!"

Strange conduct for Natasha. Why did she want Daisy so much all of a sudden? She positioned herself in front of the door, reminding me of Clarissa's odd behavior when I went to her house to tell her I wasn't seeing Spenser. "Are you hiding something from me?"

"No."

"Then why are you acting weird?"

"Sophie, I have no idea what you're talking about. If you don't mind, I'm in the middle of something."

"Is that why you closed the door instead of inviting me inside?"

She huffed at me. "No, it's because of Martha. She'll run out into the street."

Of course she would. How many times in my life had I done the same thing because of Daisy and Mochie? Did Spenser and Clarissa have pets? I hadn't seen any when we picked up the desk. No one had said anything about not letting a cat or dog out.

"Sophie!" Natasha squealed.

"Thanks. You've been very helpful." I jogged down the stairs with Natasha yammering at me.

For once, I actually ran the few houses to Nina's. I hammered on her front door.

She opened it wide. "What's wrong?"

"Aha! You don't have a dog in here. Where's Spenser's cell phone number?"

She handed me a slip of paper with the number on it. "What's going on?"

I grabbed the phone on her kitchen wall and dialed. When Spenser answered, I asked, "Do you or Clarissa have any pets?"

"No."

"Hah!" I raised my palm to high five with Nina, who looked at me in complete confusion. "I think Clarissa has Buddy."

Spenser agreed to meet us at his home in fifteen minutes. Nina laced on running shoes, and we walked over as fast as we could. On the way, I filled her in about the man who had been hurt in the alley behind my house. Spenser met us at his house, plunged his key into the lock, and opened the front door.

The house was silent. Too quiet.

"Do you think Clarissa is home?" I asked. I certainly didn't want a scene. Then again, if I was right about Buddy, it would be worth the risk.

Spenser glanced at his watch. "She's probably still having her nails done. We're safe."

But when we walked into their living room he howled. "What the blazes has she done?"

I had to admit that it looked a bit sparsely furnished.

He waved his hand toward the fireplace. "She sold the painting. And the antique tea table."

Spenser appeared dumbfounded.

"Mind if we look for Buddy?" asked Nina.

He didn't reply, as though he was deep in his own thoughts.

Nina motioned to me. In the entrance hall, she said, "I'll scout around down here, you take the upper level."

I dashed up the stairs, my optimism waning. I hadn't heard a bark or a growl. Buddy would be impossible to hide. Peering in the bedrooms and the closets was eerily reminiscent of the day we'd found Muffin's body.

Footsteps on the stairs proved to be Nina.

"I don't see anything downstairs. I think you were wrong, Soph. I'm sorry. It was a good thought."

I was having serious doubts of my own. We peered into the master bedroom. Clarissa had chosen sea foam green walls with a white ceiling and white woodwork. A fireplace served as the focal point, flanked by tall windows. A mahogany bed and matching nightstands dominated the room. White linens covered the bed, which hadn't been made. One side was covered with books. I tilted my head to look at them. All by Agatha Christie.

I sighed and entered Clarissa and Spenser's walk-in closet. I'd been so hopeful.

The closet had been expertly outfitted. Even in my dreams I hadn't conceived anything so fabulous. Clarissa's dresses hung in orderly sections. Her shoes were lined up like little soldiers on special shelving. A rainbow of purses were organized by color. She'd tossed some clothes over chairs in the middle of the closet. The sleeve of a suede jacket hung down, and on top of it lay jeans she'd worn. And there, sticking out of a pocket, was a tiny corner of yellow.

CHAPTER THIRTY-TWO

Dear Sophie,

My neighbor's dog is seriously ill after eating a piece of birthday cake. It wasn't chocolate. The vet says it was the type of sugar in the cake. I didn't know that sugar is toxic to dogs.

—Worried in Sugar City, Colorado

Dear Worried,

The cake might have been made with xylitol, a sugar alternative found in sweets and sugar-free gums. It's extremely toxic to dogs. Even a small amount can be harmful and the effects come on fast, leading to liver failure and death.

—Sophie

"Nina!"

She came running.

I seized hold of that tiny corner of fabric and pulled out a cupcake bandanna exactly like the one Buddy had worn. "I don't think I was wrong."

"I'm sure they sold more than one of those."

"She doesn't have a dog. Why would she have bought one?"

"Because she expected Spenser to bring Buddy home?"

"Spenser left her that day."

Nina grabbed the bandanna. It flew like a flag in her hand when she ran down the stairs. "Spenser, Buddy is here somewhere."

"The basement." Why hadn't I thought of that to begin with?

I ran through the hallway to the kitchen and flung open the door. Buddy looked up at us like he wondered why we'd taken so long. Nina and I cheered.

No dog had ever been hugged or patted more. His tail whipped back and forth.

Spenser came running. He fell to his knees and clutched Buddy like a long lost friend.

"He looks okay." Nina ran her hands over him. "What's she been feeding him?"

I opened some cabinets. "Looks like canned dog food and kibble." Unfortunately, they also had a box of xylitol, a sugar substitute. "Does Clarissa bake much? She wouldn't have fed Buddy anything with xylitol, would she?"

"Clarissa hasn't turned on the oven in years. We live off of takeout."

That was a relief.

"If it's okay with you, Spenser, I'll swing Buddy by the vet's just to be sure he's okay," said Nina.

"That's fine. I'll pick up the tab. In fact, I'll go with you." He was still hugging Buddy when he said, "I'm so sorry. I can't imagine what possessed Clarissa. She must have seen the flyers. She must have known we were all looking for him."

"Spenser, the day that we came for the desk, you and Clarissa had just had a big blowout of an argument. Did that have anything to do with Buddy?" I asked.

He finally released his grip on Buddy and stood up. "I told her about Buddy. I was so excited about him, like a little kid." He ruffled the fur on Buddy's neck. "The argument was about you. She confronted me and wouldn't believe that we weren't

having an affair. Then you showed up on our doorstep." He
snorted. "Kind of funny when you think about it."

Buddy sniffed the kitchen floor while we talked.

"Why would she steal him?" asked Nina.

Spenser squeezed his forehead between his palms. "I have
no idea. I feel like I'm married to someone I don't know
anymore. Why would she sell all our stuff? I can't explain
anything she does." He lunged toward Buddy, grabbed his
collar, and pulled him away from potted plants on the floor.
"You don't want to mess with that, Buddy. It's thorn apple."

"Is that the same thing as jimsonweed?" I asked.

"Might be. All I know is it's poisonous. Clarissa likes the
way it blooms out back in the summer. It's very showy, with
loads of big blossoms. I wish it weren't poisonous. Clarissa
brings it in every winter so it won't die."

Nina pulled out a leash and collar she'd brought along.

Spenser latched them onto Buddy, who appeared to enjoy
all the attention. We headed for the front door.

Spenser locked it behind us and sucked in a deep breath.
"I need to have a long talk with Clarissa. You don't think the
police will press charges, do you?"

"After what she put us through?" cried Nina.

Spenser nodded somberly. "Even after all that."

I walked home alone, wondering about Clarissa. Were
Bernie and I the only people who wouldn't want such a poisonous plant around? Even if it was incredibly beautiful?

I phoned Francie on the way back to tell her the good news
about Buddy. "How would you like to come over for a late
lunch?"

"I'll meet you in your backyard in half an hour."

I told her she'd better come to the kitchen and use my front
door.

Sometimes I wondered if Mochie was lonely when Daisy
stayed with Mars. I needn't have worried. He was sprawled
in his new hammock bed and didn't even open one eye when
I checked on him. But through the large sunroom windows,
I could see out my open gate. The police were still checking
things in the alley.

Humphrey had settled in my small family room with the drapes drawn. "To escape prying eyes," he explained. He was delighted to hear that Buddy had been rescued.

I headed to the kitchen to make a quick lunch. I poured pineapple juice into a pot with red quinoa and put it on the stove to cook. A little olive oil in a pan, and three chicken breasts were sautéing in no time. I sliced fresh strawberries, creamy avocados, juicy kiwis, and tangy pineapple spears, and set them aside. I squeezed tart lemons and added the juice to iced tea for a refreshing drink.

When the quinoa had finished cooking, I mounded it on three white plates. I sliced the chicken breasts and laid the strips across the quinoa, then surrounded them with the avocado and fruit. In case someone wanted a dressing, I whisked together a cherry balsamic vinaigrette.

I threw a sky blue tablecloth on the table and added the plates and yellow napkins. Francie barged in my kitchen door with Duke. "What in Sam Hill is going on out there?"

Humphrey joined us. We sat down to eat and filled her in on the strange events of the morning.

"I'm surprised you didn't hear anything," I said.

"I heard the sirens, but didn't think much of it. So who do you think the mystery guy could be? Any chance it's that louse Maurice?" she asked.

"Not unless he cut his hair and dyed it. The guy had nice, thick dark hair."

Humphrey's mouth twisted as though he wanted to say something but was uncomfortable about it. "Sophie, I didn't want to upset you, but I think it's Alex."

"What?" I nearly choked. "Why would you think a thing like that?"

"Right build, right coloring. Dressed kind of snazzy. I knew he was trouble."

"No!" cried Francie. She frowned at Humphrey. "I attended the cupcake feast with Alex. He was a lovely, attentive gentleman all evening. Why would you say such a thing?"

"None of this tumult started until he came to town."

"That could be a coincidence," I insisted. But I hadn't

heard from him about the general and Clarissa, either. I excused myself to call him but got his voice mail. It wasn't him, I was sure of it. At least, that was what I kept telling myself. Humphrey had been right about the size and coloring, though.

On my return, Francie wanted to hear the saga of locating Buddy. "I'm so thrilled. I've worried about him every day. I can't tell you how many e-mails I sent asking people to be on the lookout for him."

"I think Buddy will be in good hands with Spenser." At least, he would be if my newest theory about Clarissa panned out. "So tell me more about jimsonweed."

Francie put down her fork. "Uh-oh. I know you too well, Sophie Winston. What's up?"

"Just how poisonous is this stuff? Could you, I don't know, put a little bit on a hatpin and scratch someone with it? Would that kill them?"

"Oh ho! Like Agatha Christie!"

"She did that?"

"I believe she used a thorn and snake venom, but that's so hard to find. Jimsonweed is everywhere. And if you don't have any, you can order seeds from a nursery. It's all very legal."

"Or you could have it growing in your very own house."

"Yes, you could." Francie scowled at me. "Did you see it in someone's house?"

"Clarissa has it in her kitchen."

"Oh, that's terribly dangerous. There was a woman who mistakenly used the seeds in a stew and made everyone ill. I think you could be on to something. Did you know that kids try it to get hallucinations?"

I eyed her suspiciously. "You didn't just happen to know that."

"While you were busy finding injured men and rescuing Buddy, I was on the Internet researching jimsonweed. Bernie's plant got me thinking about it."

"So how come the doctors didn't find anything? Wouldn't it show up on blood tests?" asked Humphrey.

"I don't think they search for it. In most of the anecdotes, the authorities figured it out based on what the people had eaten."

"Did Agatha Christie write about causing a fall by tying a wire across steep stairs?"

"Doesn't ring any bells, but she was fond of pushing victims so that they fell to their deaths. Why the questions about Agatha Christie?"

"Clarissa had a collection of Christie's books on her bed."

"That's meaningless. I have hundreds of books in my house. You could accuse me of all sorts of things on that basis."

"Me, too," said Humphrey.

"I suppose you're right. Besides, I don't know of any reason for Clarissa to want to kill Joy. I don't think Joy ever worked for Cake My Day. I don't see a connection."

"I think we both know by now that the connection isn't always obvious. I don't see any dessert. When we're through here, how about you trot down to Sugar Mama and pick up some dessert? Meanwhile, I'll make a few phone calls to see what I can turn up."

Humphrey offered to do the dishes as long as I promised not to reveal his whereabouts to Joy.

Before I did anything else, I placed another call to Alex to be sure he was okay—and got voice mail again. Well, that wasn't reassuring at all!

CHAPTER THIRTY-THREE

Dear Natasha,

I've been asked to bake cupcake sandwiches for a dinner party. I have no idea what that means. Are they cupcakes or sandwiches? Sweet or savory?

—In a Pickle in Sandwich, Illinois

Dear In a Pickle,

A cupcake sandwich is sliced through the middle or just under the top. Frosting or a filling is applied to the bottom and the top goes over it, just like a sandwich. You can make them savory or sweet. And you can even frost the top if you want!

—Natasha

I hurried to Sugar Mama on the pretense of inquiring about buying samples for my clients. I waited until the bakery had emptied and then asked Joy to sit with me for a minute.

We discussed the samplers and arranged a date for me to

pick them up. Joy was thrilled with the prospect of catering cupcakes for large events.

"It looks like you're doing pretty well. The bakery was packed when I arrived."

She gulped. "My cupcakes are selling, and don't get me wrong, I'm grateful for that, but it's hard doing everything myself. I never get a minute off. I'm here all the time, and it's not as much fun as it was with Renee. We worked hard but we were friends, you know?"

Joy had been a lousy friend! I couldn't come right out and say that, of course, but judging from the misery on her face, I suspected she knew.

"How could I have been such a dolt? I'm not a kid. I'm not one of those girls who ditches her girlfriends just because a guy shows some interest. I can't believe I bought into Nick's lies. He had me convinced that we were going to be the next Spenser and Clarissa." She adjusted the band on her ponytail. "I abandoned all my values. He had me believing that I deserved Sugar Baby's money. Now, of course, I realize that it was because he wanted it for his own use." She shuddered. "I was a traitor. I turned my back on the best friend I ever had." She gazed out the window at Sugar Baby across the street. "I miss Renee and Muffin."

"I guess that means you no longer think Renee is trying to kill you?"

"She did steal my grandmother's ring, and I'll never forgive her for that, but . . . I don't know what to think. I've only been staying at Myra's a couple of days, but somehow I'm not scared anymore. And nothing weird has happened. Isn't that peculiar? All the terror came to a screeching halt. What do you think it means?"

"It might mean that Myra is a very nurturing person and you feel safe now. Or it could mean—"

"I know, I know. That Nick got what he wanted and no longer has a need to get rid of me."

"Joy, why do you think Renee stole your grandmother's ring? It sounds so much more like something Nick would do."

"Only Renee and Muffin knew where it was. That sort of counts Nick out."

Clearly, Renee or Muffin could have told someone else, but it could have been anyone, so I didn't bother pointing out the obvious to her. "Did you ever work for Spenser?"

She laughed. "I think I'm one of the few cupcake bakers in town who hasn't!"

"How well do you know Spenser and Clarissa?"

She opened her eyes wide. "I don't exactly run with Clarissa's crowd. Some of them come in to buy their cupcakes here, but I don't really know the charity ladies who lunch."

"How about Spenser? Didn't you tell me he was a regular at Sugar Baby?"

"He was. But I didn't know him well. Just to say hi. Exchange a few pleasantries."

I thanked her and left. That notion had fizzled to nothing. But as I walked home, I spied Maurice slinking into The Laughing Hound.

Maurice brought out conflicting emotions in me. He'd taken a chance in life with his cupcakeries, which was to be respected and admired. It hadn't worked out, and he'd lost everything. He deserved sympathy for that, even if he'd been a hardhead and hadn't listened to good advice. If only he weren't so hateful. Still, I had accused him of stealing Buddy. I didn't have to stoop to his level of nastiness. The least I could do was apologize with grace.

I followed him into The Laughing Hound and found him at the bar. Moe saw me coming, and I glimpsed fear in his eyes.

I walked up beside Maurice. "Moe," I said, "how about a drink for Maurice? On me."

Maurice didn't turn to face me, but his eyes shifted and he watched me with distrust.

"Maurice, I'd like to apologize to you. We located Buddy, the black and tan dog, this morning. It's clear that you had nothing to do with that. I'm sorry that I . . . we blamed you."

"I'll have a Guinness." He waited until I paid for it before saying, "Apology not accepted. You put me through great embarrassment by sending the police to my home."

He was treading on extremely thin ice, considering what he'd put me through with that idiotic rumor he started. I tried to take the high road. "I'm sorry about that."

He wore a short-sleeve shirt, revealing a square white bandage taped to his right arm.

"I heard you were bitten by a dog. How is your arm?"

"I'm looking for the vicious cur. If I don't find it, I'll have to get rabies shots. It shouldn't be allowed to run loose."

I hadn't heard anything about a potentially rabid dog roaming Old Town. "What does the dog look like?"

"White, with long fur, and mean, beady little eyes."

It was all I could do not to laugh. He had to mean Martha. "So it *was* you!"

Moe stopped working to listen in.

"*You* brought the golden cupcake to the dinner. What did you do, drop it? Then, when you tried to take it away from Martha, she bit you forcing you to drop it again?"

"I don't know what you're talking about."

"Oh, but I think you do. I think you know that stealing that thing was grand larceny."

"I did not steal it. It was mine."

Ohhhh! The man was so aggravating! I had to work at keeping a level tone so I wouldn't screech at him. "You sold it to Spenser."

"He cheated me. He knew I was in desperate need of money. It was worth three times what he paid."

I took a big chance. "So you broke into his home and stole it back from him?"

He faced forward and didn't look at me. "I did not! I had nothing to do with that whatsoever."

"Then how did you come into possession of it?"

"Moe, this woman is annoying me. Would you kindly escort her out?"

"She's friends with my boss. Sorry, Maurice."

He swung toward me suddenly, the limp white hair hanging in his face in the most unappetizing manner. "Tell your police friend, Wong, that if she wants to know who staged that burglary, she doesn't need to look farther than Mr. High-and-Mighty I-Have-More-Money-than-Anyone Spenser Osbourne."

"Spenser? Are you saying that he staged the burglary of his own home?"

"All I know is that I found *my* precious cupcake in a hidden compartment in the desk Renee bought from Spenser. Who else would have hidden it there?"

I steadied myself by holding on to a barstool. Spenser? I knew he was in the middle of everything that was going on, but he'd had an alibi for the burglary of his house. Had he and Clarissa been in cahoots? Was that why she didn't like to talk about it? Because it never happened?

I glanced up at Moe, who shrugged. Did I dare believe Maurice when he'd told so many lies?

Still, he'd gotten the gold cupcake somewhere, and the bite on his arm proved the validity of Humphrey and Leon's theory about Martha dropping the cupcake in Humphrey's car.

Or had he just made a very big mistake by trying to get Spenser into trouble? It was a good thing my hair couldn't actually stand on end, because it would have at that moment.

CHAPTER THIRTY-FOUR

Dear Sophie,

I'm making dinner for my new in-laws, and I'd like to bake cupcakes for dessert. I've never baked anything in my life. Any tips?

—Nervous Newlywed in Toast, North Carolina

Dear Nervous Newlywed,

Read through the whole recipe before you start so there won't be any surprises. Let the butter and the eggs come to room temperature. Be sure to beat in the eggs very well. In many recipes, you can mix together the dry ingredients. Whisk them together to blend well before adding them to the batter. Good luck!

—Sophie

I simply said good-bye and walked out, forcing myself not to run so he wouldn't realize what he'd just done. Outside of the restaurant, I sucked in air and leaned against the wall. If he wasn't lying, Maurice had just placed himself at the scene of Muffin's murder. If he really had found the cupcake inside the desk, it meant he had been inside Renee's apartment.

I called Wong and got her voice mail. There wasn't anything I could do but leave a message. I left a message for Detective Kenner, too. Why weren't they answering their phones?

I walked home, checking over my shoulder now and then. It wouldn't take long before Maurice realized that he had implicated himself. Had he snuck inside and been discovered by Muffin? Had she seen him with the golden cupcake? Or had he tried to seduce her and been rebuffed? The police would have to sort it out. They'd fingerprinted the apartment. Had they found his prints there?

Or was it all just another big lie designed to cause trouble for Spenser? If so, Maurice had caused himself bigger problems this time.

I checked for Francie in the backyard when I came home. It wasn't until that moment that I realized I had forgotten all about buying cupcakes. No sign of Francie yet. Inside, Humphrey napped in the family room with Mochie.

My nerves on edge, I busied myself in the kitchen, placing butter and eggs on the counter to come to room temperature before I baked with them. I poured sugar, water, and corn syrup into a pan and watched the sugar crystals turn golden then amber. I whipped it off the burner and mixed in cream to make caramel. It fizzed up at me, which was exactly how I felt inside—in fizzy turmoil at the thought that dreadful Maurice had murdered Muffin, the one person who had been nice to him.

I set the caramel aside to cool and preheated the oven.

Stirring a fork through flour to mix it with baking powder, baking soda, and salt, I wondered if I should ask for Daisy back. She wasn't much of a watchdog, but she might alert me if Maurice realized his mistake and came looking for me.

I creamed the butter with the sugar and added the eggs. Maybe I should wake Mochie. He would probably run to the door or window if he heard something. Or at least perk up and turn in the direction of the sound. I left the KitchenAid mixer running and went to rouse him. He was lounging comfortably on Humphrey's stomach. Carefully, so I wouldn't disturb Humphrey's nap, I swept Mochie into my arms. Back in the kitchen, I explained that I was in need of his superior hearing at the moment. He yawned.

I deposited him on one of the fireside chairs in my kitchen with instructions to keep one ear on alert. He ignored me completely and curled into a comfortable ball to nap again.

I mixed the other ingredients into my cupcake batter, divided it among twelve cupcake liners in the pan, and slid it into the oven.

Maybe I was being silly. Or maybe not. I had seen Maurice behind Sugar Baby after Muffin's murder. He'd pretended to be bringing flowers from his garden in Muffin's memory, yet he had neither flowers nor a garden. I bet he'd plucked that azalea branch off a bush on his way to Sugar Baby, just in case he was seen there. Why would he go back? Was it Maurice who had returned to Sugar Baby and tried to break in again? What did he want there?

I let out a little shriek. Of course! He'd left something there, something that could tie him to Muffin's death. That made perfect sense. Humphrey had probably interrupted him by arriving just after Maurice killed Muffin. He had to scurry out the back. Then he returned later that night to look for the thing he had left behind.

I phoned Renee at Sugar Baby. "I'm not sure, but it seems possible that Muffin's killer might have left something in your apartment. Maybe something incriminating. Have you found anything unusual?" The police had surely swept the place carefully, but if Maurice had felt the pressure to go back, he must have thought they hadn't found it.

She said she hadn't spotted anything but promised to check around that evening. I debated warning her about Maurice. I didn't want to be the one to spread false news. On the other hand, her life could be at stake. "I don't have anything concrete yet, but watch out for Maurice, okay? I have a feeling he's up to his ears in this mess."

She asked once again if I'd heard from Humphrey. *Ack*. I didn't want to lie to her. "The last time I saw him, he was going to take a nap."

Thank goodness she accepted that.

I was just cutting little divots out of the cupcakes and spooning caramel sauce into them when Humphrey staggered into the kitchen.

He opened the door for Francie with a bow and a cavalier swoop of his arm.

"Wait until you hear what Maurice said to me." I filled them in while I put on the kettle and fit a pastry bag with a frosting tip. Bending the bag over my hand, I spooned frosting into it. I positioned it over the first cupcake and stopped cold. Turning it upside down, I looked at the tip again. Six prongs.

I rushed to the telephone with Humphrey and Francie asking what was going on. Once again, Wong's voice mail answered my call.

I showed them the frosting tip. "Number ninety-six. I like it for frosting cupcakes because it makes a swirl. It has exactly six prongs. Just like the imprint on the leather jacket that guy was wearing this morning."

I frosted the cupcakes with the caramel buttercream in a hurry and removed the tip from the bag. After washing it, I brought it over to the table and smacked it onto a piece of paper. Six holes. I handed Humphrey a measuring tape.

"Three sixteenths of an inch in diameter," he announced. Francie stared at me like I had lost my mind.

"Don't you see? The man who was injured in the alley killed Muffin! I'd bet anything that the frosting bag in her hand contained a tip that will match that mar on his leather jacket perfectly! She must have fought him and hit him with it."

Humphrey shot me a look of pity. "There's a stretch of imagination."

"What about Maurice?" asked Francie. "That would let him off the hook, but he practically confessed to being there."

I finished the cupcakes by drizzling a little bit of caramel over the frosting. I arranged them on a tiered cake server and placed them in the middle of the table with more yellow napkins and tiny dessert plates.

Francie placed her fists on the table. "I don't know what to think anymore. Maurice is a sour malcontent. He lies so much that I'm not sure we can believe him."

"He wasn't lying about a dog biting his arm," said Humphrey. "And he was in possession of that cursed cupcake."

I tended to agree. "Now that we think it was Martha who bit him, that seems pretty certain. He got the bejeweled cupcake somehow. Either he was the original thief or he's telling the truth about finding it in the desk. Either way, it must have been Maurice who brought it to the cupcake feast intending to plant it on Spenser and get him into trouble."

Francie selected a cupcake. "How would we ever find out?"

"Spenser said Maurice had an alibi the night the cupcake was originally stolen. Something about singing badly in a local pub. I wonder if anyone established the exact time. Maybe Wong can check the records."

I poured tea for everyone and placed their mugs on the table along with milk and sugar. I sliced a lemon, arranged it on a plate, and brought it to the table when I joined them. "What did you find out, Francie?"

"I heard from my old friend Olive Greene. She's such an expert on plants. She thinks we could be onto something—that a prick from a hypodermic needle, or even something as simple as a thorn, that had been coated with the poison from jimsonweed could easily result in hallucinations. She confirmed that it's hard to detect in a medical examination." Francie bit into a cupcake. "Now that's how a salted caramel cupcake should taste! How did it go with Joy?"

"That was a total bust. She barely even knows Spenser or Clarissa. She may have been poked with jimsonweed, but it wasn't by one of them."

"Honey," said Francie, "she doesn't have to know them well. Maybe they needed to get rid of her for some other reason. Maybe she knows something. Hmm, if she was blackmailing them, she wouldn't admit to knowing them, would she?"

"If she was blackmailing them, she wouldn't be broke." Humphrey selected a cupcake.

"Listen to us, we're all over the place." I slumped back into my chair.

"Don't be so discouraged. We've made tremendous progress," Humphrey protested. "Buddy has been found. We've established that Maurice was in possession of the gold cupcake. Martha managed to grab it, Maurice tried to take it away, and must have been successful, because she bit him. He probably dropped the cupcake again, she grabbed it and ran. I found her and put her in my car, where Martha hid the cupcake. That's progress! The question that remains is where did Maurice obtain the cupcake? There's only one answer, of course—from the thief, the person who stole it from Spenser's house. And now it's possible, though I have my doubts, that you've identified Muffin's killer—so to speak."

Humphrey huffed. "I still blame Spenser for the confusion with the flour and the powdered sugar that caused Renee such embarrassment. Spenser must have done it to sabotage her and sink her business." He set his tea mug on the table with a clunk. "How blind I was! I thought he was being generous to offer his bakery to Renee. Meanwhile, he was scheming to put her out of business to improve his own bottom—"

A flashy neon blue fingernail tapped on the glass window in the kitchen door.

Humphrey whispered, "Which one of you betrayed me?"

CHAPTER THIRTY-FIVE

Dear Natasha,

My daughter's ninth birthday is coming up. She wants flowers and butterflies on her cupcakes. Could you demonstrate how to make them on your show?

—Clueless Mom in Flowertown Village, South Carolina

Dear Clueless Mom,

Start by making fondant. When you roll it out, you can cut out butterflies and flowers with tiny cookie cutters. I'll do a show on it because it's fun!

—Natasha

I had no choice. It would have been rude not to invite Myra in. When I opened the door, I discovered Wong was with her.

"Want to join us for a cupcake?" I asked.

"I don't want to intrude." Myra gazed wistfully at Humphrey. Her yellow tunic put the sun to shame. Skintight neon blue leggings came just below her knees.

"Yeah, well, I'm here on business, but if a cupcake is in the deal, I wouldn't turn it down." Wong promptly took a chair.

Myra scooched into the banquette next to Humphrey, who, I noticed, did not scooch away from her.

I put the kettle on for more tea.

Wong wasted no time. "Sophie, did you call me about Maurice?"

"Partly." I held my breath when I asked, "Have you identified the man in my yard?"

"If they have, I don't know about it."

I wished Alex would call! "How did you know about Maurice?"

"Moe called us and ratted on him. What did Maurice say, exactly?" asked Wong.

"That he found the bejeweled cupcake in a hidden compartment in the desk that Humphrey and I picked up at Spenser's house. And that if we wanted to find the thief, we ought to look at Spenser."

"You willing to testify to that?"

Good heavens! I hadn't expected that. "Yes. Of course. Does that mean you've arrested him?"

Humphrey perked up. "That means you can drop the charges against me. Right?"

"Not so fast." Wong bobbed her head slightly. "Kenner brought Maurice down to the station. He's questioning him now. Don't get too excited, Humphrey. There are still too many unanswered questions."

Francie squinted at Wong. "The theory being what? That Muffin caught Maurice stealing the cupcake, and he killed her?"

Myra patted Humphrey's arm. "I'm sorry, sugar, but even I don't buy that. Why would Maurice just happen to go up to the apartment and snoop?"

"Unless, of course, he knew it was there." I set mugs of tea in front of Myra and Wong.

Humphrey said, "Aha! He might have known that if he was the original thief."

Francie laughed aloud. "If he left it in the desk at Spenser's house, then he didn't steal it. I'm sorry to poke a hole in your balloon, Humphrey, but I think I understand what Maurice was saying about Spencer. He means that Spenser hid the cupcake there."

"How could he know that?" I asked.

We all looked at Wong, who had bitten into a cupcake and was the picture of contentment.

Myra shivered. "Gosh, it could have been me he murdered. The way Maurice followed me around—who knows what he might have done? I wouldn't mind seeing him locked up."

Wong finished her cupcake. "Now those are good! Wow." She drank her tea quickly. "I've got to get going."

"Just a second, Wong. Humphrey and Francie think I'm out of my mind." I slid a piece of paper in front of her and pointed to the tiny holes I'd made with the frosting tip.

Wong's smile vanished. "How'd you do that?"

I handed her the frosting tip. "Number ninety-six. Muffin had an icing bag that fell against my foot when we found her. I bet the tip is a ninety-six. It will be stamped right on the frosting tip."

"Can I have this?" she asked.

"Sure."

Wong left so fast that I didn't even have time to offer her a cupcake to go.

Francie yawned. "Time for a nap. Call me if there's another attack in our alley."

Before I knew it, I was alone with Humphrey and Myra. I wasn't quite sure what to do. My instinct was to give them some privacy, but I wasn't sure Humphrey would appreciate that.

I cleared the dirty dishes from the table.

In her soft voice, Myra scolded Humphrey with affection. "I knew you were hiding out. Not from me, I hope? You *could* answer a girl's calls."

He held up his empty palms. "No cell phone. I, uh, lost it."

"Is it Renee? Is she the reason you're laying low? That woman is relentless. I can see why you would want to escape her clutches."

I bit my upper lip to keep from smiling and stacked the dishes in the sink. From my kitchen window, I saw a furtive movement across the street.

Clarissa.

Wouldn't that woman ever give up? On a whim, I took a cupcake and a napkin out to her.

"Why are you being nice to me?" She mashed her eyes closed as though she was in pain. "You feel sorry for me." She didn't take the cupcake, but lowered her face into her hands. "What have I become?" When she lifted her face, tears streaked her cheeks. "I am officially the pathetic clinging wife that I never wanted to be. I saw you at Spenser's hotel last night. And now that your hunky honey knows you're seeing both of them, I will be the loser. Your new beau will be the one who leaves you, not Spenser. Spenser actually told me he doesn't care if you're seeing Alex. He must think I'm making it up."

She fell to her knees on the sidewalk. "Please don't do this to me. Don't you understand? Without Spenser, I'm nothing."

"Oh my goodness! Clarissa, get up."

The poor woman was reduced to a pile of nerves. I held my free hand out to her. There was so much I resented about her. The fact that she stole Buddy and put us all through such misery. Her unflappable belief that I was having an affair with her husband. Her annoying spying and following me. Yet, in that instant, I felt sorry for her. I wasn't the cause of her problems, as she believed, but that didn't change the fact that she thought she was fighting for her life.

She stood up and blew her nose into a tissue. "You can't understand. I don't have a job or children. I'm not a brilliant baker or a . . . well, anything. If I lose Spenser, I have nothing. I won't even have my social position anymore. I will cease to exist!"

"I hope you don't mean that." Was that a cry for help? Should I report it to some authority? She wouldn't take her own life—would she?

She grabbed the cupcake and ate hungrily.

"There are a lot of divorced people. And they—we—all have full lives. It's not the end. Maybe it will be a new beginning for you."

She sniffled. "Couldn't you please just date the general's nephew and leave my Spenser to me?"

"Clarissa, what can I do to convince you that I'm not dating Spenser?"

She finished the cupcake and wiped her fingers on the napkin. "Have a public breakup. And get him to come home. And . . . and never see him again."

"I don't see him now!"

"Hello? How stupid do you think I am?" Holding up her hand, she ticked incidents off on her fingers. "He came to your house. I saw you on the back porch at Cake My Day. You went to his hotel last night. For heaven's sake, you even had the unmitigated gall to come to my home!"

In a monotone, I said, "Yes, I was there to seduce him. That's why I brought Humphrey."

She stomped her foot and mashed her lips together. "You've met in all kinds of painfully public places, like the adoption booth at Cupcakes and Pupcakes."

"You saw him there? Is that why you stole Buddy?"

Some of the steam evaporated from her anger. "He told me about the dog. He was so excited and happy—in a way that he hasn't been for a long, long time. Then I confronted Spenser about you, and he said he was leaving me. I . . . I couldn't let him have the dog, and a new house, and a life without me. You wouldn't understand."

But I did. She had tied her entire existence into being Mrs. Spenser Osbourne. "I hope you find Clarissa again one day."

She seemed perplexed, but I returned to my house. Humphrey and Myra had left the kitchen. I washed the dishes, knowing I should get some work done, but I was boggled by the thought that the unknown person lying in a hospital bed might be Muffin's killer. Who had attacked him last night? And why had he been in my backyard? Even worse, what if he was Alex? Had I been enchanted by a killer?

Humphrey and Myra took off to walk, as they called it, "the scene of the cupcake caper." They intended to go over to the park where the cupcake feast had been held, then follow Martha's path through Old Town to the spot where she'd been found. I couldn't imagine that they would learn much from that, but it was worth a shot.

Too rattled to work, I called Alex again. He didn't answer, and at the general's home an answering machine picked up my call.

I had to know if the injured man was Alex. Surely they'd discovered some kind of identification on the man when they undressed him. I locked the house and drove to the hospital.

CHAPTER THIRTY-SIX

Dear Sophie,

My grandmother used to make heart-shaped cupcakes for us. She didn't have a special pan. I can't figure out how she did it. I'd like to do it for my kids.

—Nana's Favorite in Heartville, Illinois

Dear Nana's Favorite,

Make three balls out of foil for each cupcake. Place one between each cupcake liner and the pan for the top, and one on each side of the point. Presto—hearts!

—Sophie

My fears were confirmed when the first person I saw in the emergency room was the general. Always the gentleman, he used the arms of his chair to push himself up. "Thank you for coming, Sophie."

I hugged him, afraid to ask whether it was Alex or Nick who'd been so brutally beaten. "Is there anything I can do?"

"You're helpin' just by bein' here, darlin'." He lowered himself into a hard plastic chair. "He was such a pretty boy. Who'd have ever thought that would lead to his downfall? Half the nurses in the emergency room hold grudges against him."

It was Nick. *It was Nick!* How utterly horrible of me to be so happy that *it was Nick*!

What was Nick doing in my backyard? I glanced at the general. He'd been so warm toward me. "I hope you don't think I'm one of the women who is angry with him."

His fingers rubbed against each other. I could almost feel the wheels in his brain turning as they moved. "Did you ever go out with Nick?"

"No. I hardly know him. But I've, um, heard about his exploits."

His head hung low. "I never knew he was taking their money. I'd have put a stop to that, and fast. That boy needed some real discipline. I wish I'd known. He's a black mark on our family. How dare he bring shame on us like that?"

I had a hunch he didn't know about the possibility that Nick was also a killer. I figured it wasn't my place to break it to him. After all, it wasn't even confirmed yet.

Across the waiting room, I spotted Alex asking a nurse a question. He turned, and a glimmer of a smile brightened his face briefly when he saw me. He joined the general and me. I reached out my arms to him. He embraced me and leaned his head against mine.

When he released his grip, I asked, "How's Nick?"

"There's good news and bad. Nick was incredibly lucky. There doesn't appear to be any brain damage." He grinned at the general. "Seems he has a thick skull like the rest of us Germans. But it's fractured, and he suffered a concussion. His appearance will never be the same. His nose is broken, and his facial bones will require surgical repair. They'll operate when he's stabilized."

The general scowled. "The cops have been talking to you. Do they have any ideas who might have been so vicious?"

"Not yet. Maybe Sophie would give you a ride home, General."

The general's hands tightened on the armrests of his chair. "Not a chance. I need to be here for that boy."

I rose to leave, but the general took my hand in his and tugged gently. I bent over to him.

Whispering, he said, "I'm not in the habit of entertaining married women. There has never been anything between Clarissa Osbourne and me. But if she divorces Spenser, I might give her a call."

He was adorable.

Alex walked me to the door. "Thanks for coming. Nick's parents are on the way. Once they're here, I think the general will go home and get some rest. He's a tough old bird. I hope Nick inherited some of those genes. He's going to need them. His life will never be the same."

It would be even worse than Alex imagined, since I was fairly sure Nick would be facing prison on his release from the hospital. "Call me if you need anything."

I drove home thinking about Nick. Had someone figured out who'd murdered Muffin and taken revenge? Or had someone like Joy or Myra, who'd been left penniless by Nick the lothario, attacked him in retaliation?

I phoned Nina, but once again, voice mail answered. I parked the car and sat outside in my little pavilion, staring at the spot where Nick had fallen.

Rubbing my face with my hands, I tried to make sense of everything. Why would Nick have murdered Muffin? For the bejeweled cupcake? That would presume that he knew about it. When we delivered the desk, Muffin had said something about defending Renee because she had been wronged. Had Muffin argued with Joy? Nick might have come to Joy's defense. Surely that wouldn't have been enough reason to kill someone.

Besides, if Nick was Muffin's killer, then how had Maurice come by the cupcake?

My head swam with theories. I thought I was on to something with all those Agatha Christie books on Clarissa's bed and the jimsonweed growing in her house. Unless . . . I sat up straight. Unless Clarissa hadn't meant to hurt Joy. What if Joy had never been her target? At the cupcake feast, there were people milling around in a tight cluster after the general fell to the floor. Clarissa could have easily jabbed the wrong person with the jimsonweed poison.

And there was one other person living in the apartment where someone had booby-trapped the stairs—Nick.

I could feel a flush of heat in my face. Alex thought Spenser or Clarissa was trying to kill the general, but Nick could have been the intended victim, because he suffered from the same disease, and he was the one who had picked up the cupcakes every day.

But what was Clarissa's connection to Nick? The rumor. That odd rumor about Clarissa paying Nick to keep quiet about an affair she was having with the general. He'd clearly denied it, and Alex said the general never lied. Then why might Clarissa be so desperate to kill Nick? Had she lured him to my backyard last night?

Unless I missed my guess about his gloves, he had come prepared to dispatch *her.* Why had they met here? How could she have convinced him to come?

Money. How stupid of me. Money drove Nick. I had paid attention to the wrong part of the rumor about Clarissa and the general. Clarissa was paying Nick for something. And it must have been major if Nick was willing to kill her, too. Something that implicated them both?

I could only think of one thing that big—Muffin's murder. But that didn't follow, either. If Nick had murdered Muffin, why would Clarissa be paying him?

I finally wandered back to the kitchen at a loss. I debated calling Wong again, but Humphrey returned, and I filled him in about Nick.

His eyes narrowed. "Why would Nick be in your backyard?"

"Great question! Did you discover anything on your cupcake caper?"

"Actually, I did." He sat down. "Myra is fun. She's whimsical."

"So you've decided to date her?"

"Not exactly."

"Oh?"

"I'm having dinner with Renee tonight."

"I thought they were driving you nuts."

He blushed.

"*Aww.* Humphrey, I'm glad to see you enjoying yourself." To be honest, I had hoped he might hang around tonight. "Will you be going home after that, or coming back here?"

His eyes widened. "I forgot about *you*! I'll change my plans. Renee will understand."

"You'll do no such thing, but I wouldn't mind if you slept over tonight. I'd feel safer if someone were here with me. I'm sure I'm being silly, but I'm a little uneasy after the attack on Nick last night."

"I'll cut dinner short. Actually, that suits me very well. When Renee cooks up some kind of project for me, I'll tell her I promised to be here for you."

"Thanks, Humphrey."

Determined not to be home alone, when Humphrey went over to pick up Renee, I walked with him and popped into the bar at The Laughing Hound. At least I would be in public. If that loony Clarissa got a notion to get rid of me so she could have Spenser, I wasn't going to make it easy on her.

I climbed onto a barstool. Moe was less than delighted to see me there.

"What can I get you, Sophie?"

"I'll have the gossip du jour, please."

He laughed. "You're never going to let me forget that. I ought to invent a drink called Gossip. Let me think about that. It should be exciting—"

"But wrong somehow—not what it seems. And it needs to have a little kick, too."

"Sounds like a Long Island Iced Tea. Could I make one for you?"

"I think I'd rather keep my wits about me. Maybe a regular iced tea tonight?"

He nodded and promptly brought a tall glass over to me. "We're all upset about Nick. What he did to those women was the lowest. But to pay for it with his life! He pushed one of them too far."

"His life?"

"Haven't you heard? He died."

CHAPTER THIRTY-SEVEN

Dear Natasha,

I don't have the sewing skills to sew matching dresses for my dog and me. Is there something easier that I could make?

—Muffy's Mom in Golden, Colorado

Dear Muffy's Mom,

Sew a bandanna. All you have to do is hem the edges of a triangle and sew on sequin trim. You can do that by hand. Add the same glittery trim to one of your outfits!

—Natasha

If I hadn't been to the hospital myself and heard from Alex that Nick would be okay, I would have believed it. I stared at Moe. He'd been a source of so much incorrect information that I was skeptical. Of course, Nick could have taken a turn for the worse after I left. Or had the cops started that rumor to prevent his attacker from finishing the job? "I didn't know that. I'm shocked." I was. "Do the cops have any leads?"

"They were in here this afternoon asking questions. His latest conquest is that Realtor, Kayla. But Joy took a big hit, and she's been very public about it. Wonder why none of those women brought charges against him?"

I could only guess. "Maybe because they gave him the money voluntarily?"

Someone slid onto the seat next to me. "You owe me a drink. A lot of them."

Maurice. *Ugh.* The police must have released him. Maybe coming here hadn't been a good idea after all. At least I was surrounded by people. I nodded at Moe who poured Maurice a Guinness.

"You just can't leave me alone. Why do you insist on blaming me for everything that happens?" asked Maurice.

"Why did you spread a lie about me?"

Maurice rested his elbows on the bar. "Everybody knew you broke up with Wolf, and that you would date a married man."

"But it wasn't true. Why would you do that? Poor Clarissa believes it."

"That was the point, dummy."

I swung around to see his face. "You meant to create friction between them?"

"You bet. I want Spenser to know what it feels like to lose everything." He smirked. "My little plot to taint his cupcakes didn't work so well when Renee used the ingredients in her cupcakes. Didn't see that one coming."

"*You* swapped the flour for the powdered sugar?"

"Now don't go telling the cops, blabbermouth. It was a harmless prank."

He broke into Cake My Day to do it! That was a crime, not a prank. But I kept my mouth shut.

"And I didn't kill Muffin. I liked Muffin. And I don't like many people, especially not you."

That I believed. "I saw you there that night."

"You caught me coming out. I only went there to find something that would incriminate Spenser."

I nearly fell off my barstool. I didn't want to sound

accusatory, because he might stop talking. "And you found the cupcake?"

"It couldn't have been more perfect. That slimeball Spenser hid it in the desk. All I had to do was drop it in his car and report it to the cops. He would have been in so much trouble. A big, fat public scandal that would have ruined him."

"But that didn't work."

"I'll have another one, Moe," he said. "I tried to drop it into the sunroof, but it rolled off the car, and that stupid dog swiped it."

In retrospect, it was sort of humorous. I didn't dare chuckle, though.

The door to the kitchen opened, and Bernie beckoned to me. "Soph? Could you give me a hand?"

"Sure." I paid for Maurice's drinks and left a nice tip for Moe. Even though he'd spread rumors about me, he might prove a handy source of information. People undoubtedly told him all sorts of things when a few drinks had loosened them up.

I followed Bernie through the kitchen and out to the alley.

Natasha was waiting there with Daisy and Martha. "Bernie kicked us out!"

Daisy had difficulty wagging her tail. She'd been dressed in a tight outfit with ruffles all over it, including on the pants! I ran my hand over her head and rubbed behind her ear.

Bernie crossed his arms over his chest. "Natasha, you can't bring dogs into the restaurant. Everyone knows that. I'll lose my license."

"It's a business meeting! How many times do I have to tell you, Bernie? Daisy and Martha are part of the business venture. They're my models."

"Fine. Just not here."

"I can't walk out on this meeting! These are very important people. I'll lose the deal. It will ruin my name. This is embarrassing, Bernie. I'll never patronize your restaurant again!"

"If only that were true. Look, have your meeting. But without the dogs. Okay?" He took the leashes from Natasha and handed them to me. "Will you *please* take them home?"

"Of course."

"It won't be the same without them. They won't be able to see the dogs in their darling attire."

Martha wore a red doggie ensemble. *Was that silk?* The fabric matched Natasha's chic 1950s-style red dress. She'd replicated the voluminous skirt and the neckline on Martha's outfit. Natasha's purse matched Martha's leash and collar.

"Don't worry, Sophie. I made you an ensemble exactly like the one Daisy is wearing."

I swear Daisy looked up at me, laughing. I didn't want to imagine how my hindquarters would look in all those ruffles. I unfastened the dresses and handed them to Natasha. Daisy shook like a wet dog. "All right, let's go home. Good luck with your meeting, Natasha."

Bernie pecked me on the cheek. "I owe you one, Soph."

"Wait a second, Sophie." Natasha reached into her purse. "You'll need this." She handed me Martha's glittery ball.

I slid it into my pocket. The dogs strained at their leashes. Had Natasha cooped them up all day? I might have enjoyed the mild night if I hadn't been worried about Maurice catching up to us.

Two blocks from my house, Spenser and Buddy fell into step with us.

"I think I might shed some weight now that I have Buddy." Spenser breathed heavily. His white running shoes were so new that they almost glowed under the streetlights.

I couldn't help being a little bit leery. Even though I suspected Clarissa of trying to do Nick in, Spenser had the strength and the size to have inflicted those wounds on Nick's head.

"Buddy seems very happy."

"I'm looking for a place with a fenced yard. Do you go to the dog park? I think Buddy would like to romp with other dogs."

"Mars takes Daisy to the dog park sometimes."

We'd reached my house. "See you around, Spenser."

He followed me. "Um, would you mind if the dogs played in your backyard for a while?"

I hesitated. Wasn't this the perfect kind of scam to get me

alone? What was I afraid of? Spenser had no reason to want to hurt me. It was Clarissa who was the nut. "Sure."

We released the dogs in the back, and I turned on the lights that sparkled overhead in my outdoor room. Spenser sat down. He held a ball that he'd brought with him, but the dogs shot to the spot where Nick had lain in the morning. I assumed it teemed with interesting scents.

Excusing myself, I returned to the house for drinks. I mashed a banana and added coconut milk and pineapple juice for virgin piña coladas. I carried the drinks out the kitchen door but stopped short when I heard voices. Walking slowly, I peered around the corner of the house. Clarissa!

The dogs raced toward me. To be on the safe side, I coaxed them into the kitchen and locked the door.

Leaving the drinks on the counter, I slipped through my dark living room and cracked open one of the French doors to hear what they were saying.

"I'm begging you, Clarissa. This has to stop."

"What do you see in her, Spenser? I'll change. I'll do whatever you want."

"Did you know that the police questioned me today about the cupcake that was stolen? They think I lied about the theft and hid it in my grandmother's desk. You wouldn't know anything about that, would you?"

Silence.

"Clarissa, if you've withheld anything about that night, it's time to come clean. Did you hide the cupcake? Did you sell all the other things that you claimed were stolen?"

"It was Nick," sobbed Clarissa. "You and I were going through that terrible time, and Nick was so flattering. He made me feel special again. It took me a long time to realize that he didn't love me, and that when he called me his sugar mama, it wasn't cute. He thought of me as a bottomless money pit. That night, when you were in Miami, I cut him off—and he went wild. There was never a burglary—not by a stranger anyway. Nick took everything he could. I was scared out of my mind. I told everyone I was under the bed and couldn't see who was ransacking the house, but the truth is that I was so scared of Nick that I locked myself in the bathroom and didn't come out until morning. He's been blackmailing me ever since. I couldn't tell you I'd had an affair with him. I needed you more than ever. I was afraid not to meet Nick's demands for payment. I can't lose you, Spenser. You're all I have. I need your love."

I hated to eavesdrop on her confession to him. It was personal and private, and I shouldn't have listened. But given everything she'd said, I feared she had been the one who'd maimed—or killed—Nick.

I ran for my cell phone and called Wong, who finally answered her phone. I explained the situation. She said she was already in transit. Tiptoeing, I returned to my eavesdropping spot, the dogs nosing around my feet.

"How did the cupcake get into the desk? Did you hide it from Nick?"

"He's no dummy. I didn't know he'd hidden it in our house. He said it was too hot to sell. I knew he'd stashed it somewhere, but it never occurred to me that it was in our house all along. But when he saw the desk being unloaded at Sugar Baby, he called me—spitting mad. I told him it was his own fault. If he hadn't pressured me for money all the time, I never would have sold it.

"Spenser," she said, her tone hopeful, "can you ever forgive me? We're good together. And now that Nick is dead, if you'll just give up Sophie and come home, we can put our lives back together."

"Why are you here, Clarissa?"

"It's your girlfriend's fault. She told me that if I didn't know where my husband was, I ought to find out. I followed her, and she led me straight to your hotel. Tonight, I followed you. I hoped you wouldn't be with her. Now that Nick is gone, Sophie is the only thing standing between us, Spenser."

CHAPTER THIRTY-EIGHT

Dear Natasha,

I'm sewing a dog bed, but I have no idea how big it should be. Is there a rule of paw to follow?

—Crafty in Sleepy Creek, West Virginia

Dear Crafty,

Measure your dog from his nose to the end of his tail. Add six inches on each end. Then measure him from his paws to the top of his head and add six inches on each end. Those are your measurements!

—Natasha

"Sophie is nothing to me."

I never thought I'd be so happy to hear a man utter *those* words!

"I would like to believe you," said Clarissa. "But if that's true, then why are you here?"

Uh-oh. That wasn't good. Not good at all. Where was Wong?

I watched as Clarissa stood up.

Spenser shouted, "Clarissa, please!"

I threw open the door. The dogs shot toward them, and I raced behind. When we reached them, Clarissa sat on Spenser's lap with her arms around him.

"Can't a girl get a minute alone with her best guy?" she asked.

Thankful that she wasn't aiming a gun at him, I blurted out, "You were reading Agatha Christie to figure out a way to kill Nick!"

Clarissa cocked her head and pouted. "The fava-bean flour in his cupcakes didn't work. How was I supposed to know he wasn't eating them?"

"So you tried to prick him with jimsonweed."

Spenser's expression contorted. "Clarissa! You didn't!"

"Stupid Joy got in the way."

"And then you tied a string on his stairs, hoping he'd trip."

"In Christie books, they always die from a fall . . ."

"Did you lure Nick here by promising him money?" I asked. "Why here?"

"So it would look like you clobbered him."

Spenser lurched to his feet. "Clarissa, what have you done?"

Wong barreled into my yard from the gate that led next door to Francie's house. Wong was all business. "I'd like you to come down to the station with me for questioning, Clarissa."

Clarissa's chin trembled.

"How about if I take Buddy home, and we meet you there, Officer Wong? Would that be okay?" Spenser sounded reassuring.

Clarissa buried her head in his shoulder.

Wong smiled. "I'm sure Sophie wouldn't mind babysitting Buddy for a few hours."

Hah! Wong wasn't letting Clarissa slip away.

I beckoned Wong over while Clarissa untangled herself from Spenser. "Did Nick die?"

"Rumors move fast around here." She smiled at me. "No truth to that one. Hey, everyone down at the station was mighty curious about your frosting tip."

"Nick hasn't confessed yet?"

"His lawyer never leaves his side."

Aha. Everyone needed a cousin like Alex. "So we still have no idea why he killed her?"

She winked. "Nothing I can share with you, cupcake."

~~~

Two days later, I opened the local newspaper to find the headline "Local Socialite Fends Off Killer." I settled at my kitchen table to read the article.

"Clarissa Osbourne could have been the next victim of Nick Rigas, who allegedly murdered Muffin Pruitt in an apartment over the Sugar Baby cupcakery. Osbourne, charged with attempted murder, claims she saved her life by fighting back when attacked. Women have rallied to her aid, causing her to become a media sensation. Apparently Rigas had sweet-talked money out of women of every age and description."

Spenser must have hired a humdinger of a lawyer to twist the facts that way.

Nina opened my door, holding the paper in her hand, and Francie barged in with her.

"Did you see this?" asked Nina.

"Alex better be a great attorney," I said. "I'm amazed by the way they're describing what happened. Have you heard anything about Maurice?"

"He's already out on bail! I can't believe it after all the sneaky things he did."

Francie frowned. "He was an idiot to cross the police tape and sneak around in Renee's apartment. You'd think he would have realized that. I heard he claimed taking the cupcake from the desk wasn't stealing because it once belonged to him. Now, let me see if I have this straight. He wanted to plant the cupcake in Spenser's car and report it to get Spenser into trouble?"

"That's what he told me." I hooked Daisy's leash onto her collar.

Nina roared. "But Martha grabbed it and wouldn't give it back to him. When he took it from her, she bit him, grabbed the cupcake, and ran! What a feisty little girl she is! Spenser isn't pressing charges against Maurice for breaking and entering at Cake My Day, so if he has a good attorney, he might just get some community service."

"Humphrey's feeling much better now that all the charges against him have been dropped, but Renee and Myra are still driving him nuts." I locked the door, and we walked to Bernie's new house, located kitty-corner from mine.

Naturally, Muffin's murder was the talk of the neighborhood when we gathered in Bernie's backyard for a housewarming barbecue. Moe manned the grill, and all the food was catered by The Laughing Hound.

Bernie caught up to me. "I hear we're going to name a house drink Gossip."

Moe hoisted a beer. "I'm working on it."

"What's the latest gossip?" I asked.

"Sort of sad." Moe flipped a rack of ribs. "Clarissa is getting all the attention, but Muffin was the brave one who stood up to Nick."

"What I don't understand," said Mars, "is why he didn't take the cupcake with him. Why was it still there for Maurice to find?"

"I think I know the answer to that." I accepted a glass of iced tea from Bernie. "Humphrey barged in. There's a little bell that dings when someone enters the cupcakery. I'd bet Nick was in a panic and left out the back way as fast as he could. There were cupcakes baking! It all must have happened pretty fast."

Renee overheard and rubbed the base of her throat uncomfortably. "I'd bet anything that it was Nick who was trying to get in that night after I moved back."

"Think he didn't know that Maurice had removed the cupcake?" I asked.

Renee sipped from a glass of wine. "That's all I can imagine. Spenser heard Muffin shouting about Joy's grandmother's ring the day Nick killed her. I bet he found it and sold it."

Moe scratched the side of his head. "Word around town is that Sophie's devastated because Spenser went back to Clarissa."

I burst out laughing. "I can't be devastated, because there was never a relationship to begin with. And I'll share a little news. Spenser didn't go back to Clarissa. I happen to know he bought a house with a doggy door and a fenced yard in the back for Buddy."

We'd hesitated to invite both Renee and Joy, but Bernie insisted a barbecue was the perfect place to mend fences. It amused me, though, to see Humphrey caught between Renee and Myra.

Evidently Myra had taken Francie shopping. Francie's bubblegum pink top over zebra-striped leggings was a huge departure for her.

Martha the Chihuahua wore a dress of abstract pink and green swirls on a white background and a double strand of pearls. Natasha wore the same thing. It looked better on Martha.

I noticed that Leon held her leash. "Is Martha still biting Natasha?"

Leon grinned. "Every chance she gets. Natasha has come to the realization that she's not a dog person."

The rest of us had known it all along.

Natasha sidled up to me. "I don't see Alex."

"He should be along anytime. Are you giving Martha back to the breeder?"

"Heavens, no! Martha will be a show dog. She'll travel with her handler, and when she comes home—"

"She gets to stay with me." Leon picked up Martha and cuddled her. "Natasha and I will be co-owners."

Sounded like a perfect arrangement to me.

"So you're out of the doggie-clothes business?"

"It's entirely Bernie's fault. If he hadn't thrown me out, I'd be the queen of a clothing empire right now." Her scowl morphed into a beam. "Alex! I'm so glad you could make it." Natasha snaked her arm around him. "Let me introduce you to everyone."

"I'd like that, but someone is picking me up in a few minutes. I'm afraid I can't stay."

"I'm so disappointed." Natasha didn't let go of him.

Bernie, Mars, and Moe watched from the grill. A trio of maiden aunts couldn't have looked more critical.

"I hope I'll see you when I return, Natasha." He stepped out of her grasp. "Sophie, could I have a quick word?"

We left through the gate. I didn't have to turn around to know Natasha's eyes were blazing.

Alex twined his fingers with mine. "When I said I wanted to practice law here, I never imagined that my first client would be a relative. Now I guess I'll have to come back."

What could I say that wouldn't frighten him? That would let him know I was excited by the prospect of him living in Old Town but wouldn't be too sappy? "I hope—"

He cut me off in the very nicest way, by kissing me. A horn honked.

"That's my ride."

"What happened to your car?"

"I sold it. It never was my style. My law partner talked me into it. I think it was *his* dream car, actually. What I've always wanted . . ."

"What?"

He acted sheepish. "You'll think I'm silly."

"A lot of my friends are silly."

"You've probably never heard of it anyway. Ever since I was a kid I've wanted an Alfa Romeo Spider. A vintage one seems like just the right thing for Old Town."

Maybe there was hope for us after all. A spider wasn't a beetle, but it was close enough. We snuck another quick kiss, but the horn honked again.

"Impatient driver," he grumbled.

He ambled backward, still holding my hand as long as he could. When our fingers no longer touched, he turned and jogged to the car waiting in the street. His car. His snazzy BMW, being driven by the person I had to presume was its new owner—the general.

༺༻

After dinner, Renee called out, "Everybody, I'd like to show you all something."

She held a platter of cupcakes. "You won't believe what I found in the freezer this morning. Muffin must have been working on these the day she was murdered. She told me she'd come up with a recipe for a chocolate hazelnut cupcake that she loved. I thought it would be nice to share them with you."

There was something unsettling about eating cupcakes that had been baked by a deceased person. I didn't rip the paper off right away. Of course, there was no point in keeping them. Maybe Renee had the right idea. Maybe the way to honor Muffin was to enjoy her last effort.

Joy shrieked. "Is this some kind of trick?"

"No." Renee seemed confused. "What's wrong?"

"I don't believe it." Joy split her cupcake open to reveal a ring. "It's my grandmother's ring. The one from Tiffany." She looked up at Renee. "Did you bake it into the cupcake?"

Renee swallowed hard and fought back tears. "No. Muffin must have been on to Nick all along. She hid it for you some-place she knew he would never look."

Joy and Renee burst into tears.

Even some of the men wiped their eyes.

Renee and Joy hugged, and it was as though a spell had been broken.

But even as Joy and Renee chattered to catch up, I saw Renee and Myra shooting killer glances at each other. They shuttled Humphrey between them, each calling him over or dragging him away from the other one.

After a particularly nasty exchange, a hush fell over every-one, and Joy proclaimed, "It's time you two ended this. You're both my friends. I say Humphrey should pick between you and end this foolishness. So which one is it? Myra or Renee?"

I expected Humphrey to be confused, to balk. Instead, he smiled with a twinkle in his eye. "I don't think there's any need to choose right now."

Humphrey was right. I laughed aloud. He loved being sought after and deserved the attention.

I looked over at Mars. Alex had left, but he would certainly be back. I lifted my glass in a toast. "To new friends, and old ones." I didn't need to choose anyone right now, either.

RECIPES &
COOKING TIPS

Salted Caramel Cupcakes

CARAMEL

> 1 medium-sized heavy-bottomed saucepan
> 1 wooden spoon
> ½ cup heavy cream
> 1 cup sugar
> ¼ cup water
> 1 tablespoon light corn syrup
> 2 tablespoons unsalted butter
> ¼ teaspoon fine sea salt
> 1 teaspoon vanilla

Have all ingredients ready to use. Warm the cream in the microwave for about 30 seconds. In a medium-sized heavy-bottomed saucepan, mix together the sugar, water, and light corn syrup. Stir with a wooden spoon and turn the heat up to medium high. Stir until the mixture begins to bubble. Immediately quit stirring. Watch until the mixture turns a rich golden amber. Do not allow the mixture to burn! Remove from heat immediately. Stand back and pour in the cream, stirring to mix. The cream will sizzle up, but stirring will combine the ingredients. Stir in the butter and salt. When completely mixed, cool for 3 minutes. Stir in the vanilla. If not using immediately, cover and refrigerate when cool.

CUPCAKES

1½ cups flour
1 teaspoon baking powder
¼ teaspoon fine sea salt
½ cup unsalted butter (1 stick), at room
    temperature
1 cup sugar
2 eggs, at room temperature
1 cup milk
1 teaspoon vanilla

Preheat oven to 350. Place 12 cupcake liners in a cupcake pan. Combine the flour, baking powder, and salt in a bowl. Cream the butter with sugar. Add the eggs and beat well for about 3 minutes. Alternate adding the flour mixture and milk until completely mixed. Add the vanilla and mix.

Divide among cupcake liners. Bake 20 minutes or until a cake tester comes out clean.

FROSTING

6 tablespoons unsalted butter (¾ stick)
3 cups confectioner's sugar
¼ cup heavy cream
¼ cup caramel (recipe above) plus extra

Cream the butter, adding the sugar ½ cup at a time, alternating with the cream. After the second cup of the sugar is added, mix in the caramel. (Mix in more sugar if necessary to achieve desired frosting consistency.) Cool cupcakes on a rack before frosting. Drizzle a tiny amount of caramel over the top of each cupcake.

(Makes 12 cupcakes)

Strawberry Cupcakes

This recipe uses almost an entire 16-ounce box of strawberries, but it's split between the various steps. Please note that these cupcakes do not freeze well.

CUPCAKES

> *¾ pound fresh strawberries*
> *1 cup sugar, divided*
> *½ cup unsalted butter (one stick), at room*
> *   temperature*
> *2 eggs*
> *½ teaspoon fine sea salt*
> *1 teaspoon baking powder*
> *1½ cups flour*
> *3 tablespoons heavy cream*
> *1 tablespoon vanilla*

Preheat oven to 350. Place 12 cupcake liners in a cupcake pan. Mash the strawberries with a potato masher. Sprinkle with ⅓ cup sugar and stir to combine. Set aside. Cream the butter with the remaining ⅔ cup sugar. Beat in the eggs. Beat in the sea salt and baking powder. Beat in the flour, alternating with 1 cup of the mashed strawberries. Add the cream and vanilla and beat. Fill cupcake liners almost full and bake for 16–18 minutes or until a cake tester comes out clean. Cool on a rack before frosting.

FROSTING

>   4 tablespoons unsalted butter (½ stick)
>   ¼ cup mashed strawberries
>   pinch of salt
>   3 cups confectioner's sugar
>   3 tablespoons heavy cream

Beat the butter with the salt and strawberries. Add the sugar and cream, alternating until you reach the desired consistency.

FILLING

Carve a small cone out of the top of each cupcake. Drop ¼ to ½ teaspoon of the mashed strawberries into each hole and replace the top. Frost the cupcakes.

(Makes 12 cupcakes)

Lemon Meringue Cupcakes

CUPCAKES

>   1¼ cups flour
>   1 teaspoon baking powder
>   ¼ teaspoon baking soda
>   ¼ teaspoon kosher salt
>   6 tablespoons unsalted butter (¾ stick), at room
>   temperature
>   1 cup sugar
>   2 eggs, at room temperature
>   ½ cup milk
>   1 teaspoon vanilla
>   4 tablespoons lemon juice

Preheat oven to 350. Place 12 cupcake liners in cupcake pan. Mix the flour, baking powder, baking soda, and salt in a bowl. Cream the butter with the sugar. Add the eggs one at a time and mix well. Alternate adding the flour and milk. Add vanilla and lemon juice and beat well. Divide between cupcake liners, filling only half-full. Bake 16-18 minutes or until a cake tester comes out clean.

FILLING

> $\frac{1}{3}$ cup sugar
> $\frac{1}{3}$ cup water
> pinch of salt
> 2 tablespoons cornstarch
> 2 tablespoons cold water
> 1 egg yolk
> $\frac{1}{8}$ cup lemon juice
> $\frac{1}{2}$ teaspoon butter

Combine the sugar, $\frac{1}{3}$ cup water, and salt in a small saucepan and bring to a boil. Meanwhile, mix the cornstarch and 2 tablespoons of cold water into a paste. Add it to the boiling sugar mixture, stirring constantly until thick and clear. Remove from heat. Whisk the egg yolk together with the lemon juice and pour into the cornstarch mixture. Stirring constantly, return the mixture to heat and cook until it boils again. Remove from heat and stir in the butter. Cover and cool. If not using right away, refrigerate when cool.

MERINGUE

> 2 egg whites
> pinch of salt
> $\frac{1}{4}$ cup sugar

Combine the egg whites and salt and beat until they just begin to take shape. Add the sugar and beat until glossy.

ASSEMBLY

Bake the cupcakes and make the filling. When the cupcakes are cool, make the meringue. Cut a divot out of the center of each cupcake. Fill with the lemon filling. Replace the caps that were cut out. Frost with the meringue and bake at 350 for 4–5 minutes or until the meringue is set.

(Makes 12 cupcakes)

Caution: Raw egg warning. The meringue will not cook enough to kill salmonella or other food-borne illness.

Basic Vanilla Cupcakes

> 1¼ cups flour
> 1 teaspoon baking powder
> ¼ teaspoon baking soda
> ¼ teaspoon salt
> ⅓ cup vegetable oil
> ⅓ cup milk
> 3 tablespoons heavy cream
> 1½ teaspoons vanilla
> ¼ cup unsalted butter (½ stick), at room
>   temperature
> ½ cup + 1 tablespoon sugar
> 2 eggs, at room temperature

Preheat oven to 350. Place 12 cupcake liners in a cupcake pan. Mix the flour, baking powder, baking soda, and salt in a bowl. Mix the oil, milk, cream, and vanilla in another bowl. Cream the butter with the sugar. Beat in the eggs one at a time. Add roughly ⅓ of the flour mixture, then ⅓ of the milk mixture, beat well, and alternate between them until all ingredients have been incorporated. Pour into cupcake liners. Bake 16–18 minutes or until a cake tester comes out clean. Cool on a rack before frosting.

(Makes 12 cupcakes)

Coco Loco Cupcakes

Please note that these cupcakes freeze very well.

CUPCAKES

    1 cup flour
    ¼ cup high quality unsweetened powdered
        chocolate, like Penzey's
    1 teaspoon baking powder
    ¼ teaspoon baking soda
    ¼ teaspoon salt
    6 tablespoons unsalted butter (room temperature)
    1 cup sugar
    2 eggs (room temperature)
    1 ounce unsweetened chocolate (1 square)
    ½ cup light coconut milk
    1 teaspoon vanilla extract

Combine the flour, powdered chocolate, baking powder, baking soda, and salt in a bowl and mix well with a small whisk or a fork. Melt chocolate square in microwave in short bursts.

Cream the butter with sugar. Add each egg and beat well. Add the flour mixture in small amounts, alternating with the coconut milk. Beat in the melted chocolate and then the vanilla. Beat to combine.

Divide between cupcake papers, filling each about half-full. Bake 15 minutes or until a cake tester comes out clean.

(Makes 24 cupcakes)

Coconut Creme

FILLING

½ cup Marshmallow Fluff
⅓ cup unsweetened shredded coconut
1 teaspoon light corn syrup
1 teaspoon heavy cream

Mix all ingredients. Carve a divot out of each cupcake and fill with coconut creme. Replace divot.

FROSTING

2 ounces (2 squares) unsweetened chocolate
2 tablespoons unsalted butter (room temperature)
1 teaspoon vanilla
¼ cup heavy cream
3 cups powdered sugar
¼ cup milk
1 cup unsweetened shredded coconut

Melt the chocolate in the microwave, in short bursts. Allow to cool. Cream the butter with the chocolate, then add the vanilla and cream. Add the powdered sugar ½ cup at a time, adding milk as needed until the desired consistency is reached. Beat in the coconut. Frost cupcakes with a knife or an offset spatula, heaping it on and swirling. Frosting will not be smooth due to the coconut.

(For 12 cupcakes)

Dark Chocolate Buttercream Frosted Mocha Cupcakes

1 cup flour
1 teaspoon baking powder
¼ teaspoon baking soda
¼ teaspoon kosher salt
¼ cup unsweetened cocoa powder
4 tablespoons unsalted butter (½ stick), at room
* temperature*
1 cup sugar
1 egg, at room temperature
¾ cup milk
2 tablespoons instant coffee
1 teaspoon vanilla

Preheat oven to 350. Place 12 cupcake liners in a cupcake pan. Mix the flour, baking powder, baking soda, salt, and cocoa powder in a bowl. Cream the butter with the sugar. Add the egg and beat. Dissolve the coffee in the milk. Alternate adding the flour and the milk to the egg, butter, and sugar mixture. Add the vanilla and beat well. Divide between cupcake liners, filling only half-full. Bake 14–16 minutes or until a cake tester comes out clean. Cool on a rack before frosting.

SIMPLE CHOCOLATE BUTTERCREAM
This recipe makes just enough frosting for 6 cupcakes. If you want to frost 12 cupcakes, double the frosting recipe. If

you don't need 12 cupcakes, frost half a batch to serve now, and freeze the other 6 cupcakes. You can frost them later just before serving. To defrost cupcakes, simply remove from freezer and let them thaw at room temperature for 30–60 minutes. Then top with the frosting of your choice.

> *1 ounce unsweetened chocolate (1 square)*
> *2 tablespoons unsalted butter, softened but not melted*
> *1 cup powdered sugar*
> *½ teaspoon vanilla*
> *2 teaspoons unsweetened cocoa powder*
> *2 tablespoons milk*

Melt the square of chocolate in the microwave for about 30 seconds at half strength. Repeat until melted. Beat the chocolate with the butter, then add sugar and beat. Add the vanilla and 1 tablespoon milk. Beat in the powdered sugar, adding the additional tablespoon of milk. Add more milk or powdered sugar if necessary to obtain desired consistency.

(Makes 12 cupcakes)

Applesauce Spice Cupcakes

Please note that these cupcakes freeze very well.

> *¾ cup flour*
> *½ teaspoon baking powder*
> *½ teaspoon baking soda*
> *½ teaspoon salt*
> *½ teaspoon cinnamon*
> *¼ teaspoon nutmeg*

pinch of cloves
4 tablespoons unsalted butter (½ stick), at room
   temperature
½ cup dark brown sugar, packed
¼ cup regular sugar
1 egg, at room temperature
½ cup applesauce

Preheat oven to 350. Place 12 cupcake papers in a cupcake pan. Use a fork to mix together the flour, baking powder, baking soda, salt, cinnamon, nutmeg, and cloves in a bowl. Set aside. Cream the butter with the sugars. Add the egg and beat. Add the applesauce and beat. Beat in the flour mixture until smooth. Fill cupcake liners half-full. Bake 15 minutes or until a cake tester comes out clean. Cool on a rack before frosting.

CARAMEL FROSTING

¼ cup heavy cream
2 tablespoons butter
¼ cup white sugar
¼ cup dark brown sugar, packed
8 tablespoons unsalted butter (1 stick), at room
   temperature
2 tablespoons heavy cream
1 teaspoon vanilla
1½ to 2 cups powdered sugar

Place ¼ cup heavy cream, 2 tablespoons butter, the white sugar, and the brown sugar in a microwave-safe bowl. (I use a Pyrex 2-cup measure.) Microwave in short bursts of 20 to 50 seconds, stirring each time until the mixture bubbles up and is hot. Set aside to cool. The mixture must be completely cool to make the frosting. (After it cools substantially, I place it in the fridge for half an hour while the butter comes to room temperature.)

Beat the 8 tablespoons of butter well, scraping the sides and beating again. Add the 2 tablespoons of cream and the cooled caramel mixture and beat. Add the vanilla and beat. Slowly add the powdered sugar until frosting reaches the desired consistency.

(Makes 12 cupcakes)

Rosemary Bacon Corn Cupcakes

1 package Jiffy Corn Muffin Mix
1 egg
⅓ cup milk
1 teaspoon chopped dried rosemary
½ cup chopped cooked bacon

OPTIONAL GARNISH

sour cream
bacon

Preheat oven to 350. Line cupcake pan with liners. Combine all ingredients. It's okay if the batter is slightly lumpy. Fill cupcake liners just over half-full. Bake 20 minutes or until a cake tester comes out clean. Best served warm. If serving cold, garnish with a dollop of sour cream and an inch-long piece of bacon.

(Makes about 10 servings)

Bison Lasagna Cupcakes

*12 to 14 (a couple extra) pieces lasagna
    noodles*
1 to 2 tablespoons olive oil, plus extra for pan
1 clove garlic, minced
1 teaspoon oregano
*1 pound ground bison (or lean ground beef or
    ground turkey)*
1 14.5-ounce can pasta (or tomato) sauce
salt
8 ounces low-fat mozzerella, shredded
4 ounces Parmesan cheese, grated

Cook the lasagna noodles according to package and drain.
Heat the olive oil in a pan over low heat and add the minced
garlic. After 2 minutes, add the oregano. When it's aromatic,
add the meat and cook. When the meat is cooked, mix in the
tomato sauce, salt to taste, and set aside.

Preheat oven to 400.

Thoroughly grease the wells of a muffin tin with olive oil.
Cut each noodle in half and line each cupcake well with
one piece so that the ends extend slightly beyond the well.
Add a layer of meat and sauce to each well. Add a layer
of mozzarella to each well. Cut the remaining noodles roughly
to cupcake width. Lay one piece across each cupcake
well. Repeat the layering of the meat and sauce, and the mozzarella. Sprinkle a substantial layer of Parmesan on top of
each.

Bake 18–20 minutes. The cupcakes should bubble a bit at
the edges. Remove from oven and use a sharp knife to loosen
the cupcakes around the sides. Allow to stand 5 minutes
before removing cupcakes from pan. If they do not hold their
shape, allow them to stand a few minutes longer.

Lift the cupcakes out of the pan using the pasta that sticks out as little handles. The handles will be somewhat crunchy. You may wish to cut them off.

(Makes 12 cupcakes; plan on at least 2 per person)

Liver Pupcakes

(For dogs)

> *½ cup chicken livers (about 3–4 raw chicken*
> *livers, see instructions)*
> *½ cup water from cooking chicken livers*
> *¾ cup flour*
> *½ teaspoon baking powder*
> *½ teaspoon baking soda*
> *4 tablespoons unsalted butter (½ stick), at room*
> *temperature*
> *1 egg, at room temperature*
> *whipped cream cheese, optional*

Cook chicken livers in simmering water. Save ½ cup of the water. Remove livers from water, cool and mash with a fork. Preheat oven to 350. Use a fork to mix together the flour, baking powder, and baking soda. Set aside. Cream the butter with the cooled liver. Add the egg and beat. Beat in the flour mixture and saved water until smooth. Fill cupcake liners full or half-full for small dogs. Bake 15 minutes or until a cake tester comes out clean.

Frost with a dollop of whipped cream cheese or serve plain. Remove liners for dog before feeding.

(Makes 24 mini-cupcakes)

Mango Amour

1 ounce orange vodka
2 ounces peach schnapps
4 ounces mango juice
chilled sparkling wine

Pour first 3 ingredients into a glass. Add wine to fill glass.

Tiger's Paw

2 ounces citrus vodka
2 ounces lemon juice
1 tablespoon sugar
ice
orange juice
sparkling water

Combine first 3 ingredients in a glass. Add ice. Fill with half orange juice and half sparkling water.

Trouble in spades…

FROM NATIONAL BESTSELLING AUTHOR
KRISTA DAVIS

The **Diva**
Digs up the Dirt

A Domestic Diva Mystery

Determined not to be a garden-variety diva, Sophie
Winston's neighbor Natasha cultivates a plan to
shine on television—using Sophie's backyard. As the
cast and crew of the makeover show *Tear It up with
Troy* bulldoze through her backyard—and vacation—
Sophie retreats to her perennial boyfriend Wolf's to
replace a dead rosebush. But her tender deed goes
awry when she digs up a purse belonging to Wolf's
missing wife.

As speculations sprout, Wolf bolts, and then a body
crops up in a garden. Is Wolf's thorny past raising a
dead head? This is one case the domestic diva can't let
wither on the vine…

DELICIOUS RECIPES AND ENTERTAINING TIPS INCLUDED!

divamysteries.com
facebook.com/KristaDavisAuthor
facebook.com/TheCrimeSceneBooks
penguin.com